BREAKDOWN *and* BEREAVEMENT

YOSEF HAIM BRENNER

BREAKDOWN and BEREAVEMENT

>>>->>>->>>->>>->>>->>>->>>->>>->>>->>>->>>->>>->>>->>> *A Novel*

by *Yosef Haim Brenner*

Translated from the Hebrew by Hillel Halkin

PREPARED UNDER THE AUSPICES OF THE INSTITUTE
FOR THE TRANSLATION OF HEBREW LITERATURE LTD.

The Jewish Publication Society of America

PHILADELPHIA ✣ 5731—1971

B838t

First published 1971 by Cornell University Press.
This edition was published for the members of the Jewish
Publication Society by arrangement with Cornell University Press.

FH

Library of Congress Catalog Card Number 74-162545

Printed in the United States of America by Vail-Ballou Press, Inc.

Translator's Introduction

If it is appropriate that this first English translation of a full-length work by Yosef Haim Brenner should appear on the fiftieth anniversary of his death, it is also occasion for reflection that such a volume has been overdue. Of course, Brenner has fared no worse in this respect than other talented figures of the modern Hebrew revival, that remarkable literary and linguistic renaissance that began in Eastern Europe toward the end of the nineteenth century. But though the number of undeservedly still untranslated Hebrew authors of this period is considerable, it is noteworthy that Brenner alone of all his contemporaries is currently undergoing a significant revival in Israel today. One might well speculate why. Certainly it is not that he was the superior craftsman. On the contrary, as readers of *Breakdown and Bereavement* will observe, his work is marred by frequent flaws that make one fervently wish that it had passed under a firmer editorial hand than his own. Nor is it simply the passion for honesty with which he wrote, the satirist's incorruptible eye for the exposure of pretension and sham. Perhaps above all it is that in an age when to be a Hebrew writer automatically meant to be part of a national struggle whose claims upon one's energies and commitments were immense, he stayed true in his work to his own tragic

sense of man's private condition, of the prison house of the self in its ultimate isolation and anguish. That he should at the same time have been the major Hebrew author most intimately involved in the early years of the Zionist struggle in Palestine—should have, in fact, become after his death one of its public martyrs and legends—typifies the polarities that ran through his life and art.

He was born in 1881 in Novymlini, a small town of mixed Russian and Jewish population in the southeast of the Pale of Settlement, that area of European Russia to which Jewish residence was first restricted by an edict of Catherine the Great. The year of his birth marked a watershed in the history of Russian Jewry, for it coincided with the assassination of Alexander II, which brought in its wake an unprecedented series of bloody pogroms and new restrictive social and economic legislation aimed at the already impoverished and discriminated-against Jewish population. Henceforward the masses of Russian Jews could have no illusions about their future in Czarist Russia: millions responded in the decades to come by emigration, tens of thousands of others by conversion to Zionism or revolutionary socialism. Yet in Brenner's childhood neither of these contending ideologies, both of which envisioned a radically different solution to the Jewish problem, had as yet made serious inroads upon the religious orthodoxy of the provinces. He was the eldest son in a poor, large family. His temperamental father nourished high ambitions for him and he began early to study in the *heder*, the traditional schoolroom, which by all contemporary accounts, including his own—no theme is as common in the Hebrew literature of the period as that of the stolen, the expropriated childhood—was a dreary cloister of rigid discipline, rote recitation, and oppressively long hours. Still he was devoted as a boy to the stern pietism in which he was raised, and he excelled in his studies, acquiring a reputation as a scholarly prodigy. Soon after his bar-mitzvah he was sent off to a *yeshivah*, or talmudical college, to continue his education.

His years of *yeshivah* life—he passed through several of these institutions, whose informal methods of instruction and independence of student life made them not unlike a medieval university—marked his gradual estrangement from his family and religion. The loss of faith did not come easily, and the conflict between the heart that would believe and the mind that cannot was later to be a recurrent motif in his work. Here he taught himself Russian, reading Tolstoy and Dostoevsky, Chekhov and Gorky; here too he surreptitiously began to write his first Hebrew stories. When he was seventeen he abandoned his studies and moved to the White Russian city of Bialystok and later to Gomel, where he earned his living for a while as a ritual scribe. In Gomel he joined the newly formed social-revolutionary Jewish Workers Bund, soon to become a power in the Jewish community, and briefly edited its illegal Yiddish paper, *Der Kamf*. His association with the Bund, however, was short-lived, for he quickly grew disenchanted with its doctrinaire Marxism and, especially, with its hostility to Zionism, toward which he himself was increasingly drawn.

Nevertheless, when after having been drafted into the Russian army, he deserted at the outbreak of the Russo-Japanese War and was apprehended, it was his friends from the Bund who came to his rescue. In cloak-and-dagger fashion he was snatched from his captors and spirited across the border into Germany. He was then twenty-three years old and had already published a slim volume of short stories and the novella *In Winter*, a portrait of the Hebrew artist as a young man whose precociously bitter descriptions of Jewish life in Russia established a reputation for him overnight as the *enfant ter-*

rible of the small Hebrew literary world. *In Winter* was published in 1904, the year Joyce began work on his own incomparably greater *Bildungsroman,* and it shares with the latter work a number of curious parallels, for Stephen Dedalus and Brenner's Jeremy Feuermann have much in common. Both are introvert sons of a puritanical, God-obsessed race; both populate their lonely childhoods with an imaginative world of their own making, half romantic daydream, half the troubled fantasies of fear and guilt; both are sent away to religious schools, reach an adolescent height of devotional fervor, and plunge immediately thereafter into a sea of rebellion and doubt; both discover a vocation in writing, abandon the careers intended for them, and break with family and friends; and finally, both embark in the end on a journey into exile that is also a rite of passage into the inner regions of the self.

Brenner was never to return to Russia again. He wandered briefly in Central Europe, considered emigrating to New York but lacked the money to pay his passage, and in 1905 decided on London instead, where he found work as a compositor in a Yiddish print shop and started a Hebrew-Zionist periodical called *Ha-Me'orer,* "The Awakener." London was at the time a center for émigré artists and intellectuals, yet Brenner rarely ventured beyond the confines of the Jewish immigrant ghetto whose physical and spiritual squalor provided the material for some of his most cruelly satirical stories. His labors on behalf of *Ha-Me'orer* were prodigious: he not only wrote large parts of every issue himself under various pseudonyms but personally set it in type, mailed it to subscribers, and paid the running deficits from his salary at the press. The Hebrew writer Asher Beilin has left an unforgettable description of him walking down Whitechapel Road on a windy autumn evening, his back bent almost double beneath a sack of "Awakeners" which he was hurrying to bring to the post office before it closed for the day. Yet his sense of the journal's importance was not totally exaggerated: it was for a time the only Hebrew literary periodical in the world, and despite its prevailing pessimism of tone—many of its pages were devoted to Brenner's attacks on what he felt to be the blindness of the Zionist establishment of the day—it served as a symbol of continuity in what was essentially a bleak period for Hebrew letters.

In 1908 he was forced to let the publication lapse, having no more money with which to meet the bills. Already the previous year he had considered moving to Palestine—"not as a Zionist full of faith and hope," as he wrote in a letter with characteristic mordancy, "but as a man longing for sun"—and now he set out, traveling first on the Continent and arriving in Jaffa early in 1909. Conditions in the country were discouraging. The small Jewish population was itself divided into two antagonistic groups: a majority of orthodox Jews from Eastern Europe and the Levant, subsisting largely on charity from abroad, and a handful of Zionist pioneers, the success of whose efforts to create a land-based economically productive, Hebrew-speaking community hung in ultimate doubt until the period of the British Mandate that followed World War I. Brenner briefly sought to work on the land himself, but much to his disappointment, the life did not suit him, and he resigned himself to a series of editorial positions, living first in Jerusalem and later in Jaffa. Literally, his first years in Palestine were among his most productive: besides *Breakdown and Bereavement*, which was not published until later, he wrote two shorter novels during this period that were among the first Hebrew works of their kind to have their setting on

Palestinian soil. His marriage to a young teacher in 1913 soon ended in separation, though not before the birth of a son, who went to live with the mother. The details of the episode are obscure, but the breakup evidently stemmed at least in part from Brenner's own need for creative solitude and his increasingly ascetic tendencies, which grew more extreme with time. Eyewitness accounts of his living quarters in these years invariably agree on the furnishings: within four bare walls, a chair, a table to write on, a board laid over two oilcans to serve as a bed.

After the outbreak of World War I, which caused serious dislocation in the Palestinian Jewish community, Brenner's production of fiction fell sharply. Increasingly he devoted himself to translation—including a Hebrew version of an early favorite of his, *Crime and Punishment*—literary criticism, and social commentary. Though he remained on the whole aloof from local politics, both his sympathies and editorial capacities impelled him toward the infant "labor Zionist" movement that envisioned the true revolution of Palestinian Jewry coming about through the formation of collective workers' and farmers' settlements, from which the unique institution of the kibbutz eventually evolved. His position in the country during these last years of his life was anomalous, for while he remained openly skeptical about the prospects for the hoped-for national rebirth, almost defiantly so after the issuance of the Balfour Declaration, to which the Zionist movement as a whole responded with unrestrained euphoria, he increasingly became the chief literary spokesman and confidant of the most vital forces in Palestinian Jewish life. His own always great readiness, if not need, for self-sacrifice reached new heights under their influence. Much of the time he spent teaching and lecturing, often traveling long distances on foot to reach remote communities of Jewish laborers. In

1920 he lived for several months in a tent with immigrant workers building a road near Tiberias; he taught them Hebrew and lectured on other subjects.

He met his death at the hands of Arab rioters during the May Day disturbances of 1921, which were among the first serious anti-Zionist outbursts to occur under the British Mandate. He was living at the time in a rented room in an isolated farmhouse not far from Tel Aviv. Several days earlier he had been urged by friends to come to the safety of the city but had refused to leave the family with whom he was staying. Their bodies were found together; evidently they had defended themselves against their attackers and were killed when their ammunition ran out. Ironically, under the title "We Are All Brothers," Brenner had published an emotional appeal for Arab-Jewish understanding in the Hebrew press only a few weeks before.

When first published in 1920, *Breakdown and Bereavement* bore the subtitle "The Book of Struggle." The phrase might have applied to its composition no less than to its characters, for this most ambitious of all Brenner's works was also, in its creation, the most fraught with difficulties and frustration. The novel was apparently extant as early as 1914, yet it was deliberately withheld from publication for another six years for reasons that Brenner never publicly disclosed. It would appear, however, from the brief opening introduction of the author-"narrator," with its conventional apologetic device of the "found" manuscript, that the delay had to do with both his dissatisfaction with the text itself and his fears that the tremendous changes that had taken place in Palestinian life soon after the novel was written—World War I, the British conquest of Palestine from the Turks, the Balfour Declaration, the first beginnings of large-scale Zionist immigration—

threatened to make it seem badly dated, if not positively re-
actionary, in the eyes of its readers. It is indeed likely that the
published version of the novel was not originally intended as a
final draft at all and that Brenner kept the manuscript in his
drawer for so many years because he hoped to rewrite large
parts of it, reluctantly consenting to its publication in the end
only when it became evident to him that this was not to be.
Certainly this explanation would account for some of the
book's more obvious shortcomings, which even so indifferent
a stylist as himself would not ordinarily have left uncorrected.

Yet the overall architecture of the novel is far from hap-
hazard. On the contrary, it is scrupulously plotted and its al-
ternations of character and mood follow a regular, almost
symmetrical design. The imperfections are rather in the finish:
the overwritten or underwritten passages, the sometimes tedious flashbacks, the reliance on indirect discourse, the proliferation of minor characters who at times seem to be intro-
duced solely for some satirical purpose essentially unrelated
to the main body of the plot. It is generally when these figures
are "onstage" that the novel limps most noticeably. When the
main actors take their place, on the other hand—especially the
two central protagonists, Hefetz and Esther—*Breakdown and
Bereavement* assumes a genuine life of its own.

Esther is the most fully realized female character ever
created by Brenner in his fiction, which is not on the whole
noteworthy for its women. Hefetz on the other hand is the
last and most complex of a series of self-lacerating Brennerian
characters who appear in nearly all his major works. (Hefetz's
name is clearly symbolic. A not unknown surname among
East European Jews, *hefetz* is also the Hebrew word for "desire." The name Brenner itself comes from the German-Yiddish
verb *brennen*, "to burn," and several characters in other novels
bear names associated with fire as well.) If he is essentially

distinguishable from his predecessors, it is because of his ex-
cruciatingly heightened self-consciousness and the relative
freedom with which his sexual neurosis is allowed expression
—"relative," because while Brenner's handling of the subject
exhibits a curious mixture of directness and near-Victorian
reticence, it was unusually bold for the Hebrew novel of his
time, which in this as in other respects lagged a decade or
more behind its European counterpart. No doubt the reader
may find somewhat forced the thematic association of Hefetz's sexual anxiety with the physical injury incurred by him
at the beginning of the novel, but it should be borne in mind
not only that this is in itself an obsession of his neurotic imagination, but that medically speaking the condition in question was indeed a more serious matter sixty years ago than it is
today.

Breakdown and Bereavement is a novel about different
kinds of unfulfilled desire and the costly struggle of the spirit
to survive in the face of them, but in the person of Hefetz the
book assumes another dimension as well, for it would have
been impossible for its readers not to have seen in the story of
his desperate attempt and failure to build a new life in Palestine a symbolic statement on the future of the Zionist experiment as a whole—the supreme irony in their eyes being, of
course, not that Hefetz is unable to live the heroic life of a
pioneer, but rather that as the novel unfolds he is sucked back
more and more into the old-world orthodox community of
Jerusalem, that is, into the very ghetto from which Palestinian
Zionism was ostensibly an escape. And yet quite apart from
the calculated note of ambiguity on which the book ends—
an ambiguity that is heightened by the reference in the introduction to Hefetz's subsequent relapse—those critics who attacked it when it first appeared for its unremittingly black
picture of life in Palestine, and for its neglect of the new type

of Jew coming into being there, were not entirely justified even on their own purely tendentious grounds. Two such characters do in fact exist in the novel, Hefetz's cousin Hanoch and the hired hand Menahem, and though neither plays a crucial role, both are portrayed with great sympathy and hover, as it were, in the story's wings as reminders of an alternate and more wholesome form of life. This is especially true of Menahem, whose appearances in the opening and closing chapters are like two windows of light at either end of a long and gloomy tunnel.

World War I radically changed the landscape of Palestine and opened up to Zionist settlement possibilities, previously only dreamt of, that were not long in being exploited. Written on the eve of this conflict, *Breakdown and Bereavement* offers us a last, lingering glimpse of Palestinian life in the twilight days of the Ottoman Empire, when the horse-drawn carriage still vied with the railway and the country slumbered in peace if not prosperity, undisturbed by warring nationalisms and the forces of modernity, though storm clouds were already thick on the horizon. There is a vintage quality to Brenner's sketches of Jewish life as it existed at the turn of the century in the orthodox quarters of Jerusalem or on the sand dunes north of Jaffa that had yet to be named Tel Aviv—sketches which have the posed yet intimate atmosphere of old daguerreotypes. Were it for these vignettes alone, *Breakdown and Bereavement* would be a fascinating historical document quite apart from its more substantial literary merits. Yet the latter too are certainly great; they more than compensate for the novel's artistic lapses; and taken all in all, they combine to make this "book of struggle" one of the most moving and powerful works of modern Hebrew fiction.

I wish to thank David Patterson, Cowley Lecturer in Post

Biblical Hebrew at Oxford University, for encouraging me to attempt this translation and Shlomo Grodzenski of Tel Aviv for several helpful suggestions regarding the text.

HILLEL HALKIN

Jerusalem

BREAKDOWN *and* BEREAVEMENT

by Yosef Haim Brenner

❦ *Part One*

❧

Several years ago, aboard a ship bound from Port Said to Alexandria, a certain homely and unfortunate individual, who in his conversations with me, his fellow passenger, had repeatedly stressed the need for an attitude of good will toward all men, fell mentally ill. He was about thirty-three at the time, and his face, which even previously had shown the strain of perpetual tension, now expressed utter confusion. When he was taken ashore he left behind a small abandoned object—a little knapsack, whose contents yielded several notebooks, from which I learned that this was not his first attack. Once securely again on dry land, I took these notes and wove them in a conventional fictional manner into several chapters dealing with the life and inner world of this man during the preceding few years. For a variety of reasons, however, these chapters have remained unpublished to this day. Among those having to do with the work itself, the most important, perhaps, were my qualms at having made insufficient use of the material at my disposal, much of which I did not include in my account at all, and at having failed to adapt successfully even the little that I did use, so that it retained a memoiristic flavor, and in many places even preserved the dialogue in an indirect form. . . . But be this as it may, and despite my reservations about the form, which have not and of course cannot cease to exist, I have resolved in the end to offer this story to the reader exactly as it was written, without a single correction. In doing so I am forced to brush aside yet another misgiving, which though peripheral in nature is still a cause for concern, namely, the time of publication, which is neither suitable nor conducive to the consumption of such tales. For my own part, to be sure, I, the author, occasionally delude myself into thinking that this is not so serious an objection, inasmuch as there can be no clear line to begin with between what is "contemporary" and what is not: the sufferings of the wretched, like as not, will always be with us, and suicides and madmen who can no longer bear the shame of their private lives will be found in the most glorious of times. (Have we ourselves not seen how even in these momentous, tumultuous days each of us continues to be pettily preoccupied with his own individual ennui?) Still, this doubt persists and deserves to be considered further.

I

It was an afternoon in the middle of April when the accident occurred. The year was a leap year, rainy and warm, and on that summery spring day in the commune he had already been given the job of getting in the hay. He and Menahem, the hired hand, were at work in the field; Menahem up above, on top of the wagon, and he, Hefetz, down below; Menahem at a leisurely pace, without visible exertion, like all the migrant help who were one day in Dan and the next in Beersheba,* and he, Hefetz, the regular member of the commune, zealously straining every muscle, as had always been his way, particularly since his last return from abroad. Rivulets of sweat streamed down his face and his eyes shone triumphantly with the effort, as if to say, "See, I too can hold my own!" He worked without letup, tiring his partner and driving himself ever closer to exhaustion with each bale of hay he pitched upward. Before Menahem, quick as he was, had finished setting one load in place, an even bigger one would come flying at him like a mad bull.

The wagon filled bale by bale; the distance between the two men grew gradually greater and with it, Hefetz's exertions.

* Dan and Beersheba are the northernmost and southernmost outposts of Palestine. [N.B.—All notes are the translator's.]

His Arab *kaffiyeh* * slipped unnoticed from his head. The
sun beat down with its usual fierceness. Suddenly the man
below uttered a soft groan and staggered slightly with the
load on his pitchfork. Menahem looked down to see a large
bale of hay, the heaviest yet, overturned on the ground, and
Hefetz squirming beside it. "The devil!" he cried, slipping
down from above. What could be the matter? Sunstroke?
Malaria? Chills?—No, a sharp pain . . . a pain below the
waist . . . ach, what an ass!

That evening the members of the commune assembled in
the kitchen and decided to send Hefetz to Jerusalem at the
expense of the sick fund. True, it was nearer to Jaffa, but in
Jerusalem, it had meanwhile been discovered, the injured man
had some distant relatives. The elected head of the commune
even recalled how several years previously there had been
some other trouble with Hefetz, on account of which (Hefetz himself had not been consulted) it was decided to send
him to Jerusalem too, only then (how times had changed!)
there was no choice but Jerusalem, either Jerusalem or Beirut,
because . . . because in Jaffa they didn't have the right sort
of place for him . . . only meanwhile Hefetz had decided to
leave the country, which put an end to the affair. It seemed,
though, that a man couldn't escape his proper destiny. No,
indeed. . . .

Indeed, so it seemed. In the course of the evening two or
three other old settlers also recalled Hefetz's journey abroad
and the events that led up to it. These were described most
vividly by "the Master-of-intrigue," a scarecrow of a man
with two left thumbs whose favorite tactic was to boast and
threaten at once that he was imminently about to receive a
ticket for passage from his brother in Brazil; in the meantime

* The cloth head-covering commonly worn by the Arabs of Palestine.

—for this had been going on for five years—he did his best to turn one friend against the other, and particularly, to complain about the cook, who wasn't fulfilling her duty, the duty of a cook in an agricultural commune in the Land of Israel. Ah yes, Hefetz' madness. "I tell you, we should all have the luck to be as mad as he was!" (If only his brother in Brazil would come to his rescue already . . .) The business with Hefetz had happened several years before. The commune was not then in existence; in fact, there were no communes at all; in other words, the new form of life developed by the pioneers in Palestine, the agricultural collective, had not yet appeared on the scene. In those days they all worked in the "colony," or more precisely, passed the time there, Hefetz as well. Several days before the first night of Passover ("Hasn't anyone noticed? This time it's almost Passover too!") he had fallen ill.* "Still, his illness then, gentlemen, was of a different sort." It was a nervous, a . . . what was the word? . . . a *psychic* disturbance. In fact, he seemed to have gone slightly mad. On the other hand, there was no need to exaggerate: he was far from completely deranged. In any case, there was nothing dangerous about his condition. What was it someone had said? Yes, someone had hit the nail on the head: it was the sort of illness that concerned the patient alone. It was an attack of . . . what was the word? . . . of *anxiety*.

"But it wasn't just that," added some of the other old-timers. Anxiety . . . of course . . . but in general . . . morale at the time was terribly low. It was a critical period, a time of transition, for the Jewish workers in the settlements

* The first night of Passover is annually a time of tension for East European Jews. For Hefetz—as emerges later in the chapter—Passover is associated with the traditional fear of pogroms and of the blood libel or Christian accusation against Jews of slaughtering Christian children and using their blood in the baking of unleavened bread eaten on the holiday.

. . . and Hefetz, who had a bad case of malaria, had been on a diet of quinine and was very weak. To be sure, there was nothing out of the ordinary about this; but because of his weakness and his inability to work during the day, he had decided to become a night watchman. The dangers of being a watchman, of course, were not then what they were now, but since his nerves were on edge and the work was new to him ("After all, he was no great hero to begin with," observed a voice from the side to the general approval of all) . . . on account of all this, it was said, he panicked one night while on duty and imagined he was being attacked. It was this fright that undoubtedly brought on his illness.

"In any case, you can't but feel sorry for him," remarked the Master-of-intrigue in an unusually mild tone. "It wasn't wise of him to go abroad. Others could have left at the time and didn't—and he could have stayed and he left. It all goes to prove that he was already out of his mind. After all, we all know that you have to be mad to want to leave this country, don't we, my friends? Still, looking back . . . abroad, you know, the cooks are better than ours, ha ha . . . say what you will, he came back with his belly full. He must have feasted like a king over there. What a character, that Hefetz! The man runs away, so it seems, because he's gone quite berserk, shows up again, I won't say recovered, but anyway, with some . . . what's the word? . . . *flesh* on his bones, and then goes and loses that too. And all in a few months. Our commune simply has no luck, my friends."

"But who's going to take him to Jerusalem?" asked the head of the commune deliberately interrupting the talk; his heavy eyes stared down at the ground, as they always did when it was a question of general concern.

The posing of a practical question led to discussion, dissent, innuendo. Those who were disinclined to make the trip to

Jerusalem with the injured man were quick to put forth their candidacy, offering to sacrifice themselves for the common good, while taking care at the same time to present their case in such a way as to make their going clearly out of the question; while those who would have been only too happy to take a few days off from work and see Jerusalem at no cost to themselves did their best to seem reluctant—though if duty called, of course, they would have no choice but to comply. . . .

"Gentlemen, it's one o'clock in the morning," tired voices called out. "We've got to put an end to this." They had just resolved to cast lots when Menahem, the hired hand, volunteered his services.

This young man of twenty-two had already been "everywhere"; indeed, he had even met Hefetz once before somewhere in Western Europe, before coming to Palestine, and had taken a liking to him. Menahem's knowledge of geography—he could all but tell you the exact distance in kilometers between any two cities in Austria, England, Germany, France, even Belgium and Holland—did not come from books. He had a weakness for stations and train tickets and his favorite saying was: "The devil take it! Fish look for deep waters, men for sweet!" His eyes, though round as an owl's, were not owlish at all; they were merry, open, honey-colored, but not too sweet or cloying; they were rather like the honey that is fresh from the hive and still dripping bright with pure brilliance. Menahem took to new surroundings as no one else, plunging straight into them as into a clear mountain pond, lazily greeting each stranger with a fond hello, as though inviting him to partake of his honeyed essence. He liked to go barefoot and even took pride in the fact; yet somehow this failed to annoy Hefetz the way the exhibitionalistically barefoot types generally did. The simple, childish way he enjoyed things made up for everything. He liked to swear—"the devil take it!"—to stake all on an oath—"upon my life!"—to break into laughter, to gossip about the girls in the nearby settlement, to tell an occasional indecent joke (at times such as these Hefetz would become strangely pliant and laugh submissively); none of this, however, offended a soul, for it was done without the slightest malice, in a comical, almost piping voice. "I don't like to talk about my troubles," he would say to Hefetz. "If talking about them could drive them away, why not? Then I'd talk about them all day long, I'd do nothing else, just like you. But as it is—I leave it to you. . . ."

The debate over Menahem's proposal gathered strength. Those who were averse to going and feared to draw the unwelcome lot threw caution to the winds and declared (it was really too late to keep up pretenses) that it was only right for the hired hand, who had come with Hefetz from abroad, to go with him too; the opposing party, however, had persuasive arguments of its own, the most powerful among them being that a nonmember of the commune should be made to travel at his own expense. Menahem's acceptance of this last condition hastened the final decision in his favor.

And so Menahem went with Hefetz to Jerusalem.

On the way, as they approached Jerusalem, Hefetz thought he felt better and began to regret having come. The whole thing now seemed to have been something he'd imagined. Why must he blow up everything out of proportion? He had collapsed while at work—was that any reason to go running to the doctor? What an amateur he was at suffering! It was really just like him.

Menahem spit through his teeth in his fashion and tried to console him. If the condition wasn't serious, so much the better. The pain was real enough. Since he would be unable to work for a few days anyhow, what did he stand to lose?

Hefetz listened and felt reassured; still, he announced in advance that he had no intention of seeing a doctor in Jerusalem. The latter would only laugh at him, that much was certain, and he was not going to make a fool of himself. In fact, it had already once happened to him that he had thought he was ill and had actually been in great pain; by the time he'd arrived at the doctor's, however, the pain had disappeared and he hadn't known what to say! He wouldn't say anything to his relatives, either, simply that he had come to Jerusalem for the holiday. If he should have to stay a while longer, he could always tell them the "truth": he was malarial, the quinine no longer helped; he needed a change of air, and so he had decided to stay in Jerusalem and not go back to the farm. . . .

And yet, when all was said and done, he needn't have come. It was really just like him. Always on the run. . . .

His trip abroad, for example—what made him take it? He had been about twenty years old when he first came to Palestine, strong, healthy, undemanding, a little bit odd perhaps, but still—popular enough. Elsewhere, abroad (in Hamilin's circle of students, for example), he had been a dull-witted, clumsy, solemn young man, at a loss to get on with the weaker sex and in general having no luck with it, in short: the very opposite of well-liked. No, elsewhere someone like him had no chance at all. In the workers' inn in the colony, on the other hand, surrounded by bearded, bookish, ascetic votaries of labor; there where everyone was an eccentric of sorts, a bit of an "original"; there and only there could he too, Hefetz, be a good companion, even if he wasn't contentious like the rest of them and didn't argue at the drop of a hat or take sides in every quarrel or play politics out of sheer boredom and the need to pick a fight. . . .

And yet he went abroad. It was just like him. Even before that, all the time he was in the colony—a period of several years, all together—he had gone about with a strange feeling.

He had felt as though he were trapped in a long corridor, but only for the moment; somewhere ahead was a room that was still to come, that had to come. He was incapable of saying or describing what this room was like; yet there was no end of fantasies about it, bizarre, impalpable, but sweet nonetheless. At any rate, it was clearly intolerable for things to go on forever without these dreams coming true . . . and not only because life as it was wasn't good and deserved to be better. Of course, he wanted this too, and at times the desire would actually get the best of him, but deep down it was not the main thing. The main, the overriding thing was . . . if only everything weren't so dry and bitter and hard: the burning, sweat-sucking air, the filthy inn, the sickening, poisonous food, the alien cold surroundings; it was impossible not to dream of a comfortable place to live, a good meal, shade, a cool stream, tangled woods, tree-lined streets . . . but in any case, it wasn't this that mattered most . . . on the contrary: sometimes he would deliberately resist the slightest improvement in his life, refuse to escape the desolation, the apathy, the packed quarters, the filth, even for a moment. No, what never failed to crush him was the utter pointlessness of it all: it seemed monstrous to him to have to go on living like this, for no reason, as a Jewish "farm hand" always looking for work; monstrous when he found it to have to go out every morning and compete with a horde of strange Arabs; monstrous to have to fight all day long with the ill-mannered foreman; and then to return to the inn at evening and gulp down a sour, gassy gruel that boded ill for the stomach; and afterward to drop by the workers' club to yawn once or twice and read an old newspaper; and then back to the inn again, to a bachelor's sleep bitten into by all kinds of bugs; and once more to rise with the ringing of the clock and work all day long until evening. And the work had no meaning, and the end was far, unclear, invisible, non-existent . . . to go a year like that, two years, ten years, forever . . . and never any change; no relief, no progress, no hope. . . . *What? Everyone lived that way*, Menahem said? Yes, of course, everyone did; his spleen and his ennui had been banal, of course, but he had suffered from them all the same. A kind of apathy had come over him, a total indifference to what he ate, the way he dressed, where he slept. He could have gone for months without changing his clothes or lain in an unmade bed from one week to the next and let his mind wander or not wander as it pleased. He loathed it when his roommates took the trouble to tidy up. It was a strange thing, his illness . . . the word "melancholia" did not exactly fit it . . . it was as though some horror of life had taken hold of him, a revulsion toward everything around him. Food disgusted him; he grew thinner every day, and the less he ate, the more he dreamed and talked, as if to escape his inner fears. He had never been much of a talker before.

What did he talk about? About everything except his un-speakable fantasies. . . . *The darling little girl whom he had seen in the school in the colony would grow up to be a young beauty. A woman's grace, a man's strength, would join in her soul. One day she would be seventeen . . . and he would be thirty-five, twice her age, a weary castaway . . . but she would say: "It doesn't matter . . . I've seen all your suffering and I want to share it with you. . . . Father is the richest man in the colony, and I'm the most beautiful woman, I know. . . . But I'm leaving it all for you because it's you that I want. . . ." No, she would not say it that way; she would not speak so commonly. . . . She would put her hand in his without a word—everything would be understood, transformed into infinite bliss. . . .*

Hefetz talked about practically everything during those

terrible, garrulous days, but he did not talk about things like these, not about his wild, insane imaginings. As though by itself, with no effort on his part, his conversation turned to matters of the general interest—matters, that is, which might have pained him, even moved him deeply in ordinary times, but which at bottom, and especially now, meant nothing to him at all. The more remote a problem was, the less he or anyone else could do anything about it, the greater his concern. He talked a great deal, for example, about the Arabs; he spoke of their national awakening and of their hatred for the Jew; he was obsessed . . . by the possibility of a pogrom, over which he wracked his brain, soliciting advice and making endless plans for rescue and relief. Once an Arab woman from one of the families in the village had stopped by the inn, which was near her house, to inquire of those seated on the bench outside whether they had seen her little brother, who had gone off somewhere unannounced. He, Hefetz, who had been sitting in the doorway, turned as white as a shroud. He didn't attack her or lay hands on her—it hadn't yet come to that—but when he heard the word *zrir*, meaning child, he jumped to his feet like a shot and leaped backward over the threshold as though looking for a place to hide, from where he began to stamp his feet and to shout: "*Zrir, zrir*, I know what she's after! We're not cannibals here! We don't drink human blood! But just try to convince her that we don't have her brother when the Arabs are awaking and the germs of hatred have infected them too. . . . See where it gets you!"

Under the circumstances, as long as Hefetz carried on this way his companions were understandably not upset; they saw that he had changed, of course, but while his preoccupation with the common good lasted, they did not give it much thought. They were all, after all, neurasthenics, cosmic worriers, who bore the world's burdens on their shoulders and judged everything in terms of the group. If one of them traveled abroad, for example, he had not simply gone someplace else, but had "given up" and "betrayed the ideal"; if someone stood guard in a vineyard he was not just a lookout, but "a watchman in the fatherland"; if the cook burned the food in the inn—and when did she not burn it? and who really cared, anyway, except that it was something to talk about?—she was an execrable cook, of course, but she was also "an irresponsible woman with no sense of duty to her comrades."

Soon, however, a reaction set in and everyone realized that Hefetz was not just another victim of general conditions. His final metamorphosis made this apparent. He looked as unwell and distracted as before; but now not only his mind, but his tongue too, seemed to have gone out of order. It was all very well for him not to talk, but there was silence and there was silence! For days on end he refused to say a word. It then became obvious that his previous chatter had been one thing, his illness another, and that the latter derived not from the common predicament, but had private origins, underlying irritations, which were purely personal in nature and had nothing to do with anyone else. Only what was to be done? During several meetings held in the sick man's absence, though not without his knowledge, much was said about the need for treatment, namely, for "bandaging up the old wounds" that had come open and begun to bleed again, etc., though at the same time, of course, a "permanent cure" was perhaps "out of the question," "but as a temporary measure" . . . Jerusalem or Beirut. . . .

But when Hefetz, overcome by inner desire, sheepishly announced that he was about "to take a trip," in other words, to go abroad completely, respect for him reached a new low. As always, it was a time when the number of settlers who came and went far exceeded the number of those who stayed;

still, the custom persisted, and not always as a mere matter of form, to grumble aloud about all those who "fled the field of battle" and betrayed the national cause. . . .

Hefetz was ill . . . but with what? Hefetz was going . . . but where? To others he murmured that he wished to see the world a bit, but to himself he would add: *I want to live, to live.* In spite of the privileges conferred on him by his illness, he didn't, he couldn't, tell this to anyone else; he himself, however, was perfectly aware of the drives that impelled him—primitive, ugly drives, if you will, which in any case, would never, could never, be fulfilled. Yes, he was tired of this monotonous, unbearable life, without a spark of pleasure, without a woman; he had to free himself of it, somehow cast its yoke from off his neck. Even his distant, feckless dreams had come to disgust him. He knew them only too well. . . . *There in Europe there were great cities with all the good things of life. . . . There was no end of possibilities. . . . He would get a job, he would work hard, harder even than here. . . . But the pay would not be bad. . . . And at night, after work, his time would be his own, to do with as he pleased. . . . He would enjoy himself, he would live like a human being and forget all this. . . . He would walk the streets in the evenings, visit the music halls, the theaters, whatever he desired. . . . There would be piquant, fantastic encounters. . . . And other houses, too, which he would not shy away from. . . . Perhaps he might even meet a gentle, attractive young girl. . . .*

Hefetz wandered for some three years in Western Europe, from city to city, from place to place, without rest. Penniless and hungry, he lifted eager, curious eyes to the twentieth century's civilized glitter: to the busy, magnificent streets with their modern traffic, the giant department stores crammed with riches, the brightly lit marquees, the sparkling restaurant windows, the exhibitions of art and trade. Languages he had never heard before rang sharply in his ears; elegant strange men and proudly-mincing women passed before him. In Paris he worked for three months in a Jewish philanthropy for "our unfortunate brothers from the East"; then his time was up, and again out of work he wandered somewhere else, and from there to French Switzerland . . . by which time he realized that the change he desired was not to be had by changing place. Wherever he stayed he slept in the same foul bed in the house of the same immigrant peddler in the same foul Jewish quarter; only the speech of the men and women who lived in these streets (their children already went to school and spoke the local tongue) no longer seemed Jewish, was not the Yiddish he knew, but another patois, new, queer, and unfamiliar. . . . The cities changed name, the bed was the same. . . . And when work was not to be found he passed the same tediously slow time in the same "Jewish Workers' Club" in the ghetto, which was the same gathering place as always for the same bored, down-and-out, unwanted, discontented drifters like himself. . . .

Life in newer pastures had proved no greener. No, not only no greener; he was worse off now than he had been before, much worse. Whereas in Palestine, at least, he had been a person like everyone else, here he was of a distinctly lower standing, something that was impressed on him in various ways. There, for example, he had spoken the native language of a Jew from Eastern Europe, and this had seemed perfectly natural, certainly nothing to be ashamed of; and if now and then he had actually conversed in Hebrew with a teacher, or a student, or an aspiring young girl, they had all felt a bit superior. But here, if he turned

in Yiddish to some immigrant from Russia, to say nothing
of the immigrant's children, he was made to feel that he
was speaking some pitiful jargon, while his partner in conversation addressed him condescendingly in Russian or the
language of the country. How differently one expressed
oneself then! Here the question of language was no longer
a "Jewish Problem," but something that life took care of
quite casually, cruelly, on its own.

After Hefetz had been abroad for nearly two years, however, his racial instinct for adjustment got the upper hand, and
objectively, his situation began to improve. He obtained a job
as a clerk in a Jewish old-clothes store and gradually set
about to transform himself into another person. The spiritual
caprices of the past, his "oriental whimsies," seemed, as it
were, to disappear by themselves, and at the time that Menahem first met him his name was not even Ezekiel, Yehezkel
Hefetz, but something entirely different and not in the least
prophetic or oriental or Palestinian.

Menahem met Hefetz in the city in French Switzerland, in
the home of a Jewish *emigrée* from Russia who had wandered
with her family to England only to be refused entry there,
and had finally made her way to one of the Swiss provinces,
where she had hoped to find a certain rich relative. The relative, however, could not be located, and meanwhile the woman's husband went off on some business in search of a com-
mission and never returned. It was said that he died on the
way of the same illness that had barred him from England,
but there was no way of knowing for sure.

This abandoned woman was something of an eccentric.
Despite her poor health, which kept her from working and
supporting her large family, and the infirmity of her children,
"the poor little orphans," she obstinately insisted that each
single one of them, from the youngest on up, should continue

his education through high school—grammar school, mind you, was not enough—and that none of them, if she could help it, should have to work, but should study, study all the time. What little strength she had left she devoted to seeing that her brood was respectably dressed. (Whether or not they had enough to eat concerned her less, and here her standards were lower.) To accomplish this she was ready to sacrifice her eldest daughter, who had never been consecrated to learning, but who was in her opinion an extraordinary beauty whom she was determined to marry off to the first good earner to come along, despite the fact that the girl was still very young, perhaps not even sixteen; however, as she was developed for her age, her mother pretended that she was two years older than she was, a daughter, thank God, of whom there was no need to be ashamed. In fact, the girl was not pretty at all and had a sickly nature; yet there was something attractive, pleasingly frail, about her pinched face, her high breasts, her straight but slender neck, and the tiny, almost invisible freckles on either side of her turned-up nose which she had acquired in the Swiss city, to whose climate she had never adjusted. She liked to dress in bright colors: in her flaming blouse and darkly hued skirt with its unfashionably long blue hem she made one think of some magical, tropical bird. And yet unconsciously, without knowing quite what she was doing, she adjusted her style to suit whoever was staying in the house at the moment. Once, when the boarders were several young men who had some connection with the military, she developed a sudden interest in dancing and even in women's athletics. Later, when these were replaced by a group of college students, she took up calligraphy, geography, and grammar. One of the students, in fact, managed to teach her world history as far as Alexander the Great.

Hefetz alone, though he too became a permanent lodger in

time, inspired no change in her. But he did have a decent job, and the girl's mother, who took to calling him "our commissioner," did all that she could to persuade her daughter that he would provide her with everything and mustn't be refused (the woman was actually mad enough to believe that Hefetz had laid away a small fortune of which no one but herself was aware), especially since he loved her to distraction and would devote his whole life to making her happy.

To begin with, Hefetz's "love" and its symptoms amounted to nothing more than the overcourteous, slightly cynical manners of a weak single man toward a delicate girl. When he first discovered the house—he had been looking for a "Russian" home to eat in—he felt sorry for the abandoned family and did everything in his power to help out, perhaps even more than was in his power; the girl, however, he ignored completely, because she wasn't to his taste. As though on orders from the doctor he deliberately sought someone healthy, healthy and strong, though at bottom this too was a sham. Of course, he thought about marriage; orders were orders; it was impossible not to think of it, after all, impossible for his heart not to quicken when he did; there were even times (most often when he was made to remember some revolting thought or scene that none but a bachelor's four walls ever witness) when he resolved to make up his mind, to have done with it no matter what; only he was so unsure of himself and had so little self-respect, that he didn't take, didn't dare try to take, the first practical step. All his dreams of "encounters" and "affairs" had come to less than nothing. He would be drawn to someone, he would tremble with emotion —and he would get cold feet. In the end he developed perfect contempt for both his feelings and his fears. The one thing he couldn't decide was which derived more from his weakness, his outward correctness or his cynicism in private, and this made him more bitter yet. And yet he was genuinely pleased when the forsaken mother scolded him affectionately in front of her daughter for his "spendthrift ways" . . . on himself he spent nothing, only on them . . . what did he see in them? Why did he do it? He would blush with pleasure and stammer that it was nothing . . . nothing at all . . . he earned well . . . he had more than enough . . . it was only a loan . . . they could always pay it back. Then the mother would look significantly at her daughter, who would go to the window and stare at the people outside. . . .

And then all of a sudden, one overcast day, Hefetz noticed the girl and was smitten by her special frailty. The next morning he declared to himself: "I love her and I'm going to marry her." His doubts as to whether they were truly meant for each other were short-lived: he was poor, after all, and she was spoiled, unused to hard work (the boardinghouse, which was always untidy, was cared for by a chambermaid); besides which, he felt sincerely guilty for a while for "having realized"—a realization which he knew was in all probability untrue, but which he was disinclined to disbelieve—that all his kindness to the family had been on account of the girl alone. Once this brief period of uncertainty was over with, however, his love grew even stronger and he began to actively woo her. The doubts, of course, did not vanish completely; as always in these matters, in all matters, really, there remained a subtle residue of intangible, ephemeral, indefinable emotion.

And yet even in the period that followed, when her heart was officially his and he considered himself, both with her mother and in public, to be her "fiancé," there were times when all the tedium, the insanity, of his life in Palestine would come back to him as in an echo, overpower him, call upon him to return; then his interest in the girl would flag; his feelings would cool; and he would suffer immensely both because of the unnecessary relationship in which he was trapped and because of its weakening hold on him. He had already begun to regret the loss of his frightful, voluptuous dreams, the unwilling surrender of his bachelorhood, to which he had grown comfortably accustomed. And yet at the same time, he was struck with horror when he contemplated the collapse of the entire venture, horror for the girl, of course, for the way he was making her suffer, but also for the evanescence of his own infecund feelings, which weighed on him like an unpaid debt. *So this too has gone up in smoke*, said a terrible voice inside him. *How do you like it now, your "eternal love"?*

And still he pulled himself together and persisted. He forced himself to overlook many things and resolved to drain the cup come what may. There were fine, clear days on which he went with her for long walks, drank the fresh air by her side, dismissed each uncharitable thought, fondled her, cried in her lap, thought himself the happiest of men, marveled at his good fortune—yet all along he was haunted by a vague sense of dread that he did not believe in his happiness, that he was pretending to be someone else, that it was all a delusion. And the trouble was not only with her—though it was obvious to him that she did not deserve to have him cry in her lap or to make him happy—but above all, with himself . . . in spite of which he now spent all his time in his future mother-in-law's house and gave her every penny that he earned, even borrowing from his salary in advance. He was not yet convinced that the girl was right for him; he was still gnawed by doubts that robbed him of what peace he had left; yet his other self, the clerk in the old-clothes store—and perhaps not only the clerk —was content, sure that he had found bliss at last in this faraway city. He would sacrifice everything if he had to, but he would keep things from falling apart. *Then they could, then they might fall apart?* No, he mustn't think of it. It was too frightful a prospect.

Among his acquaintances at the time was a student named Hamilin, who hailed from the woman's home town. Though Russian by birth, in manner and appearance he was more like a Levantine who had somewhere acquired a smattering of European education. Yehezkel Hefetz had met many like him in Palestine and en route there among the Greeks and Armenians who had married and mixed with the Christian Arabs of Syria, or among the enterprising Arab guides in the cities who catered to the tourists. Hamilin's voice was hoarse and husky, like a syphilitic's, but his complexion, though swarthy, was clear and smooth. Yet despite its youthful good looks, his face was far from good-natured; a kind of sullen, bullish obstinacy leaped out at you even from his smile, which was thick and greasy, and in any case, infrequent. Among his student friends he was careful to make a point of his bourgeois, well-to-do, nonplebeian origins by eating and dressing especially well. Unlike others of his type, however, he did not particularly pride himself on his immunity to spiritual distress, or feel the need to express contempt for all "idealists"; poses such as these were foreign to his nature and he couldn't have cared about them less. If anything troubled him at all, rather, it was his desire to play a more brilliant role in life than either his talents or powers permitted, so that he worried over every new wrinkle in his face or clothes, though professing to pay it no attention. Among the careerist Swiss students there were many who were just as vulgar and complacent and no more concerned about hiding it, though all this was generally concealed by a thin, two-century-old veneer of culture, something that Hamilin, the middle-class Jew, was totally without; in the pell-mell, helter-skelter world of the immigrant Jewish students, on the other hand, he was absolutely unique, and he treated them without exception, as he put it, "like a pack of grinning beggars." More exactly, he simply ignored them, as though they were so many more wrinkles to disregard. He went his own way and looked for better company.

And yet from time to time, Hamilin dropped by the Russian woman's boardinghouse.

And then a little episode took place which Hefetz was still retelling to Menahem with much self-mockery several weeks after his return to Palestine. In fact, he even had a name for it, to wit, "A Tale of Two Houses, or, 'The Making of a Skeptic.' "

Across the street from the boardinghouse, far in the Jewish quarter, there was another house, a "house" in quotation marks. Though he occasionally paid his countrywoman a visit, Hamilin, it must be said, would have nothing to do with her cooking, a gentleman like him being used to other fare. Naturally, the woman held this against him even more than she did his having abandoned his wife and children in her home town (Hamilin, she knew, had married a woman with whom he had never gotten along, though he continued to let her support him along with his parents); to her daughter she broadly hinted that while the young student came only rarely to see them, this was not at all the case with the house across the street. *There* he was indefatigable, he didn't miss a night. More than once she had gone out to do her shopping in the morning and spied him on his way home. . . .

Of course, she exaggerated. The "indefatigable" Hamilin, particularly in recent years, was a lover of moderation and not at all the *roué* she made out. The young bride, however, believed every word of it and was duly impressed. She was also impressed by Hefetz's imprudent warning, coming on top of her mother's, that she must never be seen any more in Hamilin's company. The debauched scoundrel, it seemed, had already taken to boasting about town of his "little affair with the innkeeper's daughter." . . .

One evening Hefetz and Hamilin met in the street. Without a word of greeting they walked together as far as the two houses and parted ways. "He to his house and I to mine— which is the better off?" thought Hefetz, not without a flicker of pride. A feeling of warmth stirred within him, fed by the certain knowledge of the future that lay ahead, the family and home on which he would securely build his life. He was then at the very height of his epithilamial mood and had even begun to buy a few gifts for the wedding, which was only a few weeks away. But when he stepped inside the house, the girl wasn't there. Where had she gone? Her mother, who didn't know, insisted crossly that she must have waited for him and left when he hadn't come.

"But how could she have waited?" This was the usual hour he returned from work. He always came home at this time.

"Ah, what does it matter? She must have gone for a walk with some friend."

But when an hour went by and Hefetz had finished his meal and she still wasn't back, he went to look for her in the public park. She was nowhere to be seen. He started back in a foul mood. And then, as he walked toward a bench on a small arbored lane that adjoined the street of the two houses, he saw the young couple: she was lying in Hamilin's lap.

Hamilin didn't remain in the city much longer, because meanwhile he had been discovered cheating on some kind of examination and was permanently expelled from school. But despite the favorable prospects created by his departure, Hefetz too was soon on his way. It was no consolation to tell himself that while he, Hefetz, had acted all along in perfect good faith, without the least deception, Hamilin had taken advantage of the girl's inexperience to seduce her with his wiles—no, none at all. He was hurt to the quick, more hurt than in love. It did not even matter that he could now "have her all" to himself, in the words of her mother, who did everything in her power to patch things up between them and simply could not understand the ravings of the wretched groom.

"Suppose you're right . . . suppose I'll be the reality, since he's no longer here. But what kind of reality will I be? The heart is also real . . . and he still has a place in her heart. . . ."

"Heart?" The woman argued. "What heart? What does a girl like her know about hearts? She's a child, she doesn't feel she's done wrong . . . if she did, she'd never be able to look you in the face. See for yourself. . . ."

Yes, Hefetz saw everything, knew everything too, even . . . even that now that it was over he was glad it had turned out this way, glad that nothing had come of it. Was not this the inevitable fate of all "loves" like his? But he still could not settle down. More and more he felt a single urge: to get away . . . away, no matter what. . . . It was then that he began to regret having ever left Palestine. How could he have made such a mistake? There the people were different, completely different, and relations between them were different too. Ah! If only he had been able to appreciate life in the colony. Now he was being made to suffer. There such an episode could never have taken place. There was simply no way for it to happen—that much, at least, was certain. He would go back. . . .

II

The courtyards of Jerusalem's hospitals, like the corridors of its charities, were filled to overflowing with the sighs and groans of the ill and the afflicted, the indigent and in need, invalids on crutches and in bandages—all just as it was two thousand years ago when a young gentleman from the Galilee, who in the innocence of his delusion and the foolishness of his pride believed that he could cure the sick, the suffering, the weary and the burdened, appeared on the scene. The sextons of the burial society rushed through these courtyards every day, hurrying to dispose of the dead so as not to be late for the distribution of the dole, while the crowds lined up in the charities anxiously scanned the faces of the officials in charge, fearful lest they miss the visiting hours in the hospitals.

"Come, Brocheh," said an old woman to her companion in the courtyard of the hospital "Physick for the Soul," to which Yehezkel Hefetz had come at the appointed time to see a doctor. "Come, let's sit together on this bench. There's room here for the two of us."

"Come along then, Golda," Brocheh acquiesced, hastening to sit down first.

"I'm an honest woman and you're an honest woman and the Holy One has brought us together," Golda continued.

"Listen, I have something to tell you. The Lord preserve us
. . . Soreh. . . ."

"From Mishkenot?" *

"Eh? Yes, from Mishkenot."

The conversation groaned along. *Oy, oy, oy:* the Lord preserve us! She, Golda, wouldn't have minded if they had taken
everything that Soreh owned . . . the pillow that she slept on
if they liked . . . but to throw her out of her rooms—how
could they have done such a thing? It was robbery, robbery in
broad daylight. The poor woman was an orphan, there wasn't
a soul to look after her. . . .

Yes, I'm in Jerusalem, Hefetz said to himself. He sat down
on one of the stones.

The old woman was carried away by her words. Saliva ran
from her mouth and she struck her sunken chest with her fist.
Still, Hefetz thought, *it's nothing compared to the scene that
Soreh herself must have made when they threw her out with
her pillows a few hours ago.* As he sat huddled over, waiting
for the doctor, verses from the Prophets buzzed in his ears.
In his mind's eye he saw the ragged blond beard of the young
Galilean. The verse *And I have seen the tears of the oppressed*
ran through his head. *And they have no one to comfort them
. . .* no strength . . . *strength in the hands of their oppres-
sors . . .* no one to comfort . . . no one. . . .

Brocheh, who seemed the less perturbable of the two companions, murmured with a burglar's cool cheek:

"They'll take it all, the pillows too. They'll throw her from
her rooms. Of course they will. . . ."

"But they've taken it already!" cried Golda. "It's already
happened."

That's just what she, Brocheh, had been saying. They

* One of the first Jewish neighborhoods built outside of the old
walled city of Jerusalem.

would take it all. Everybody knew it. Golda should hear *her* story. . . .

And now Brocheh unburdened herself and poured out her own troubles. She knew a widow who had just given birth in the hospital—Boruch-Bentsia's wife from Kerem Shlomo.* Her husband had died several months ago of some trouble in his throat; he had already been in a bad way when they brought him to the hospital, and as it happened to be the Sabbath they wouldn't admit him, and he had died right there in the yard. Freyda, his wife, had no parents, and since her little boy was to be circumcised today, Brocheh, who had been looking after her in the hospital every day, suggested that she ask Reb Yankev to be the child's godfather. Reb Yankev would be glad to accept and was sure to give the mother half-a-mejidi for the honor.

Brocheh grew sarcastic. "What do you think? She could afford to turn up her nose at it? She could throw it away?" She herself stood to gain a quarter-of-a-mejidi for her pains; to be the godfather of an orphan, after all, and an eldest son at that, was no trifling matter. She was at Reb Yankev's yesterday and again today; it had all been settled in the morning. But when she was admitted to the hospital (she had arrived, in fact, much earlier, but they wouldn't let her in)— when she was finally admitted—she could hardly believe her ears: the circumcision, it seemed, had already taken place.

"Taken place? Without Reb Yankev? What are you saying?"

Golda had heard rightly. Believe it or not, the attendant told her that the circumcision had already taken place. The doctor, he said, hadn't wanted to wait, so he had roused the circumciser early in the morning and performed the operation at once; he himself had held the baby on his knees. But she,

* Another early neighborhood beyond the walls.

Brocheh, didn't believe that he could have been in such a hurry. He had simply wanted to be the godfather himself.

"But what about Freyda?"

"Freyda? That animal? She let them lead her by the nose like a cow!"

"It's a crime, a perfect crime!" grumbled Golda in protest. How could they have done it? Such an injustice! Freyda deserved a good scolding.

Brocheh went on complaining. "I'll ask her, 'Freyda,' I'll say to her, 'What have you done to me? Is that how you thank me for my trouble?' How can I face Reb Yankev if what they say is true? He'll spit in my face and he'll be right. He's not a child to be made a fool of. He took my word for it, he prepared himself this morning. . . ."

I'm in Jerusalem. Hefetz bit his parched lips.

Another woman was talking on the bench in front of him.

"I came to have my eye bathed and so I said to myself, 'I'll go see how my old one is doing' . . . he always comes to say hello at the door . . . at this time of day you can't go inside . . . the plague take those horrible attendants! If it weren't for them I'd never budge, I'd stay here all day long. Only now I don't know what to think . . . my man isn't up . . . he must be feeling worse if he didn't leave his room. . . ."

"And my boy," volunteered a man who was sitting beside her, "has been lying in bed for three days with a fever of forty degrees." *

Oy, oy, oy! The sighs came from another corner. A grown boy leaned weakly on his mother. In her other arm she held an infant that wailed and stretched out its hands.

"Forty is still less than forty-one," the sick boy's father's neighbor comforted him. When a man met with misfortune,

* Forty degrees of fever centigrade is 104 degrees fahrenheit.

it always seemed to him that things couldn't be worse; but they could, they certainly could be. He himself, as a matter of fact, knew a Jew, a scholarly man from a good family, but poor as the dickens (the Lord spare us the same!), who had a household of unmarried daughters and was himself sick in the legs. Words simply couldn't describe the poverty in his house. He had come to Jerusalem several years ago from Russia, this Jew, and hadn't earned a penny since. There was no need to mention his name, but in any case, you'd think that he couldn't possibly be worse off than he already was. But what did the dear Lord do? On top of all his troubles, He sent him a new one: a relative from one of the settlements whom he had to take into his house. Go sue!

That's me that he's talking about. Hefetz blanched.

Oy oy oy. The sighs and complaints didn't cease for a moment. But the light Jerusalem breeze, blowing over the bare hilltops, scattered them all and turned them to nought, to a meaningless cipher. Here a poor woman evicted from her house, thrown into the street without even a bed, so that she shore off her hair, beat her body with her fists and screamed in a voice that wasn't hers: "I've been robbed!" And here an old man about to die, his wife pining for him in the yard; a boy on fire with fever and his father waiting on burning coals for his recovery, while his neighbor on the bench tried to comfort him with the thought that it was better to be dying than dead; mothers wilting in their sorrow, their children wailing in their arms, the thread of life about to be cut forever. *Take them too you thieves, take them to the grave; what good to them is life. Oy oy oy* . . . distress upon distress . . . and yet it aroused absolutely no feeling. Even the hopes of Reb Yankev, Reb Yankele Goldmann, who had counted on being a godfather today, had come to nothing. So many sorrows in the world—and nothing ever came of them. . . . *In the yard, on the stones, lay the father of the circumcised infant, because on the Sabbath he grew worse, because on the Sabbath it was time to die, because on the Sabbath you can't come in. Weep not, 'tis the holy Sabbath.* Nothing. The breeze blew through the yard of the hospital, the stones lay idly about. The world was turned to stone. *Stone.* It was all one. He whom the evil had reached, let him suffer. *And we?*

"Now I'm a real Jerusalemite," said Hefetz to Menahem, who was waiting for him in the yard when he emerged from the hospital. "What I mean is, now I'll stand around and do nothing. Or rather, I'll sit. And with relatives . . . yes, with relatives like mine. Well, there you have it."

The two friends strolled slowly through the streets of old and new Jerusalem. In a store within the walls of the old city Hefetz bought the truss that the doctor prescribed for him and put it on right away. Then, because he was annoyed at having nothing to do and was bothered by wearing it, he began to talk freely, though not about what he was thinking. Once again—just as he had done then, years before—he talked about things that really didn't matter to him in the least.

He thought: *What an ugly way to suffer . . . what an ugly way to suffer. . . . In the book of Job the Leper it is written: "And he took a potsherd to scrape himself with." . . . Only I am not Job: I have no complaints against God. In fact, I have no God. I have nothing to do with God. And even if I could complain—I'm not complaining and I don't wish to protest. I'm not Job. And I don't sit in ashes, either, but in refuse, in the refuse of my own ugly suffering. Only I don't let go of the potsherd. I can't stop scratching. Yes, a potsherd is probably the one thing I can't do without. . . .*

Yehezkel Hefetz, farmer, or rather ex-farmer, had thoughts such as these, but to Menahem he spoke about—the "social reality" of life in Jewish Jerusalem. There were about fifty or sixty thousand Jews in Jerusalem, or so it was said, for no one knew exactly. ("No one knows! Ai, ai, what a pity!" mocked someone inside the speaker.) "But even if we grant," he earnestly went on, "that it's an accurate estimate, is there anything about such a number—a number one and a half times as great as that of the exiled Jews who returned to Judea from Babylonia—is there anything about it that's the least bit encouraging?" ("Encouraging to whom?" asked the same voice inside him.) "Sixty thousand! But ninety percent of them, for the most part, live off the donations that they or somebody else get in the mail. Their main occupation is trading shares in their beggarly charities. All of these fat cats whom you see going by in their carriages are stuffed with the blood of the miserable paupers whose dole they've made off with. There isn't one of these frock-coated, ignorant leeches who doesn't eat up the shares of ten others along with his own!

"It's too horrible for words!" Hefetz's heart wasn't in it, but he struggled to keep talking. "A large city completely dependent on the whims of philanthropy! A city which if you deprived it of the handouts it gets from all over the world—would die of starvation! Do you have any idea, Menahem, of the kinds of things that go on when it comes to doling out this dole—of all the vile intrigues that take place between the officials of these almshouses and those who speculate on them?" He, Hefetz, happened to have looked into it. ("Now's the time to look important!" said the voice.) "Did you ever realize that this dole, which comes from the four corners of the earth, isn't all handled in one central place, but is divided up among various charities according to the country of its origin? Do you know that there are poor charities and rich charities, and that in Jerusalem it's the lucky man who gets born into a rich one? Did it ever occur to you, Menahem, that when these same Jews assemble on the Day of the Rejoicing of the Law to dance and sing 'Happy art thou, O Israel,' what they really mean to say is: 'Happy art thou, O Israel, that thou hast the dole'?"

Too horrible for words!

But by the time he arrived at the house of his uncle Reb Yosef Hefetz, where he lay down to rest until his "discomfort" (of which no one in the house was aware) felt better, his judgment had mellowed a bit. The language he used no longer pricked and jabbed like a needle, but had become casual and almost bookish, as though he had resolved to put his impressions of the last few days into a final form.

"But in general, Menahem, Jerusalem, after all, is a city like any other," he declared. "The details and barely visible nuances can be easily overlooked, but on the whole—a city! People live and die in it, love and hate, weep and make merry, get sick and get better, get better and get sick. Weddings . . ."—here he permitted himself a jocular tone— ". . . take place with or without a matchmaker; funerals are attended by great crowds or by none. We've made the rounds today, haven't we, and seen for ourselves: natives, tourists, people in the streets; carriages rolling; plenty of priests and missionaries too. Only instead of factory chimneys spitting their clouds of soot here, there are minarets, church spires, columns of dust. Yes, Menahem, there's no lack of dust, and the pious housewives nearly faint from it in the streets whenever they go out. Haven't you seen them, Menahem? Listen! What a wonderful image! Listen! At the very same time, their menfolk, who really aren't men at all, are sitting in their study houses, or in their shops, or by the Wailing Wall, and drinking dust there too; and their children, the children of the

ruins—weren't we in the synagogue they call 'the Ruin' *
today and didn't we see?—yes, their children, Menahem,
whose heads are full of the dust of prayer books and Talmuds,
though none of it means a thing to them, so that even the
blood in their veins is diluted with dustwater—their children
sway back and forth and daydream feebly of distant lands
. . . do you understand what I'm saying? Distant lands,
where the people are rich, rich, rich, like they are in America,
and without whom—I mean without those rich people—
Jerusalem would be destroyed in the twinkling of an eye. A
sublime poem, isn't it? A poem of dust! But what does it matter? For the time being they're rich and have mercy and give,
and Jerusalem prays and goes about its business, while the
hope for some miraculous windfall flickers on in its rheumy,
half-blind eyes. We're in Jerusalem, Menahem!"

But Menahem was not in Jerusalem for long. Even before
the Passover he returned to the commune, where he reported
that the injured man's condition was good. In fact, it was a
joke, there was nothing serious about it; on the whole, it was
safe to say that he was staying in Jerusalem because he liked
it there and was making out well. If only everyone were no
sicker than he! True, it could hardly be said of his uncle
(Hefetz, Menahem related, had a real uncle in Jerusalem, and
not just some distant cousin as had been thought; Hefetz's
mother and the uncle's late wife, in fact, were buried in the
same cemetery in Gomel. Truly, an uncle from the dead!)
—it could hardly be said of him that he was a particularly
rich man. "But he does have two grown daughters. The older

* The Synagogue of Rabbi Judah the Hasid, the largest of the
synagogues in the old Jewish quarter within the walled city, commonly called "the Ruin" because of its state of disrepair from its
destruction by Moslems in 1720 until its reconstruction in 1869.

one, comrades, is really a little too old—" ("She can't be any older than our cook," volunteered the Master-of-intrigue) "—but upon my life, the other's in the bloom of youth! In a word, if you care to be jealous, here's reason enough: it's a Turkish paradise, comrades, he won't be leaving it any too soon. He's lost and gone forever, your Hefetz . . . the devil take it!"

III

"And whereas experience has taught me . . . experience
has taught me . . . that all phenomenal events . . . all con-
tingent phenomena as we know them are vanity and evil. . . .
And whereas I have seen . . . I have seen . . . that all the
causes and objects of my fears . . . are substantially . . .
neither good nor evil . . . but only as they affect the spirit
. . . I made up my mind . . . my mind . . . to inquire after
the true good. . . ."

Reb Yosef Hefetz, Yehezkel's uncle, pored over the book
that lay on the long table and whispered to himself as he read.
The food which was brought to him by Miriam, his youngest
daughter, stood before him untouched. He munched on a
piece of bread, chewing his cud and looking at his book,
whispering the words out loud and chewing on them too.
Yehezkel, his late wife's nephew, sat idly across from him and
understood nothing of what he heard. *All phenomena as we
know them are vanity and evil.* There was reason neither to
weep nor rejoice, yet somehow one was supposed to inquire
after "the true good." *The true good?*

Reb Yosef continued his recitation. ". . . From which one
may postulate . . . the necessity of knowing. . . ."

Yes, the necessity of knowing . . . that he, Yehezkel

Hefetz, wore a truss and had the kind of injury that he was embarrassed to talk about. Why couldn't he have broken a leg? Or lost the sight of one eye? Why did he have to be injured in this of all places? Below the waist . . . after having been rescued—temporarily—from the crisis . . . above the waist? In any case, the injury was a fact. Only his heart, his prophetic heart, was still in one piece. From which one might postulate . . .

"Father, eat!"

The voice was Esther's, Reb Yosef's eldest daughter.

The lenses of the unanswering man's glasses glittered frighteningly. Yes, they frightened him: substantially they may have been neither good nor evil, but as they focused on his daughter, whose eyes shone back with a glassy blackness of their own, he was frightened. He, Yehezkel Hefetz, who was bound by a truss, and who a few days later was finally to be sent to a hospital, though not to one for the physically ill; who here, in this house at the city's end, turned his heart—the only strong and healthy organ he had ever had—to inquire after the true good; was frightened by the glasses of his learned uncle, the scholar Reb Yosef Hefetz.

Reb Yosef placed his handkerchief on the open page of his book. He gave himself the benefit of the doubt by not shutting it, straightened up, moved closer to the table and cast an inquiring eye on what lay before him. And yet there was something strange about the way he sat on the hard stool by the table, as though he were not really in his own home surrounded by his family, but rather crouched in hiding in the back of some wagon bumping from place to place in Germany or the Low Countries during the Middle Ages. In any case, he sat up straight only for a moment, then reverted to the habitual slouch that he had acquired from constant reading. Lastly, he removed his glasses and placed them alongside his handkerchief. One corner of his sparse, delicate beard strayed irregularly outward, while the other, which was longer and narrower, pointed sharply at his chest. The look in his large, almond-shaped, scholarly eyes was one of suppressed anger, the expression of a man who has fallen among unappreciative strangers, while his broad-brimmed new hat, which did not match the rest of his clothing, but rather left the impression of having been bought especially for some impending journey, slanted over his eyes, giving them, in conjunction with his long, straight, neatly-trimmed earlocks, a rather pedantic and demanding appearance. . . .

Still, his remarks as he ate were pleasant enough at the outset. Some books, he observed, were especially good strengtheners of the faith. The particular one he had been reading (here he cast a glance at the volume he had pushed to one side) was practically all that was left of his treasure. In Russia he had many books, a portion of which, though only a small one, he had brought with him to Palestine. But to this day they were lying in the customs house in Jaffa: perfectly good books, only the duty was too high and he hadn't the money to pay it. There they lay, no doubt rotting away, while without them he felt as helpless as though he'd been deprived of one hand. Wherever his books were, there he was at home; among them he was in his element and possessed his true powers. Let the slightest question arise on the subject of Hebrew law, legend, philosophy or language—his books were there to rely on. Back in Gomel, there hadn't been a gap on his shelf: he had his plain edition of the Talmud (he had given away his annotated set to his son in Kiev on his wedding day), two collections of the Midrash, the Vilna edition of *Jacob's Spring*, a Bible with all the commentaries, Ben-Ze'ev's *Lexicon* *of Roots,* several concordances, Zunz's history of the Jews in German, Spinoza's *Tractate,* also in German, *The Inquiry into God,* Mendelssohn, Salvador (ah!), *The Contemporary Guide for the Perplexed,* yes, even Schleiermacher. And then there was Rabbi Samson Rafael Hirsch's *Horeb:* that he still missed.* If only he at least had his *Horeb,* which was such a great strengthener of the faith! In fact, if it wasn't boasting to say so, he, Reb Yosef, had even looked into Kant, though were it not out of respect for such a famous philosopher he would have said that there wasn't a new or original thought in his works. His ideas were all borrowed from Hume; Reb Yosef had come across this opinion, which happened to coincide with his own, in a book by a well-known German philosopher whose name he could no longer remember. Kant

* The Midrash—the corpus of early rabbinic legend and homiletic commentary on the Bible.

Jacob's Spring—a midrashic anthology by the 16th-century Palestinian scholar Ya'akov ibn Haviv.

Lexicon of Roots—a Hebrew dictionary compiled by the 18th-century German-Jewish grammarian Yehudah ben Ze'ev.

The Inquiry into God—a 19th-century Hebrew translation of Spinoza's *Short Treatise on God.*

Spinoza's *Tractate*—The *Tractatus Theologico-Politicus,* Spinoza's attack on revealed religion and rabbinical authority.

Zunz—Leopold Zunz (1794–1886), German-Jewish historian of Judaism.

Mendelssohn—Moses Mendelssohn (1729–1786), German-Jewish philosopher and seminal figure of the Haskalah or Hebrew Enlightenment.

Salvador—Joseph Salvador (1796–1873), French-Jewish historian of Judaism.

The Contemporary Guide for the Perplexed—Hebrew work by the Galician-Jewish philosopher Nachman Krochmal (1785–1840).

Schleiermacher—Friedrich Schleiermacher (1768–1834), German Protestant theologian.

Samson Rafael Hirsch—German orthodox rabbi and theologian (1808–1888).

disproved and tore down but he never replaced it with any-thing. *The Critique of Pure Reason?* A perfect case in point: the destructive outweighed the constructive. It was all about cause and effect, just like Hume, but even Hume said nothing new. You could find it all in Spinoza. The theory of the phenomenon? Bah! There was no real contradiction. It was one and the same thing, only so long as it remained *in posse* it was cause, while once *in esse* it became effect. . . .

Reb Yosef popped a pickled green olive and about half an oliveweight of soft bread into his mouth. As he talked he cut away the crust, which was too hard for his worn teeth to bite into, and left it on the table. For a moment his face lit up with phenomenological satisfaction; then it darkened again and he exclaimed:

"If a person tells you that he understands the *Ethics*—laugh in his face! They excommunicated Spinoza as a heretic and an atheist, but the man was a saint, a great saint. Now every-one drinks from his waters and sees by his hidden light. The things he says about the appetites of the senses, about honor, about wealth! Mirages, he calls them! Such possessions don't help us live our lives at all, but undermine them completely, do you follow? Here you have the height of wisdom, true philosophy: 'For the moral law is not a commandment in it-self, but only seems so relative to the imperfect human will, which is led astray by ephemeral sensations and naturalistic, experimental reasoning.' Or again: 'The moral consciousness is experienced as something imposed from without because the will is impure; but for the pure, holy and ethical will it is not enslavement to a yoke, but freedom itself.'"

He, Reb Yosef, praise God, knew the whole *Ethics* by heart. What a great moral handbook! There was nothing that it didn't treat of: jealousy, prodigality, love of humanity . . . yes, love of humanity. . . . He, Reb Yosef, had nothing but contempt for those who talked about the famous philosophers solely on the basis of having read about them in some history book. No one read the original works themselves any more. (This was an allusion to Shneirson, Miriam's volunteer tutor in Hebrew and Bible, a young man from a well-to-do family who was certainly no worse than the run of his contemporaries, but who was disliked by his pupil's father perhaps for the very reason that he was young and well off.) All his life, praise God, he, Reb Yosef, had sunk his teeth into the sources.

"Would you believe it? There are people who actually think that they know all there is to know about the attributes! Well, let them think it. . . . And in general, *The Inquiry into God!* Has any of you ever read or studied *The Inquiry into God?* Has any of you understood it? In order to understand such a book, a person first has to be familiar with Descartes and with Spinoza's commentary on him. Then you can go on to the little book that Spinoza wrote on human happiness, which was 'discovered,' as it were, fifty years ago. And then the letters—Spinoza's letters! Only once you've read them can you understand the question of . . . of . . . even of determinism and free will! The fact is that God himself, as it were, has no free will. He too is subject to his own laws, but at the same time he's their master, his own legislator! Knowledge is free will! Therefore—" Reb Yosef cocked his head at Yehezkel "—therefore, the more a man knows, the more intelligently he inquires after the truth, the more he frees himself from necessity and the laws of the environment and cleaves to God. An unfathomably profound thought! The *Tractate*, you understand, is already easier. True, there are things in it that a Jew oughtn't to know, oughtn't to know at all . . . the biblical criticism, for instance . . . but here too it's a question of grasping the true meaning. The intelligent reader simply won't. . . ."

Reb Yosef spat out the pit of the last remaining olive, whose taste hadn't pleased him at all (ach, that Miriam! The olives the storekeeper gave her! Bitter as wormwood!), and washed his hands in the fingerbowl preparatory to reciting the grace after meals.

Despite the fact that according to the *Ethics,* "honor," like wealth and the other "mirages," was ultimately a "self-defeating possession"; and despite the fact, too, that both in thought and out loud Reb Yosef was used to making short shrift of Shneirson, Miriam's tutor, who regularly lunched in their house; he could still never resist the postprandial temptation to relate to the latter his "biography" (yes, always to Shneirson, never to Yehezkel, and not just once or twice, but time after time), the story of his odyssey on earth.

The life and times of the autobiographer Reb Yosef Hefetz, as he was in the habit of narrating them, naturally divided themselves into the following three periods:

1) *The first period.* Until his wedding. Study on his own and tutoring in Talmud, the Talmudic commentaries and the medieval codes. What more could be said about it?

2) *The second period.* Long arguments with his father-in-law. (Also a Hefetz . . . Yehezkel's maternal grandfather. . . . the whole family a stubborn, prideful lot. . . .) Bible and Hebrew grammar. But talk about grammar! There wasn't a book on the subject, from *The Compendium* to *A Guide to Language* * and *An Aid to the Vowel Points*, which he, the punctilious Yosef Hefetz, hadn't studied—and completely on his own, too. A true autodidact! Not only that, but he had a

* The *Compendium*—A Hebrew grammar by the medieval French-Jewish scholar David Kimchi (1160–1235).

A Guide to Language—A Hebrew grammar by the Russian-Jewish Hebraist Haim Zvi Lerner (1815–1889).

memory like a steel trap, praise God! It was during this period, too, that he first ventured into the field of philosophy, from which (the Giver of Knowledge be thanked!) he emerged completely unscathed, having embarked on it not for selfish ends of his own but for the sake of wisdom alone, as he wrote at the time to his father-in-law (the two of them, it was true, were living in the same town, but he wrote for the sheer pleasure of setting down his thoughts in the holy tongue, as was the common practice in those days) in a lengthy apologia for devoting himself equally to the two things, the sacred Hebrew language and the philosophy of the Gentiles. In fact, if he wasn't mistaken (for he hadn't the patience to look for it), a draft of this letter was still in his possession. Of the study of Hebrew he had written: "For as the splendor of the Israelitish speech is all that hath been bequeathed to the House of Jacob from its glorious antiquity, let us bountifully pride ourselves on it, for it is to us as a vine of beauty and choicely spiced wine; neither hath its eye grown dim nor its vigor abated; its sayings are pleasant refreshment to those parched with thirst; though twice one-thousand years have passed since e'er it graced the lip like other tongues," and so on and so forth. To tell the truth, he could no longer remember the rest of it. Juvenilia! As for the philosophy, apropos of which one might well quote Isaiah, Chapter 2, Verse 8, "And they strike hands with the Gentiles," he had written as follows: "Faith and reason, my dear father-in-law! From time immemorial they have walked together in sweet and brotherly friendship, guiding mankind between them, clearing the way for it to set its foot lest it stumble or swerve from its path! Yea, like the bright stars that shine in the firmament above, they show it whither and how to guide its steps across the trackless sea of life's trials and reversals. . . ."

Yes, those had been the days. His father-in-law, a timber merchant, and a hard Jew to deal with as he had already had occasion to mention, turned a deaf ear to his pleas and demanded that he, Reb Yosef, decide "whither and how to guide his steps" on some practical course in life; but he, the youthful scholar, refused to listen, nor had he ever regretted taking the road that he took. Both in Kiev and later in Gomel, he had always managed to make ends meet on the income from the private lessons that he gave to the children of wealthy Jews. In fact he even gave one lesson, an hour a week devoted to German and logic, to a Gentile, a Russian Orthodox Christian. God knew that he had never been one to mix with the Gentiles or court their good graces, but say what you will, this was something he had never forgotten. Yes, he was proud of the fact that he had taught in the home of a Russian official—and without committing a single *faux pas!* It was enough to recall that the people of Gomel would whisper as he passed: "Do you see that Jew over there with the earlocks? He's a tutor at His Excellency Kultonov's. And not just an ordinary tutor, mind you, for they all look up to him and call him 'our teacher,' "—all of which was perfectly true. Moreover, he, Reb Yosef, did not sit there with his head uncovered, but actually wore a skullcap, to which no one thought to object . . . so it was whispered . . . and in fact, though it went against his grain to comply, several times Jews approached him to ask that he intercede for them with His Excellency in this or that suit. And once a large dealer, also a Jew, came to the house on some business. Naturally, he remained standing in the doorway, but when he saw Reb Yosef inside he plucked up his nerve, as it were, and stepped in. "How dare you take the liberty of intruding in my house?" asked the official. "But I can see I'm not alone," the Jew replied. "Not every Jew is alike," the official retorted. "Don't think it's to your credit, Yankel, that Gospodin Hefetz tutors my son. Gospodin Hefetz is a learned man—but who are you?"

The excited autobiographer surveyed his audience with naïve pride, mingled with curiosity to see what impression his story had made on Shneirson—yes, on Shneirson most of all. He himself, the protagonist, made no attempt to conceal his satisfaction, as though it was not really himself who was being praised, but someone else, an entirely different person.

And after all, was there really any call to boast? Only . . . only take, for example, the science of geometry: at first he himself didn't know how much he knew. You could count on an autodidact never to know the true extent of his powers; in some cases he tended to exaggerate, while in others he sold himself short . . . and he, Reb Yosef, sold himself short. Only it chanced to happen—not that he, Reb Yosef, really believed in chance—that he and a pupil of his, a student at the polytechnicum (who, he recently heard, had converted to Christianity and was soon to receive a professorship at some university in Western Europe), were discussing higher mathematics—and when they came to Lobachevski's theorem, he, Reb Yosef, expressed an opinion which so startled his pupil that he exclaimed: "Gospodin Hefetz, I simply must tell this to the professors!"

Reb Yosef lapsed for a moment into sweet memory without bothering to finish his story, the details of which only an expert could have appreciated in any case, thus ruling out—but a word to the wise was sufficient! Instead, he returned to the tale of the high Russian official and to an incident that took place in his home. Once, on a Friday—it was right before his pupil's final exams—he was requested to come back on the following day, which his employer had forgotten was the Jewish Sabbath. He was getting a ruble an hour at the time, but he answered without hesitation: "I'm much obliged to you for being my providers, but I happen to be a Jew, and no Jew would profane or make light of the Sabbath for any amount of money in the world." They hadn't meant to make him betray his religion, of course, having simply forgotten what the next day was, but when they heard his reply, both father and son were quick to beg his forgiveness . . . and yet the fact of the matter was that the man himself was no great lover of Jews . . . on the contrary, it later turned out that when the pogroms came to Gomel he nearly joined the "Black Hundreds" *—or so it was said! But even the worst anti-Semite admired a Jew who was truly a man of faith, that is, who insisted on keeping his religion. And the proof of it was that when he, Reb Yosef, returned on the following Sunday, the family simply couldn't do enough to make amends (the boy, it so happened, had done exceedingly well on his first set of tests). His mother, the official's wife, invited him to have a cup of tea in the sitting room—tea! tea with Her Excellency!—while his pupil literally danced around him: "Whom do I see? Gospodin Hefetz! *Golubtshik!*" †

From this incident, which Reb Yosef never failed to include in his account, telling it, especially lately, with such unusual relish that it banished all moroseness, he continued on to—

3) *The third period of his life*, which was—alas!—the Palestinian period.

To be sure, Reb Yosef did not proceed directly by announcing "now we will move on to period number three";

---

* The popular name of the antisemitic League of the Russian People, founded in 1904 and so called because of its organization in cadres of 100 men each.

† Russian: Dearest!

rather, he approached the subject roundaboutly, taking one step toward it and two away. One had the distinct impression that he was loathe to part from the second period, that golden age of sweet illusion, to plunge all of a sudden into a maelstrom of setbacks and misfortunes. As though seeking to delay things a bit longer, to forestall them a little more, he would begin to spin endless anecdotes, the first of which was as a rule to the point, only to be followed by one tale after another until the overall thread was completely lost. Reb Yosef's favorite—and most relevant—story concerned Czar Nicholas I, who had heard of a Jew in his kingdom whose piety was no bar to his wisdom, so that his observance of the Law went hand in hand with his intellectual enlightenment—a combination as rare in those times as it was in these. The czar, who took a special interest in such cases, commanded that the Jew be brought before him in order to put his wisdom to the test. But when he received the czar's message, the Jew was overcome by fear and made haste to shave off his beard and buy fashionable clothes so as to appear presentable before the throne. "Is this the man you told me about?" asked Nicholas when he saw him. "But I have many like him, I see nothing special about him at all!" And he had him dismissed at once.

And again Reb Yosef's weary eyes, which smoldered with suppressed irritation, lit up with a childish, innocent, almost unearthly light. A helpless smile, typical of poets and absentminded professors, whose heads, so they say, are always in the clouds, spread over his face, while his agreeably clipped earlocks, as it were, repeated silently after him: "No, Reb Yosef isn't one to cringe before the czar; *he*, you may be sure, has always stuck to his guns. . . ." But immediately his venerable beard, whose hairs had been shed in the pages of many a sacred text, began to wag with resentment; recalling his pupil, the Russian official's son, who used to affectionately call him "dear teacher," Reb Yosef compared the bitter present with the glorious past and declared:

—The younger generation in Palestine simply didn't know how to honor its elders and betters. In Gomel his house had been open to students of every kind, Jews and Gentiles alike: as far as ideas and religion were concerned, he had learned from his masters the philosophers to be a tolerant man. No, it wasn't the irreligiousness of the younger generation in Palestine that concerned him. Even if they never went the length of converting, many of his old students, after all, whom he had taught in the course of twenty-five years of pedagogical labor, had gone on to become *Privatdozenten* * (many others, alas, had gone the way of apostasy completely); yet there wasn't a one of them with whom Reb Yosef hadn't been on friendly terms, and by whom he wasn't well liked, not to say respected. Only here, in Palestine, ever since the moment he'd arrived. . . .

For some reason, Reb Yosef fell silent. A moment later, however, unable to restrain himself, he went on:

—Here . . . to tell the truth (and the truth wasn't easy, wasn't easy to listen to—he was only asking for trouble if he told it—but he would tell it anyway!)—here a person counted for nothing. He didn't want to mention names—A or B or C—but the truth was the truth. Philosophy began with a search for the truth, and he, Reb Yosef, was for the truth. True, it had been proven that the human brain could never grasp the truth in its entirety, but the power of human

---

* *Privatdozenten*—In German and other European universities, private tutors or lecturers recognized by the university but receiving no salary other than fees from their students. Generally speaking, this was the highest university post that a Jew could attain without undergoing conversion.

intelligence, whose defining mark was the truth, was great nonetheless. Let the fool refrain from boasting that he knew as much as the wise man! "The beginning of all knowledge is to know that we don't know," said the philosopher, and yet there was a considerable difference between he who knew that he didn't know and he who did not. Yes, it was his, Reb Yosef's opinion that there was all the difference in the world between the philosopher and the nonphilosopher, a difference in knowledge of the truth. Yehezkel, who was sitting across from him, should realize how foolish it was to scoff at philosophy. *Vernunft und Wahrheit! Die Wahrheit!* It was no small thing, *die Wahrheit!* He had been a teacher for thirty years, thirty consecutive years; he had taught young and old, beginners and advanced; but the schools in Palestine ("I'm sure you all know about our wonderful schools here in Palestine . . . our Jewish school system . . . feh!")—the schools in Palestine hadn't thought he was good enough for them! And why? What had he done that was wrong? He hadn't spoken Hebrew with the Sephardic pronunciation—as though it were in that very accent that God had talked to Moses on Mount Sinai! Not that he denied its correctness— no, he himself was ready to admit that it was historically authentic. True, at first he had been against it; the question had troubled him no end; but now, having thoroughly looked into it, he had come to revise his opinion. He, Reb Yosef, did not like to decide things in the contemporary fashion while standing on one leg; he had spent many days and nights studying the two accents, the Sephardic and the Ashkenazic,* and he was now finally convinced that Rabbi Joshua Steinburg,†

---

* The two traditional systems of Hebrew pronunciation, the first prevalent among the Sephardim or Jews of the Balkans and the Arab world, the second among the Ashkenazim or Jews of Eastern Europe.

† Russian scholar and Hebraist (1839–1908).

in the introduction to his book *An Outline of the Language of the Hebrews,* had been mistaken, and that there were irrefutable proofs in favor of . . . only what was the use? One might as well talk to the wall!

No one uttered a word. The parties to Reb Yosef's tirade stared at the floor and said nothing. This made him angrier yet and he added abruptly:

"Here there's a place for people like Hamilin!"

"Hamilin?" Yehezkel was startled.

"Yes, Hamilin, Goldmann's brother-in-law. Do you think I don't know the rascal? He was once a pupil of mine when he was a boy in Kiev—and not one of the better ones either, I can assure you! A brain like an ox! A rotten apple only breeds worms . . . but here . . . here every little pagan is a huge success! Yes, here the doors open before you if only you can chatter away in a few European languages. Tell me if I'm not speaking the truth! He isn't even here yet, but a thousand jobs are waiting for him because he can call himself 'doctor.' This institute and that institute are bidding to get him . . . he has more offers than he can count! Whereas the fact of the matter is—but perhaps you don't know what a magnificent college they have in Beirut?"

Yehezkel was curious. "Beirut?"

Shneirson explained that Doctor Hamilin had received his degree in Beirut, though he had studied in Europe before that. As for Reb Yosef, he should know that his rancor was groundless: he, Shneirson, had learned from a reliable source that Hamilin was coming only to visit and had no intention of staying for good.

Reb Yosef, however, refused to hear of it, while Yehezkel kept his amazement to himself.

Hamilin?

IV

Miriam's two short chestnut braids flashed fondly at Shneirson, her tutor and guide. Ah, all she wanted, her one real desire, was to go on learning! Education was the only true happiness. What was an uneducated person? What was he worth? Look at her Uncle Haim or at any of her girlfriends. Look at herself, for that matter. What was she worth? If only she would be accepted by the Teachers' Institute—who could compare to her then? How happy that would make her! Her two braids, slipping from beneath the white scarf on her head, bobbed against the well-shaped shoulders visible beneath her sailor suit. She bent over the "optimus," the large, smoky kerosene stove, on which a pot of thick soup boiled and foamed while several cracked egg shells lay whitely beside it, her face tanned and pretty, if not finely featured, her dark blue, flirtatious eyes flecked with a catlike gray-green, the lines of her mouth fresh and attractive, for all their stubborn, uninviting, unfeminine energy. The lively chatter of her speech, jumping from one thing to another, rose above the drone of the sewing machine and the plaintive hum of Esther, her pinched, wasted sister, who sat singing softly over it.

Miriam threw the egg shells through the open window and observed to Shneirson that he was absolutely right. A person

had to stand up for himself. There was nothing more important than to be stubborn, particularly for a woman. Her father, for example, thought that a woman had no business studying at all; as far as he was concerned, her only job was to marry and be some man's cook. It was enough for him to be educated himself—what happened to other people didn't interest him. In general, her father didn't think much of the other sex. Her brother in Russia, for instance, who had only girls—father behaved as though he were completely childless! Too much to do with women, he said, was bad for the memory. Ha ha! What did Mr. Shneirson think about that? It was really her luck that she had an older sister: otherwise she would have no peace at all. No, if it weren't for that he would be at her constantly with his one refrain: "A girl your age ought to be married!" As it was, it was her sister who bore the brunt of it. She, Miriam, was embarrassed to repeat the things he said. "Esther drives the men away with her own two hands. . . . She just won't think about her future. . . ." Those were his very words . . . to think of it . . . wasn't it awful! Only what future did she, Miriam, have in Jerusalem? If she didn't get into the Institute she would either go to Jaffa or to Cairo. She could take in sewing half the day and study the other half. Here she was just a burden to everyone, including herself. What kind of a cook was she? Was this the work she was meant for? Here she simply saw no future for herself at all. Father was always in a bad mood. "Poor tempers make poor teachers"—where was that written? Where? In *The Ethics of the Fathers?* Yes, in *The Ethics of the Fathers,**
now she remembered. . . . And in fact, father once said—as a joke, of course—that this was why he had stopped being a "teacher" and had become a "tutor." But he still had a temper —and that was no joke! She, Miriam, couldn't recall a single

* The Mishnaic tractate *Pirke Avot*, a collection of moral precepts.

time when he had managed to control it. And not only his pupils enraged him, but everyone and everything. Nothing pleased him, nothing seemed right or true or fair. He gave no one any peace with his demands. And yet, though he appeared to be satisfied with himself at least, even this was not true. And his temper had gotten much worse since they'd come to Palestine. The doctors had advised him ten years ago to move to a warm climate, but as long as mother was alive, nothing could be done; she was afraid to start over in a new place . . . she too, mother, had trouble with her kidneys . . . and in fact, last summer father had begun to feel better. Father believed that the Land of Israel could cure anything——it was only the people that he didn't like. How he loved Jerusalem! How beautiful he thought it was! Jerusalem, he said, was the navel of the world. . . . But ach, here was Uncle Haim coming to eat already—and the food wasn't even ready! Some cook she was! What must they think of her? And just look at what she was doing now! Why didn't someone speak up? Why was she cooking in the middle of the house instead of in the kitchen? What madness! She would move the stove to the kitchen . . . wasn't anyone going to help? But Mr. Shneirson really needn't bother . . . needn't bother at all . . . he too must be hungry by now . . . why didn't he chew on a slice of bread in the meantime? He mustn't be embarrassed to ask . . . ach, they were all out of water. She was going to fetch water . . . she had completely forgotten that there wasn't a drop left . . . she had no memory at all . . . but she would leave her apron on . . . she would drape her little sweater over her shoulders and go . . . wasn't it a lovely sweater? Tra-ta-ta. . . .

Once Miriam had disappeared and Shneirson, having thought the matter over, had come to the conclusion that he should go help his pupil draw water, Esther awoke from her frozen trance, cast a dull glance around her at the walls of the room, and noticed her Uncle Haim, her father's brother, who had come to eat. *Had he said something?* But what was his opinion? What would be the end?

"The end? Why nothing . . . father will get a job in the end . . . lord yes . . . only where is he anyway? Has he gone to the synagogue?"

Esther withdrew inside herself once more. The sewing machine droned on. It was useless to talk to people—they never understood a thing. Miriam agreed with Shneirson that the best thing was to be stubborn. Ah, if only she, Esther, were a little more stubborn herself! If only she could learn to stand up for her rights and not always give in for somebody else's sake! How much longer could she go on working day and night at this machine? For whom and for what? And what would it all come to?

"Are you also on Miriam's side, Uncle?" she asked, unable to restrain herself in the end.

"On Miriam's side? In what?"

"In what? She says that a person should be stubborn and look out for himself, only for himself . . . that everyone should be stubborn. . . ."

"Stubborn?" Uncle Haim took his time in answering. But one word led to another and he went on: "Yes, stubborn. . . ." He too had been stubborn once. When the colony of Jezreel had first been founded, he remembered, Goldmann somehow got it into his head to make everyone pray according to the liturgy of "the divine rabbi," Rabbi Isaac Luria.* What for? he was asked. They all preferred the Ashkenazic liturgy, to which they were accustomed. But

---

* An influential cabbalist (1534–1572), who settled in the northern Palestinian town of Safed and established a school there to teach his doctrines. His use of the Sephardic liturgy, which differs in certain points from the Ashkenazic, was subsequently adopted by his disciples.

Goldmann insisted, that was the kind of man he was. It came to a quarrel and in the end Goldmann won: little by little, those who favored the Lurianic liturgy gained the majority. "We're not far from Safed," they argued, "and Safed, as is known, was where Rabbi Isaac lived." Only lord, he, Haim, knew perfectly well that it wasn't the divine rabbi whom they feared, but Goldmann. And so he made up his mind to be stubborn: he held his ground and went on praying like the Ashkenazim even when it was his turn to be the cantor. He thought a lot of himself in those days . . . and in fact, the only Torah scroll in the whole colony belonged to him, the reason being that once when he was still a young man and happened to be in great danger (he was dealing in contraband—Esther knew the whole story), he took a solemn vow (he had two thousand rubles' worth of goods on him at the time) that if God saw him safely through he would buy a Torah scroll for a synagogue. And so when he came to the Land of Israel and became one of the founders of the colony, he kept his vow and bought a scroll with the last of his money. Ai, ai . . . even his Torah scroll . . . no, Esther knew where his scroll was now . . . what good had his stubbornness done him?

No, he was no longer stubborn any more. Why be stubborn? She could see for herself: what was the use of it? Once in those days he had been stubborn enough to insist on planting potatoes. There were potatoes in Russia—why not here? An expert tried to warn him that the soil was too clayey, but he wouldn't listen. And sure enough, it rained so hard that year that the seed all rotted in the ground. Another time a local official came along and began to mouth words at them like a *goy* speaking Yiddish: "intensive farming," "the European method," "mixed cultivation"—in a word, they were being asked to plant sesame. There wasn't any choice: they planted sesame. But they used a European plow, the kind that turns the dry topsoil under and brings the moist subsoil to the top. In no time at all the sun had dried this bottom layer too. The spring rains didn't come, the sesame was sewn in the dry earth—and that was the last they saw of it. That's what he meant—it took a special kind of luck to be stubborn. The Arabs were stubborn too, only they got away with it. When they were asked to do the plowing in the colony, for instance, they refused to go ahead with it unless they were allowed to use their own plows. The colony was forced to lay aside the big European plow that had cost it so much money and buy new wooden ones for the Arabs. But lord, by then they had a foothold in Jezreel anyway. They filled the colony as hired hands and squatters; they took what they wanted, whatever they laid eyes on; and not only that, they stole the land away too. The directors spent thousands of francs on getting it back, they threw money around as though it were dirt, scattered it right and left, but the officials, once they had stuffed their pockets full and grown rich from it, proved perfectly useless. The only thing they were good for was sucking Jewish blood. . . .

Lord, what good did it do to be stubborn? It was out of stubbornness that his son had married Goldmann's daughter. Not that Goldmann himself had been against it. At the time, after all, he had not yet become part of Jerusalem's upper crust, a man with an opinion about everything, a "big wheel" in all the institutions. No, then he was still a poor, would-be farmer with an unworked holding in Jezreel, and his daughter —that high-and-mighty woman of the world with her French and her satin dresses—a lazy young thing run after by the Arab boys in the colony, with whom she stupidly played the coquette. (Esther should forgive him for not mincing words!) Goldmann had been worried about his daughter and was only too glad to give her away to the first person to want to take her in hand; she herself, in fact, was not even consulted, though she could hardly have kicked up her heels at Hanoch's offer in any case, seeing that he was the last eligible man in the colony, from which nearly everyone had departed. He, Haim, had of course warned his son: "Look, Hanoch, you're only asking for trouble. Believe me, it's not that I care about her father, even though there's no love lost between us—but it isn't him you're going to have to live with. Only she . . . you . . . how will it ever work out?" But Hanoch, lord help him, insisted on having his way, though he always had been and still was a good-natured boy. . . .

Yes, his son Hanoch had a good disposition, a good nature, thank God. There weren't many like him. In fact, there was no one like him at all and never had been—a healthy, robust, hard-working lad, and full of life too, though far from a chatterbox. And motherless since the age of ten. . . . He'd had trouble with his speech, but ever since he was a little boy he'd been unusually strong and fit. The moment didn't go by that he didn't put to use. It made him smile just to think of it; when Hanoch was still a child, he loved to rummage through the rags and old clothes that his mother used to keep around the house and throw them outside. And he did this, it was no exaggeration to say, with a kind of devotion, a special delight, while his mother, might she rest in peace, would cry: "Good heavens! All my rags. . . ." But it would absorb him completely. And when he grew older he took to sleeping in the stable with his horse. It wasn't just an ordinary horse, either; no, it was a headstrong, crazy Arab stallion, more suited to fighting than farming, as wild as the Bedu who bred it. You'd think it had been bitten by a mad dog to see it act up when hitched to the plow. Hanoch would grab hold of the reins as hard as he could; the Arab might throw him, drag him, but Hanoch, who was far from an expert plowman, would hang on for dear life. Did she, Esther, understand? He wasn't strong enough to stop or control him, but to let go completely —never. There was stubbornness for you! Not only that, but once he, Haim, had told him: "For a horse like that, Hanoch, you should buy a smaller plow—you'll never get him to work with the big one." But Hanoch had answered: "I'll plow with what there is." Stubborn as stone!

Only what good had it done them? In the end they were forced to leave the abandoned colony anyway. Where were they to go? Goldmann, who was planning to move to Jerusalem himself, offered to set up his daughter and son-in-law in business in Beirut. His daughter, who was an only child, wouldn't hear of any place else: she wanted to mix with people, to see the world. As if there could be any question! But Hanoch was dead set against it: he wanted to go to Safed or Tiberias and become a builder. And just then he was offered a job as a watchman. Several years before a Jewish company had bought some land, which it never worked, about half a day's walk from Jezreel. Eventually word was received that the Arabs in the area had begun to farm the Jewish property. The company decided to take action; if it didn't, the land, which had cost hundreds of thousands of francs, would end up in the hands of the squatters. And so, as a temporary measure, it was decided to build a small house and hire a Jewish guard to live in it. The job was offered to Hanoch and he immediately said yes. But Henya, his wife, put her foot down. Did he think she was crazy? The thought of her going to live in the wilderness! "After the wonderful life you've given me here," she railed, "I should go live with you in the desert? What will I do with all my servants that you've gotten me . . . ?"—and so on and so forth. She had a tongue, Henya did, and a sharp one! Lord . . . Hanoch, bless him, told her:

"If you don't want to come with me, I'll go myself." But the fact of the matter was, that though Henya was Henya, any other woman would have done the same thing. Even he had tried to talk his son out of it. What was the sense of it? He was taking his life in his hands. Not that he, Haim, had been one to run from danger when he was young; but still, a man had no business cutting his own throat, not even to earn his bread. One single house on thousands of dunams * . . . somewhere across the Jordan or the devil knew where . . . right in the lion's mouth—lord! But Hanoch, bless him, was as stubborn as ever. "Father," he said, "the Arabs have driven us from here and they're driving us from there, and there isn't any end to it. The company has made it clear that if they can't find a Jewish guard they'll hire an Arab one. But there aren't any Jews in these parts who could go except me; how can I say no? They've taken over everywhere—let me at least be the one to take over there." Perhaps those weren't his exact words, but that was the spirit of it. Hanoch had always been a silent one, a stammerer—that Esther knew. He, Hanoch's father, was a sociable being who liked company and good talk—lord! But Hanoch was different. There were times when you couldn't pry a peep out of him with a pair of tongs. And that still wasn't the end of the story. Goldmann, it happened, was looking for a caretaker to keep an eye on his land, which he still hadn't sold—and Hanoch turned this down too. "A c-c-caretaker? I don't want to be a c-caretaker," he said. In the end he had had his way, every bit of it. And he was a watchman there for a long time too, until he was finally dismissed—so it was rumored—because the company had found a group of colonists to settle on the land. Since then Hanoch was working in a nearby mill whose Arab owner had taken him on. When an Arab was willing to hire a Jew in his mill,

* A dunam is a quarter of an acre.

how could the Jew possibly refuse? In a word, though it was easy to tell, it had been a long time happening. Years, in fact; and all this while Henya—both when Hanoch was a watchman and afterwards, when he began to work in the mill (which was still before she moved to Jerusalem)—never once went to see him. Even when he came to Jezreel for the holidays, she made life miserable for him. But by then she was only looking for an excuse to throw him over. "I'm sick and tired of him," she used to brag to her Arab friends. The first time that Hanoch came to Jerusalem for the Passover (this was before Esther and her father's time) she didn't even try to see him, but sent Goldmann in her place to ask for a divorce. There were your modern women for you . . . an easy life was all they wanted . . . smoking and what-not . . . and there was nothing that could be done about it. Stubbornness was no use. Could stubbornness keep the smoke from getting in your eyes? Ai, Miriam and her smoking! But to serve a meal at the proper time—that she couldn't do. It seemed that he was only wasting his time by waiting . . . lord . . . Miriam certainly wasn't in any hurry; it was already time to go for afternoon prayers.

As soon as Uncle Haim departed, an oppressive silence settled over the house. The shadowy walls of the room loomed closer around Esther and her cousin, who for some reason was occupied with a jumble of dusk-drawn thoughts about Miriam, about what Esther was going to say about her in another minute, and about a certain something that she, Miriam, had in common with the heroine of his last adventure. Two such different personalities . . . and still it seemed there was something in common . . . or was there? And what could it be? Perhaps the same quality of not belonging? Perhaps . . . but

in any case his thoughts were proof that the entire episode
had still not been forgotten—no, not even now, during this
most recent crisis in the latest chapter of his life—had not yet
yielded its place to his subsequent misfortunes. Worse: now,
of course, there could no longer be any question of a "relationship," any kind of relationship at all, but even if there
could be, the girl in Switzerland would still stand in its way.
He felt sure of it . . . but could it be? Could it be that that
slender-necked thing had not only the power to consume all
his strength over there, but to go on haunting him forever, to
the end of time? But how could it! It wasn't possible that a
chance encounter could ruin a man's whole life . . . no, he
was free of her! He was free of the whole thing! He almost
shouted these words out loud, then looked up and saw her
sitting before him.

Esther was still bent over the sewing machine, tall and
slightly stooped, but her hands were idle. She had stopped
working. Alternately she bit her lip and opened her mouth,
revealing her dull, decaying teeth. Her neatly arranged clothes
made a strange impression, as though they belonged to some
wealthy and refined young lady who had suddenly gone
blind but still remembered how to dress. At first glance everything seemed correct, impeccable, even in the latest fashion,
until one realized how mechanical it was. Missing was the last
tasteful look in the polished mirror.

Hefetz sat lost in thought, in his own misery, but at the
same time he felt an overpowering need to say something
(*just let it not be some stupid joke!*), to do something, in
order to break the harsh, malignant mood—if only some
feeble remark to the effect that now that spring was over and
the holidays were ended, there would no longer be any work
writing addresses in Russian at the post office, which meant
that he stood little chance of earning the few piastres he had
hoped to make—but he could not find the words, could not

play himself false, and so he kept silent instead. A moment later, furious for taking part in so uncalled-for and demeaning a dumb show, he was glad he hadn't spoken; yet only for a moment; then, once again, he felt guilt at his own indifference, as though by his silence he were deliberately cutting himself off from a drama that dripped with live blood. Without a word, his mouth too opened slightly.

Esther suddenly rose to her feet. Her stingy body and her bony, masculine, greenish face expressed a kind of self-restraint, but a restraint which was flagrant, accentuated, almost meant to be noticed. She gave the impression of a person who was pretending to be pretending—an impression as grim and depressing as slow death itself. The silence, however, remained unbroken. At last she crossed in a turmoil to where Hefetz was miserably sitting. As though to mask her agitation and ensure an escape back to the safety of an ordinary conversation, she looked away, her two thin arms extended for some reason before her, and whispered feverishly through her frightfully thin lips:

—What was it that had caused her to notice for the past several days, to feel, that he, Yehezkel, was keeping aloof from her, as though he were angry? Could that be it? He was angry? But why? Why be angry at her? He must tell her, honestly, what he was angry at. He could tell her everything. There was nothing he need hide from her.

Hefetz had nothing to tell, nothing to hide. *She had noticed for the past several days . . .* but he had only been there several days altogether! Yet seeing her face and her pale thin lips and the buttons which fastened the long sleeves of her jacket at the wrists, closing over her slim, anemic arms, and hearing the excited eructation of her breath, he couldn't help murmur:

—Angry? He? But what for? She mustn't even think such a thing! How could he be angry? *He angry?* On the contrary

. . . what could he possibly have done to make her feel that way?

—Not angry? Then she must have been mistaken . . . it had seemed to her . . . but she was suspicious by nature . . . she couldn't bear to think that it was impossible to speak openly even to a cousin, to be his friend. . . .

Her sharp, stinging speech, which like the limbs of her body had no roundness to it, no give, lost some of its edge. As if she didn't know . . . one could never do enough for other people. And it always seemed to her that she ended up owing them something, that they were angry with her. No, she was not a good person by nature. Why should she boast if it wasn't true? On the contrary, she was bad . . . which still didn't mean that she was as bad as some. Miriam was far worse, every inch an egotist. She, Miriam, was possessed by the idea that she had to get an education and become a professional at any cost—nothing else mattered to her any more. She was even ready to go abroad! Father was powerless to prevent it and he was willing to let her go to Cairo just to keep her from running away to the settlements in the Galilee or Judea. Hadn't he seen what had happened to his eldest daughter after living in them? But in any case, whatever happened, she, Esther, would not let Miriam get away with it. She had learned from experience, and once you had learned the hard way you couldn't be good. And she was not good at all, she thought only of herself . . . except that she had always forced herself to be good in spite of everything. Yes, she was capable of being a good, a loyal, a devoted friend! She had trained herself to be that way—and had succeeded. (Much of the credit, she thought, was due to the idealistic atmosphere several years ago in Russia, at the time of the Revolution,* when people forgot their selfish cares. "Another

* The Russian Revolution of 1905.

factor," perhaps, was her father's constant preaching, his moral demands.) She had sacrificed herself for the Party.* And who knew, perhaps she had only been deceiving herself . . . now, at any rate, there were times when she thought that . . . three or four times a week she would be up all night: meetings, lectures, standing guard . . . she spent entire days walking the city collecting for the revolutionary "Red Cross" . . . had anyone paid attention? No, there had been no one to see it, no one to appreciate her devotion, all the things that she had done. Her sacrifices had been taken for granted with never a word of thanks. And later, when she had used up all her strength, when she was at the end of her rope, when she came to Palestine, when she went to work in the settlements . . . yes, for a while she had actually worked in the settlements . . . there was even a famous photograph, a picture postcard of "Harvest," in which she appeared among a group of farm hands with her wide-brimmed straw hat and a basket on her shoulder . . . hadn't Yehezkel ever seen it? She had it right here . . . there she was . . . but she hadn't worked there long. Once again she had been disillusioned. The men thought that a woman was good only for cooking . . . and cook was all she did: the life wasn't fit for a dog! Forty mouths to feed, and each with its own pretensions and demands: one wanted sour cream, another four eggs in his omelet, another stewed fruit, another pudding every day! Serve them the soup and they spilled it like pigs . . . or else they set their bowls in a row on the table and poured it from bowl to bowl as a joke until her blood boiled within her . . . or banged their spoons until her ears ached . . . not to speak of the vegetarians, who made life unbearable . . . to say nothing of all the complaints: The food bill is too high! Just look

* The Jewish Workers' Bund, which played an active role in the 1905 uprising.

at those deficits! A man hasn't the strength to work on such food! While in the meantime pieces of bread lay around un- eaten and the men on duty in the kitchen forgot to bring water and wood, so that the meals weren't ready on time. And for everything the cook was to blame! Really, a cook in Palestine was no better than a slave. She had no human rights. If only she had known how to act the flirt, then she could have gotten along, then she might have found a protector. Yes, she, Esther, had worked in the kitchen for a month with a girl who had found herself a "champion" and who left all the work up to her, while she, the girl (and she didn't even have a vote at meetings!) went walking in the fields. "Esther, darling, why don't you wash the dishes!" "Esther, be a dear, look after the bread in the oven!" It made no difference whether it was her turn or not. Sometimes she felt an urge to forget about the bread . . . let it burn, let it be ruined . . . let them eat it and choke . . . revenge! No, there was noth- ing good about her. Just imagine: before she came to Palestine she had thought that it was inhabited by angels! Not that she was so naïve, but she had hoped nonetheless . . . and in the end—the way the young workers behaved toward a woman! Such crudeness, such indifference . . . as though she weren't a human being . . . no one had lent a helping hand . . . no one had talked to her as you talk to a friend . . . nothing but disdain, sarcasm, stupid jokes. Not one of them had known her when she was still young herself, when she had sacrificed all. And now . . . now they made fun of her because she wanted . . . because she wanted to live a bit . . . yes, she too. . . .

Esther talked on and on. She spoke about this and that, now with a frank allusion, now with a cryptic hint. Her words were logical, contradictory, philosophical, even lyrical, in turn. But in any case, her voice was different and more eloquent than anything she said. *It* did not contradict itself, though it shifted with each fresh train of thought. Her words failed to reveal the full abyss in her soul, the utter extremity of her state, but her voice told all, everything; her words were confused, sometimes more and sometimes less precise, but her unpleasant voice lent weight to them all, made each single one of them important, comprehensive, symbolic. The unrewarded one! She had sacrificed all for the Party, for her ideals. It was then that she had learned to be altruistic in her relationships and to look down on any sign of weakness between the sexes; despite her regrettably passionate nature, she would never have forgiven herself had she allowed any man to take liberties. But her "nasty" character, or rather her inherent bad temper, together with these natural tendencies, which were neither good nor bad in themselves but had been suppressed due to the revolutionary atmosphere of the times, were now rebelling within her, causing yet another revolution at the very moment when her physical powers had deserted her. . . .

Hefetz tried to reply:

—Nevertheless . . . she should realize . . . what was she lacking? She lived a productive life . . . a decent life . . . a life that was of value to others . . . she helped her sister and her father . . . what more did she want?

Esther looked at him and said nothing. A silent plea, along with the barest shadow of a reproach, was in her glance. Suddenly Hefetz felt infinitely cheapened by the lying words he had offered her, the foolish, commonplace comfort. A woman like her needed to be kissed, needed to be taken in someone's arms and hotly, fiercely, passionately kissed. Let her be fed the strong meat that she craved! Let her remember forever that a man had stroked her thighs with fierce hands, kissed her chapped lips, her coarsened cheeks, her eyes full of long-ing and desire—let her remember and take pleasure!

Miriam re-entered the room.

V

Shneirson, Miriam's tutor, was a young Hebrew nationalist, certainly no worse than any of his Russian friends and contemporaries who had debarked at one time or another off the coast of Palestine's Jaffa. They admired the splendid scenery from the deck of the ship, went into town feeling dreadfully moved, lost their temper at the Arabs who approached them on the way, ordered their meals at the hotel, told tales about the local farmers who weren't hiring Jewish workers, went out to work one morning with a hoe on their shoulder and a bottle of water and half a loaf of bread tucked under their arm, wandered about the settlements, made the pilgrimage to Jerusalem for one of the holidays, looked forward to seeing the Galilee, and when they were through tramping about— ended up with some trivial post as a secretary or teacher in Jaffa or Jerusalem. Shneirson, however, never went out to the fields with a hoe or looked for a job at all, for he came from a well-to-do home, received his monthly allowance punctually from his parents and didn't spend much on himself. He lived in the Harel, a cheap hotel in the neighborhood of Sha'arei Yehudah,* where he shared a small, untidy room with a bachelor named Kahanowitz, who was preparing to enter the

* A quarter outside the old walled city of Jerusalem.

Teachers' Institute. The latter was a stubbornly determined fellow, an ex-pupil at the Yeshivah of Telz * and an authority on all the intricacies of ancient Jewish lore—none of which, however, gave him any satisfaction. His one ambition was to study in a "modern" institution of learning, it being his firm persuasion that unless he started all over from the beginning by sitting on a modern schoolbench and learning the alphabet from modern schoolteachers and schoolbooks, he was doomed to a life of inner conflict, or to put it more literarily, to suffer from "intellectual insecurity." At the age of twenty-eight or twenty-nine, therefore, notwithstanding all his erudition in the Talmud and its commentaries and the literature of the Haskalah,† he was preparing to enter the lowest form of the college and sit there side by side with fourteen-year-old Sephardi boys from Jerusalem. To this end he applied himself without stinting, worrying only that he might be cruelly rejected.

Shneirson also (though in a profounder, more contemporary fashion, of course) was outspoken in his conviction that a man should have a unified outlook and not just a patchwork of opinions. He too, in fact, was something of a student, though no one seemed to know exactly of what. He liked to expound with a genial sigh on the need and obligation "to work," that is, to study intensively ("It not only orders your life, it also—and this is the main thing—gives it a sense of purpose!"), but when left alone with his roommate he would regard him with a pair of intimate, reproachful eyes and groan significantly as though to say: "Well, what do you make of it? A bad business, a bad business!"—meaning that study had given his own life neither order nor purpose enough.

* A prominent Talmudical college in Lithuania.

† The movement toward modernization in Hebrew letters that began toward the end of the 18th century.

After giving Miriam, "the nymph," her free evening lesson, Shneirson used to roam aimlessly through the streets and quarters of Jerusalem, for his room in the Harel was too cramped for comfort and made him take pity on his own appearance, which was far from unhandsome and was only going to waste. Encountering an intelligent acquaintance, he was sure to remark straight away that Palestine was a land of twaddlers and dilettantes who knew nothing about study and the need for a unified outlook; if the same were a woman, however, he would make a show of not talking at all, only to relent in the end and say something about silence, which was ever so more eloquent than speech, supporting himself in the pinch with a choice quotation from Maeterlinck or perhaps yet another poet. Thence he would proceed to the impressions that he had gathered two years previously in Europe, where he had managed to see a great deal. In the Hotel Harel, on the other hand, there was nothing to see at all—although to tell the truth, the place was a den of strange characters. Did he make himself clear? Not people—*characters!* Having made his point, *it seemed to him*, there remained nothing more for him to say . . . (Shneirson stressed the "it seems to me" in particular, in other words, it only "seemed" to him because as a European man he knew better than to set himself up as an authority and force his opinions on others. In reality, though, when one compared his "it seems" or "my opinion would be" with the "I assure you" of somebody else, somebody who hadn't seen what Shneirson had seen or gathered the same impressions, and who didn't, therefore, deserve the same deference, having no standards, no *cultural* standards of his own, and having never lived in a den of strange characters—could there be any doubt as to whose word one would take?)

Shneirson prided himself on his insight, that is, on his perspicacity as an observer; consequently, when meeting a new "character" he felt obliged to transfix him with a piercing glance, staring intently and at length as though to probe him to the bone until he had divined his true nature and could define it with a single word. Admittedly, there were moments when the crease lines between the brows of those penetrating eyes gave everything away by revealing that he felt less the judger than the judged: more than he was striving to form an opinion of the other, he was straining to record the impression that the latter was getting of him . . . in spite of all which, he was still officially the tribunal that handed down names to all. The owner of the hotel, for instance, was "the dilettante innkeeper"; Uncle Haim—"the retarded one"; Hefetz—"the invalid" and "the maniac"; Reb Yosef—"the phenomenon" and "the conservative progressive"; Miriam—"the nymph"; Esther (behind her back)—"the old virgin" ("A typical case of the Jewish girls who come here from abroad!"), and (to her face)—"the bluestocking." She, for her part, referred to him as "the student without a university."

His roommate Kahanowitz, Shneirson called "the phlegmatic," an appellation based on an abundance of facts from Kahanowitz's life that had not escaped his sharp eye. For instance, Kahanowitz refused to start wearing his white summer suit before the Feast of Weeks,* even though it would already be hot by Passover; once he put it on, however, he'd insist on going about in it until Hanukkah. Or again: he was a hearty, almost a ravenous eater, but only . . . as long as the bread was already sliced and laid out for him on the table. ("I mean," explained Shneirson, "the big trunk in our room which we use as a table.") But if it meant commencing a fresh loaf, he, Kahanowitz, preferred to make do with a single

---

* The holiday of Pentecost or *Shavu'ot*, which falls usually in late May or early June. Passover generally comes in April, and Hannukah in December, by which time the Jerusalem winter has set in.

stale slice rather than perform the honors himself. In a word: "A phlegmatic!"

Shneirson was a freethinker, almost a radical in his views, though hardly any more so than most of his peers; in fact, he was a progressive in general, an intellectual in the true sense of the word. When speaking of intellectuals, however, he would hasten to point out that the word no longer meant what it used to. Once to be an intellectual had meant to be . . . yes, a rationalist. "Do you follow me? Rationalists!" His own, Shneirson's, outlook, on the other hand, like that of all contemporary intellectuals, was historical. Everything was a historical development and needed to be seen in that light. "Do I make myself clear?"

Lest anyone object that he didn't, he, the volunteer tutor, offered an example. Take the legends in the Talmud. The old Jewish intellectuals either thought that they were nonsense or else—like Reb Yosef, "the conservative progressive"—tried to read ideas into them that didn't belong to that period. The fact of the matter was, however, that the historical perspective alone could reveal the true beauty in the legends of the Talmud!

Having mentioned Reb Yosef, Shneirson felt obliged to explain. He hadn't meant to imply that Reb Yosef was an intellectual of the old school, not at all. Reb Yosef, one might say, was a case in himself, a phenomenon! You couldn't discuss him in any terms but his own. In him, to tell the truth, light and shadow were mixed together. On the one hand you had a man familiar with the latest findings of science, philosophy and history, and on the other—a believer in all kinds of superstitions and old wives' tales. "Would you believe it? Reb Yosef actually believes in fetishes and incantations! He believes in magic and reincarnation!" What? Kahanowitz wished to argue that in the Middle Ages too there were philosophers who believed in astrology and alchemy? But the two things had nothing in common! He, Shneirson, would explain it in his own special way. It seemed to him . . . that is, in his opinion . . . the struggle between religion and science in Reb Yosef's mind was a struggle of the old with the new . . . h'm . . . which was why he, Reb Yosef, sometimes held the rope at one end and wouldn't let go, and sometimes at the other. . . .

"That's true!" declared Miriam. When the subject was her father, she too had had a right to be heard. In father one found both things together. He was a great intellectual, but he also observed every jot of the Law and enjoyed it. He was accustomed to it since childhood. It was his entire life.

—That's just what he, Shneirson, had been saying! Reb Yosef held on to both ends of the rope and wouldn't let go. Reb Yosef liked to say, for example, that he knew why prophecy had existed in antiquity and what was needed in order to revive it now. He, Reb Yosef, also said that he knew why spells, demons, metempsychosis, charms and sorcery had been realities in the past, in the days of Menasseh ben Israel,* for one, as was stated in his *The Soul of Life*. To disbelieve in these things was impossible, as there were reliable witnesses to the contrary. Now such powers no longer revealed themselves, but at one time they had: this was Reb Yosef's opinion. It stood to reason that a person who talked that way could have no true conception of the development of ideas, of beliefs and opinions, of religion! And yet only the concept of development, to reiterate, could shed light on the intellectual achievements of Judaism, on its ancient literature, on the Midrash, on Talmudic legend. . . .

"But why stop there?" Shneirson challenged his audience.

* Dutch-Jewish scholar, statesman, and author of works on Judaism (1603–1657).

"Take the Holy Scriptures themselves! Take the stories in the Bible! Take the Book of Genesis! Take the most sublime, the most eternal things in . . ."

"Look at Uncle Haim," Miriam interrupted. "He's so tired he's fallen asleep."

"Never mind!" cried Shneirson rapturously "Tired or not . . . the Bible is eternal for everyone, even . . . even for the tired! Let the weary read it and take strength. 'Ponder it and ponder it for it is all in all.' And you don't have to be a religious man to believe that. On the contrary! Free biblical criticism, the national-historical perspective, are the best guides to what the Scriptures are really about and to their national significance. It's only when you learn how and when these classics were created that you realize the truth of Heine's remark about the value of this one little book!" He himself, Shneirson, could not imagine a day going by without reading part of the Bible. Whoever it was who had said that the Bible was the greatest gift the Jews ever gave to mankind was absolutely right! He, Shneirson, a modern Jewish intellectual and an adherent of the concept of development, could not imagine Europe, the human race, without the Bible. Generations came and went, but the Bible remained forever. The Bible was eternal. What? Hefetz wished to say something? No? Was the invalid tossing and turning again? The maniac was still in bed? For shame!

VI

Hefetz lay sick in bed. Esther took care of him.

His injury bothered him. But it wasn't about it that he thought. He was already used to the pain, which he could bear with equanimity, or at any rate, without groaning excessively. And yet he groaned nonetheless. He groaned like a man with typhoid and a fever of forty-one degrees when he is thrown into an ice-cold bath. His injury took on a strange shape in his mind, as though it were a metaphysical essence, and she too, when he looked at her minding him, was transformed into some *substantia* of his deranged brain. He experienced for some reason the strangely painful sensation of a man who looks at the picture of a girl he had loved many years ago with a terrible passion, and had then forgotten, utterly and completely, so that now he wonders incredulously what ever possessed him . . . Merciful heavens!

The real, the physical Esther who took care of him, made his bed, emptied his chamber pot, simply didn't affect him, as though she weren't there at all—and this too made him feel bad. Was that any way to treat a woman? Besides which, a single thought kept bothering him. What if she knew—what if she knew the whole truth, knew what was really the matter with him—would she still be taking care of him then?

What a curious question!

Because if she did know and still took care of him, something would have been proved: it would have been proved that there was actually an other than himself; it would have been proved that there was something selfless after all in life and in the world. . . .

He fancied himself a great sinner who feared to be punished, to be found out, and who thought in the presence of people: *Suppose they were to know that it was I who did it . . . suppose they were to know.* A queer desire palpitated within him to suddenly stand and shout: "It's I who am the criminal!"—and to observe their reaction, the expression on their faces. . . .

His injury wore him down, made him utterly despondent, but through it all he pretended that it was only a fever, an attack of malaria. He prayed that the thermometer which Esther put under his arm would show at least thirty-eight or thirty-nine and not slip any lower. He coughed whenever he could, cleared his throat, spit on the floor, shook with chills. Terrible chills shook Hefetz's body!

At the heart of it he remained apathetic, or rather, without hope. And yet underneath this emptiness stirred the strange yet familiar feeling that it had already all happened to him before. Not just the apathy and the hopelessness, but even the pretended fever and chills. Then too—only when? in a previous existence? in some bad dream?—it had been like this. Exactly like this. The same apathy and the same make-believe. And he had foreseen then, had felt, though he hadn't known what it was that he was feeling or foreseeing, that it would end like this . . . yes, then . . . who knew how many thousands of years ago . . . but the wheel had come full circle . . . full cycle. . . .

The odd, familiar feeling suddenly assumed a new shade.

And yet it was still the same thing . . . the same thing . . .
repeated over . . . endlessly over . . . so that some time ago
—fifty years, or two years, or one year, or maybe even yesterday or this morning—he had foreseen, but perfectly clearly,
that now, right now, that is, fifty years, or two years, or one
year later, or tomorrow, or tonight, but now, at this moment,
that it would be like this. And once more before his death he
was sure to foresee that it would happen all over again . . .
that he would lie once more in this house . . . in Reb Yosef's
house, his uncle by marriage . . . and that Esther . . . Esther would warm him some milk. . . .

The sick man continued to cough, clearing his throat queerly
and spitting on the floor. He uncharacteristically called attention to his presence, making a point of it as though that would
make him feel better. He did it on purpose, suspecting that it
annoyed her. And yet it never crossed his mind that this
annoyance, like everything else, was a source of strange and
incomprehensible pleasure to her, that it only seemed to draw
her even closer, to impel her to him bodily from her place so
as to scold, "How long must you go on coughing? Enough!"
—and then, a moment later, to bend and collect his mucous
in a bottle, as though for a memento.

Only toward evening, when he felt better—a sure sign that
it wasn't malaria!—and she sat silent and submissive by his
side, did he return to the central question that had been
bothering him: why really was he so cold to her? Why
couldn't he be more friendly, if it was that important to her,
if that was what she wanted?

If only she weren't so pinched-looking, said a voice inside
him, *or rather, if only she'd do what other women do to make
their breasts look a little higher, then at least you wouldn't
play the pampered epicure.*

"Ahhh-h-h!" Hefetz doubled over in pain.

He understood as soon as he heard his own voice, understood that he was cracking above again, that all was lost. . . .

He held her hand and considered. He thought: *if some respectable bourgeois or poet of beauty and high ideals* (the two were not as far apart as seemed at first glance) *were to know what I was thinking at this moment, he would surely look the other way.* He would sniff categorically and say in a single breath: "How cynical!" "How ugly!" "How disgusting!" And he would be right. The bourgeois and the beautiful were always in the right. He, Hefetz, the dross of the human race, was in no position to argue. All honor was theirs, all beauty was theirs, all justice was theirs. . . .

He suddenly laughed grotesquely, then gave a faint groan. "Sweet melancholy . . . the poetry of sweet melancholy . . . they can agree to that . . . they can accept it . . . fair poesy! But my own pain, hah ha . . . feh! That they don't want . . . a ruptured man . . . how repulsive . . . sweet melancholy won't hear of it . . . won't accept it . . . no ruptures allowed. . . ."

"Accept?" she whispered. "Who? The hospital?"

"They won't forgive!" the sick man moaned.

"Forgive? Who? What are you talking about? Are you delirious?"

"I'm not delirious and I know what I'm saying. Now I know. They . . . people . . . life . . . their minds are made up. They don't want to hear any tragedies . . . they don't want to know that this week they're going to take me to that place . . . that it's already been settled . . . and when I remind them they point at me with their fingers: Look at him! What a fuss he makes! Look at the underman showing off his flaws—his upper flaws! Oh they're kind enough to mock very gently . . . but it's a mistake, honored life! It's all a mistake, normal sirs! Your excellencies are mistaken! I'm not proud at all and I'm not glad to be entering . . . the place you just mentioned. I'm only reminding you—and I agree: there's no need to defile the world with my ugliness . . . no reason why my pain should count . . . truth is what's charming, sublime . . . and I—I'm an interested party, you can't take me at my word. Don't waste your pity on me . . . don't spend your compassion on a poor, ruptured fool!"

Esther placed a cold compress on his forehead.

. . . *He stood in front of the Jaffa Gate, just as he had then, several weeks before, during his stroll with Menahem through the streets of old Jerusalem.* The gate was made of iron and was shut. The Jaffa Gate was not shut as a rule, but this time it was iron and was shut. And this surprised him. The sun beat down on his head, yet a chill ran through his body, which surprised him too. But he chose to ignore it and went on talking to Menahem. Menahem was not here, Menahem was there, in the kitchen of the commune, in the same kitchen where Esther was the cook (Yehezkel Hefetz was sure of this!), but he, Yehezkel Hefetz, talked to him here. And once again he was surprised. ("Three surprises!")

He said to Menahem in words like these:

"I can't go on living this way. I've come as far as I can. Only to live any other way—isn't permitted. It isn't permitted because I haven't the strength. I've been sustained by just one thing: my compassion. But I've discovered, ha ha, that I have no compassion, that I haven't the strength to have compassion, that I'm not allowed to have compassion, because my compassion is all a lie. Across from me are the Jaffa Gate, the Valley of Jehosephat, the Vale of Gehenna." *

* The Jaffa Gate is one of the main gates of the old walled city of

Menahem answered him:

"You can't always say no. Sometimes you've got to put all that behind you. Sometimes saying yes shows you sides of things that you never even dreamed of. As long as you're still alive—long live life and all experiments to live it!"

And he confided in him further:

"You, Yehezkel, have kept away from life. You haven't lived yet, you haven't really been tested. And without experience you haven't the right to decide a thing. What do you know? What experience have you? It's so limited, your experience! It's only your private fever, only your private fever! You know only your own self, only your own world! What poverty! You have to find the strength in yourself to try! What, you'd rather go on living the easy life you have now? But new sufferings must come. New ones! Do you understand?"

Menahem disappeared—and the iron gate began to labor on its hinges. "Labor pains!" cried the sick dreamer and tried to get up, only to fall once again. His eyes closed once more in nightmarish slumber. He was in a field, on a work day, during the lunch break. Here there was nothing to be surprised at; here everything was just as it should be. His friends, the field hands, stood quietly by doing nothing. Then, quick as a flash, the clang of their hoes was ringing in his head. They had all gone back to work without eating (Miriam's spinach cakes were a burden to digest) while he alone hid under a bush. He was much too weak to work. He lay pleasantly sprawled on the ground, his heart beating in fear of the foreman. There was no foreman in the commune, but this was before all that, when he still worked in the colony. "What's this? Shirking?"

Jerusalem, which faces west onto the road leading toward Jaffa. The Valley of Jehosophat runs along the foot of the eastern wall of Jerusalem, south of which it connects with the Vale of Gehenna.

The foreman was suddenly upon him. "On your feet!" But now Esther appeared too. "I'm on your side!" she said. "Stay where you are, you're weak! Let me do the work! Just don't drink the groundwater. The water from Miriam's well is bitter, you'll get malaria . . . here, drink the milk that I've brought you." But he refused to drink, though he was fearfully thirsty. He was waiting for a miracle. "Toadstools and spinach cakes!" he cried out and was silent. But the voice went on speaking inside him: "A miracle, there has to be a miracle! It's no longer possible without one. Nothing natural, nothing in nature, can do any good . . . nothing . . . there has to be something beyond all that!" Yet even as he spoke to her—he spoke inaudibly, moving his lips—he was perfectly aware that the miracle would never come, that there were no miracles. . . .

It was then that Menahem got to his feet and told him:

"Here and now in this world—there's your miracle! We're out in a field—there's the great wonder of it, the *mysterium tremendum!*"

"Why all those foreign words?" the sick man argued. "But what's true is true; it doesn't even surprise me to hear myself say it; even she would be an improvement over what I have now. And I know something else now too: now it's permitted. Because now, since it's not just for her that I'll do it, not just to be charitable (what a horrible thought!) out of some kind of *noblesse oblige* (but now I'm using foreign words too!), but for my own sake, because I realize how things stand, because I must know what I must know, because I must go through what I must go through . . . only what was it I was saying? She's only an experiment, you say? 'And she in herself? Is that any way to treat a woman? And what if your experiment should fail?' But I'll take all the blame, I tell you! If there won't be any love, that's only because there's no such thing, because it's all a figment of the heart to begin with. Suppose she were a princess—would I love her any more then? Then too it would only be a different kind of selfishness . . . always selfishness . . . but I'll go ahead and do it, selfishness and all! I'll love her . . . it will be a great miracle. A great miracle? But even if it won't be . . . even if it turns out that it was a mistake to have tried—that too will have been worth it. Because then, finally, there's bound to be a point beyond which is the end: somewhere there must be such a point . . . and then it will be time to pay my last respects. One way or the other, for me there's only one way left: up off the rack!"

Only meanwhile he lay bound on the rack.

Neither a gate of iron nor of wood. A top-floor room. A stone tenement in New York.

He stood there and stared at the small, old revolver that lay before him on the window sill.

The gun was small, old and slightly defective. Just two bullets stood out in the six-chambered cylinder. The other chambers were empty. Engraved on top of the short rusty barrel, the half-effaced name of the firm glinted in foreign letters.

He stood there by himself. His wife wasn't with him in the room. She was a seamstress, she had left to go to work.

He thought about her, about himself, about his and their life. He stared at the gun with unseeing eyes.

Would everything really soon be over? asked his stare. Could it really be that simple? Was he really going to find the strength at last to blot out the pestilent hell within him with redeeming nothingness?

Safe harbor! O haven! Come O come! Come save him from it all: from the hell in his own heart, from his utter self-contempt, from his terrible hatred for others—yes, from his terrible weakness, too, which had kept him from keeping his promise to himself. . . .

For he had promised himself, he had sworn it . . . then, in taking the step he should never have taken. . . .

Then (a moment ago . . .), in taking the step, his brain had been lit by the vow that he would either love and live or put an end to it all. An end—and no more. Ah, how sweet not to be any more!

Sweet? Not so. How much better if it weren't to happen! There must be some way. Just let it not end all at once. Anything but total nonbeing, total annihilation. . . .

No! He would get away from it all, away . . . he would go somewhere else . . . where nobody knew him . . . among the Africans . . . it wouldn't matter how he lived there as long as he kept alive . . . there he would see. . . .

Only this too was a lie. He had nowhere to go. Nowhere. His grave must be here, right now. A defiler like himself, a defiler of himself, could never be pardoned. There was no atonement for self-defilement ever. The self-defiled deserved to die.

And she? What would she say? But he deserved to die for that too, for having thought—and wrongly!—only of himself, not at all about her. He had thought about the children such a marriage might produce, yes, he had thought about that, but not about her. She was sure to be wretched—and he hadn't thought of it. And when it did cross his mind, he reflected: *It doesn't matter . . . she isn't any better than you are . . . all cripples despise each other anyway . . . it's been tit for tat . . . no one has been cheated . . . there's been no great loss!*

So that now—now there was no need to think about her

any longer. Now that there were to be no children, no one to poison—now he must free her as quickly as possible. He must make amends, destroy what he had botched . . . for having lived like that with a woman one surely deserved to die!

The minutes went by—and the hateful potion remained where it was.

Potion? Poison? Then the revolver must not have gone off. . . .

He seemed to himself like someone whose creditor—the hangman!—demanded to be paid, threatened to throw him in irons and have him strung up, while he, who had nothing to pay with, who was doomed to be hung, pleaded and prayed for time: one minute more . . . just one minute more. . . .

What good did it do? Why put it off? But he did put it off, put it off until the last unendurable moment.

He couldn't wait to be dead. How dreadful his own breathing seemed to him. How badly he wanted not to live! Every minute was unbearable. Why was he putting it off?

Ai, ai, ai, ai. . . .

He dug his hands into his matted hair, he pulled and pulled at it, he stared at the revolver. . . .

A tap opened somewhere in his brain and something cool began to flow. A spittly froth, like ashes mixed with water, trickled over his lips and throat. Incredible! His body had not been consumed. Rotten it was, yet not decomposed. Just ashes and sweat. He was like a drowning man, drowning in the spittle of his hatred and physical disgust for life. The revolver winked from far off but he wouldn't go near it or touch it. "A gun? How did I get it past the guards on Ellis Island?" All else was forgotten; this question alone annoyed and kept bothering him until he began to awake. Then everything went blank and he fell weakly to the straw mat on the floor. "A straw mat?

Then they lie on straw mats in New York too? But how can
it be!" He gritted his teeth, pulled at his hair, shivered, half
awoke and whispered through parched lips:

"A man when he falleth . . . a man when he falleth . . .
will perspire? Am I perspiring?"

"Yes, you're perspiring, Yehezkel. Your fever's going
down. Would you like to turn over on your other side?"

"Esther, leave me alone! Any way that you make me lie,
it won't ever stop hurting me," the sick man replied, as though
he had drawn some conclusion at last from his idle reveries,
which had apparently lasted for over a quarter of an hour.

"Of course!" thought Yehezkel Hefetz shortly after awakening about the "interpretation" of his dream, which was of
absolutely no consequence in any case. "It would be criminal
of me if I were foolish enough to try to lead 'a new life . . .
elevated by suffering.' As far as I myself am concerned—
which is to say, concerning everything—because after all, I'm
everything to myself—there's nothing left to try. Any suffering will always be the same: nothing new, nothing elevat-
ing. It's all so transparent, so obvious whatever happens. I
would like not to be any more. But even now that I haven't
stopped being, it's as though I had. I've said good-bye to life.
I'm all through. There: it's interpreted."

He covered himself with his coat and tried to doze off. But
this proved impossible, for no sooner had those present recovered sufficiently from the curious gibberish spoken by the
sick man in his sleep about "toadstools" and the like (the
things that didn't pass through the brain of a man with a
fever!) than the house filled up with "interpretation" in
earnest. Every evening Reb Yosef's bare apartment (rooms in
Jerusalem were expensive but if one didn't bother with furni-

ture they could be made to look spacious and not at all small) brimmed to the walls with study. Only Uncle Haim, who had meanwhile returned from his day's work, sat quietly on a bench without a book. In one corner, Reb Yosef was busy with his only pupil, who came to him nights, while Miriam, hungry for knowledge, sat in the corner opposite with her tutor Shneirson.

With the aid of medieval commentaries Reb Yosef was teaching a lesson from the Five Books of Moses, the *Humishl* * as he affectionately called them, while Shneirson instructed Miriam in the identical subject from a volume called *Tales of the Bible*.

The head of the household felt duty-bound to reply to all that he had heard Shneirson say about the Bible a short while before upon his return from the evening prayer. Instead, however, he held his tongue and kept silent. It was clearly out of the question that he, Reb Yosef, should seriously debate the Bible with a young stripling. Only when the last murmurs of Shneirson's voice had died down completely did he decide that it was time to have his say.

—The philosopher Spinoza, he began by declaring, once wrote that the Mosaic Law was a constitution. Of course, it was the popular view among the younger generation that the stories in the Bible were nothing but myths. He, Reb Yosef, believed this too, only his opinion was closer to Maimonides', who took a somewhat profounder view of the whole matter. . . .

It soon became obvious, however, that the profundity of Reb Yosef's opinion derived entirely from the fact that he confused his terminology and failed to distinguish properly between "allegory" and "myth." After setting out to prove

* Yiddish diminutive of the Hebrew *humash*, the Pentateuch or Five Books of Moses.

that Isaac's blessing of Jacob and Esau was really "mythical" (in other words, allegorical), he was quickly carried away by his own keen discernment. The Tower of Babel as well, he explained, was really a lesson in systematic philosophy. Or take the pregnancy of Rebecca: *And the two children struggled within her. . . .* Then she said to herself: *If it be so—* if reality is really dualistic by nature—*wherefore do I live.* Why does it say *I am the Lord thy God,* meaning "I and no other," that is: in no wise polytheism but only pure monotheism? Eh? While concerning Jacob and the ladder . . . according to Descartes the existence of man himself was the ultimate proof of the reality of God. Even supposing that the world was nothing but a dream—yes, let it be nothing but a dream!—there was still a dreamer to apprehend it whose existence was beyond doubt. And the same held true of the Creator. Even in the absence of man, the Creator of man would exist . . . reality demanded it . . . as was written in the story of Jacob: *And he dreamed . . . and said: Surely the Lord is in this place and I knew it not.** In other words: "Suppose it was only a dream that I dreamt . . . still, the Lord is in this place, for *I* knew it not, ergo, there is clearly still an I, a dreamer, which no one can possibly say I didn't know. . . ."

"So, what do you think of that for an explanation, eh?" The interpretation of *if it be so, wherefore do I live* was an old one, but the other, that of *surely the Lord,* had providen-

---

* *And the two children struggled within her, and she said, if it be so, wherefore do I live?* is from the Biblical account of the birth of Jacob and Esau (Genesis 25:22).

I am the Lord thy God is from the prologue to the Ten Commandments (Exodus 20:2).

And he dreamed . . . and said: Surely the Lord is in this place and I knew it not is from the story of Jacob's dream of the angels (Genesis 7:16).

tially occurred to Reb Yosef himself only a month ago. Hah? God be praised, he had many such ideas of his own. Only a fool would want to argue that the text was to be taken literally. But that was nothing: if it weren't universally accepted at face value, so that he, Reb Yosef, was unable to find a single commentator to give him moral support, he would have said that the whole story of Israel in Egypt was simply a myth as well. Yes, he must look it up in Ibn Ezra or Gersonides . . . except that he didn't have his books.* The *Humishl* spoke of the Land of Egypt, *Mitsrayim*.† "I suppose you think that's all there is to it? Not at all!" *Mitsrayim* meant "the two straits," from the Hebrew word *metsar*, a mythical reference. Only in order to slight neither school of thought, he, Reb Yosef, was prepared to concede that the story was both mythical and true.

Having had no choice but to listen to all this, though not without unconcealed impatience, Shneirson seized upon a momentary pause, waited another fraction of a second for politeness' sake, and hurriedly said to his pupil:

"Now then, suppose we continue. What did God create in the beginning?"

Miriam stole a glance at *Tales of the Bible* and answered in a naïvely young voice:

"In the beginning God created heaven and earth."

Yehezkel Hefetz couldn't sleep. He heaved in discomfort on his cot at the end of the room while every word of Miriam's answer cut into him deeply.

* Abraham Ibn Ezra (1092–1167) was a Spanish-Jewish philosopher and Biblical commentator.

Gersonides is Levi ben Gerson (1288–1344), a French-Jewish philosopher and commentator.

† The Hebrew word for Egypt, which has a grammatically dual ending, though its etymological connection with Hebrew *metsar*, "strait," is doubtful.

He thought:

"God . . . Shneirson and my uncle—both of them, each in his own way—like to talk about seekers of God, seeking for God. But those who seek—aren't really seeking him. They talk in his name—'He created'—and they leave it at that . . . it's as if the whole thing didn't really concern them. . . ."

He shivered abruptly. " 'In the beginning God created'— but that only proves that once upon a time there were Jews, no matter how enlightened, who had ideas like that about the world. What does it tell us, what can it possibly tell us, about the creation of the world itself?

" 'In the beginning God created'—hah! The hand that wrote that—what could it have told me that I don't already know about the riddle of the world, about the riddle of my own life? Heh! Those lines were written by one of a million million ignorant souls, yet it alone deceived itself into thinking that it knew!

" 'In the beginning God created,' is that it? Then there really is a God and a creation and a beginning to heaven and earth and a beginner and a prime mover and a first cause. But what if there are no causes and no beginnings and no beginner, just a ghastly, bottomless pit of meaningless, endless accidents and an I that feels and is conscious of a few of them? At any rate, no universal laws or order, no 'And the earth was without form and void,' no 'In the beginning God created' "——

The clock struck nine. Haim had fallen asleep in his seat; his drowsing head drooped nearly to his knees, where it nodded up and down as though agreeing with all that was said. The sick man's burning eyes struck it from afar and he thought:

"Haim is sleeping . . . and when Haim sleeps his thoughts sleep too. Perhaps he doesn't even see things in his dreams like I do . . . but if he were to see his son in a dream, his divorced son Hanoch, Hanoch from the mill whom he was telling us about only yesterday, I'm sure he would tell him: 'Father! Don't listen to what they tell you about the greatness of "the eternal book"! The eternal book—what does it have to say about all the solitary years that I've spent here by the mill-stones? What does it have to say about my anguish, my life, and my approaching death? At the very most—a word here, a word there—some paradox about the justice of God . . . about the justice of what doesn't exist. Or is it that my years simply don't matter at all? That my life is unimportant, in-significant, undeserving of mention? Two or three years on the job in some forsaken mill . . . ah? You say they're noth-ing to speak of against the background of eternity? The book of eternity passes over them in silence? Eternity?' "

The sick man gave everyone a fright by suddenly crying aloud:

"Eternity! Cold eternity! I stick my warm tongue out to greet you!"

Several days later, on a hot, sunny afternoon toward the end of April, Yehezkel Hefetz was brought in a carriage to the house on the outskirts of town.

❦ *Part Two*

I

A few months went by in the course of time, the harsh Jerusalem summer—that airless, waterless time of year—went by too, the holidays came round, November passed as well, and with the onslaught of rain in that wet, bitter month Reb Yosef Hefetz's illness took a turn for the worse. The whole left side of his body and both his legs seemed to have become strangers to him. He could hardly read any more; most of his time he spent lying in bed, an open book, a pair of glasses marking the place, to his left or to his right. The verses "And his soul was vexed to death," "Now the days of David drew nigh that he should die," "And I will lie down to sleep with my fathers," droned one after another through his tired brain. Sometimes in the mornings he still went to consult the doctors, either in their homes or in the corridors of Jerusalem's many hospitals, led slowly by his youngest daughter Miriam whenever she had the time or the inclination to take him; but the doctors, as their diagnoses bore out, were unable to define his ailment with any precision. In any event, the consensus seemed to be that the word "rheumatism" was not entirely inappropriate to the patient's condition. Yes, rheumatism—it generally got worse at this time of year.

Late one morning Reb Yosef returned from a visit to the

doctor and began unlacing his shoes before getting back into bed. As he pulled the shoe from his left foot, the pains in that leg seemed to get suddenly worse. Reb Yosef's thin, irritable face grew even longer and angrier than usual, just as it had a few days before when Goldmann, his rival in the *kloyz* *— that is, in the little group that regularly met for prayers in the guesthouse downstairs—had chosen to contradict him. At a time when the entire overheated city was thirsty and dry, so that rumor had it that the Rabbinical Court was about to decree a special fast, he, Goldmann, had said—and it was just to annoy him, just to annoy him!—that drought was not a good enough reason for calling a fast. Yes, just because he had his little "nest egg," namely, several cisterns full of water to be put up for sale; and because he was a director of the guesthouse and an Important Person who had many of the local charity politicians under his thumb; and because his brother-in-law was Hamilin, the new doctor, whom some said was even going to marry his divorced daughter—he, Goldmann, thought that he knew everything, even when the evidence was against him. There was nothing that he didn't know, that "great rabbinical authority," so that he, Reb Yosef, the real scholar who was equally at home in both philosophy and the Law, and who hadn't missed a single work on the subject of fasting from *The Book of the Covenant* to *The Threefold Ram* †—he, who even felt free to criticize the Rabbinical Court itself—*he* was obliged to prove to that vulgar, illiterate boor (of proofs, praise God, there was an ample abundance) that regardless of the court's opinion, one needed

* Yiddish: A small synagogue.

† *The Book of the Covenant*—A Hebrew work by the 15th-century scholar Pinchas Eliezer Horowitz of Vilna.

The Threefold Ram—A Hebrew work by the 18th-century rabbinical scholar Elijah Gaon of Vilna.

only to consult the Biblical story of Jephthah, etc., to realize that a public fast was not at all ineffective. As it was written: "Be not silent but cry unto me!" What a topsy-turvy world it was! He, Reb Yosef, had to go to the trouble to prove—and to whom? To Yankele Goldmann! Ai, ai, the paradoxes there were!

Reb Yosef laughed bitterly and continued to tug at his shoe, groaning out loud so that Miriam, who had just come home and was already busy in the kitchen fixing dinner for the family and its boarders, should hear him and lend a hand. But Miriam didn't come. The drumming of the rain on the rooftop must have drowned out his voice. Or hadn't she heard because she had other things on her mind?

—Yes, Miriam had ceased to obey him and had begun to rebel. She was up to something strange, that girl! Only yesterday she had announced out of the blue that since prices had risen they could no longer afford to feed extra mouths, especially the capricious Shneirson, who paid too little and expected too much. Let him eat at the Harel!

The sick man raised his large, almond-shaped, rabbinical eyes, unshielded by their glasses, to the low, dark ceiling, and held weakly on to his half-removed shoe with both hands. *I don't want to suffer, I don't want to*, said his glance. . . .

But the beads of moisture in the corners beneath the ceiling seemed to patter on and on: *It won't do to be angry—there's no way out.*

In the afternoon Reb Yosef's brother Haim came to pay a sick call and no sooner had he walked through the door than in stepped Esther too. Haim entered slowly and took a seat in silence. He had been laid off the last few days from his job as a stonecutter, partly because of the general slack in the building trade and partly because of the heavy rains, the likes of which, according to Reb Yosef, hadn't been seen "in years." As far as the rain was concerned, Haim knew that this wasn't exactly so: two years ago, for example, it had rained even harder, so that midnight prayers, if he remembered correctly, had to be said in all the synagogues—which made it something of an exaggeration to say that it hadn't rained so much in years. Why exaggerate? And yet on the other hand, why not? In any case—but lord! If his elder brother said so, his suffering scholar of a brother, then let it be. Anyway one looked at it, he had been unemployed for several days, as a result of which he had no lack of time to sit up with his sick brother. He went home to sleep at night, but nearly all day long he sat without a fuss, and generally without a word, on the bench by his brother's bed, from noon until the hour for evening prayer, and then again until bedtime.

Esther, on the other hand, had been working in recent months in the women's ward of the hospital for the mentally ill on the outskirts of town and could tear herself away to visit her father only at rare intervals, and even then, always without warning in advance. This time, too, she arrived on the run, her costume thrown carelessly together, determined to stay "only for a minute." ("It's just that Miriam can't be trusted. She's not the type to worry about others, and Father, after all, is ill.") During her half year in the hospital she had learned to say "ill" like a bona fide nurse, with a nonchalant pride like an artist's when he speaks of his work, and to pronounce the technical terms of her trade—*temperature, thermometer, enema*—in a special tone of proficiency. Taking off her glasses with a movement like her father's, she placed them for some reason on the table, shook her head at Reb Yosef's worn, cobbled shoes with the assurance of a specialist who knows the reason for every complaint, and made some remark about not catching cold and the need for warm baths for the feet.

Reb Yosef groaned in bed. In order to bathe, he observed, one needed either to borrow a tub from a neighbor or else to spend good money buying one. Neither alternative was realistic. Borrowing, it went without saying, was out of the question: who in Jerusalem would lend them a tub? Jerusalem wasn't Gomel or Kiev. There he'd had friends, there everyone knew him; whereas here—but why go on? He, Reb Yosef, hated to speak ill of Jerusalem! . . . As for the second of the two alternatives, buying one—that, ha ha, was an even greater absurdity: it would cost a whole gold napoleon! Besides which, the truth of the matter was that the really pressing problem was not a bathtub at all, but rather an apartment, which was a question of five napoleons, not one. The renting season was just around the corner: they would need to find an apartment and pay the whole year's rent in advance (such was the custom in Jerusalem), to raise five napoleons at once —and where was the money to come from? Goldmann had already announced that their present apartment was to be "requisitioned" for the guesthouse downstairs, which was running short of space.

"For the guesthouse?" Esther's greenish face flushed with fury and a fiery, consumptive hatred shone in her eyes. "Maybe it's really for his brother-in-law that he wants it, for Hamilin?"

Seventeen-year-old Miriam, who was standing right there, controlled herself and refused to answer her spinster sister's taunt, which was completely baseless and had been made for no good reason, out of the sheer irritability of growing old. Instead she waited for a moment when her father was engrossed in conversation with her uncle and then whispered to Esther:

—The one thing that really needed watching, she, Esther, hadn't even noticed. Her tongue was sharper than her eyes! Father had bought another book yesterday. Some strange kind

of Bible with a new commentary for four francs. When he'd
come home with it he'd told her that he'd borrowed it from a
friend; he was afraid to tell her the truth. But Shneirson had
inadvertently revealed the secret; father had bought the book
without even asking permission. He'd been given it on credit,
since naturally he hadn't had the cash. But he'd promised to
pay and he would. What a strange passion: to go on buying
books when you didn't know where your next meal was coming from! It was simply terrible. They must tell all the book-
stores not to give him more credit. She just couldn't put up
with it any more.

"And now I have news to tell *you*," Esther rejoined,
abruptly changing the subject.

"News? What can it be?"

"Oh, as if I didn't know you. You won't even care."

Reb Yosef sat up. "What did you say? News? What kind
of news?"

"Yehezkel may be leaving our hospital in the next few
days."

"Then he's better?" Haim too was eager to hear more.

"Yes. The doctor from the men's ward told us this morning
that if he keeps making progress, perhaps. . . ."

"You don't say!" Reb Yosef's eyes shone unaccustomedly.
"Well, well, God be praised! God be praised! He afflicts and
He cures. Providence works in such wonderful ways! God
be praised!"

"God be praised!" Esther mimicked angrily. "And yet all
these weeks and months . . . and no one could even find the
time to visit him . . . you call yourselves family!"

"There's no excuse for it, no excuse," Haim admitted.
"Granted, Yosef has been sick, but still. . . ."

Miriam feigned innocence. "Visit whom?" she asked.

Esther could have scratched out her eyes. "Yehezkel!"

"Ye-hez-kel?" Miriam repeated the name after her, drawling

each syllable with flaunted *sang-froid*. Her eyes laughed with girlish mischief.

"Yes, Yehezkel!" raged Esther.

"Goodness gracious . . . Yehezkel . . . who's Yehezkel?" Miriam knew that the barb would strike home and it did.

"He's not Shneirson!" Esther snapped at her.

"Shneirson?"

"Not the student without a university!"

"Ahh, now I know . . . Yehezkel, our cousin . . . the lunatic. . . ."

"That's none of your business. You're a lunatic yourself. And your tutor. . . ."

But immediately Esther regretted losing her temper. It galled her to be reminded that the riposte "Shneirson" was no longer really to the point: hadn't Miriam informed her just the day before yesterday that her lessons with him were over? Having given up hope of admission to the Teachers Institute, what did she need a Hebrew tutor for anyway? She'd made up her mind to go abroad, most likely to America (indeed, where else did one go?); instead of studying Hebrew, she should be beginning to take up English. Cooking, too, was something she was done with; from now on Shneirson would dine with them no longer! And after all this—she, Esther, was still goading her sister with the same rusty weapon. *Your tutor, your tutor* . . . no more! She must think of something to say that would really be cutting . . . something to put her in her place . . . only what?

Unconsciously almost, her feelings and thoughts still awhirl, Esther had a sudden inspiration. With no visible connection to what had come before, she remarked as deftly as a pinprick:

"Or maybe Doctor Hamilin will give you lessons, my fine English lady? I'll wager he studied at the college in Beirut— just so he could teach you the language. . . ."

"What makes you think you're so funny?" Miriam replied

in a stung tone of her own. "What makes you so sure I haven't already asked him?"

"And he agreed?"

"Suppose he did?"

"And he'll come here to teach you?"

"That's none of your business, either. Who are you to stop me if I decide to go to him?"

"No, of course I won't stop you. No one will stop you. You can go to his hotel. Go. . . ."

"I will go. What of it?"

"Of course. Nothing at all. After all, it's only to study. And he comes from father's town . . . he was his pupil . . . a fellow townsman . . . of course! Only what will happen to father?"

"Father? Does father want to study too?"

"Is father going to be left alone in the house in his condition?"

Reb Yosef sat up again. "What? What? What about father? What hotel are you talking about?"

"Lord!" Haim tried to calm him. "They're talking about Goldmann's brother-in-law. He was supposed to arrive at the beginning of summer and came only at the end of it. He's staying at the Harel."

"Ah, the Harel . . . Goldmann . . . so that's it. . . ."

Reb Yosef resumed his conversation with his brother. Haim was also worried about the renting season—he too had troubles with his apartment. As a rule the apartments in his court-yard were raffled off each year, but this year, he had heard, there was another "interested party." Once again Goldmann was at the bottom of it. What the Bible said about Ishmael, that his hand was "against every man's," could well be said about him, only unfortunately, the second part of the verse, "and every man's hand against his," did not apply in this case. Yes, Goldmann had a finger in the pie here too. The man could hatch six different schemes in a day, damn his clever soul! He had plans, the devil alone knew what, to start some sort of school in which the students were to learn languages and secular studies, but the whole thing to be strictly God-fearing and religious, "one hundred and one per cent." True, the school itself was not planned for Haim's building; but in order to find a place for it Goldmann had dickered and dealt with a number of people who in turn had some claim on the courtyard. All kinds of mortgages, deeds and charity pledges were involved as well—Haim himself was unable to grasp the half of it, much less explain all the fine points to his brother. This much, however, he knew: when the residents of the courtyard had gone to Reb Yankev to complain, the latter had told them that they hadn't a leg to stand on, for he'd had nothing to do with it all and had even publicly advertised his withdrawal from anything involving the courtyard and its apartments. He was in no mood to be bothered and refused to speak to anyone. Besides—so he said —everything hung on the raffle. Since the lucky winners would have a place to live in any case, what was all the fuss about?

The older of the two brothers rambled on again from his sickbed. The unthinkable, the insufferable things that were done these days! And these were the servants of the public, the great philanthropists . . . what paradoxes! Philanthropists indeed! Yes, once, he remembered, when he had still been a youngster, there had been a cultivated Jew, a teacher in the government rabbinical school . . . Ochsenfeld, his name had been, or maybe Ettinger . . . and he'd written some sort of book, a "broadside". . . .

Yet try as he did, Reb Yosef was unable to recall a thing about this "broadside," not even such relevant details as its date of publication and contents. In fact, he wasn't even sure of the title itself: had it been "Sarkele" or "Etkele"? It pained him to have forgotten. His memory was deserting him completely.

His brother's distress was too much for Haim to bear. With an uncharacteristically resigned sigh, he too began to mouth words at random, as if to cover over some unspoken void.

"Lord! He's got a hand in everything, in absolutely everything. Goldmann'ke! He even runs the raffle, he calls the tune there too. And he says that he's never interfered in any of the charities. He's lying through his teeth. The man is everywhere, he's got his hand in everything. How can you deal with someone like him?" Did anyone think that he, Haim, was going to go running to him? No, he would never in the world ask him for a personal favor. He knew him well, too well—how he wished he had never known him at all! His "in-law" . . . yes, whenever he happened to remember that while Hanoch, bless him, had still been married, Goldmann had been his kinsman, his daughter-in-law's father—whenever he thought of it— lord! Ever since then he, Haim, had gone out of his way to avoid him; and not just to avoid meeting him, but to avoid thinking of him too. Just the thought of him was enough to give him fits! Worst of all was their argument over his security. Had or hadn't Goldmann kept his security and refused to give it back? It had been outright robbery! Yes, it was easy enough to speak of "security" . . . one might think it was nothing but a ring or a watch or a coat . . . *security*, h'm . . . but a Torah scroll! His own Torah scroll which he, Haim, had vowed to have written the time he was in danger and had to escape from the customs agents . . . his vow which he had been able to keep only in the Land of Israel . . . and this scroll of his had fallen into the hands of that vulture! His *reinigkeit* * had been snatched away as security! And why? Because Hanoch, bless him, hadn't the money to pay Henya the alimony fixed by their marriage contract, although it was she, the *grande dame*, who had insisted on the divorce, she who had forced him to give it to her with her wailing that she couldn't live with him. No, nothing in the world could have ever made him, Haim, go to that thieves' den on business of his own, if it weren't . . . if there hadn't been . . . er, another matter, which concerned his sick brother. After all, it was nothing to make light of: a sick, jobless man who if forced in his present condition to leave his apartment—when and where could he find another as cheap? He, Reb Yosef, would be forced to sleep in the street . . . on the rocks in front of the Hotel Harel——

"I hope you at least gave him a proper talking to!" It was almost as if Reb Yosef had divined the end part of Haim's thoughts, which the latter had kept to himself, alluding to them out loud only disjointedly. "You needn't have felt embarrassed in front of him. I can tell you the man's no genius! Just at the start of this month I had an argument with him over the custom of prostrating oneself during the High Holy Day prayer. He was stubborn as a mule and simply wouldn't admit the truth. And such disrespect, such vulgarity. Finally I brought out the prayer book *Celestial Light* and showed him in black and white . . . heh heh . . . I'm telling you! But that's just it: you have to know how to deal with people like that! Only you still haven't answered my question . . . you should have told him everything, spelled it out for him in plain words. . . ."

"Well, what do *you* think happened?" It was the best Haim could manage to reply.

But the sick man was relentless. "Well? What did happen?"

* Yiddish: literally, "purity," i.e., a sacred object.

"What did happen? What did happen?" Haim's temper too was wearing thin. "Do you think he would listen to me? There's just no way of getting around him. He kept saying that it was none of his business. The way he can lie, lord! One minute he's telling me that it's not up to him to decide, that there's some sort of 'board,' and in the very next breath he's making propositions on his own! The swine! He'd tear out your eyes and not feel the least bit sorry." To prove that he had his former in-law's interests at heart, Goldmann had offered him the sextonship of the guesthouse chapel, which was presently vacant because the former sexton was somewhere overseas. The "board," of course, might not wish to approve, but Goldmann promised to support him, and what he, Goldmann, set out to do was as good as done. And he'd said all this in so many words, as though it were none of his concern that just a minute ago he'd been protesting that he hadn't the power to decide a thing on his own! In a word, according to Goldmann, he, Haim, would have an apartment waiting for him and would be able to help Reb Yosef, for whom Goldmann—as God was his witness—could no longer do a thing.

Reb Yosef reached out from the bed with his good right hand, picked up a book from the chair nearby, replaced his glasses on his nose and began to read. The conversation, it seemed, had become a burden to him and he wished to put an end to it. But the pause did not last long. Raising his thickly knit brows, Reb Yosef massaged his numb leg with the cover of his book and asked without looking at Haim:

"Then you don't think it's worth considering?"

"The sextonship of the guesthouse?"

"When I'm left without a roof over my head you can help me find a place there . . ." added Reb Yosef in jest, as

though to mitigate the special harshness surrounding Goldmann's crude offer.

"They don't accept local residents," his brother replied in
earnest. "It's only for visitors and even then there's never
room."

"I was only joking," said Reb Yosef to apologize.

Haim sought to apologize too: "Anyway, no one is allowed
to stay there for more than three weeks at a time."

Reb Yosef said nothing.

"I'll tell you the truth, Yosef. Maybe I'd be wise to accept.
Lord knows I'd make a better sexton than a stonecutter! Between the two of us, what kind of stonecutter was I cut out
to be? Besides which, how long can I go on milking Hanoch,
God bless him, for ten francs a month? It's not as though he
lives off the fat of the land himself. But to be a slave to that
man when I can't even stand the sight of his face! Even when
they lay me out with shards on my eyes, I'll never forget the
day of the divorce, his rudeness in court. Lord, anyway you
look at it I was in the right! It wasn't my son who divorced
her, but the other way around; why should he pay her alimony? He saw that the judge was seeing things my way, so
he called me over to one side and said, 'Why make fools of
ourselves? Let's settle out of court. I know that you haven't
any money'—he meant Hanoch and me—'so what difference
does it make whether the court decides that you have to pay
alimony or not?' My Hanoch, bless him, stood there dumb as
a lamb and said nothing. But I began to shout. 'What do you
mean?' I said to him. 'If we don't have to pay, then I'll get
the court to make you give me back my Torah scroll . . .
my Torah which you've taken for security. . . .' 'Oh no,' he
says to me, 'you're not getting the scroll; a scroll is worth
good money. My daughter Henya has every right to ask for

a divorce and he has to let her have it and pay alimony.' 'But on what grounds?' 'Lord,' he says to me, 'if that's how you're going to be, what will you do if I claim that your Hanoch hasn't given his wife her just due, *her food, her raiment and her marital pleas* . . .* Do you follow me?' And all the time he kept winking his eyes at me. I can see them before me this minute as real as life. Hanoch said nothing, but I was fit to be tied: What did he mean, he wasn't going to give it back to me? He would have to perjure himself! But he wouldn't give an inch. 'I'm ready to forget about the food and the raiment, but what about the third clause?' 'What are you trying to say?' 'I'm saying that we'll claim he's not a man, that he's not able to give her . . . the third clause. A smart fellow like him should realize. . . .' Those were his exact words. Tfu, damn his soul! How can you even sit in one room with an unclean thing like that?"

Reb Yosef nodded over his book, in which he hadn't read a word, and cut short the conversation. This wasn't the first time he had heard his brother's sad story. *Great was the evil of men. . . .* Besides which, as far as the law itself was concerned, he was still not entirely satisfied that a woman who claimed incompatibility with her husband was not entitled to alimony. To the best of his knowledge, the later rabbis had taken issue with the Talmudic ruling and revised it in favor of the woman. Indeed, if his memory wasn't playing tricks on him—and lately, alas, it had become enfeebled completely —there was a long and commendable note on the subject in the third volume of the Hebrew translation of Graetz.† . . . *What? Esther was already getting up to go?*

* . . . *her food, her raiment and her marital pleas[ure]* is from the Biblical passage prescribing the marital duties of the husband (Exodus 21:10).

† Heinrich Graetz (1817–1891), a German-Jewish historian of Judaism.

"What can I do?" the departing visitor asked lamely. "I told you I could only stay a minute. . . . I've left all my patients. . . ."

"Your patients? You just finished telling us that your patient was all better."

Before Esther could reply in kind, however, Shneirson entered the room, leaving her with her comeback still stuck in her throat.

"I say, Shneirson, see how sick I am," Reb Yosef called out in a tone of childish indulgence.

Shneirson arrived with sensational news, a revelation which couldn't wait to be told: he had just this minute learned from a reliable source in his hotel that Hamilin wasn't a doctor!

"But how can that be?"

It was perfectly simple: he still hadn't finished his studies. All the hoopla about him had been in vain. In fact, this was why he had come, in order to see Goldmann. It was the latter who had advised him in the first place to leave Europe and study in Beirut. But the rub had been that in Europe he'd had a wife who supported him and sent him money, whereas now—or anyway, so it was said—he'd left her for good and had to turn elsewhere for help. And so he'd come to his relative Goldmann, who had meanwhile gone and announced that Hamilin was already a doctor.

Shneirson addressed his remarks to Reb Yosef, but at the same time he kept a sharp eye on Miriam to see how she was taking the news.

How much "the nymph" had changed lately! Or rather, not she herself, but her relationship to him. Only a while ago she had been so different . . . whereas now she hardly even listened any more when he was teaching her or telling her stories. *Tales of the Bible* lay forgotten; she no longer prepared her lessons and had taken to sticking a pin between her lips in the middle of them and picking continually with it at her teeth (all, to be sure, in the most genteel, the most ladylike manner), while her eyes went strangely dim, like an exhausted porter's under his load. . . .

At first Shneirson had adopted a policy of sarcasm, had said "hail, gracious lady" instead of "hello" and the like, partly in order to get back at her and partly in the hope of winning her back, but all to no avail. Nothing seemed to do any good. And once, at dinner, when she had given him a sardine tin to open, and he broke off the key and couldn't open it and was full of self-reproach (it seemed to him to be symbolic of something: he, Shneirson, was not in the habit of quoting Maeterlinck for nothing!), she had laughed at him in front of everyone and wouldn't stop . . . all of which, of course, made him exceedingly cross and demanding; whereas once he had simply nodded his head at everything as a sign of approval, now there was nothing that he didn't find fault with. There had been a time, for instance, when he had amused himself with the thought that although the food always reached the table in a jiffy, the meals, alas, went on and on, thanks to Reb Yosef and his endless talk; now, however, the waiting took longer and longer, while the meals themselves were over before they'd begun—some salad, a bit of soup, a glass of tea, and *voilà*. And today, in her haste, Miriam had actually handed him an unwashed spoon with somebody's leftovers still on it, which had made him want to rise from the table with a sudden desire to puke. . . .

Enough! He would go back to eating at the hotel. He would tell them that starting with the first of the month he would take his meals at the Harel. He lived there, and so he would eat there; that was all there was to it. He didn't mean to lead two lives any more.

Still he controlled himself and said nothing. It was hard to come out with it. For the present he preferred to observe the impression that his news made on Miriam.

And she was certainly not unimpressed! True, the business about Hamilin having been married and then divorced didn't affect her so much . . . a single man was worth more to her than a married one anyway . . . what was it to her whether he'd ever had a wife or not? *She* wasn't going to be his bride in any case! But it saddened her to think that he wasn't yet a doctor . . . a man like him *should* be a doctor . . . though on the other hand, this had its advantages too . . . still not a doctor . . . only a student . . . it brought them closer together . . . he wouldn't be able to put on such airs any more. . . .

Miriam was overcome for some reason by a feeling of joy; her face brightened, and with it, her mood. In a fit of sudden tenderness she even offered to serve her father supper in bed, but Reb Yosef wouldn't hear of it. No, he wasn't so sick that he couldn't manage to get out of bed now and then. It wasn't easy to have to lie on his back all day long. He would put on his shoes and get up to go to the table.

Haim heard his brother's intentions and threw himself at his feet without a word to help him with his shoes.

"Ai, ai!" Reb Yosef expressed his displeasure. "I'm not such a great scholar that I should be waited on hand and foot." But his eyes, which were turned toward Shneirson, seemed to plead: *Come, say I'm mistaken, so that Goldmann, who's always against me, shouldn't think. . . .*

Haim was upset. "In your condition, Yosef, in your condition . . . lord. . . ."

"Nonsense!" Reb Yosef interrupted. "Ask the know-it-all in our synagogue—he'll tell you what kind of scholar I am!"

Water still dripped from the corners of the ceiling. There was a chill in the night air, the drizzly end of a rainy day.

The shoe was tied at last but Reb Yosef remained sitting on the bed with his eyes half shut. To no one in particular he uttered a word that sounded like "nevertheless." *Nevertheless,* even if he, Reb Yosef, was no scholar, no *great* scholar, that is (he didn't wish to appear overly modest), nevertheless . . . let it not be held against him . . . it wasn't as if he had meant to flatter himself . . . but still . . . he was critical by nature, severe on everyone, that was simply the way he was. According to Spinoza, good and evil had no existence in themselves, but only in the impressions, pleasant or painful, that they made. So too, he, Reb Yosef, knew that man was not a free agent. What was man like? Like a stone that someone had thrown. If the stone could think like a man, it would think it was going its way of its own free will. And yet nevertheless! That was his nature. He divided people up into categories . . . it was only natural, it was something he'd learned from his studies . . . Goldmann too was a category . . . so was Hamilin, doctor or no doctor . . . even he, Reb Yosef, was some kind of category. Nor did he think that his own category was better than anyone else's . . . he was equally distrustful of himself . . . only would someone be so kind as to inform him what there was to suspect him of here? He had known that rain was needed, he had supported the court's decree of a fast, he had said as much—what had he done wrong? Was it his fault if just because he said "yes" Goldmann had to say "no"? Was it his fault if drought happened to be good for Goldmann's business? He himself, after all, had nothing to gain from the rain . . . nothing but rheumatism . . . oy, oy, no good would come of it. . . .

II

The black-skinned wife of the Arab watchman focused on him with the whites of her eyes, then opened the small gate in the fence for him with her huge key. The mass of clifflike boulders in the field across the way met his glance: to the north, in the crimson glint of the rocks piled before him, their color heightened by the reddish beams striking against them from low in the southwestern sky—it was nearly four o'clock and the December day was already on the wane—there was no suggestion of a father's forgiveness or a mother's sheltering breast, but neither was there anything sinister or somber any more. Just a few days before he had paced wildly about in the garret above him, and softly groaned "rocks, rocks, rocks" without knowing why . . . knowing only when he did know that he would not be killed by the mob . . . it was enough that he had been imprisoned on a false charge . . . a charge brought against him by the Arab woman in the colony . . . before the Passover . . . the woman who had lost her child . . .—And he knew then too, knew he would prove that his blood wasn't Jewish at all . . . Gentile blood flowed through his veins . . . he had been born exactly nine months after the first pogroms . . . he wasn't a Jew at all, but a *goy*, eighty

per cent Slav . . . how could the woman not understand that he didn't have her *zrir?* *

He had been obsessed by strange fantasies like these, terrified by his own weird dreams. What had he imagined these rocks to be when he had stared down on them from above, his shirt hanging open, his nerves shattered, his mind in a fog, gripped with fear? At the moment he neither remembered nor wished to remember. All that was over with. The dread concealed in those groans . . . yes, he could feel it even now . . . only now it was over. The gate was wide open. He stood with his suitcase, his old companion, in one hand, wearing his own worn street clothes in place of the long, torn hospital frock which he himself had ripped, completely on his own, leaving it all, inmates, institution, everything, behind him. In another minute he would turn to the right and walk east, toward Sha'arei Yehudah, Mishkenot Yisrael, Oholei Ya'akov, hardly recognizable to anyone who hadn't seen him during the six long months of his imprisonment. *Onward to freedom then! Fresh air at last . . . and the rocks?* He watched their outlines blend with the backs of the goats browsing down the hillside among them. The sunlight turned everything the same golden red. . . . No, it was pointless to groan. The rocks were just rocks. Soon they would recede into the distance and be gone.

Behind him the watchman's wife shook her head. "Look how the poor devil runs! How happy he is to be gone."

"And little wonder!" It was the head attendant who spoke in Hefetz's defense, a Syrian Jew whose pock-marked face and burly waist, so un-Jewish in its powerful girth, made him seem someone special, one of a kind.

Unconsciously, Hefetz slowed his steps to listen to the voices behind him.

* Arabic: little child.

"Go, go and God bless you!" The Syrian urged him on deliberately but gently. "And don't look back! Be healthy and whole. Just don't talk too much, don't talk any more than you need to . . . and don't look where you needn't either . . . take my word for it . . . keep a tight grip on yourself. I've got nothing against you . . . you can consider me your friend . . . take care not to say any more than you have to."

And again the attendant made a point of stressing his friendship, as though there were reason to assume that Hefetz could not help but doubt it. But the latter, though his well-wisher's words meant little to him, bore him no grudge for what had happened in the hospital. Indeed he could not have, for at the moment of his release all that had slipped his mind; it was only an instant later, when he was already through the gate, when suddenly *she* appeared out of nowhere from the side, as though to talk down the attendant this time too, and to get at him, Hefetz—it was only then that the memory flared within him . . . why, it had been like that then too . . . when he'd been beaten . . . then too she had appeared like that out of nowhere, from the side. . . .

"*. . . to beat a sick man like that . . . and such a quiet one . . . it's sheer murder. . . .*"

"*Such a quiet one, such a quiet one!*" *The attendant furiously mimicked the nurse's aide from the women's ward, who refused to mind her own business.* "*He tears his clothing to shreds . . . he fouls his food. . . .*"

"*But I told you that he didn't eat tomato stew. Why did you have to give it to him?*"

"*I gave it to him because I felt like it. And if he doesn't want to eat—fine, he doesn't have to—but no games with his food!*"

"*As long as a patient isn't harming anyone else, one has to show restraint. The idea is . . .*"

While he, the subject of the discussion, the object of the blows, reasoned out loud in an imploring tone of voice as though he really weren't in the least bit mad at all:

*"Tomato stew . . . to mate or stew . . . so that's it, is it? But I'm a broken man . . . bric-a-broke . . . above, below, between . . . the heart is between . . . the heart is at the heart . . . but to stew? To eat is a sacrament, the greatest saints worry that there won't be enough . . . for everyone, everyone . . . that is, for every one of them. Only you mustn't call it socialism! Never! To hell with socialism! Everything all planned and arranged and decided in advance —pooh! What a lot of nonsense—they'll never get it right! The planners will take the pudding for themselves—of course they will! Only of course, there should be enough to eat too . . . enough for myself and my neighbor . . . and you're giving me stew? Wasn't I created in God's image too? Er and Onan * abused God's image—it's all in the Bible, the Humishl isn't ashamed to say so—the bastards stewed in their own juice. Bastards, not bastards . . . all of us are bastards, none of us are bastards . . . there aren't any bastards, so those who aren't mustn't feel proud . . . it's just that it says: 'And the sons of Judah did evil in the eyes of the Lord.' And myself? Good, evil, it's not that I deny it, it's just that I don't understand, don't know . . . I don't deny that I'm ill . . . that I need to be in the hospital. . . . 'And it came to pass on that day'—that the whole world was put in a hospital. But in prison? Is that any place for me? Here, where even the prisoners' horses eat halvah?"*

"What? Their horses eat halvah?" The attendant winked at the meddlesome nurse's aide and grunted twice in triumph under his breath.

---

* The sons of Judah, of whom it is related in Genesis 38 that the latter, rather than fulfill his levirate obligations to his deceased brother's childless wife, deliberately cast his seed to the ground.

The patient hastened to explain. "That is, I didn't mean to complain. Halvah without bread . . . halvah with toadstools . . . it has to be, of course . . . there are worse prisons in the world than this. In The House of the Dead * *it's far worse . . . they suffer more there. But the things you give me to eat—it's just too much for me . . . believe me, it's too much! There are so many prisoners—and only one of me . . . how can you give me so much? A glass of plain water would be enough . . . water without milk . . . and an onion if you happen to have one . . . an onion . . . it can't do any harm . . . but no tomato stew. I'm not what you think . . . the doctor can say what he wants . . . you mustn't listen to him. . . ."*

"We mustn't?" she asked curiously. "We mustn't listen?" She bent over to fix his cap, pressing against him with her long, thin body, breathing on him with her mouth. "Do you mean the doctor is wrong?"

"What is it you're suggesting? That I'd rather stew? Tomatoes! Feh, what ugly names these Italian vegetables have . . . of course! It happened in Italy . . . it's quite a story. . . ."

And he proceeded to tell her the whole long story, which concerned a poor Italian who was a total failure in life, a man who had nothing to give. They had done their best to help him; he had been in great misery; he had wandered about for years, he had tried to escape his fate—but he couldn't avoid it. The inevitable happened. Sooner or later the wheel must come round. Four years went by—and the same thing happened again. What good had being in Italy done him? What good had it done him to be on the farm? Now he had gone and left it again . . . had she heard the song about the farmer's wife? La, la, la, la, the farm-er's wife, la, la, la, la, the farm-er's wife. . . .

"How does the story end?"

* Dostoievsky's novel of Russian prison life.

—The end was simple. He had nothing to give because he was poor; poor and weak and terribly unhappy. But his love for life was even greater than his poverty and it triumphed. Because the poor Italian loved life, and even more than he loved it he felt rooted in it, rooted just like an onion. The whole trouble was that here, in Palestine, he hadn't seen a single onion. Not one farm grew them. . . .

"La, la, la, la, the farm-er's wife. . . ."

And he was off again on another tack:

"They say that Palestine is the center of the world . . . what a joke!" Why, he himself was the center! In his present incarnation he was . . . a central switchboard. That is, every time they pulled the switch he tapped his head and another telegram arrived. The telegrams came flying from all over and each one announced that its sender had gone mad. Burning wires led to him from the far ends of the earth to transfix him and tell him everything. . . .

. . . Yes, word had been received: the widow in Italy had lost her husband and was left with her six children, not counting the girl. The girl didn't count at all: she simply got in the way, she made a nuisance of herself, she sang "The Farmer's Wife." She was in a stew over Hamilin, she did whatever she pleased—the tomatoes were for her! But the six children were hungry, they lay sick, three in a bed. The oldest was ten, the next nine, the third eight, the fourth six, the fifth four, the sixth three, and she, the mother, made seven! Yes, he knew how to count, he was almost a socialist, he wasn't crazy at all. And they were all hungry, naked, sick . . . Hamilin had studied medicine but there was nothing he could do . . . there was no one to help. Even he, the poor Italian, couldn't help. Seven wires transfixed him (the girl didn't count at all): the first was ten cubits long, the second nine, the third eight— but the fourth, what was the fourth?

"*The fourth? The fourth what?*"

"*What makes you think that just because I have no visitors the world is dead? You're wrong! I know everyone and I visit everyone . . . at night . . . in the dark pit at the bottom of my dreams . . . rock bottom . . . a pit full of eyes . . . my friends' eyes, people I know . . . the eyes of the other prisoners . . . what, you don't believe me? You mustn't think . . . life hasn't come to an end. . . .*"

All of a sudden, as though he were in complete possession of his senses, he went on:

"*Nothing here says anything about the world. It doesn't prove a thing about life itself. Here it's just the broken little revolver of a little man. What is man that Thou shoulds't remember him? An individual. A single sick individual. And an individual has no right to judge the mass of men. An individual can only say: 'What have I to do with them? If I'm unhappy—well then, I must be hard to please.' But the others are right too. 'So you're unhappy, are you? Of course, you can tear your hair out if you like, but what are we, the mass of men, supposed to do about it?'*"

And just as suddenly his face went foolishly blank again:

"*It's just that the world hasn't gotten any clearer! Life hasn't come to an end—but the world hasn't gotten any clearer! The central switchboard is all confused. The telegrams make no sense . . . the telegrams from the front make no sense. It's dark here in the pit . . . there's not a ray of new light . . . only without the switchboard it would be even worse . . . a bare bit of truth gets through . . . a bare bit gets bared . . . the naked truth . . . you can give a man tomatoes but you can't make him stew. I'm not what you think . . . not even Onan . . . Kenan not Onan . . . because Kenan begat Mehalalel and Mehalalel begat Jered and Jered begat Enoch . . . and Enoch Ezekiel . . . dost mean*

Ezekiel the Priest, son of Buzi? Why, nothing of the kind, nothing of the kind! Just plain Yehezkel. 'And he shall set the stumbling-block of his sin before him.' * *He said that too, Ezekiel. . . ."*

"Yehezkel! Yehezkel!"

She. His closest kin. The nurse's aide from the women's ward. Esther Hefetz, She—with her lashless eyes. She—with her tall, stooped body, taller than his own; with her mannish chest, more sunken than his own; with her hurried, flustered walk, her dry, jarring, agitated voice.

"Wait! Wait a minute!"

His first thought was an angry, a healthy, an almost youthful one; it came to him from across the years, from a time before all his illness. *I don't need her,* his first thought was, *why must she run after me?* But his second thought was already more considered. What did she want from him? Could it be that she simply needed him for his weakness? Only why must it be him? Was there no one else from whose sick, rotting body she could hope for attention? His third thought was more yielding yet, almost agreeable . . . who was he, chronic cripple that he was, to be displeased by her chasing him? Even if she didn't know the whole truth—who else beside her would reach out to a man just out of the madhouse? What other woman would even condescend to stand in his presence, to breathe the same air as him?

"Yehezkel! Stop! I want to talk to you."

She caught up with him at last, out of breath, coated lightly with perspiration from the exertion of running and her unwholesome excitement. Her tightly drawn face was full of misery, hardly less so than his own. A delectably warm wave of compassion swept suddenly over him. For her? For himself? It hardly mattered. . . . *My poor, pitiful sister in sick-*

* Ezekiel 14:3.

ness! All my cold comforts be upon thee! After whom are
you running so?

The late afternoon December air was chilly though not
damp, yet the early sunset promised a night of scattered
clouds, a rare, misty, pale-mooned Jerusalem night such as he
loved, with a handful of half-hidden stars. Suddenly his head
started to ache again, to hurt him fearfully, even worse perhaps than it had then, a few days before, in the little room up
above. He began to shake all over and then his hand was un-
steadily clasping hers. At the touch of it Esther's eyes somehow lost all their fierceness; in the dying twilight a con-
strained yet immense, infinite expression of gratitude filled
them instead.

"Yehezkel! Where are you off to?"

She pressed his hand firmly and bent over still more, as
though she were about to go limp against his shoulders.

"Why do you ask?" he parried her question. "Isn't this the
way to Sha'arei Yehudah?"

She let herself be guided by his answer. "Yes, of course it's
the way. Did you think I didn't think you could find the
way?"

"I didn't think anything of the . . ."

"But that's not it at all. You don't forget your way in six
months' time. You know that's how long you've been here
. . . you do know that, don't you?"

"But why do you ask? Do you think I'm still ill?"

"Of course you're not. If you were they wouldn't have let
you go. But you have to take care. The doctor said . . . yes,
the doctor said that the sooner you left the better. The staff in
the hospital had a bad effect on you . . . what a strange collection of idiots! But you should be sure to keep in touch with
a doctor . . . you should consult a specialist . . . you should
come visit us. . . ."

"I didn't know you were a doctor."

"I meant in general. You should drop in on father. Where are you staying tonight?"

"I don't know yet. I'll find a place."

"You won't stay with us? But why?"

"I didn't know you were a hotel either."

"I didn't . . . actually, we don't have room. Uncle Haim . . . but you mustn't isolate yourself from people, Yehezkel. I know that . . . that after leaving here you're embarrassed to be seen . . . aren't you?"

"Maybe I am."

"That's why . . . that's why I came here to tell you . . . but I only have a minute . . . I don't have time now. I'll be at home tomorrow, perhaps I can fix a bed for you there. I have to go now . . . but take my advice, don't stay at Goldmann's guesthouse . . . it's filthy and unsanitary in every sense of the word. Pay half a bishlik and stay at the Harel. Do you have money? Here, let me give you some."

She took another step closer, trembling with longing, totally wretched.

"Esther'ke," he suddenly whispered. All the anger that he had felt a moment ago, when he had seen her coming, had vanished like a breath of bad air. "Esther'ke, sister, what do you want from me?" His voice was completely submissive. "Neither of us are young any more . . . or healthy . . . we have to be more careful with each other. . . ."

"You mustn't say that! You mustn't say that!" Her face twisted idiotically and she clapped her small, grimy, unpleasant hand over his mouth. Nothing stood between them any longer. Her eyes as though shut halfway and for an instant she seemed about to forget that they were standing in a public place.

The terrible part of it was that he too, for all that he didn't care for her, for all that he didn't want her, for all that he certainly didn't want her to want him—he too couldn't tear himself away, as though he sensed that with her would go his last, his only support.

She was murmuring hysterically. "Yehezkel . . . one minute . . . I'm coming with you . . . all the way. . . ."

He managed to prevent her with the last of his failing strength, bade her goodbye, kissed her furtively once and then again, and left her, walking on the tips of his toes as though leaving a dying man's bed, with the same careful steps with which she must have left him . . . back there in the yard . . . after they'd beaten him. . . .

And the truth of it is that she doesn't even need me! He grew calmer as he walked, making no attempt to suppress the thoughts that assailed him. *But she gets an excruciating pleasure from it all . . . yes, pleasure . . . the pleasure of the pariah . . . and I too, after all, get the same pleasure as she . . . how confused I must be! Pooh, what an idiot! And she— she's just a sick, pathetic nun . . . as sick as I am . . . just as sick . . . only she doesn't know it and I do. . . .*

His legs gave way and he stumbled against a rock on the road and sat down. The pale moon rose to shed its common, customary sadness. Yehezkel Hefetz stared at it for a long time. He thought of the cold metal of her glasses which had come between them when they kissed and of how they'd fallen to the ground a second later but magically failed to break. *Yes, pathetic*, he murmured, *we're all so pathetic, pathetic. We all deserve to be pitied. Who dares to be angry! Who dares to look down! To mock? Ay, let the mockers mock if they can. . . .*

A caravan of heavily burdened camels passed earnestly before him.

III

Goldmann's guesthouse in Sha'arei Yehudah had three rooms, two that were of average size and a third, larger one that was open to the public for prayer. At its eastern end was a small ark containing a single Torah scroll; a high table that served as both lectern and podium stood in the middle; and a quorum of ten met to pray in it three times a day in accordance with Jewish law. The prayer group, for the most part, did not consist of the boarders of the guesthouse itself, whose number never exceeded two or three and who lived together in cramped quarters under a soot-blackened ceiling in the narrow room next door that separated the chapel from the lodgings of the sexton; the latter, rather, on Goldmann's instructions, filled his quota of ten with neighbors, passers-by or whoever else came to hand. The one steady member of the little congregation was Haim the stonecutter, who was occasionally joined by his older and more eminent brother who lived with his daughters in the apartment overhead. But the sexton, though he never refused to call on Reb Yosef if needs be to be the "tenth man," and would even boast now and then to some new lodger of the "professor" upstairs who came to pray in the chapel, was in fact of two minds about his learned neighbor's appearances, for Reb Yosef was free to a fault with the water for washing his hands in the ritual before prayer, though as it was only September and the rainy season hadn't begun, so that the cisterns were empty and water cost a pretty penny, one would think that he might be more sparing. "Hmmmph!" the sexton would comment with a nasal snort. "It's easy to be generous at someone else's expense . . . yes, indeed!"

The sexton lived with his pale wife and delicate children in the guesthouse's third room, which faced in on the courtyard. He was a Jerusalemite by birth, an alert and by no means un-intelligent young man, though without a drop of blood in his system and with two small rheumy olives in the place of eyes. He had already been far out into the world and back again, and was in fact about to depart for New York once more, only meanwhile ("far die present time," as he put it in En-glish to the representative of the American charity, whom he had come to ask for some favor and wished to impress with his knowledge) he had taken on the sextonship of the guest-house, or as he called it in his Anglicized Yiddish, "die shel-ter." Of the typical Jerusalem costume, which he had long since abandoned, he continued to wear the colorful frock coat alone, and even that only on Sabbaths and without the customary striped jacket with large buttons underneath; the rest of the week he wore his clothes "short," in the American or European style, though then too he dressed with unusual color and flair, even after the Jerusalem winter had set in. In his bright cap and shoes, his rumpled red tie which hung crookedly from the pleated London collar of his shirt (the shirt itself was covered with blue polka dots), his striped gray pants and belted overcoat (on Sabbaths this same belt was wound around his dark yellow frock coat, while a white wool-knit skullcap protruded from beneath his best hat), and his green socks which flopped unabashedly over his dusty sandals, he seemed to have assembled his outfit at different times and in different places all over the world, giving him the appearance of a man of many seasons, a not uncommon type in the capital of Palestine: part "ritual director," i.e., cantor and leader of prayers; part "author," i.e., circulator of gossip in the Jerusalem newspapers; part "administrator," i.e., secretary and general hanger-on to one of the local societies or organizations; and part independently active in his own behalf whenever the hour seemed ripe. Mister Bassin (such being the sexton's name) belonged to the Volhynian charity, which was one of the poorest of its kind, so that his entire *yoks*, as the dole was called, amounted to no more than twenty or thirty francs a year, a figure that made him greatly dependent on the good graces of his wife, the product of a rich charity who had fallen to him like a gift from the blue, it being all but unheard-of for a young lady of means to marry a young man without them of her own free will. Because he had hopes of raising the necessary sum for his latest trip abroad from his wife's parents, Mister Bassin curried favor with them too; apart from that, however, he was one of Jerusalem's angry, disillusioned young men, a rebel, as it were, who went so far as to challenge the very system of the dole, the injustice of which, or so he claimed, was in large part responsible for driving him from his native land.

"Just think of it!" he would argue at length before the gathering at the "shelter" after the evening prayer was over. "Doesn't it say in the Good Book 'For the whole congregation is holy' * or something of the sort . . . well, doesn't it? Weren't we all born in Jerusalem? Is it right that Jews themselves should discriminate, or however you call it, between one Jew and another . . . is it right? If one person, for example, comes from Volhynia, and another, let's say, from

* Numbers 16:3.

Hungary or Holland, and Hungary sends more—is it only for its own Jews that Hungary is sending or is it for all of us? Am I right or not, gentlemen? Who ever heard of such a thing!"

It reminded Mister Bassin of his first visit to New York, where he had wandered into a public library and seen notices in one of the Yiddish socialist newspapers for the *Bebroisker Revolutsioner Untershtitsungs-farein*, the *Slutsker Revolutsioner Untershtitsungs-farein*,* etc. How far did they think it was, after all, from Slutsk to Bebroisk? He, Mister Bassin, would tell them. "No more than a hundred miles, that's how far. But—" —hmmmph!— "—what may be all right for the socialists, gentlemen, is definitely not all right for the charities of Jerusalem, which are meant—" —hmmmph!— "—for all who worship the one God of the one people of Israel. The Minsk foundation, the Pinsk foundation, the Slonim, the Karlin, the Brisk foundation †—what difference is there between them? Why, nothing but the few piastres a year more that one gets than the other! And yet—" —harummph!— "—they're always at sixes and sevens, or however you say it . . . yes, indeed!"

"*Ja!*" Here the sexton's complaint was interrupted by Herr Kauffmann, the Jew from *Ost-Preussen*, a regular lodger and one of the guesthouse's permanent fixtures. Herr Kauffmann was a short, round Jew in his forties, with a grayish-black beard, which was also round, that had already begun to turn white, a plucked-looking mustache, wide, almost distended lips, and clothes which though old and patched were always

* The Bebroisk Society in Support of the Revolution and the Slutsk Society in Support of the Revolution. Both Bebroisk and Slutsk are towns in Russia.

† Minsk, Pinsk, Slonim, Karlin, and Brisk are cities in Russia and Lithuania.

spotlessly clean and showed signs of the ironing board. Once he had been a salesclerk in the large shops of Lyck and Königsberg, where he had earned a respectable living and led a burgherly life, when suddenly—it had happened only two days after his marriage to a German Jewess who was eight years his elder—he had been possessed by a spirit of modern Orthodoxy, by a sort of *Offenbarung,** as he put it, which caused him to abandon everything, including his wife, and embark for the Holy Land. Arriving in Jerusalem with a pittance in his pocket, he had declared his intentions of "building up" *einige käufmannische Tätigkeit* † on an extensive *Massstab,*‡ yet five or six years later he was no closer to his goal and hadn't a penny to his name. On the strength of some old dealings with Goldmann he had taken up residence in the guesthouse; the overall impression that he created, however, was that he no longer hoped for success and was even somewhat frightened of the prospect. Not that he didn't still send letters abroad larded with terms like "export" and "import," or hurry to the post office each morning with a small attaché case under one arm; but he would be back again almost before he'd set out and the attaché case—if it hadn't by chance grown fatter by an onion or a slice of bread—would be as empty as before.

No one could deny that the business methods of Herr Kauffmann of East Prussia were rather peculiar. Each new failure of his speculations was only a "temporary setback," for all that such setbacks had been going on for years—in fact, ever since his arrival in Palestine. It was hardly any secret that this same man, for whom there was no language too extravagant in the guesthouse chapel with which to describe the future of trade in Jerusalem if only the charity foundations

---

* German: revelation. † German: a commercial operation.
‡ German: scale.

would establish a Savings and Loans Association of their own, was at a complete loss for words when actually obliged to approach someone on a matter of business. Instead of coming straight to the point and saying plainly what he had in mind, he would begin to hem and haw and endlessly clear his throat —the words just wouldn't appear! Each time the cat got his tongue, that devil of a cat . . . and yet on the face of things he was always so careful to lay the "groundwork" in advance, proceeding with his grand presentation only when he'd judged it thoroughly prepared:

"My dear ————! I've come to propose that Your Eminence grant me a moment or two of his time, as I have something of the greatest interest to impart to him." —"Well," the answer would be, "let's hear what you have in mind." —"But I can't . . . Your Excellency must realize . . . now isn't the proper moment," Herr Kauffmann would murmur. "Couldn't we set another time, perhaps later today or tomorrow?" —"Fine, come at . . ."

And again Herr Kauffmann would appear at the agreed hour, only instead of making a concrete proposal at last, he would start to lay the groundwork all over again from the beginning, beating forever around the bush and ending once more with the request: "If only Your Eminence would grant me a brief appointment, what I have to relate to him is of the utmost importance."

As Herr Kauffmann prayed with great devotion and took longer than anyone else to recite the evening service, he would still be in the middle of the concluding prayer by the time the others in the chapel were already idly chatting. Then he would finish in a hurry and plunge headlong into the discussion. This wasn't the first time, nor would it be the last, that he wished to make it known that he would tolerate no attacks on the Orthodox community of Jerusalem—in a word, he would simply not put up with it! Not that he felt any need to always *haben sich* * to argue, but he was determined not to spare himself in defending those most necessary of institutions, the charity foundations of Jerusalem, to the best of his ability! If *jemand* † wished to speak in the name of unity, well and good, *Einigkeit ist nicht kein Kleinigkeit;* ‡ but nonetheless, *meine Herren,* the charity foundations had yet to have the last word and a brilliant future awaited them. All that was needed was to increase the amount of trade in Jerusalem through Mutual Loans and Savings Associations—and it was sure to come! He had already broached the subject to a good many people. All *die Leute* § agreed with him, there was no lack of enthusiasm, in fact, the project was already underway—*im Werden.*° He, Herr Kauffmann, wished no one to doubt that if only he knew a little *Chemie,**′ he would personally travel the length and breadth of Palestine to investigate the earth, for he had complete faith—no, absolute conviction!—that great treasures lay buried beneath the soil of the Holy Land. Only to get at these treasures mutual associations were needed, yes, mutual associations established by the charity foundations, for the *Zukunft* †′ belonged entirely to the Old Orthodox community. As for the Zionists—*na,* they were nothing but *Phrasiologen* ‡′ and traitors to their religion. Yes, now he had said everything, he had said it all.

When Herr Kauffmann faced the other way the blondish-white curls that were eccentrically combed on the back of his neck gave him an air of confidence and determination, yet when he turned to face back again his wide, distended lips, which were the color of baked mud, wore a foolishly mystical

---

* German: have to.   † German: someone.

‡ German: Unity is no small trifle.   § German: the people.

° German: in the process.   *′ German: chemistry.

†′ German: future.   ‡′ German: phrasemongers.

look. And in fact, Herr Kauffmann made no effort to conceal that he saw mystical powers at work in everything . . . as a result of which he was constantly at odds with Reb Yosef, who, enlightened man of science that he was, would have nothing to do with "invisible presences" and "supernatural illuminations" of any sort: grant that they existed in but a single case, and there was simply no end to it, the laws of logic would have to be thrown out! On the whole, Reb Yosef had his own special tactics for dealing with Herr Kauffmann from the guesthouse downstairs, for whereas in his arguments with Goldmann he played the strict constructionist, sticking to the letter of the law throughout and citing such erudite texts as *The Basis of Worship* and *Celestial Light*,* he became the very soul of toleration when disputing with the Prussian, siding with the young Zionists against their Orthodox elders and defending them with all the dialectical skill at his command and with quotations from *die Bibel*, the Book of Books. Herr Kauffmann thought that the young folk were *Phrasiologen* and traitors to their religion? He, Reb Yosef, would say nothing about *Phrasiologen*, lest he be forced to resort to the proverb about people who lived in glass houses, ha ha . . . but as for the accusations of impiety and irreverence, his own opinion was that the younger generation was less sinful than rebellious, and that it rebelled out of a sense of anger and frustration at its own lack of faith—"Do I make my point clear?"—which was an entirely different thing. Besides which, if the youngsters did sin, their parents were partly to blame. Pull too hard on the reins, as the saying went, and they were bound to snap. Which was why he, Reb Yosef, kept insisting

---

* *The Basis of Worship*—a work on Jewish ritual by the 18th-century cabbalist Alexander Süsskind Ben Moses of Grodno.

"Celestial Light"—a part of the 13th-century cabbalistic work, the *Zohar*.

that if only the rabbis hadn't forbade the trimming of beards, for example, which was actually permitted by law, the young people wouldn't go about completely clean-shaven and break the Mosaic command. In fact, this was how he chose to interpret the difficult passage in Isaiah, where it said, "precept upon precept, line upon line, here a little, there a little," and again further on: "And the word of the Lord shall be unto you precept upon precept, line upon line. . . ." It was really quite simple. Because the Children of Israel insisted on adding one superfluous ordinance to another—*precept upon precept, line upon line* *—the word of the Lord, that is, the prohibitions of the Law, were multiplied too—yes, precept upon precept, line upon line. And yet Israel refused to pay heed!

For a moment the Jew from East Prussia actually lent an ear to the Jew from West Russia's liberal point of view, but only for a moment; then he not only refused to hear any more but went so far as to declare that he could detect a mystic power even in Reb Yosef . . . namely, that of Satan himself in the guise of a learned Jew. As for Herr Kauffmann, it was not his desire to reinterpret the Bible—such was not his stock in trade—but simply to express his opinion on the commercial prospects of the charity foundations and the Orthodox community of Jerusalem. He himself had come to Jerusalem with great plans and if his *Spekulationen* had so far come to nothing—such were the hazards of commerce. But he was confident nonetheless that Providence would not fail him; he refused to be discouraged or to abandon his enterprise; and why? Because he wasn't a Russian-Jewish atheist, that was why! Because he had an *Idee!* And to have an *Idee* was everything.

Here Herr Kauffmann departed from the realm of commerce and went on to the sphere of *Politik,* which too was

* Isaiah, 28:13.

no subject for "the wise men of the *lizhanka*" * but needed
to be discussed in terms of the secret powers at work in it.
Whenever two rulers clashed, for example, or two nations
went to war—what was behind it if not that two *Ideen* were
in conflict? Every *Nation* had its own *Idee* without which it
couldn't survive even for an instant. . . .

"How terribly original!" Reb Yosef fumed, unable to swallow the sarcastic reference to "the wise men of the *lizhanka*,"
which the ignorant *Daitsh* had heard him use on a previous
occasion and was now turning against him. "You'll find it all
in Krochmal . . . *The Contemporary Guide to the Perplexed* . . . the Idea . . . the Spirit of the Nation. . . ."

Herr Kauffmann, however, refused to surrender his *Position;* instead, he commenced to explain *konkretisch* just what
the various *Ideen* were, starting with the Franco-Prussian
War of 1870. Or take the war between France and Russia in
1812. Yes, believe it or not, even Ivan the Pig had an *Idee* of
his own!

"Lord, anyway you look at it," put in Haim Hefetz, who
on days when his brother wasn't ill liked to linger for a while
in the guesthouse chapel after the evening service to enjoy a
friendly conversation, "anyway you look at it—*Russland* or
Deutschland—a plague on them both!" But to say, to say—
here he tried to change the subject back again—to say that
everything in Jerusalem was just as it should be—why, it
simply wasn't so! That at least was his opinion—could he possibly be wrong? But no, it was impossible to say that Jerusalem was a model city. Why did there have to be so much
fanaticism? Why all the bickering and backbiting? The chairman of the board of the guesthouse, for example, was as
zealous as they came in the service of the Lord—but when

* *Lizhanka*—the extended mantle of the stove, used for warming
oneself in Russian peasant homes.

Goldmann and the Lord sat down to eat, who was to say how the dumplings were divided? On the subject of Goldmann, however, it was best to keep silent, for the man, after all, had once been his in-law and people would say that he was nursing a grudge. Yet the guesthouse had other officials too: "They're always complaining about their expenses—but who knows what they really are?" He himself, at any rate, happened to know that they took in more than they spent. Why, every year thousands upon thousands of letters went out to ask for donations just for the guesthouse alone—"the one place in Jerusalem where our indigent brethren can find a home." ("Mind you, the owners of the other rooms to let in Mishkenot Ya'akov and Zichron Yisrael say that theirs are the only ones too—lord!") In a word, they fleeced you coming and going. And in the end, there was only one room the size of a chicken coop, and that too they were careful to keep empty, there was hardly anyone ever in it. It cost a whole bishlik just to stay the night, and even then you had to be somebody special, with a letter of recommendation from, for example . . . but lord! Wasn't it so? He, Haim, was a simple unsophisticated man, but was he telling the truth or not? All one ever heard was "sorry, no vacancies." True, now they were talking about expanding . . . but even if they did, they would just cut back some-where else . . . they took from one pocket and gave to an-other. Lord, there was never enough room, there was always shouting, swearing, insults, accusations—there was everything but common decency, everything but that. That was the truth of it. Say what you will. . . .

Haim rejoiced over "Hatskel" * and his return from the hospital with all the simple goodness of his heart. It was really

* Yiddish affectionate form of the Hebrew name Yehezkel, or Ezekiel.

Reb Yosef who was Yehezkel's relation, and he too of course was pleased that the Healer of the Sick had seen fit to succor his late wife's nephew, yet his pleasure was tinged with sadness: when he looked at Yehezkel it was as though from afar and he was careful not to mention the unspeakable fact of his half year in the asylum. Instead he resorted to circumlocutions and spoke cryptically of "the prudent soul which avoids strong sensations, as philosophy warns us to do," and so forth. But Haim, on the other hand, made no bones about his happiness. At the time, lord help him, he had been terribly upset: to see a man take leave of his senses right in front of your eyes! All during those six months—and they were over now forever—he had kept inquiring about him from Esther. . . let Yehezkel ask her if it wasn't so . . . but to actually visit him in the madhouse—it was easier said than done. Only in any case, lord, it was best not to talk about it . . . he just hadn't had the time . . . it was only recently that he'd been laid off from his job . . . yes, he was out of work now and was living off the twenty francs a month that his son Hanoch— God bless him and keep him—was sending . . . of course! Hadn't Hatskel known? Only lord, even then it only went to show that the Almighty sometimes put the salve before the wound . . . because had Hanoch remained a married man he would never have been able to support his father now. Not that he, Haim, was glad that his son was divorced . . . it would have been far better had he remained a normal husband and father . . . but nevertheless: the dear Lord struck you down with one hand and raised you with the other. Now that Hanoch was without dependents (for Hanoch's son, too, was living at Goldmann's with his mother Henya)—now he could afford to look after his father, who'd felt like a useless limb ever since he'd been laid off from his job as a mason on the new hospital.

The "useless limb" hadn't changed at all during the half year since Yehezkel had last seen him, that is, during the time in which he'd become useless. Only the lines of his cheeks had multiplied, to the point where they now exceeded those of his forehead; but his short goatee—short and ungodly indeed for a Jew over fifty!—was the same thick, tangled mass of grayish-white hairs as before, the still blondish ends of which seemed to promise some future renascence, a return to the days perhaps when their master roved back and forth across the Russian-Polish border dealing in contraband. All in all, Haim was a broad-shouldered Jew of not less than average height whose build expressed a certain masculine strength. His voice, which was quiet and on the hoarse side, suggested an affable good nature, though in his small, restless eyes, which were flecked here and there with clouds of inky blue, beneath the coarse, dusty pupils, something seemed to be hidden, buried perhaps underneath the dust or not yet brought to light; while the characteristically Jewish features of his face, which reminded one of a worn coin, were tempered by the old cap that was perched habitually on top of his head, covered with grime and stone dust like the rest of his clothes, giving him an almost earthlike appearance, as though he'd sprung straight from the soil.

Haim hadn't always been a mason. As a young man he'd been apprehended by the authorities in a small border town in the district of Souvalk,* where all would have been up with him had he not somehow managed to escape abroad, at first to Prussia, and from there to Austria and Rumania, where he joined a party of Rumanian Jews on their way to Palestine. It was only in Jerusalem, to which he'd come after the colony of Jezreel had been abandoned, that he'd set about learning the mason's trade, which was hardly a common oc-

* Polish Suwałki, a district on the Russian-Polish border.

cupation among European Jews. Still, he'd stuck to it ever since, like his son Hanoch to his mill. . . .

No, he, Haim, had no reason to complain about his luck. True, he rarely thought any more about his narrow brush with the law—but whenever he remembered it he thanked his stars anew. What right had he to complain? As long as there was work for him to do and a bit of strength left in his bones, so that old age, God forbid, shouldn't jump on him all at once—and so that he shouldn't have to go on taking money from his son, either—because otherwise—phew! Of course, Hanoch was a good fellow, praise God, not much on book learning perhaps, but a good soul who would never desert him . . . no, he had no complaints on that score, there should only be more like him . . . but the poor fellow . . . it wasn't right to deprive him so . . . how much did he earn there in the mill, after all? And surrounded by Arabs! One Jew in the middle of dozens of Arab villages. . . .

. . . Yes, surely Hatskel could see that the really unlucky one was his brother Yosef! Here was a man who'd had no luck in Palestine at all, no, not since he'd arrived a few years ago—though he, Haim, thank God, was at least not responsible for that. He had never advised him to come, and Yosef too hadn't built his plans around his brother. Indeed, there was really no comparison between them, for he himself was just a simple working man who had come to Palestine to keep body and soul together, whereas Yosef, it was safe to say, had had other things in mind: where more than in the Holy Land, he had thought, would his learning be in demand? And Haim too, when he had heard that his brother was coming, had been sure he would have no trouble earning a respectable livelihood among people who looked up to him. But lord, there was no need to tell Hatskel about his uncle! The man was a great scholar and a truly pious soul, not—God forgive him for what he was about to say—one of your Jerusalem Jews! Here in Jerusalem, he had heard it said, there was little real learning, while as for piety—why not admit it?—it was only an outward show. A Jerusalemite would sell anything for his own gain . . . whereas Yosef was almost a rabbi, besides being an expert at grammar and history. Why, before the disorders in Russia *—and may those days never come again—he had supported himself with dignity by giving lessons, and had been honored and welcomed, so he had told his brother, in the wealthiest houses in town, Christian no less than Jewish. Professor Hefetz! There people had known who Yosef Hefetz was—lord! But then the wheel had turned. In the pogroms, it was true, he hadn't been hurt at all, but what did it matter when the whole town was reduced to ruins? And he had thought that in Palestine he would find provision. . . .

"Provision?"

—Yes, as in the story about Jacob and Joseph. *And Jacob saw that there was no provision in Egypt* †—wasn't that what it said? He too, Haim, had been sure that his brother would not want for recognition: after all, here the schools were entirely run by Jews, and who was to teach in them if not he? Why, Yosef was a rare expert in the Hebrew language! He had been sure that they would receive him with open arms. Only when a man has no luck . . . not a single job was offered him. Among the younger generation, the freethinkers, he was considered too old-fashioned; what did it matter if he knew a thousand times more than they if his beard—grievous sin!—was too long? Yes, and he wore earlocks too, trimmed though they were. While as for the Orthodox schools—there

---

* The outbreak of pogroms in 1903 that centered around the Bessarabian city of Kishinev.

† Genesis 42:1.

too there was no place for him. That is, perhaps there was a place, but no one wished to hear of it. Here in Jerusalem it was all a matter of connections . . . and his elder brother had none to fall back on. *For the wisdom of the poor man is despised* *—wasn't that how the verse went? During his first years in Jerusalem he had sought to give lessons in Talmud and grammar, a few of which he retained to this day . . . only now, on account of his legs, he could no longer go looking for pupils. Of course, his eyes were much better; his vision, which had suffered greatly during his first year here, had improved; but his legs . . . yes, he suffered from rheumatism, God spare us the same. . . .

One way or another—lord! God spare us was all he could say. To tell the truth, he too, Haim, was not without rheumatic pains of his own, twinges in his left side, bless them, a souvenir of his smuggling days; but these were nothing new and had a special origin of their own, apart from the usual chill which he used to get every night from his work in the villages along the border. One night the synagogue in the town where he was staying happened to catch fire. The fire department was hardly more than a name, it being just a small hamlet, and even the two or three volunteers who existed were late in coming. Well, to make a long story short, he, Haim, was still something of a daredevil in those days, and so when he was awakened in the middle of the night, he didn't think twice. It was already too late, but when he reached the site of the blaze and saw that the flames had taken hold of the Ark, he leaped inside in an effort to rescue the holy books. In the end this too proved unsuccessful, only he paid dearly for the attempt. Returning to his quarters, utterly worn out and covered with soot and sweat from head to toe, he decided to take a cold bath—and immediately his whole body went into

* Ecclesiastes 9:16.

shock. Lord, the illness he came down with didn't last for more than a week or two—he was stronger in those days than he was now (not that he wasn't thankful for what he was now too, mind you!)—but ever since then the pains kept recurring: they would come for a while, go away, then come again. Really, though, it was nothing. But his brother's rheumatism, where did it come from? That was another question. Reb Yosef always took care of himself, worried about his health and was careful not to catch cold. Could it be due to his hotheaded nature? Anger, they said, could cause anything —and Yosef tended to anger. But of course this was understandable. He had a great deal to be angry about. Had anyone else been in his place, you would think, he would be teaching in a university by now, while Yosef, God help us, didn't even have enough to eat. And he hadn't any luck with his children, either. His wife, Yehezkel's mother's sister, was a good, kind woman who had died young, leaving him a son and two daughters. The son, it was true, was really not much of a burden: he still lived in Kiev and was even well off. (Of course, he too had problems, namely, four daughters and not a single son, which was why Yosef wanted to bring him to Palestine: perhaps in the Holy Land he would be able to have boys. Yes, Yosef actually believed in all that and could even prove it from his books!) But as for the two daughters, whom Hatskel knew . . . Esther had been a seamstress all her life, only now she was working as a nurse in the in- . . . the insane asylum . . . yet she didn't seem to like it very much . . . no, she wasn't at all happy there either. What did Hatskel make of it, eh? Today, for instance, she had told him that she wanted to leave . . . she quarreled with everyone . . . how contrary she was! She had been there only five months and she was already tired of it! Miriam, on the other hand— true, she was healthier, one could even call her good-looking, but she would never marry well here. Worse yet, she didn't even seem to care. It was her job to do the housework, the cooking and the rest of it (no need to tell Hatskel about that), but she too was unhappy . . . yes, like all the young girls these days. She wanted to go to America; when the sexton left, she planned to accompany him; only where was she to get the money for the trip from? Of course, she had thought of going to the settlements too, but Yosef had forbade it—anything but that! In the meantime, she spent all day in the Harel, the hotel next to Goldmann's house. (Was it true, by the way, that Goldmann had offered him, Hatskel, a job as his private secretary?) Yes, Miriam spent her time with a girl friend in the hotel, with whom she proposed to learn English from Hamilin. And on the sly too, without so much as telling her father! Yes, Hamilin knew English—he knew a great many languages. Hamilin . . . once he had been Yosef's pupil . . . and now. . . .

The small oil lamp was lit. In the guesthouse chapel matters of local interest were being discussed: the latest crises in the charity foundations, shares and speculations, the drift of population out of the city ("which is being completely ignored by our leaders, who aren't doing a blessed thing to stop it"), illness ("where else in the world is there so much of it? There just isn't a house or a day here that you don't find someone sick!") and other similar subjects. At last Herr Kauffmann began to pour fire and brimstone on the Christian mission, "which is gaining ground by our own negligence; yes, it's due to our own carelessness that the Devil is making hay!" Yehezkel Hefetz sat or rather lay listening on a bench in the corner, partaking of the distant world of conversation and enjoying himself immensely. So life still went on apart from the obsessions that had surrounded him ever since his departure from that house, from his own closed circle of relationships, from problems of morbid eroticism and religious collapse! Here were men sitting and talking—and yet it would never have occurred to a single one of them to speak of the torments of sexual jealousy and sexual weakness, or of the crumbling pillars of good and evil, torments that were everything to a subject like himself. And not only that—if he himself were suddenly to come to life and tell them of everything that was stirring and simmering inside him, they wouldn't even raise an eyelid or sniff "erotomania" or "free thought" with a shrug of disgust; no, they simply wouldn't understand what he was talking about; and if he were to insist on repeating it—then, no doubt, he would be sent packing back to the hospital that very same night.

Ah, get a grip on yourself, Yehezkel, be strong! Learn to think of yourself as one of them, Yehezkel Hefetz! The weakness in the flesh—think of yourself as an old man and make your peace with it! Make your peace, old man Ezekiel! Life is generous enough without all that, even an old man's life is still a life. And if you can't, if you don't know how to—then lie in your corner and stick out your tongue at yourself. Let it even be so, let it be as you say, let it be that as far as yourself is concerned you always know best; yes, as for you, perhaps you're entitled to dismiss all this, all of it; as for you, you needn't even ask permission, needn't ask it at all . . . because who is there to give it? But stop your struggling—because there is no one to rescue you either. Resign yourself—and live as best you can. It would all have had to end someday anyhow, just as your life too will someday have to end. Oblivion is waiting for you, waiting. Try to live each minute with what other feelings you have: live as the crushed fly lives with its wings pulled off or as the blind, mangy dog. Nothing will ever change, resign yourself once and for all. Accept what comes

your way—and be still!—Be still, thou soul of Ezekiel Hefetz!
Speak not of life, speak not of good and evil; speak not of
that which is beyond thee, whose essence thou lacks't. What
dost thou know about life, thou that are all the ravings of
death?—Bear with it, Hefetz! Lie in your corner and bear
with it! Yes, hide in your corner and keep your groans to
yourself. Not another word out of you, Yehezkel Hefetz!
And then . . . then . . . then everything will be all right.
Then you can remain here among them. Then no one, noth-
ing, can drive you from the dungheap of your own failure and
insufficiency, on which you've sat and whimpered to yourself
all these years. . . .

He picked up the bundle of his pants and jacket which had
been serving him as a pillow and moved it to the other end of
the bench. The lamp had gone out and the room was deserted.
Lying down on his other side, he began to pursue an entirely
new train of thought. The bench was hard and extremely
narrow, no wider than his own thin body, which could not
turn comfortably from side to side without falling to the
floor. Hefetz laughed to think of the solution he had hit on:
after one side had absorbed as much pain as it could stand
from the pressure of the hard wood, he would rise and move
his pillow to the other end of the bench, thus relieving his
stiffness in the course of changing sides. In this way he spent
the night traveling with his bundle from one end of the bench
to the other.

Yes, he would accept Goldmann's offer. He would work
for him in his office. What did it matter? It was all the same
to him. He would work there, he would continue to sleep
here, he would give his salary to his uncle. He knew of
course that he was taking the position with Goldmann only
on account of Reb Yosef, to help him in his need. He, Yehez-

kel, was a good person, yes, good, why bother to deny it? He wasn't harmonious—where look for harmony?—but he was certainly good. Not that he believed in any "religion of goodness"—no, nothing of the sort. In general, it had nothing to do with religion . . . it was strictly a private affair . . . because as soon as it became a religion there was always room for disagreement—room for someone to ask: "What kind of religion do you call this? Religion is for the many, while you, Yehezkel Hefetz, wouldn't be who you are, wouldn't argue as you're arguing, if you were anyone but yourself. How can you expect anyone else to share such a religion with you?" But if it wasn't a religion, if it was simply something private, then no one could object. Yes, it was true: he was who he was because that was who he was—had he been someone else he'd be different. But since he was that way he had every intention of continuing, of being as good as he pleased, of feeling as morbid as he pleased, of living as abjectly as he pleased. With harmony or without! He would sing hymns of praise to his abjectness, his disability, his bad luck . . . or better yet, he would do without them. Why sing hymns? Hymns only undermined the whole structure all over again. Better a blind acceptance of being abject, disabled, unlucky . . . while as for his goodness, who knew what it really was worth? At bottom he wasn't good either . . . yet here was no paradox. Not that he need be afraid of paradoxes, but in this case there were none. Let it be both ways instead of just one! Let it be that because of his luck he still retained a bit of simple love for the lives of others, like the love of those old Jewish women of mercy in the villages of Eastern Europe in generations gone by. And this love of life was redoubled and intensified further for those who were closest to him, for their trials and tribulations, for everything that was most immediate and concrete. It was not for him to worry about the World,

Humanity, the Nation—no, *his* thoughts were for the members of his own household alone, among whom he had come to live by pure chance. And he wasn't doing them any "favors," either (as if a person like himself was capable of favors!): it was simply that he overflowed with it, overflowed and was alive in every vein. It was something tangible—and he had use for what was tangible only: not for "relationships" in the abstract, but for the daily contact with the people who surrounded him, which however tacit was real. The trouble with all this was, though—because it wasn't easy, it wasn't easy at all—that none of it came to him as naturally or nicely as it did to those old women. And yet not only wasn't he to blame for this—let the flaw in his character take the blame!—but what difference did it make whether he was or not? Who was to judge? And still he wasn't to blame: How was he at fault if he wasn't natural or nice, if his character was flawed, if he had nothing constructive to offer? Then let there be nothing constructive! Why be constructive? With what?

. . . Where look for the constructive? Where look for the harmonious? Where look for the aesthetic?

And again—why look for the aesthetic? What did the aesthete know about life? He might know the name of each precious stone that hung around his mistress' marbled throat— yes, that he knew; but how did this make him better than anyone else? How was his fatuous wish to have himself and his lady love fitted out in frills by the finest tailor in town more important than his own, Yehezkel Hefetz, the man of ugliness' desire that his uncle not sleep in the streets? Didn't all feelings have the same right to exist? What made the dogmas of the aesthete profounder than those of the moralist? Didn't everything that flowed from an inner human need have equal value? The moral code was false, baseless, absurd? But what if this same code were to turn into instinct and become flesh-and-blood of some abject individual? Nay, let not the priests of the beautiful boast of their beauty, nor the heroes of the harmonious of their harmony, nor the saints of morality of their morals, but of this alone let each man boast—to himself and if he so wished: "I'm free to follow my instincts as I please."

. . . *Whereas I . . . even if I'm only invalid, my motives can't be questioned. The subjective demands of morality are instincts too . . . and if such demands should conflict with other, weaker instinct-demands and overcome them—so much the better! Let there be morality! Let there be good! Let there be everything, because as for me—"the victorious instinct can't be questioned."* . . .

In his Bible now it was written: *And it was very good—it was Life.* Life was good, the only good, there was none other beside it. For it to be very good, of course, especially good, the people you were close to had to be alive, healthy, happy and contented; all your senses had to function, enjoy, receive pleasure; there had to be meaning, the "common meaning of Life," the only real meaning there was. But even if there was nothing to rejoice about but only to mourn; even if Life had left you crippled and choking on your own caul; even if its treasures were barred to you and this was bad, so bad, and you had no comforter—even then, Life, your life, was good: lying in its embrace, with nothing beside it, you could learn to love it, bless it, esteem it— *No, it's not something that can be taught and I'm not a teacher; but I do know . . . I do know how to be thankful for the little that I have, and for me this is happiness.* . . .

In the early hours of the morning he added more clearly:
The crux of the matter is within the House of Life itself and not somewhere beyond it. Even the ancient rabbi who said

prepare yourself in the Antechamber to enter the Chamber *
thought that the goal was still not beyond the Chamber, that
is, in the last analysis, within the House of Life. Anyone could
say if he wished, "This house doesn't agree with me—if only
because it's too big and I'm too small," but a fool alone would
insist: "I demand to know what this house is for, because until
I do you can't possibly expect me to like it!"

Life was good not only because it could be filled with good
deeds or because there was room in it for love, happiness,
ideals—in a word, not only because it offered all kinds
of fulfillment—but in and of itself. True, there were times
when one's suffering obscured Life's face until it could barely
be made out and then one might say, "it isn't worthwhile."
But even this—was Life; one said it only with one's lips. The
truth of the matter was that everything was Life and everything was worthwhile, and only the person who understood
that everything was worthwhile—yes, *everything*, even if
meaningless—could appreciate Life in all its manifestations,
could find meaning everywhere, could bless each radiant
smile, each stone and blade of grass, the good with the bad,
yes, though the bad *was* bad and it hurt, because it too was
Life. . . .

—*A fine theory?*

—*Yes, a theory if I were to tell it to others,* he answered
himself, *if I were to try to persuade them of it, because then it
would just be another hypothesis, and they could believe in it
or not, accept or reject it, as they pleased. But when you come
to it from your own experience, in a house on the outskirts
of town—then it's no longer a theory but Life itself.*

In the windows looking out on the city the dawn was beginning to break.

* A quotation from the Mishnaic tractate *Pirke Avot.*

IV

Goldmann's residence, in one of the side rooms of which Yehezkel Hefetz had begun to work daily in the former's service (particularly in connection with his latest project of a modern Orthodox school), was different indeed from Reb Yosef Hefetz's. Here was a home that had never known the lack of five napoleons for the yearly rent or of a half a napoleon to pay the baker's bill, and that was filled with the best of whatever was available in a small Asiatic town like Jerusalem. The appeals that went forth from it in the name of the master of the household's charitable foundations, however, were not just the usual pleas for help in the lachrymose Jerusalem style; in addition they played, with no little profit and success, on the "economic argument," explaining and illustrating the value of the institutions concerned to the development of both the Orthodox and modern communities, for which they were "a source of livelihood and a blessing in every area of endeavor." Even the divorced Henya, Reb Yakov's daughter, who a few years before had been the ignorant peasant wife of the inarticulate Hanoch, was now in the habit of regularly visiting the German bank downtown, where she stood half-hours at a time by the teller's and cashier's windows, her bankbook in her hand and her heart beating with indescribable bliss, the sweat pouring from both cheeks as though they were made of red sealing-wax, depositing more than she withdrew. Nor was it any secret, least of all to Goldmann's stockholders, that his mother, who had come from Rumania to spend her "last years" with her son in Jerusalem (her tongue would fail her and her voice grow weak whenever she used this expression: the fact of the matter was that her life was just beginning and that she hadn't the least credence in these "last years" at all), hadn't arrived empty-handed either, though she'd done her best to conceal the sum that she'd brought for fear of the Evil Eye. It was from this ample and amazing woman in fact that Henya had come to learn the great thesis-and-antithesis that ultimately became her byword: *Dos iz praktish—dos iz nit praktish.** In general, the two women, the mother of the father and the daughter of the son, each of whom put her money to work in the shares of safe charities and did what she could to help her father/son in his career, had a great deal in common, the difference between them being no more than that of a red Rumanian kerchief that is nearly new and a much older one that is beginning to tear here and there and to show the effects of age. The old lady, to judge by all the signs, had been a handsome woman in her day too, and generously proportioned; while Henya, for her part, whose plump body, especially at a distance, seemed more Levantine than European, lacked the same domestic, protective, womanly-as-opposed-to-feminine flair as her grandmother. ("She's a type!" was Shneirson's epithet for her, meaning: *A man can't turn his back on a woman like that for a minute, but you can't deny she's irresistible, damn it all!*)

Goldmann himself, Reb Yakov Goldmann ("less a business-man than a new type of busybody," according to Shneirson's definition), had a flaxen beard that appeared to be trimmed

* Yiddish: That's practical—that isn't practical.

with a scissors and an Adam's apple that resembled a parched lemon. In past days as well as present a high-strung and hot-tempered Rumanian Jew, he had liked to declare while still a farmer in Jezreel:

"Everyone complains but what do I have to complain about? If I'm poor, so is everybody else. If everyone is rich, then I'm rich too. I haven't a cent to my name, but what farmer in Palestine does? A house, young fruit trees, fine investments like that—if that's wealth, why, then I'm wealthy too!" What was that? You couldn't eat a house and young trees? They weren't cash? The speech would begin once again. "If I'm poor, so is everyone else. I'm not the envious type. Not that I don't have my faults. Of course I do. And I like to be honest about them. I'm no bleeding heart. I don't want your advice and I don't ask for it. You go your way and I'll go mine. But I'll never nurse a grudge either, which is more than I can say of our village council."

When Goldmann wasn't quarreling with the council or the villagers, he was shamelessly lording it over both, making friends and enemies as he pleased. He was forever defending "the village honor," speaking up for "the Truth" and harping on "the Dreyfus Affair"—the latter to convey that he, the Dreyfus of Palestine, whose sole guiding light was the Truth, was being driven to despair by the unconscionable goings-on in the village, which were ruining its good name. At the same time he liked to play the humble spirit and preface his remarks opportunely with such apologies as "but what does a simple farmer like me know," etc., it being obvious to all concerned that he considered himself the sole authority on everything and would let no one else get a word in. But though he was constantly handing out advice and meddling in everyone's business, the fact was that he hadn't the slightest use for anybody or anything that didn't help line his own pocket. His neighbors loathed him like a spider; while he, in turn, between preaching against the dangers of soft living, "which should grieve every mother's son of us, because it isn't right for pioneers like us," consorted with the local officials and fought with his wife, a fretful, peevish, overworked creature whose every other sentence was the cry: "Oy, the work I have to do! Oy, I'm going to collapse!"—a litany she repeated over every dirty curtain (not that Goldmann cared one way or another about the appearance of the curtains in themselves, but simply because "we aren't Moldavian *muzhiks* * that everything we own should be filthy and torn!"). On the whole, his changed status and removal to Jerusalem had done little to alter his character or philosophy: true, whereas Farmer Goldmann had insisted on "the good name of the village," Chairman-of-the-Board Goldmann now stressed "the good name of Jerusalem," but in general he clung to his position that "expenses here are more than a man can bear," so that "it's impossible to exist in Palestine without some kind of backing from abroad," and that all things considered . . . yes, all things considered it was good to be a Jew. One need only compare the Jew's life with the Gentile's to see which was better: consider how the Rumanian peasant or the Arab *fellah* † toiled and slaved and think of the Jew; or what the same Rumanian or Arab ate and the Jew. . . . People were always complaining that the Jew was a *luftmensh*,‡ that he lived on thin air, but he, Goldmann, simply laughed. What was so bad about it? No, there was no reason at all for the Jew to envy the Gentile!

And yet if neither Goldmann's character nor opinions were markedly different, if his Adam's apple still bulged in his throat and his paunch drooped as before (a consequence of his temper, since even in Jerusalem he'd remained a light

* Russian: peasant.   † Arabic: peasant.
‡ Yiddish: an "airman," one who lives from the air.

eater), the way he walked had changed completely, so that he seemed more irritable and high-strung than ever. He went about these days with a kind of nervous scurry, as though he were forever plotting something, forever chasing someone, forever coming home in the end tired and exhausted and with the same complaint in his mouth:

"The expenses are more than a man can bear. . . ."

Despite the expense of doing business in Jerusalem, however, Goldmann's house, as Hefetz had seen, lacked for nothing. There were tender, grilled birds, fish fresh from the Jordan, bottles of wine with genuine labels, all kinds of sweets and desserts; there were quantities of linen and of silver, furniture from the workshop of the German cabinetmaker, pearl necklaces in little cases; there were "social calls" and pleasant conversation, accompanied all day by sips of coffee, concerning houses, marriages, the price of goods—in a word, whatever people of the world discuss in their leisure hours, the men seeking to turn the talk to some modest theoretical conclusion, their hostesses cutting them short time and again with an unconsciously impatient "yes, but . . ." to continue the chatter unchallenged and uninterrupted by themselves. It was a house that had everything—everything one could desire. *Just one thing is missing*, Yehezkel Hefetz thought, *one thing alone that this house has never known, which it would be almost impolite to name: a bit of real laughter.* Of such there was none in his uncle's apartment, none in the guesthouse chapel, but least of all was there any in Goldmann's own house, for all that it had prospered in recent years and begun to emit new odors that were hardly familiar to the traditional Jerusalem street.

But if there was never any laughter in Goldmann's house, it was never really quiet either. In the absence of visitors—

and at times even their presence didn't help—there were constant violent outbursts mixed with curses, tears, the gnashing of teeth. For this provocation or occasion weren't lacking, though in any case they were hardly needed, since the slightest pretext was enough to touch off a family row: a broken egg, an apple that proved wormy or rotten when opened, a piece of meat snatched by a rat, someone's underwear that hadn't been properly patched, an oil stove that wasn't working, a cup of tea served at the wrong time. But there were more important things too: extravagant spending that couldn't be afforded, swindling by Goldmann's own agents, money stolen by the children (who attended a Jesuit school), and finally, Henya's refusal to accept the offer of the Hungarian charity official's son, who was worth a small fortune. As if it wasn't perfectly clear whom the fat cow was making eyes at! To think that she should turn her back on a guaranteed sure thing to go on a wild-goose chase after the lord knew whom (meaning Hamilin)! And what was he, Hamilin, going to do with her? He hadn't even finished his studies yet, but supposing even that he had, supposing that he'd be willing to have her—in the first place, he happened to be a close relative, and secondly, he was no "great catch" to begin with . . . and of course, he wouldn't have a practice that quickly . . . to say nothing of bringing money into the family now . . . besides which, what could he possibly see in her? A fat cow like Henya didn't know the first thing about getting along with people!

The "fat cow" herself, however, resented this opinion of her greatly. It simply wasn't so, the fact was that she knew perfectly well how to get along: the manager of the bank treated her with respect as though she were an important lady . . . and *he* too looked at her gallantly and said *bon soir* when they met on the street, and not just like a relative either, not at all like a mother's brother . . . and she knew the right reply too, she had learned all the words correctly—just let that slimy Hungarian try to step across her threshold! His money meant nothing to her—why, she too had a bankbook full of numbers!

On the whole, Henya was not easily pushed around: "Mother, keep quiet! Do you hear me? It's none of your business!" But besides being a daughter she was also a mother herself, a capacity in which she made life thoroughly miserable for her three-year-old son, whom she had been crazy enough not to want to give to her husband at the time of the divorce when he had asked for him. How she regretted it now: regretted it and took out her regrets on the guilty party! Her demands on the child had grown especially since "gentleman callers" had started coming to the house—a development that the little brat, by refusing to relinquish his disgusting habits, seemed determined to ignore. The torture and the screams would start early in the morning. Already at eight o'clock, when Hefetz would be passing through the kitchen in order to get to his workroom, "scene one," the scene of the potty, would be under way. Each day he was greeted by the wailing little boy, bare bottom turned to his mother, who would be flailing at it without mercy.

"Eh? Now will you learn? Now will you stop disgracing me in front of everyone?"

Though the young divorcée did not ask much from her son, she expected to get what she asked; and this was that he learn to tell the maid the minute he felt the urge to go, so that she might whisk him away in time. Only he, the willful creature, insisted on making all over the house, and only then, when the damage was done, would he come and confess: "Momma! I've done a doody!" It was enough to give a person a fit! Not only that, but when you spanked him and warned him that he'd better be good and learn to call "potty" in time, the little pagan would begin to cry, throw a tantrum, stamp his feet and wail at the top of his voice. Then neither kind words nor harsh had the least effect on him. Sometimes he would even stare at you with innocent eyes as though he didn't know what a potty was, though he'd been told day after day that he was to ask for one! Worse yet, when his stomach was upset—and when wasn't the wicked boy's stomach upset?—yes, when his stomach was upset, it happened every half hour. You could hit the filthy savage as hard as you pleased, beat him half to death for his wildness—half an hour later it would have happened once more! And not only would he be at it again, this time it was worse than before. What had he done? Merely hid where no one could see him and made between the closet and the door in the guest room! It was just his luck that the maid hadn't cleaned there yet, that she'd still have a chance to discover it . . . because otherwise . . . if people had come and found the . . . the stink themselves . . . ai, ai, the child was more bitter than death!

The "callers," namely, the young uncle Doctor Hamilin (*so spiffed up and spotless*, Hefetz thought to himself. *Ah, Europe!*), were not late in coming, though never before eleven. No matter what time it was, though, some frightful new mess had always preceded it. By then Henya would be back from the bank, decked out in her fashionable best, while the black-and-blue child would be somewhere out of sight, safely away from the guest room.

Hamilin's arrogant eyes, which had a way of looking through you when he talked as though he neither knew you nor had the slightest wish to know you in the future, played at such times in spectral hues against the tender gooseflesh of his niece.

There was nothing new. What should they talk about? In Jerusalem a bit of spicy news was a rare delicacy. But they were never oppressed by silence. Doctor Hamilin was never at a loss for words. (*And what eloquent words! And what a voice!* Hefetz observed. *You can be sure that the voice with which he'll speak to his poor patients someday will be nothing like that!*) "Eh? That portrait of Montefiore? * Not badly framed at all. There's a museum in London where you can see his carriage and even his pipe."

"Montefiore's?"

"Yes. They have a whole collection there. All sorts of rare things. Whatever belonged to Jews. There's a whole room set aside just for that."

"Ah, it must be wonderful. I'd love to see it!"

But there were even nicer things than that in the museum. There was a collection of old coins, for example. In one of the rooms. There were many more rooms than one. And among the coins was one belonging to Titus † . . . a coin minted by Titus . . . but why did she look so bewildered? There was a man named Titus . . . a famous figure in history . . . and he minted coins . . . from gold. . . .

"Gold?"

Shneirson criticized Hamilin severely to his roommate Kahanowitz. He was willing to forgive his behavior to the owner of the Harel's daughter (the girl, after all, was already engaged; and he, Shneirson, had seen things that nobody else even knew of!); he was even ready to ignore his assimilationist views; nevertheless, he'd come to the conclusion that Hamilin was a perfect dilettante, an extremely limited type

* Sir Moses Montefiore (1784–1885), Anglo-Jewish philanthropist.
† Flavius Sabinus Titus (A.D. 40–81), Roman conqueror of Jerusalem and later emperor.

and the epitome of pure vulgarity. Granted that he couldn't care less about Hebrew culture and that everything Jewish was foreign to him and of absolutely no interest—yes, granted; but that wasn't the end of it; no, he had to go and boast yet that he was sure that he wasn't missing a thing by never looking at a Hebrew book! Not that there was any need for him, Shneirson, to tell Kahanowitz what Kahanowitz already knew, namely, that he himself, Shneirson, was far from satisfied with the state of Hebrew letters in recent years. There was simply nothing to read. The newspapers were full of dirges—why was there no real journalism? Where was the intellectual leadership? Where was the effort to instruct, to shape new paths of thought? All the wonders of the world, the achievements of science and of progress, the poetry of existence and the like, were a closed book to Hebrew literature. There wasn't a single fresh idea, not one! All this was true enough. But what did Kahanowitz say about the way Hamilin openly abused everything that was precious and sacred to them? He was so cocksure that he even laughed at the idea of Palestine itself. A moribund country, he called it. Of course, he too, Shneirson, sometimes asked himself when depressed what the whole venture amounted to at the present moment. There was no real life here, no variety, not even any sin, no, not even the opportunity to sin—in short, they were living in a veritable Kingdom of Heaven. Was it so or not? Of course it was! But the trouble with Hamilin was that he didn't speak of it in these terms; in fact, he didn't speak of it in any terms at all. And the nerve of that *kallé bromatom* (Shneirson's medical nickname for the young doctor) to have said what he did the other night about the religious yearnings and gropings of people like himself, Shneirson! Not that he'd put it in so many words, but it was clear enough what he'd meant when he said during dinner: "If only all these tender souls could be married off, they'd get over their tragic tears soon enough." That was how he'd phrased it . . . almost another Max Nordau * . . . and he'd actually under- lined the words "married off." The lummox had a sharp enough wit in some things! "Married off"—*ergo*, they could never find a woman by themselves, though once married off to one—yes, then Hamilin, the student of medicine, was pre- pared to guarantee each weeping prima donna a cure for his melancholy.

Shneirson recited all this to Kahanowitz with great though somewhat calculated anger not once but several times, on a number of which occasions Hefetz too happened to be pres- ent. At such moments he thought: *He can't stop talking about Hamilin and I can't stop thinking of him. It hardly matters who's better off. But isn't there some way out of his eternal noose?*

And the noose was indeed eternal, unfrayed, well-greased. There were infrequent days, to be sure—his last days in the hospital, for example—when it had seemed to widen and loosen, as it were. More recently, however, Hamilin had ceased entirely to be a real person in his eyes, one who lived in the Harel, played with the affections of the owner's daughter, if Shneirson was to be believed, and conversed with Henya about Montefiore's pipe. Instead he had turned into something abstract—a Hamilinoid substance that had stolen the Russian widow's daughter from his arms—an almost hal- lucinatory nightmare. . . .

And yet from time to time he still struggled to pry the noose loose. *How ridiculous!* he told himself then. *If it's ab- surd to make a cult of my sexual disaster, that is, of the ab- stinence that I can't help, why is it any less so to make one of someone else's successes, someone luckier than I?*

* Austrian-Jewish Zionist, author, and iconoclast (1848–1923).

"Luckier" in quotation marks? Perhaps, but perhaps not either. What is it to me? He's young, strong, self-assured, he comes from a good home, he has a healthy appetite and looks after it. More power to him, to the many who are like him! And not just because there's nothing I can do about it, no, not at all. He dresses well, his eyes have an insolent charm. The women run after him (and not just the sick or the silly or the sex-starved ones!). They hang on his every word, on every movement that he makes. Bravo! Only why make a cult of it? Why moralize about it? Why let it make me depressed?

To each his own, to Hamilin too. And yet the truth was that he hated him, hated him with a passion, had hated him ever since the incident in the widow's house. Why deny it? And he didn't deny either that his hatred had nothing pure or ideal about it, like the hatred that anyone honest might feel for a scoundrel; no, for the most part it was simply the product of his irrepressible envy. But what did it all prove? Only a Hamilin could think that he'd said the last word by declaring he was hated out of envy alone. The fact of the matter was that he, Yehezkel Hefetz, was well aware that at bottom he wasn't suffering from envy at all, that is from the actual feeling of it, but simply from the possibility, the possibility of envying Hamilin and suffering from it. Because to be perfectly truthful, there was nothing to be envious of; certainly not of his talents, but neither for that matter of his wealth of experience or character; while as for his actual accomplishments, his triumphs and their consequences—these too were hardly enviable. What then was it? That Hamilin had always had it easier? Perhaps that was it. One wanted life to be easy. He, Hefetz, wanted his share of success and pleasure too, of course, but most of all, he wanted life to be easy. He didn't deny it in the least. He despised Hamilin and he envied him. But what did it prove? All this, after all, was still before the noose had begun to tighten. . . .

The noose had tightened for real only at the point that Hamilin began to lose his real existence and become a hallucination . . . a terrifying nightmare. . . .

The real Hamilin . . . only why not admit it? It wasn't pleasant to live in fear of a devil without horns, but this particular devil, as disconcerting as he was, was hornless. Even Shneirson imagined and read things into him that weren't there. The fact of the matter was that Hamilin wasn't even a personality in his own right, but simply a sexual category, a masculine one of course, but an empty, swinish person just the same, not really any different from the gross Arab *effendi* * with his flock of fat wives who had rented out his house to the owner of the Harel. Not only wasn't he a thinker, it was actually to his credit that he never said a word about the ultimate problems of existence. Hamilin and the mysteries of the universe—good god! No, his goal in life was perfectly clear and precise: to be rid of his wife whom he couldn't abide, to finish his studies with a decent degree, to follow this up if possible with a leisurely and not too frugal "postgraduate tour" of Europe for "purposes of research" in order to establish a reputation in the *urbs caelestis* of Jerusalem as a specialist who had traveled professionally on the Continent for an entire year, and finally, barring the prospect of a more lucrative offer elsewhere, to be appointed to one of the few available positions in one of the City of Charity's many charitable institutions. Such was the full extent of his ambition, the realization of which was first and last a question of money, which could best be obtained through a suitable marriage, a "good adjustment," as the one-eyed matchmakeress who frequented the Harel liked to put it. Hamilin, then, was

* Turkish title of respect.

seeking an "adjustment"; and since the "higher things" in life—and not just poetry in Hebrew, mind you, but in any other language as well—would help get him nowhere, he simply refused to be bothered with them. There was enough to worry about as it was. What could be less diabolical? It was perfectly simple and aboveboard; there was nothing fiendish, not the least trace of personified Evil in Hamilin at all. What was so terrible about him that he should be hounded, maligned, called all sorts of names, pictured in terms of a wide or a narrow noose?

And yet this was exactly what had happened. Hefetz wasn't sure himself why or how, but Hamilin had become his private obsession, as though he alone now contained the solution to numerous insoluble problems, if not in the actual flesh then at least in some essential part of him, some ultimate metaphysical kernel. In his feverish state, however, Hefetz had taken to dividing this elementary substance too into finer and finer particles, dissecting it further and further, until the problem of it, the problem of Hamilin, had come to absorb him completely. He thought of him continually; both at work and when free he waged spiritual warfare against him at all hours of the day. . . .

. . . Hamilin might be in the guest room with Henya; Esther (who had left the hospital and was now sewing for Goldmann's wife) might be in the room next door; and he, Hefetz, sitting in his office, would invent dialogues between them, dialogues that never had and never could have taken place. All of a sudden, for example, Hamilin might say that he recognized no such thing as the moral law; that the only thing that mattered was to express one's feelings and satisfy one's desires; that he himself valued only strong, pleasurable sensations; that he loved Power, Beauty, Love. . . . And now Esther would answer from behind the wall that she couldn't understand such vanity at all, that she had always despised vain people and would continue to despise them. Power? But the Czarist government in Russia had absolute power . . . Beauty? Yes, she too loved beauty; beautiful landscapes, sunsets, autumn days. Only . . . only what was there to boast about? Either you were lucky enough to be beautiful or you weren't. She had never envied anyone's beauty. You could have a beautiful appearance and be ugly inside. The important thing was inward, not outward beauty. Outward beauty was simply a gift of nature. What was there to be vain about?

Hamilin didn't answer. ("You don't discuss the execution in the condemned man's house," said the expression on his face.) Instead he turned to Henya (*but how insane all this was!*). He, Hamilin, was a doctor whose job it was to treat the sick, yet how he really loathed them! How disgusting they were and how weak! It was ingrained in their nature to avenge themselves on the healthy and strong. All their talk of morality amounted to one great act of vengeance, the vengeance of lowly, groveling cripples. They actually prided themselves on their ugliness and deformity; they openly displayed their wounds so as to poison the lives of the healthy and beautiful, whom they hated. . . .

But at this point he, Yehezkel Hefetz, could no longer contain himself. *Yes, fine, we've heard all those arguments before; only they don't mean a thing; they simply can't be taken seriously.* Strong sensations? But every sensation was strong if only you let it be; in fact, it was the very impressionability of the weak that made their lives particularly intense. Except that in any case, who was to say whether a given sensation was strong or not, pleasurable or not? Everything was strong and everything gave pleasure. Everything was

Life. Every single breath. But supposing even that a sensation could be disagreeable—what difference did it make? Why should the disagreeable be objectionable? Or the unpleasurable? Why rule them out, refuse to cherish them too? In every disagreeable sensation there was pleasure as well, the pleasure of being alive and still sentient—who knew this better than the truly impressionable man? Beauty, Power— by all means! The man who said, "Blessed are the poor, blessed are the wretched, blessed are the oppressed," was only a poor, wretched, oppressed soul himself who preached the other cheek because he was incapable of the slightest action, and whose terrible love for life so agitated and upset him that he was moved in the end to offer up his humiliation and futility as a sacrifice on the hilltop. *But that's nothing for us to be thankful for. As far as we're concerned he needn't have done it. Why should he have? Just because the "beautiful," the "strong," the "healthy" lord it over us, insult us, trample us in the dust, is that any reason to pay them back in the same coin? As if it could possibly work! No, we simply wish to make clear that we who can't act, we who are too weak. . . .*

"Begging your pardon, Mademoiselle Helena," Hamilin *interrupted him in the intonation of a Gentile parodying a Jew, "begging your pardon, we who are ruptured will please to take our vengeance on whomever is not. . . ."*

"Vengeance, Monsieur Hamilin? Then you really think that we vile creatures are capable of so sublime an act? How amazing that you should want to raise us to your level, to compare us to you at all! Only it's nothing but 'psychology,' this vengeance of the envious and base, this weak, envious vengeance of the weak—'psychology' and nothing more, Monsieur Hamilin! Envy and vengeance simply don't enter into it. Perhaps not even hatred. We the weak . . . my only point is, I just wish to say . . . we too are alive . . . period!

We too are part of Life . . . period! Not the salt of the earth, but still needing ourselves and caring for our own lives. And to Pilate we'll say—or better yet, we'll say nothing; we won't hide from him behind 'Truth's' skirts; we'll sit facing him by ourselves in silence, because we're weaponless against him. No, against those who revile us we need no weapons; against those who crush us, alas, we have none. (But please realize too that only those who merely think themselves strong wish to crush anyone; the really strong, the strong in actuality, crush no one!) All the same, as for those who threaten us, who insist that we give in to them because of their bravery and beauty . . ."

"*. . . real or imaginary . . . . .*" *Esther put in.*

"*. . . we'll stick out our tongues at them,*" *Hefetz concluded, as though welcoming her remark. "Yes, we'll stick out our tongues at the metaphysics of those who call themselves masters. 'We don't begrudge you what's yours,' we say to these preachers, these cultists of the modern masterclass, 'you go your way and we'll go ours. Because for us, wretched as we are, our own lives are the supreme value. And the rest of life, life in general—we'll judge it as we please and we'll say what we think of it. Not just to spite you, not to take our revenge, not to ruin your lives—what good is any of that to us? Besides which, how can we possibly ruin the juicy roasts that you gorge yourselves on, the fragrances and lotions that you perfume yourselves with, the beautiful women you acquire? No, we simply propose to live for ourselves and to judge life for ourselves, so that our standards of good and evil, of what profits us and what doesn't, will be our own. When life goes badly with us we'll call it bad, and when it goes well we'll call it good. What do we care that it's in our 'interest' to do so, that we're not capable of being 'objective'? We aren't philosophers. To hell with philosophy and objec-*

tivity! What do we care that the part can't sit in judgment on the whole? The whole is invisible to us, perhaps we don't even wish to acknowledge its existence (we can leave that to your wise men, who embrace what they can with rounded arms and call it the totality), because for us, the part, that is, we ourselves, is everything.' " . . .

Goldmann entered the room. Hefetz roused himself.

"Have you answered the American charity yet?"

"No, not yet. I haven't had the chance."

"Why not? What's the matter with you today? Have you mailed that acknowledgement to Stamford Hill, London?"

"Not yet. But it's already in the envelope."

"Let me see how you copied it."

"Here it is."

"But what's this here?"

"Ah, nothing. I'll take care of it. . . ."

The letter had been copied correctly. But all over the margins of the envelope the copyist's hand had scribbled in pencil:

Two Hamilins, two Hamilions, two Ham-millions.

V

The "moving season" was on hand. The whole city buzzed
with talk of places to live. The words "rental" and "apartment" were on every lip. Ordinary tradesmen dropped their
work to dabble in real estate. Even the notables of the Sephardic community, who generally conducted their affairs in
dignified retirement, now canvassed the city, singing the
praises of their properties in Arabic, French, Ladino, Yiddish,
or to the prospective tenant who spoke none of the above,
in a combination of sign language and the Holy Tongue itself: *Much good houses . . . no have too much sun . . . no
have nothing.* . . . It rained steadily, so that the carriages
that sped from Me'ah She'arim and Mahaneh Yehudah to the
Jaffa Gate and back again sprayed watery mire in every
direction, while the more modern-minded passengers complained *en passant* about the traditions of Jerusalem, poked
fun at the "extra holiday" whose one disadvantage was that
there was nothing about it to celebrate, and protested the
absurdity of changing dwellings in the middle of the rainy
season. What kind of sense did it make? At the very least
one might wait until the summer! Or take, for example, the
custom of paying a whole year's rent in advance. Who could
afford to pay for an entire year all at once? Such irrational

procedures had no parallel anywhere—yet no one did a thing to try to change them. . . .

"But it's exactly the same in Jaffa!" submitted a fellow passenger in Jerusalem's defense.

"Will you be staying in town?" The women in the carriage asked one another the question that was on everybody's mind.

"Of course I'm staying!" one answered loudly.

"In town? Why in town?"

"I want to live in town!"

"My husband insists on Nahalat Shiv'ah.* He says the air there is better."

"Air!" snorted the matron who had chosen to live "in town," that is, within the confines of the old city walls. "As if I had nothing better to do than to run after air!"

At last, with the coming of the month of *Muharram* † and the first days of the Moslem New Year, the moving commenced in earnest. The poor put their shoulders to the wheel, loading themselves with rusty tin buckets, crushed, battered cartons, empty oilcans stuffed with old clothes, bedboards marked with strange stains and charred with holes from which the bugs had been smoked, and the large blackened water jugs called *jarras* by the Arabs. The better-off citizens resorted to donkeys, while the rich moved themselves and their possessions by porter and horse-drawn wagon. The Kurdish porters in particular, with their Assyrian beards and mild, innocent eyes, displayed amazing strength by hoisting huge chests of drawers weighing hundreds of pounds on their backs with casual un-self-consciousness, supported only by a solitary rope that passed around their foreheads. Yet everyone, even the handful of people who for some reason

* Jewish quarter of Jerusalem outside the old walled city.

† The first month of the Moslem year, at the beginning of which leases in Jerusalem were traditionally renewed.

stayed where they were and were spared the upheaval, was in an irritable mood—and not without reason. As the entire city was moving at once, changing apartments in practically a single day, the homes to be occupied were never vacated in time, their former tenants having not yet left because the old tenants of their new apartments were also still there. And why? Because the latter too were waiting for someone to move out, and so *ad infinitum*. . . .

The air was filled with shouts:

"Get out of my house or there'll be trouble!"

"*Shu haddha?*" *

"How long are we supposed to wait out here?"

"What can I do? The people in our new apartment won't leave. What are you doing to my chair? What are you shouting for? *Shu haddha?*"

Husbands raised their voices too:

"Get on with you. Out! I'm not moving until I plaster my new house first."

"What, plaster it? And wait for it to dry too, I suppose?"

"And what will you do to me if I do?"

"Do to you? I'll smash everything you own! Do you expect me to camp out in the street?"

"Smash everything, will you? I'd like to see you try!"

The arguments multiplied; no one could make head or tail of anything, no one seemed to want to. . . .

"Lord, it's more of a curse than the day before Passover," Uncle Haim exulted.†

He spoke of the "curse" with great glee, as though it were really a blessing. Indeed he was one of the few happy men at

* Arabic: What's that?

† The day before Passover is the day on which all leavened bread and houseware that has come in contact with it must be removed from the home.

this time of year, for the art of plastering which he had lately taken up was in great demand and he had all the work and money he could handle. He went about each job conscientiously, at a sure, methodical pace, growing almost festive toward evening as the day drew to a close; yet the general pandemonium of the season failed to affect him and he would even pause to chat a bit with the lady of the house instead of rushing straight home after work. Yes, he hoped God would grant her and her husband and their children enjoyment from their new apartment. The main thing was to be healthy and well and not to have to worry about one's daily wants or anything else. He too, Haim, could not enjoy himself when he was worried or troubled by anything. It was now two months, for example, since he had last received a letter from his son, which worried him greatly. God grant that she, the mother of a family, know no such sorrow. . . . But he must be off now and have a bite to eat—he hadn't tasted a thing since morning—lord! And even then he'd merely swallowed a slice of bread and a few ounces of dates, without even a cup of tea to wash it down. But one way or another that was how he was—the more tired he became, the less he ate. If God would only—but what a job of plastering! Heavens above . . . it put you in a holiday mood. . . .

Reb Yosef's daughter Esther was caught up in the whirl of the moving season too, in fact seemingly more so than others; yet this was at bottom an illusion, for her heart was not really in it; her heart, on the whole, was off somewhere else, somewhere completely unrelated. Yes, outwardly she might complain that she had returned to her father's after six months at the hospital only to find him homeless, a man without a roof to call his own, but deep in her prepossessed heart she had every confidence—in Yehezkel. She knew that during the few weeks he had been working in Goldmann's office he had made himself so indispensable that he had even been able to arrange the difficult matter that Reb Yosef's top-floor apartment, while being officially transferred to the owner-ship of the guesthouse, which had, in the language of Gold-mann's annual "Report," "grown and expanded with God's help and added several attractive and commodious new rooms," should remain for the present in the possession of Reb Yosef, who would henceforth be considered "a deserving needy individual from abroad," etc., etc.—to all of which Goldmann, albeit grudgingly, had agreed. In addition it was all but settled—and on Yehezkel's advice once again—that Uncle Haim would accept the offer of the sextonship of the chapel in return for free living quarters and twenty francs a month. Outwardly once more none of this kept Esther from repeatedly protesting that she would not, could not, possibly agree to let her father—*her* father, whom no one else knew as she did—continue to live in the guesthouse. She offered no alternative herself; she even neglected to mention the small sum that she had safely put away somewhere which might have helped solve the problem; nevertheless, she was "cate-gorically opposed" to Yehezkel's plans for the apartment, and even more so, to her uncle's obsequiousness toward Gold-mann and "the terrible degradation of his being Goldmann's sexton." . . . She remonstrated, flew off the handle, wouldn't sit still—it would have to happen over her dead body!—yet her heart wasn't in it; *there* she was satisfied no end that Yehezkel chose to look upon the family's affairs as his own and even wished to play an active part in them. So too she made a show of great furor over Miriam's plans to travel to America with Mister Bassin. How could she? What on earth for? Why all of a sudden? It was sheer madness! But here too her heart was somewhere else; in recent days her thoughts

were only for Yehezkel . . . for no one but him . . . and
he was almost hers now . . . completely hers! Not that any
woman was about to envy her on his account; but still he
was hers, she was no worse off than anyone else. Worse? On
the contrary! She knew more about loving than all those wax
dolls put together! They could die a hundred deaths before
they would learn to love like her! Because she herself was no
doll. She was different—and her love was different too. She
wasn't attractive, so people said, so she had heard them say.
People said! Public opinion! What was any of that to her!
Perhaps she had never paid much attention to the way that
she dressed . . . she was not so young any more . . . or so
full-blown . . . she had never chased after men . . . it had
never been like her . . . she had never made herself up or
made faces at herself in the mirror . . . she hadn't tried to
make the men run after her like all the others . . . but she did
know how to love! Yes, she too knew how . . . she too—
she alone . . . and O how she loved! Her love was faithful,
passionate, fierce . . . Yehezkel. . . .

Nor was Esther lying to herself. Not about this. Not about
her love. The few moments of special intimacy that had been
granted to her with a shattered man, intimacy such as she had
never known before in her life, had slowly nurtured, at first
the hesitant germ of the idea in her anguished heart, and
finally the firm decision, that he alone, he and no other, was
the man who was meant for her, that at long last her time had
come to be married like everyone else, to have a husband
come what may. And it wasn't a question of pity, either, of
a cousin's pity for a cousin, not on her side and certainly not
on his, but of a true, an absolute love. Why shouldn't it be?
Why must she deprecate it? Was love something only for
brainless coquettes? To the devil with all the silly thoughts
that kept creeping into her head!

Yehezkel . . . what a darling he was! (It was only at times that a flicker of incomprehensible dislike for him would pass for some reason through her weary mind.) She was drawn to him wholly. She knew all his weaknesses, of course, every one of his failings; but she knew too that he was one in a thousand, the dearest man alive, a unique human being. God of her fathers! What a crude romance, without flowers, parties, balls, sweet flirtation, any of the romantic trappings; but a romance nonetheless. Her love was dreamlike, poetic—and so prosaic in its calculation as to be almost frightening; it was irritable, pent up—and like an open book. She was like a coachman traveling an unknown road on a dark, rainy night and afraid that his coach will stick in the mud at any moment, so that even before reaching the swampy ground that he dreads he whips on his horses with all his might and urges them ahead. . . . Esther knew that the man she was going to marry had a weak will and a poor opinion of himself—yes, she was practically sure of it. Who knew whether he would ever have taken the first step by himself? Each shared intimacy between them had started with her—of course it had. But she would never have undertaken it had she not known that he loved her deeply even "before the hospital," more in fact than she had loved him, except that then he hadn't dared show it, while afterwards, of course, he had dared even less. She need only keep her head and act sensibly to be sure to get what she wanted. Yes, she knew exactly what went on in Yehezkel's mind; it was simply a question of "getting down to the job," as her old sewing instructor used to say. . . .

And Esther got down to the job, on the results of which her future, her hopes, her entire life depended. The first thing she did was to resign from the hospital and return to her sewing, which she had left off when Yehezkel was taken away. She had to prove to him—to herself it was hardly necessary

—that her love was something sacred, romantic, whatever a love should be. She had already gotten past the worst of it, the terrible fear of rejection when she had first reached out to him, and now that events had proved her right to have begun, had shown that she'd not been rejected and that he cared for her at least as much as she for him, she could no longer force herself to be content with a few miserable crumbs; she wanted their love to be grand, spacious, overarching, to demand great sacrifices of them both. And just as she had made the first overture, had she not made the first sacrifice too? She had gone to work in that place half a year ago just to take care of him, she had freely chosen him when his life was at a low; now, no sooner had he left there than she'd left too. Once more, of course, it was simply to be close to him. Yes, she would speak to him about it. He should know. He *did* know. Yehezkel!

And Hefetz knew, knew without being told, nor was it at all ridiculous in his eyes. Rather he saw in it the symbol of his entire human tragedy; he accused himself incessantly of being completely inhuman toward her, of lacking true compassion and the unselfish capacity to forget himself entirely just once; and he suffered for it. Most of all, however, he suffered from his feelings of gratitude, which rose and swelled in him harshly and became a terrible burden; and he suffered even more from the realization of it, that it should be too much for him, that he should begrudge her even this, that here too he should refuse to be tied to her. He knew that all her talk about self-sacrifice wasn't devious or meant to deceive (whom could she deceive with it? himself? but why should she want to deceive him? who was he to be worth deceiving? what could she possibly gain from it?), that she indulged in it naïvely out of the simple faith that her love for him alone had brought her to work in the hospital and to leave it—and it was precisely this that he found unbearable. He felt a duty to belittle himself in her presence whenever he could, to make her see that he didn't deserve her love, that he was a miserable man who would make anyone who got too close to him miserable too; yet at the same time he couldn't stop reproaching himself and suffering that now, when he felt "happy" at last, he should refuse to let her share in it. He spoke to her a great deal about his poverty, about his illness, about his being a wreck of a man, but in all of this he felt as if something were still missing, some ultimate disclosure in more ways than one. The little that he revealed to her only seemed to cry aloud that he was concealing twice as much. Not that she was unaware of this, of course; but she persisted in understanding it in her own way. In any case, the result was that she felt more drawn to him than ever; she wanted to know everything about him, everything; she not only failed to grasp the compound horror of what he told her, she actually seemed amazed at herself that none of it could shock her or come between them in the least. Could it be that he still hadn't told her all? But no, the likelihood was rather that he had even exaggerated, that he thought far too little of himself. . . .

Yes, Hefetz could talk on about being a wreck of a man—but did she follow him? Did she understand? And no sooner had he finished, then full of contempt for his own fear of telling the truth, of the final humiliation of calling each thing by name, he would stammer almost involuntarily: *a wreck . . . malarial . . . up in the air . . . without a thing to fall back on* . . . did she understand? But no, she did not. Of course, she thought from time to time of the weaknesses he spoke of; she even magnified and intensified them in her own mind, took them fully into account and made allowances for them, while furiously hating him at the same time for speaking of them so openly, for smashing all her dream castles, especially since no one was really as good as he, so that in the end she told herself each time: *A wreck? Of course. A sick, shattered man, a spiritual invalid; but still not incurable, no, not by any means. . . .*

And unwittingly Esther was right. Her intuition proved true, though only in one respect. Hefetz grew stronger, healthier. The truss had come off some time ago though the symptoms were not all gone, but his spirits, which convalesced more slowly, were now completely recovered. He was now, in the middle of this Palestinian winter, healthier of mind than he had ever been before he fell ill. The sun shone on him with full brilliance and warmed him with full warmth. The words "future" and "hope" no longer seemed remote to him, but what was even more important, they hardly seemed to matter any more. The present was plenteous enough, each blessed day of it. True, there were still times when waking at night in a sunless place with a raw, wracking cough that echoed of the past, he would feel as though a dim red pall had been cast over his consciousness. The next day, however, his feet on the sun-steeped earth once more, his sense of well-being would sparkle within him like a bottle of sweet wine downed all at once. Truly, he was then like a drunken man, though the effect of his health on him was the very opposite of drunkenness. The first few glasses of wine made a man merry but the next few made him dull, so that the more he drank the more the giddiness of the second glass yielded to the depression of the fifth or sixth; but such was not the case with Hefetz. All his nerves were opened wide to sense the world and to delight in it. In December, when he was first released from the asylum, he still had not gotten over his dread of facing people; his thoughts were still suffused with the fear of *what now?*

What would he do now? If something gladdened him then, he rejoiced more in his gladness than in the thing itself. The further it got into January, however, the more his happiness grew (for everything! the slightest thing was enough to add to it!) and the better he felt. He no longer went about whispering to himself, *the sun still hasn't set for me—why shouldn't I live too?* Now he could actually feel its vigorous warmth and think: *yes, it's shining for me too; there's a breath of life in me yet; I'm still a member of the brotherhood of all that creeps and crawls upon this earth.* He no longer thought of his life, all life, as an inescapable surrender, a forced coming-to-terms, but rather as a great and precious gift that had been given to him no less than to those who had been healthy all their lives (and how pleasant it was now to be like them!). Even the peculiar work that he was reduced to doing for a living, this writing of all kinds of letters and editing of accounts, did not seem onerous to him as such work had in the past whenever he had been bound to a job (and often a much better one than this) which simply couldn't hold his interest. No, he was now oblivious to such conflicts; he was prepared to do anything that would help bring in money so that he might make life a bit easier for the family of his uncle, Miriam's father. . . .

Miriam! Everything seemed new to him but she seemed newest of all. He thought of her as though he had seen her only yesterday for the first time. She had always been pretty, he thought, but now she was beautiful. And not just because people in Palestine generally looked better in the cold weather than they did in the hot. No, she had a special beauty of her own now that she hadn't had before. Then she had reminded him of a sun-dried fruit, whereas now she was enveloped in a wintry halo and the snow-white purity of the Slavic lands from which she hailed.

Hefetz was twenty-nine years old when he left the asylum, nor was this the first time that he had been drawn to one woman or another in his life. All of these previous attractions, however, had been infatuations from a distance, accompanied or not by the desire to marry as the case might be, but in any event, incapable of changing or subjecting him. In the last analysis they had been merely unpleasant involvements; he had never believed in them, had easily gotten over them. Even when some part of him, for whatever reason (or perhaps for no reason at all), had lacked the strength to disengage itself or break free, as in the case of that slim-necked creature to whom he had been bound for an entire year, and who now seemed so utterly, so completely forgotten, as though she had never existed—even then he'd often had to ask himself whether it wasn't just a passing aberration, his naked need for sex perhaps, cunningly dressed up (because weakling that he was, it by itself was not enough for him), or his desire to have pity on her family (which again had seemed insufficient to his unreasonable state of mind). The certain fear of impending disaster had been greater than his hope for anything new or good, so that when the whole thing came to nothing he'd felt a sense of emancipation along with all the pain; his ambivalence had been like a prisoner's before his trial, who on the one hand wants to get it over with as quickly as possible, yet trembles with relief when he has another month in which to be free, to feel safe, to harbor the illusion that he may yet be acquitted. . . . Now, however, in his new relation with Miriam, he confessed to himself with a feeling of almost total happiness, though not without embarrassment as well, that this was not another infatuation but love itself; yes, he loved this flower of a girl with an innocence that was perhaps out of character, that in certain ways and from a certain point of view was perhaps even absurd—yet why should he care? Far

less than in his previous attachments he was not out to con-
quer or reach any goal, it being enough for him simply to feel
his own love; yet just as it would not have occurred to him
to simplify or idealize what was happening, so he was prepared not to shirk certain responsibilities if they should ever
come, in another year or two. But even if this should never
happen—and it was almost certain not to, mainly because of
her, but also because of circumstances that neither of them
could control—then too it would be perfectly all right. There
was no compulsion about it. There were only his own
awakening feelings toward her. And whatever might happen,
however it might happen, he was grateful that these feelings
existed.

To what end? With what in mind? Why she of all people?
Naturally, had he chosen to ask himself these questions, he
could never have answered them. In the past, of course, he
might have found the answers, or more precisely, a single
answer which would have answered nothing: human beings
met by accident, he would have told himself, and love, if such
a thing existed by the same or any other name, was an accident too. What was new about his present situation was that
he rarely stopped to ask himself what it meant or whether it
would last but was simply glad of it with all the lucid rapture
in his heart. He loved to stand to one side and watch her, especially when she had just arisen in the morning and was
rubbing the sleep from her eyes, the traces of which would
still be etched in the lines of her young face; he loved to look
at her vivacious braids that were knotted at the ends, to follow her pert walk with his eyes, to listen to her voice whose
muffled quality made him think of longing and satiety at
once; he loved her round white hat with the pink band above
the brim, and her black apron, which she wore tightly pressed
against her dress and the curve of her thighs. She reminded

him of many things he had forgotten, many faces that were blurred in his memory and yet lived on, while at the same time remaining always true to herself. In her facial and physical gestures, he observed, there was a mixture of the local traits of Jerusalem with various features of Jewish womanhood from all the many places that he had ever set foot in: the Ukraine, Podolia, Lithuania, Bessarabia, Bukovina, the cities of inner Russia and of Western Europe—an indigenous blossom whose leaves and petals came from all over the world. True, such a combination might have been found in any number of the young women he had met in Jerusalem, but he had chosen to notice it in his uncle's daughter alone. Not that he sought to convince himself that there was any special advantage in this; on the contrary, he considered it to be no advantage at all. And yet he loved her for it too. Had the old question of what he had in common with so ordinary a girl risen again in his mind, he would have gladly answered this time without hesitation: *everything!* He loved her; he loved her because she was young, because she was full of life, because she was there . . . Miriam!

VI

From the Fast of the Tenth of Tevet on,* the days in Jerusalem were clear; Reb Yosef Hefetz readjusted to his new, which was to say his old, apartment, in which he had been allowed to remain thanks to his late wife's nephew, and everything returned to normal. Whereas in the past half year, particularly in the recent months of having to worry about his rheumatism and a place to live, his life had been one vexed uncertainty, so that he had even ceased to hold forth as usual in the presence of company and had thrust his Biblical and grammatical studies into the background, now that the situation had stabilized, his apartment having remained in his possession and his illness having taken a turn for the better, he resumed his sententious chatter and his burrowing in borrowed concordances, perused the new commentary in his latest Bible which he had bought on credit the week before and Yehezkel had had to pay for, and added new interpretations to the writings of the Rabbis, each of which kept him occupied for several days at a time. It took him several days, too, to get over his feelings of gratitude for Yehezkel's

* The Tenth of Tevet—a fast day, generally falling in the month of January, commemorating the onset of the Babylonian siege of Jerusalem in 586 B.C.

bounty, which he concealed on the one hand so as not to seem greedy for yet more favors, while alluding to it incessantly on the other hand lest this precaution be uncalled for, inasmuch as the cause that had led Yehezkel to behave so considerately in the first place would doubtless prove operative in the future as well, it being a self-evident principle of logic that an existing thing could more easily continue in existence once it already existed than come into existence in the first place.

An incidental though by no means unprovidential consequence of this chain of reasoning was that Reb Yosef was granted a major insight into the rabbinic text in the tractate of *Berakhot* * that declared, "It is forbidden to pity a person without knowledge." On the face of it, the text seemed inexplicable: could it be that human beings were less deserving than animals, for whom it was commanded to have compassion by the Bible, as was explained by the Rabbis in their commentary on the verse in Psalms, "And His mercy is over all His creation"? Only in order to answer his own question Reb Yosef had first to point out that it was an axiom of moral philosophy that a man who performed a good deed should never expect a favor or even gratitude in return, lest he reveal thereby that he had acted not out of pure sympathy for the other but merely for the self-gratification of priding himself on his action. And yet though the philosophers were undoubtedly right, it stood to reason that the recipient of the favor should express his appreciation of it and his intention of reciprocating nonetheless, since by doing so he encouraged his benefactor to perform yet another good deed and vice versa. This then was the explanation of the text in question, in which the word *knowledge* signified *acknowledgment*, as it did in the verse in the first chapter of Isaiah, "Every ox

* A tractate of the Mishnah.

knoweth its owner"; in other words, the man who failed to acknowledge a favor weakened his benefactor's determination to do good in the future, and this made him less worthy than an animal, which was why he needn't be pitied. . . .

"Well? What do you think of it, eh?" Reb Yosef's eyes twinkled with a fond, affectionate light, so that it was almost impossible to tell which pleased him more: Yehezkel's considerateness, his own appreciation of it, or the fact that he had been led by it to such a marvelous insight. The latter, in any event, provided him with food for conversation for the next four or five days. Each evening, forgetful that he had already expounded it on the previous day and again the same afternoon, he would begin as though about to divulge a new divine dispensation:

"In the course of my reading today . . . I discovered with God's help . . . in the tractate of *Berakhot*, on the thirty-third page. . . ."

The weather remained clear and Reb Yosef spent his days "relaxing," as he put it, from his trials and tribulations. It was especially restful to be able to leave the house and chat with company on the nearby rocks, so that he could almost have been happy, if only . . . if only he hadn't had to worry about his daughters. His eldest, of course, he hardly saw any more, since she was busy working with two other seamstresses from eight in the morning to seven at night, and sometimes even later, for Goldmann's daughter, who was assembling her *garde de robe*. Indeed, in his heart of hearts Reb Yosef had despaired of Esther completely; she had never hit it off with men to begin with, so that now there was no longer anything to lose; if her plans concerning Yehezkel should bear fruit (though convinced that no one could possibly suspect them, Esther secretly wanted everyone to know and dropped constant hints about it wherever she went), so much the better; and if not—no one would be any the worse off. Still, though there was no arguing with the Rabbis that two were better than one, and for all his kind feelings toward Yehezkel and his disinclination to rule out any prospect in advance, this particular match seemed somehow ill-suited to him; in spite of which, Reb Yosef began to befriend the "young man" more and more and to confide in him his latest textual discoveries, of which some were purely original and others culled from old books. He even went so far in his enthusiasm as to reveal to Yehezkel that the whole story in Genesis about man being created last, after the fish, the birds and the mammals, was perfectly in keeping with the latest findings of science, from which Yehezkel was free to draw his own conclusions if he liked.

As for Esther, then . . . well and good . . . but the problem of his youngest, Miriam, who insisted on going abroad, was much more difficult. The trip in itself, of course, was not so terrible; everyone was making it these days, and besides, she would be traveling with a family she knew. Travel, after all, was nothing to frighten a Jew—and yet nevertheless . . . why did it always have to happen to his family? She was only a child yet whenever he heard her complain "What am I doing here?" or "What can I possibly make of myself in this place?" his conscience would torment him and he could scarcely set his thoughts straight. Only where was the money for her passage to come from? Was he expected to pull it out of a hat? She too worried about it . . . except that she was hardly at home any more in any case . . . yes, she went looking for advice elsewhere, just like a man . . . these modern young women! Not even eighteen yet and such ambition! And meanwhile she was neglecting the house, she had simply stopped looking after it. In fact, it had already once happened that the laundress had come to help with the wash, as she did every month, and Miriam hadn't been home. Nothing was cared for any more, nothing was cleaned or mended. He was ashamed to tell a soul that for several weeks now even the linen hadn't been changed!

The exodus from Jerusalem was a constant subject of discussion among those gathered regularly on the rocks, which were occupied each evening by young men and old; storekeepers and sharetraders; artisans and Talmudists; landlords who lived from their properties and beggars who lived "from the wall," that is, who solicited by the Wailing Wall for alms (the most downtrodden of these sat listening to the others in silence); men of vision like Kauffmann, the Jew from East Prussia, and representatives of the younger generation like Shneirson and Kahanowitz. The older men reminisced with nostalgia and a kind of elderly pride (though not for some reason with any of the expansiveness that might have been expected to accompany such memories) about the not-so-distant days when the very place where they were sitting had been a wasteland without a single one of the houses that they could now see all around, so that no one had dared to venture beyond the old city walls. Now of course all that was changed. Yes, now the residents of Jerusalem no longer feared to leave the city altogether. . . .

Shneirson, on the other hand, having investigated the situation personally and come to conclusions of his own, was convinced that the emigration from Jerusalem had been greatly exaggerated, the proof being that rents were not going down; on the contrary, they kept rising all the time, so that it was impossible to find a decent place to live. In fact, this was exactly what had happened to Hamilin, who wished to prolong his stay in the city but couldn't find a suitable room.

Having mentioned the *kallé bromatom* by name, Shneirson

could not resist the opportunity to take an extra dig at him and his vulgar theories about the romanticism of certain young Jews. On the subject of the young doctor, particularly as regards the latter's practical affairs, he was supported by Kauffmann, the Jew from East Prussia, who though he hated Shneirson, *der russischer Student,* with a passion, just as he hated all Russians and all newcomers to Jerusalem in general for "polluting the air of the Holy City *im geistigen Sinn* * and leading it to wrack and ruin," openly declared that he considered Hamilin to be in the employ of the Devil and the Powers of Evil no less than the scourge of emigration itself.

Their rival in debate on this particular day was Kahanowitz, the Yeshiva student from Telz, whose command of Talmudic dialectic, while equipping him to find each hidden contradiction in the argument of an opponent, in no way prevented him from straightforwardly grasping the same problem by the horns himself. ("So you don't think it's true," he had mildly remarked after listening to Shneirson wax rancorously lyrical over Hamilin's opinions about marriage, romantic young Jews and the dissipation of despair. "And yet suppose he's right after all?" No, the only trouble here was that whether one married or not was ultimately not up to Hamilin!) As for the problem of emigration, however, which Herr Kauffmann claimed to regard as the work of the Devil (Kahanowitz happened to know for a fact that Kauffmann had written a letter to a friend in Galicia, which he kept in his pocket in case the occasion for sending it should ever arise, in which the latter was requested to help him "to escape from this Vale of Tears in whatever way you can"), here too, he, Kahanowitz, begged to differ. Not that he didn't agree with Shneirson that things were far better than they seemed, but for a totally different reason. Emigration, of

* German: in the spiritual sense.

course, was nothing new; it was growing and would continue to grow—and not to the agricultural settlements either (the situation of the farmers there was well-known) but rather abroad. In his own unprejudiced opinion, however, not only was this nothing to grieve about, it was actually a cause for rejoicing that fresh young talents (it was primarily the young, after all, who were leaving) should get out into the world where they could be of some use to themselves and their comrades instead of wasting away in this rubbish-heap of idleness that people called Jerusalem. This was his unprejudiced view.

Here Reb Yosef felt compelled to speak up. He had listened collectedly to everything so far because none of it seemed worthy of argument or rebuttal. It was all so much childish prattle. Jerusalem! Did anyone present really know what that meant? In *The Kuzari* * it was written . . . words that were worth their weight in gold . . . and about the Promised Land in general, too . . . except that this was not the place for all that . . . but Jerusalem! A widowed, desolate, deserted city, crying for mercy like the Israelite nation itself, which was like unto a scattered lamb. True, nation lived off nation—Rome had only been built on Jerusalem's ruins. But Jerusalem was still Jerusalem! The city was precious not only because it was a sacred site to every Jew and to many Gentiles as well but also because of its beauty; yes, there was a special place set aside for it in Reb Yosef's heart, it was inscribed there as though by a legendary hand. Jerusalem was his home . . . right up above in the guesthouse, in fact . . . that is, where he lived was not actually a part of the guesthouse . . . only none of this was what he had started out to say. Yes, what he had started to say was that his house

* A work by the Hebrew poet and philosopher Yehudah Halevi (1085–1140).

was full of mosquitoes which wouldn't let him sleep and whose bite was worse than being stuck with a needle. They were more bothersome than bedbugs, begging everyone's pardon. These insects were inhabitants of Jerusalem from time immemorial, particularly during the summer, though there was no lack of them in his apartment in winter too. In fact, he had recently heard someone say (the allusion was to Hamilin, whose anonymity Reb Yosef preferred to preserve) that medical science had discovered that they alone were the cause of the fever called malaria . . . the mosquito itself was called "anopheles" . . . the word was even to be found in the commentary of Rashi * . . . except that here was not the place for all that. He, Reb Yosef, had observed the nature of these creatures: they could stand in one spot on their crooked legs for hours on end without moving a wink, but just let him rise in a rage to swat one and away it would fly in a second! No matter how he crept up on it or tried to outwit it, the same thing happened each time: this little native of Jerusalem was always a step ahead of you. It had a special sixth sense. He must look into it in the works of the naturalists. Though he himself was not well-versed in this field, he had discovered on the basis of his own observations that animals in the Holy Land had faculties that they didn't have elsewhere. The divine poet knew what he was saying when he wrote, "Bird and beast in Thee grow wise." And it was not only in mosquitoes that Reb Yosef had observed such things. Take the cats of Jerusalem, for example, those emaciated strays that never had enough to eat. Once the cat that lived in his building—that is, there was a cat that had lived in his building from time immemorial, and after his younger daughter had begun to prepare for her trip there was no one

* Rabbi Shlomo Yitzhaki (1040–1105), a Biblical and Talmudic commentator.

to look after it any more—once this cat gnawed an entire
loaf of bread that should have lasted them all for two days,
so that Reb Yosef lost his temper and struck it to teach it a
lesson. Only now—wonder of wonders!—it never set foot
in the building when it knew that Reb Yosef was there; the
minute it sensed his footsteps—in fact, it was enough for it
merely to smell him behind the door—it would scamper out
of the house as fast as its legs could carry it. Yes, by the time
he opened the door it would be gone like an arrow from a
bow. What paradoxes! In Russia and other countries cats had
no memories because they ate rats, whereas this cat remembered everything . . . which simply bore out his point . . .
Jerusalem! The very idea of trying to say . . .

Jerusalem was under discussion in Goldmann's house too.
"Jerusalem!" Goldmann sucked on the nargileh that had
been brought him from the nearby Arab coffeehouse and
spoke as he inhaled. "You can't trust a soul in Jerusalem!"
Hadn't the Council promised him that his new school
would be ready for the dedication ceremony immediately
after Hannukah? And here it was weeks later and there was
still no sign of the money! Not only that, he hadn't even seen
the sum that had been promised him for the new rooms upstairs that he was donating to the guesthouse.
The Hungarian charity official sat across from his host
sipping tea and nodding his agreement to the urgent need
for a modern school to be founded upon the principles of the
Torah and the pillars of religion. The good Lord preserve
him if just the other day he hadn't seen two youngsters from
a well-known charity playing in the nursery of those dese-
crators of the vineyard of the Lord who were leading Jerusalem down the path to perdition! Merciful heavens! Merciful
heavens!

The house was in a hubbub. The children, who had stayed home from school today because it was the eve of the Feast of Epiphany, ran wildly about on the balcony, while Henya sat with Hamilin in the parlor next door and complained with the gesticulations of a *grande dame*, which she had recently begun to cultivate, that even at St. Joseph's *l'education* was not what it should be: you would think that at the very least they would teach the children not to make such a racket when they came home! Ach, the schools in Jerusalem . . . they were positively unbearable. . . .

Goldmann's mother was out of sorts with Jerusalem too. She stared with disbelief at her son's nargileh, at the water bubbling in the strange glass bottle and at the peculiar pipe which reminded her of the long tube of a certain instrument which the doctor occasionally prescribed for her when she suffered from constipation, and cursed the bad taste of all Jerusalemites. At last she rose and waddled off through the house like a fattened goose to ask for a cup of coffee, only to encounter the one-eyed matchmakeress, who had just dropped by to pay a visit. Making a sour face to mask her satisfaction at this turn of events, the old lady quickly sat down again. Cakes were served. With a slyly deferential gesture the match-makeress declared:

"I'm in luck again. Wherever people are eating and drink-ing, that's where I turn up."

Goldmann's mother, however, refused to swallow the bait. The honey-sweet words of the half-blind marriage broker failed to go down with her. Say what you will, the matches that were made in Jerusalem didn't please her at all. They simply weren't to her liking. She had been living in the city for months now without hearing of a single decent match. The doweries that they gave here, the wedding gifts, even the grooms! (She was referring, of course, to Jerusalem's men.)

The way they behaved toward their mothers! In Piatra,*
where her son Kalman'ke still lived, everything was different.
Once, believe it or not, when Kalman'ke had to travel to
Bucharest, she had given him fifteen days to be there and
back, and though he still hadn't finished his business when
his time was up, he didn't dare disobey his mother and returned the same day! That was Rumania for you! Not like
her son in Jerusalem, who contradicted her every word. And
to think of the match that Kalman'ke made—every man
should be so lucky! One day her *gottseliger* † husband had
announced that it was high time Kalman'ke got married, for
he had sewn enough wild oats as it was and was throwing his
money away . . . yes, the time had come for him to take
the bit in his mouth. To make a long story short, that is, he
was a hard-working lad but one who liked to live well: three
hundred francs a month he made, spent it all on himself and
went about dressed like a *Graf!* Not that you could work for
a huge agency like he did, of course, and not live well . . .
and when a bachelor spends three hundred a month on himself, don't think he doesn't know it! A fine young gentleman
like that thinks nothing of traveling a hundred miles just to
find a tailor he likes. And to hear them gossip about the
woman he would marry—none but the finest, the wealthiest,
the most beautiful girls were good enough! "Momma," he all
but begged, "I'm not ready yet, it's still too soon"—and this,
mind you, when they were parading princesses before him,
living dolls. But no one could ever guess what happened
next. Yes, they offered him Reb Berish's daughter. To be
perfectly honest, she was no old maid, but she was far from
a spring chicken either, and at least three or four years older
than he was. But a mother is a mother and the match was

* A city in northern Rumania.
† Yiddish: blessed of God, departed.

nothing if not practical. She may not have been a beauty like the others, but such intelligence, such a housekeeper! And she was an only child as well—after her parents had lived to be a hundred and twenty, God willing, it would all be hers. At first he began to whine. "Momma, have pity!" But in the end he came to her and said: "Momma, do what you want, I'll listen to whatever you say." And it wasn't that he couldn't do without her—why, he was making three hundred a month as it was. But he knew that a mother knows best . . . ten thousand in cash didn't grow on trees . . . and an only daughter at that—after one hundred and twenty years it would all be hers! And now? All her well-wishers should only be as well-off as her Kalman'ke. God be praised, in the whole city of Jerusalem there wasn't a living soul that enjoyed life as he did. Jerusalem . . . heh heh . . . that too passed for a city! God forgive her for her sinful speech. . . .

"Jerusalem!" snorted Goldmann, his voice rising once more above the din. "A den of swindlers—that's Jerusalem for you!" He, Goldmann, would not be swindled though, No, nobody cheated Goldmann. In his entire life he had been cheated only once, by a Yemenite Jew, and the thief got his proper comeuppance. It had happened while he was still living in the colony. One of the Yemenites who worked in his wine cellar had begun to smuggle home grapes in the bottom of a basket covered with old rags and the leftovers from his lunch. Once, however, he, Goldmann, happened to glance through the cellar window and saw what was going on without being seen himself. What did he do? Instead of letting on that he knew, he waited for a moment when he could send the Yemenite off on an errand; then he took the basket, replaced the grapes with stones and covered them over again with the rags and the food. But the best part of the joke was still to come. On his way home the Yemenite met an Arab friend whom he innocently invited to share some grapes with him. The Arab tucked his legs beneath him and waited to be served. But when the Yemenite opened the basket— there was nothing in it but stones! The insulted Arab nearly gave him a hiding . . . let that be a lesson to all thieves . . . no, from Goldmann, gentlemen, one didn't steal!

"But what are you getting at, Mister Goldmann?" implored the American charity official who was now sitting in the Hungarian's place. He sipped from the tea in the glass in front of him.

"I tell you, I won't put up with it . . . to think that I should ever have trusted philanthropists like you . . . never again, gentlemen!"

"But what have we done?" the official complained, taking two more sips from his glass.

"There's more here than meets the eye, I can assure you of that!" Goldmann persisted, sucking in smoke with each word.

"But what for example? Reb Yankev!"

"You're out for your own good, I tell you. I know you philanthropists!"

"But what good?" the American asked impatiently.

Goldmann stood firm. "I'm not saying any more for the moment."

"Not saying? But you're being unfair. Surely you're not suggesting that Reb Zalman took the lease?"

"He didn't take the lease but he took something else."

"But what?"

"I've already told you I'm not saying. Reb Zalman giveth and Reb Zalman taketh—blessed be the name of the Lord. But make no mistake about it, I don't intend to put up with it! The good name of Jerusalem is being dragged through the streets."

"Well then, if I can't get a single word of truth out of you. . . ."

And loudly reciting the grace after drinking:

"Blessed art Thou O Lord our God, King of the U-ni-verse . . . who createth myriad souls and fulfilleth the needs of each one . . . and bringeth life to every living thing. . . . Oy, fine times! Fine times!"

The American official was through with his tea but Goldmann still sat by his nargileh and groaned: "Jerusalem . . . Jerusalem. . . ."

VII

Uncle Haim went to work in the guesthouse chapel, for though Mister Bassin was still in Jerusalem, he was busy preparing for his trip abroad and could no longer attend to his duties. Haim had agreed to accept the sextonship against his better judgment, on the urging of Yehezkel, who had argued that there was really no choice: Goldmann's new school would sooner or later force Reb Yosef out of his apartment upstairs and it was necessary to plan ahead. In addition, Miriam too would need to be helped and Yehezkel himself would have to find a new room once Reb Yosef moved below. At first Haim had wanted to stipulate that Goldmann should at least release him from the rest of his debt (at the time of the settlement he had actually paid the bulk of the alimony in cash, so that the sum against which his Torah had been seized was far less than the worth of the scroll itself), but here too he acquiesced in the end on Yehezkel's advice. At heart, however, he continued to be oppressed by a nagging feeling. He felt like the Canaanite slave in the legend, condemned to exhaustion carrying water to his master in a leaky bucket that was always empty when he finally got there. He was damned if he did and damned if he didn't! Previously he had been helpless to retaliate against Goldmann too: yet as long as he wasn't employed by the man he had been dimly but proudly conscious of the fact that his head was held high, that he still fought on for his rights as best he could, whereas now even this was denied him. When Yehezkel had first briefly hinted that it would be his duty to accept the sextonship, his instinct had been to speak his mind completely, unreservedly, as had always been his fashion; yet suddenly, uncharacteristically, he had found himself dumb with emotion, not because he was physically unable to speak, but because of some strange, unrelenting, incomprehensible conflict within him. There had seemed to be so much, so much, that he had wanted to say, yet no sooner did he open his mouth than it vanished into thin air, leaving only the nagging feeling behind.

He didn't go about sulking, of course . . . lord no . . . he did what was asked of him without a fuss . . . but within him the mournful feeling persisted that everyone, his own son, Yehezkel, his brother's two daughters, yes, everyone, had let him down. The lord only knew what had become of his son Hanoch who regularly used to send him ten francs a month with a letter. (True, the letter hadn't been written by Hanoch himself but by a scribe in Safed, and he too had to have it read to him by his brother Yosef, but the fact remained that it had come, with ten francs inside it, every month!) He was buried alive in his mill up there—that is, if he was still alive . . . how terribly long it was since anything had been heard of him . . . three months, at least, if not longer. And his brother Yosef! He, Haim, had hoped that in Goldmann's new school, where the children would learn Talmud and Codes,* there would be room for Yosef to teach. With a regular job things would look up for him. True, he would lose his apartment, but he could then rent another; he would be a man of means independent of the guesthouse.

* Codes—the medieval compilations of Jewish religious law.

Yes, he would start a new life, the cloud would show its silver lining. Indeed, Yosef had spoken in this vein himself all week long—and in the end . . . in the end . . . but it was pitiful even to think of it! Still, incredible as it seemed, there was nothing to do but accept the fact that his brother Yosef was merely going through the motions of applying. Even had he made every effort, of course, which was what a poor man had to do in Jerusalem if he wished to get anywhere, his prospects, though good, would have been far from certain, for there was no end of applicants for such a position—much less now, when he refused to give a straight answer whether he even wanted it or not. And why didn't he? Because of the Hebrew pronunciation! Yes, the Hebrew to be taught in the new school was to be of the Ashkenazic variety, while the classes themselves were to be held in Yiddish. As far as the Yiddish was concerned, Reb Yosef did not object too strenuously, for while he held that German-Jewish jargon in contempt (*feh!* was how he generally expressed his opinion of it), he was equally opposed to the "Hebrew through Hebrew" method that had recently become popular. This, then, was no obstacle; but the pronunciation, the Ashkenazic pronunciation . . . no, he could never agree to it . . . it would be impossible to teach in such a school. . . . Hadn't he himself fought against the Sephardic accent all these years, armed with the weapons of scholarship and science, in the mistaken belief—a belief buttressed by innumerable proofs and citations—that it was incorrect? And now, having come to see the light at last and having confessed that the Sephardic pronunciation was indeed the historic one after all, was he seriously expected to teach in a school that made a special point of insisting on its rival? The idea of even suggesting it!

"But father, don't you also teach your pupils in Ashkenazic Hebrew?" Esther tried to reason with him.

"Eh? In Ashkenazic Hebrew? Far from it! I'm not referring to the phonetic details, mind you . . . besides which, private pupils are a different case. But what does that have to do with it one way or another? The Sephardic pronunciation is difficult for me because I'm accustomed to its faulty sister. Only that doesn't mean a thing. What matters in a school is the method—and mine is the very opposite! What difference does it make what I'm accustomed to? Who pays it any attention? The main thing, daughter, is the awareness. How many times have I told you that it's the conscious awareness that counts and not the mistaken habit?"

Haim listened without understanding. He was loathe to agree with Esther that her father was simply frightened of a regular position because he was getting old and hadn't taught classes in years. How could one possibly believe such a thing of Yosef? Esther was too hard on him when she said, "All father can do now is sit and talk. The whole of his grumbling about not being offered a job is just so many words. He himself doesn't want one. He's been lazy all his life and now he's given up." No, he couldn't believe it was so . . . because if it really was—why didn't Yosef come out and say it? Why did he hide it from them? He could have told them quite frankly, "It's too much for me, I'm just not up to it," and that would have put an end to it. Why hide it? Yet he too in turn hid Esther's suspicions in the back of his mind and refused to consider them further.

Esther, Miriam . . . Miriam, Esther . . . oy, oy, oy . . . nothing but trouble . . . trouble everywhere . . . Hatskel too . . . would he ever be anything but trouble? A fine chance of that.

Haim went out to the street to assemble ten Jews for the afternoon prayer.

Esther's attitude toward her younger sister's travel plans kept changing for the better. In the beginning there had been nothing but reproaches: "Miriam! You heartless thing! How can you leave me alone like this with father? How can I do everything myself?" Eventually, however, she had come around to agreeing that Miriam should go to Jaffa or to Haifa and learn a trade there. Let her even do housework if she liked! In the new Jewish quarters that were going up there was a great demand for maids. Yes, let her go, why not! Whereas now, Esther no longer seemed to care whether Miriam traveled to America or the mountains of the moon. Not only that, she was even prepared to pay her way for her, that is, if her modest savings, which she had given to someone for safekeeping, would suffice. Just so long as the crybaby agreed not to flood the whole world with her tears! She, Esther, had worked like a dog all her life, day in and day out, without ever thinking of herself. She would give Miriam what money she had now too if Miriam couldn't find it elsewhere. Anything to stop her whining!

But according to Miriam it was already too late: Mister Bassin's party was setting out this week, a second group would not be formed soon, Esther's money was not enough in any case (this she had learned from Mister Bassin and the other travelers), and there was nowhere else for her to turn. She refused to go to Jaffa or to Haifa; Beirut too had lost its attraction; and now it appeared that she would not be going to America either. It seemed that there was nothing left for her to do but take poison and die.

Those were her exact words to Esther; her young voice, however, seemed to be saying something else; at any rate, it gave no cause for fear that she might actually pour such a silly thing as poison down her full, young throat. . . .

The two sisters' conversation turned to the subject of Yehezkel. He had moved to a new room without even telling Esther. He was living in Mister Bassin's old mother's place now. He paid seven francs there. She slept in the hallway and he in the large room.

Mister Bassin's mother, a little, wrinkled, deaf old lady, lived all by herself. She received no aid from her son and eked out a livelihood by calling on a few acquaintances each morning with fresh meat from the butcher shops. Her entire life was given over to her butchers, her customers and her special "cuts," apart from which she understood nothing and could not have even had she wanted to. Rising early every morning, she wrapped up her few copper coins in a bundle and tottered to the marketplace, where she waited for hours on end to receive her "cuts" while arguing and quarreling with the butchers, who were always out to cheat her, the bastards! Then she slowly made the rounds of her customers. She brought her meat into the kitchen, spent forever and a day making out the bill (her mind was none too keen and she had to rely in the end on everyone's honesty, including her own), accepted her payment with trembling hands, wrapped it carefully in her bundle as though wrapping up her own lifeblood, returned home before noon, cooked herself a bit of buckwheat porridge, ate it all up and lay down again until the next morning. As for her son, she went weeks at a time without even seeing him, for he never came to visit her and she never went to him. Every Sabbath and every free hour of the week she whiled away in sleep.

Esther flared up. How could a person not even bother to inform a person he was moving? In the end, of course, she had found out where he was and went to visit him.

—Might she come in? Was he sure she wasn't intruding? (Who ever knew, after all, what another person was thinking?) She believed she'd take a seat. Might she? Might she sit down? Yes, when relations weren't . . . weren't open, one had to ask permission for everything. In general, she had never understood how . . . how it was possible for two people to be so intimate with each other one day and to say good-bye on the next, as though everything were automatically ended, as though it had never all happened in the first place. . . .

She scrutinized Hefetz with burning, lifeless eyes. His expression was like an animal's after it has just been saddled and harnessed. He was stricken with panic that the entire inner structure that he had built for himself ever since his release and his return to health was about to collapse again, to be ruined, hopelessly smashed. Not that he actually reproached himself at that moment for lacking the supreme strength to say to her, "Esther, for the love of God, leave me alone!" Nor did he chide himself for not having the opposite power, the strength to reach out to her, to behave as a saint might behave, to be for her all that she wanted him to be. No, at that moment he was totally overwhelmed by the simple fact that a human being in a dress was squirming in agony before him: a miserable, terrifying, saddled-and-harnessed feeling of pity swept through his body for her, and even more, for himself, her "beloved." Her beloved who had jilted her! He—beloved and jilting. Great God! To what depths of misery was it possible for some people to sink?

In the hallway the old woman was sleeping like a log. After a few torturously long minutes of silence, Esther tried as usual to break the ice. Her eyes filled with excruciating torment and she whispered in a tremulous voice:

"Well, you might at least shake hands."

And for an instant she ignited fearfully, as though equally touched off by the effort she had just finished making, the moment of indecision that had preceded it and Yehezkel's sweaty, extended hand.

"You're afraid of life," she shuddered. "Shame on you!"

"I'm a coward . . . always have been . . . all my life. . . ."

"A coward? You can say such a thing about yourself?"

"If it's true."

"But why?"

"Why what?"

"Nothing. Why are you one?"

"I just am."

"You always think you're doing me favors. That's the one thing I don't want!"

"Favors? What kind of favors? Do you think I'm any better off than you? On the contrary. . . ."

She groaned deeply and began to whisper words that seemed to have no logical connection. Yes, she knew . . . he was rotten . . . rotten through and through . . . there was no love in his heart . . . only lust . . . he didn't know what love was . . . it meant nothing to him . . . he didn't even care that she had come to him . . . she was only a cousin . . . he would treat any woman who befriended him exactly the same. . . .

She hushed and waited for an answer. Had he told her she was right, it would not have distressed her; far from it, it might perhaps have helped soothe the no-longer-fresh pain that she had been carrying about with her for the last ten or fifteen years, the pain of not being looked on as a woman, of not being desired by men. *Yes, he was treating her as he would treat any woman, he was incapable of anything else—but then he did at least desire her. . . .* Yet Hefetz knew that such an answer, though it might not distress her, could not make her happy either. It was against human nature to settle for such cold comfort; nothing but the very best, the most idyllic, was ever enough. What she was really trying and hoping to elicit from him with her incoherent accusations was an emphatic denial, and perhaps not just a denial, but a sacred, eternal oath that it was not merely lust at all, so help him; that he swore it wasn't true that she meant nothing to him; that he loved her with a great, a supreme love; loved her truly, loved her alone, loved no one beside her.

Alas, he hadn't the heart to tell her anything—neither what she wanted to hear nor what she wanted not to. He saw only that, for the time being at least, this wretched woman loved him, yes, *him*, loved him all by herself, she and no one else. There was no one else. It would have been far better if there had been, but there wasn't, and she did love him, really she did: naïvely, painfully, poisonously, neurotically, hatefully, yet truly all the same, without ulterior designs, to the very marrow of her being, with the last of her strength, with the meagerness of her wasted body, with the remnant of what vital powers she had left. . . .

Suddenly he softened, as on the day of his departure from the hospital; what had seemed to him only a minute ago to be foreign, impossible, out of the question, now, in an instant, seemed not only thinkable, but absolutely simple, self-evident, necessary. In a flash he became all feeling, emotion, compassion; everything was forgotten; every barrier was down; yes, every barrier, without exception. He clutched her to him weakly in his arms, listened to the pounding behind her smooth rib cage, showered her hair repeatedly with wordless, burning, sibilant kisses. She gave a horrible groan and gathered herself against him in complete self-oblivion. For a long time she would not let go of him; as though half-crazed, she kissed him on his cheeks, on his neck, on his lips, kissed and bit him until she drew blood. Suddenly she hiccuped; something had happened to her dress; a button on the back had ripped and come off. Her chest seemed to heave up and down with its last breaths, sucking back blood, like little waves that could not reach the shore. A bad smell, an odor of decay and indigestion, began to give off from their mouths and bodies. Yet when the tiredness overtook her too, she grew terribly sad. For a long time afterward she could think of nothing to say to him. Only before leaving did she ask in a whisper: *What was it that had happened? What did all those kisses mean?*

Afterwards she began to come to him every evening: with enigmatic remarks, with fond, ingratiating phrases, with tender diminutives. Sometimes when she left him she wanted to cry, at other times she felt like laughing and dancing with joy. What was happening to her? And ah, how she longed for him all day long, all the while that they were both sitting and working in Goldmann's house! She would be busy sewing on the other side of the wall, yet her thoughts would carry her far, far away from the drudgery she hated. Then she thought of him alone, only of him.

Sometimes he sought to be stern with her:

"Esther! I can't be for you what someone else might have been. Do you understand me?"

"Of course I do! Of course! No one could be for me what you are."

It was hopeless. Deliberately or not, she insisted on standing his words on their head. She couldn't help it. Who could reach into the back of her mind and set them right again? She couldn't possibly understand all that he expected her to and never would. *Give up on it, Hefetz! You can never tell her everything!*

He would try changing the subject but she would change it back again. Then he would knit his brows and attempt to explain in a special tone of voice, which was far clearer in itself than anything he said, what it was he had meant when

he'd told her that he couldn't possibly be for her all that she
wanted and expected him to be. He had no way of knowing,
of course, what her inmost reactions would be should they
ever really link lives. But he couldn't help thinking—he was
sure of it—that they wouldn't be good, that she couldn't be
happy with him; while as for himself—he was certain that
he would always feel that he had been a catastrophe for her,
that she had been sacrificed up to him, that she would have
been happier with a hangman or an epileptic. Yes, she was
bound to suffer from the fact that it would seem to him—
of this he was certain—that he had forced himself upon her,
that is, forced her to marry a man wh-who . . . who was a
physical and mental wreck and . . . wh-who . . . had once
been in a house for . . . for . . . and who might return
there again some day, so that whatever respite of health and
happiness there had been would simply go up in smoke. The
wheel was sure to come round again.

Esther's eyes opened wide and filled with dread. Whenever
he spoke like this she would really be convinced that he was
headed for a relapse. The maniac! Scenes from the past half-
year sprang to life in her imagination; fragments of his mono-
logues echoed in her ears; and she was gripped by horror. And
yet she wouldn't, couldn't, let go of him. In her was a power
that overcame the horror too.

"What are you saying, Hehezke'le, what are you saying?
Why must you frighten me so? I'm not a coward. . . . I
only know that I can't live without you. . . ."

And she would go on talking to him about love until all
hours of the night, sometimes reciting the very phrases that
she had heard ten or fifteen years ago from one of her comrades in the movement and that had repelled her at the time.
Now, in these panicky moments, she would remember them
unconsciously and repeat them word for word, without sens-

ing in the least how utterly inappropriate they were for two people in their situation.

"All day long while I'm at work I think of you, Yehezke'le, only of you. And you?"

"But Esther, perhaps we should talk about something else . . ." he would try again.

"I know, I know. I won't listen to another word. I haven't anything else. I don't need anything else. I'm not one of your idealistic young things who talk all day about their fine ideals and have something else in mind. I—I don't say one thing and mean another. I've made enough small talk to last me the rest of my life. . . ."

"Then . . . in that case . . ."

"In that case nothing. Come, sit with me for a minute, Yehezke'le, what are you afraid of? Don't you love me? And I love you so. But you do love me a little bit too, don't you?"

"I don't love anyone. Not even your father. But even if I could . . . I'm a sick man. You should keep away from me . . . it's neurasthenia, it's my nerves . . . what kind of husband would I make you?"

—But why should that bother him? She went on clinging to him, as though she hadn't heard his last words at all. What was he worried about? That she might be making a bad bargain? That it wasn't a fair exchange? That she would be giving more than she was getting? But she was prepared for all that! She wasn't a shopkeeper, she didn't keep accounts. Or perhaps he thought she was asking for guarantees in advance? But she didn't want any! They would begin a new life together. What good to him was the way he lived now? She knew everything about it.

"You do? Everything?"

"But you live in a pigsty!" she cried, changing the subject. Just look at his room . . . what filth, what a mess . . . and the ceiling . . . there wasn't a chair to sit on . . . she would be good for him . . . she would serve him. . . .

"But Esther'ke, you're forgetting . . ."

—No, he mustn't, mustn't talk! She refused to hear a word of it, not a word! He must, must, must, tell her the truth: Whom did he love? Who was she? Whom did he want to marry? Who? Her sister would never marry him, never! He'd better get that straight in his mind. Yes, she knew, knew perfectly well: he was sick for her, only for her; for herself, Esther—not at all! He'd better get it straight: Miriam would never marry a misfit like him. She had her heart set elsewhere. It was Hamilin whom she loved . . . did he hear her? Hamilin. . . .

It was a nightmare for Hefetz to actually hear it said, yet it came as no surprise. In fact, he had known about it even before Esther. Yes, Miriam had fallen in love with Hamilin, with the emphasis on *fallen*. It wasn't love but a childish crush—no more, though no less, either. Not that Miriam was incapable of real love; she was not only a woman already, after all, but one of character as well; in spite of which, what had happened here was merely an infatuation, a slight effervescence, a nervous excitation of the kind easily produced, say, by an evening of hypnosis. None of her dreams about the future, about her studies, about being on her own, about all the other nameless things that adolescents dream of, were in any way connected with Hamilin; they had their existence and he had his; except at the moment it appeared that the balance had shifted in his favor. Of course, Esther's choice in love too was lacking in common sense; she too refused to be realistic about her chosen one's capacity to provide her with a home and to look after her when she herself no longer had the strength to work (a prospect that seemed to grow more imminent with every passing day); but at any rate, she at least was not waiting for a miracle; her chosen one, unluckily, was on the same level as she, perhaps even a level lower; he had been salvaged from the asylum, scraped from the bottom of the barrel—whereas Miriam was well aware that she was a nullity compared to the glorious Doctor Hamilin and that she hadn't the ghost of a chance with him. And yet that was precisely it! It wasn't as if she were pinning her hopes on anything. Did anyone seriously think that she expected him to . . . to . . . propose to her? She wasn't as insane as all that! He simply appealed to her as a *chevalier*. Of course, Esther was right: she had enough problems as it was; why must she add to them with fantasies like these? Yet the word *chevalier* had as though cast a spell over her ever since she'd heard it used in connection with Hamilin by the daughter of the owner of the Harel, whom she had recently made friends with. *Chevalier*—what exactly did it mean, this word, which she had scarcely heard spoken in all her years of living in Jerusalem? For all practical purposes, after all, she was a native of the city; not only hadn't she known a great many *chevaliers* in her life, she was not even sure what one was. (Not so her friend, who had recently arrived from Poland and was something of an expert in these matters.) And yet the word for some reason pleased her. Lately she had even begun to use it disdainfully of Shneirson; he too was a *chevalier*, she told herself, he hailed from the wide world too . . . that same world in which there were so many different kinds of *chevaliers* . . . *chevaliers* who escorted their ladies on their arms to the opera (*opera*—that too had become a much-discussed word with her friend) . . . even in Jerusalem she had once or twice seen some official of the *Alliance* * or some European Christian walking home like that

* The *Alliance Israélite Universelle*, a French-Jewish philanthropic society that was widely active in Palestine, especially in educational and cultural fields.

with his wife . . . but no, no, no! Only he, only Hamilin, was a real *chevalier.* . . .

No, it was completely out of the question. Might she hope to die if she had ever thought of Hamilin as a husband! Absolutely never! What kind of talk was that? *He* should pay attention to *her?* What was a poor, ignorant young girl like herself compared to him? She hadn't taken leave of her senses completely.

And yet, Hefetz thought, *who knows.* Who was to say that she was not like the consumptive who knows he is going to die, who is aware for a fact that the specialist whom he believes in as in God has recently told a relation of his in so many words, "I'm afraid it's a matter of weeks, my friend, at the most"—and yet who in the face of all this, in spite of all this, continues to hope—no, has the absolute confidence—that he will go on living for a long time to come, for months and even years?

She schemed and planned and looked for ways to get to America, but to herself she thought: Jaffa, and from there to Beirut. In Beirut she could manage just as well . . . she had heard that there were schools there where you could study to be a nurse. She held long, fanciful conversations about life abroad with her friend, who was prettier than herself and closer to *him,* because he stayed in her father's hotel; her mind was filled with the names and images of many women, women whom she knew and whom she didn't, women from Jerusalem and from all over. A single question gnawed at her brain: which one of them would he marry? Her instincts, her powers of anticipation and an invisible voice all told her that it was not as farfetched as everyone seemed to think that Hamilin, who was not so young himself any more, should decide despite his greater education and merit to say "be mine" to the fat divorcée, who was positively rolling in money (it was surely no accident that Henya had all but turned her house into a sewing factory lately!); for the most part, however, she too was sure that this could never happen; she refused, yes, refused, to believe in it; yet no sooner did she enter Goldmann's house every day to bring Esther her lunch and hear Hamilin's voice as he chatted with his "intended" in the other room (Henya, departing from local custom, declined to feed her workers from her own kitchen) than her face unconsciously assumed the superior expression of a woman in the presence of her rival, whose wealth and good looks must be combated with all the delicate refinement, the intellect, the nobility of emotion at one's command.

No, Miriam expected nothing, yet not only was it enough merely to gaze on Hamilin from a distance for her heart to start pounding like a murderer's, she actually seemed to enjoy it. His very presence put her in a trance. In her dreams she saw his firm, straight legs, his clear-cut jaw, his strong, satisfied lips, the confident flair of his nostils. *But what do nostrils have to do with confidence?* the dreamer curiously asked. Miriam couldn't answer; she did not even understand the meaning of the question; yet his nostrils did seem confident to her even when she was awake. (*The two of them were in Cairo*, she would daydream on . . . *on a burning hot day . . . they were walking barefooted together on the fiery terrazzo.* . . .) Had she stopped to ask herself what the color of his eyes was, on the other hand, she would have been at a loss to reply; but she did not stop to ask nor did it occur to her to. Her one aspiration was that he should happen to be standing there when she entered Goldmann's house, that he should detain her for a moment and speak to her, ask her some question. Yet there were days too when it was impossible to say that she was simply suffering from the sweet pangs of lovesickness in their usual adolescent form. No, the pain she felt then was less a symptom of sickness than of an antibody in her blood, an inoculation she had been given to render her immune to the disease itself. At such times it might almost appear that she was the one healthy person in the midst of an epidemic: she alone could be sure that she wasn't secretly carrying the infection within her, that she wasn't living on borrowed time, for the air was full of the amatory bacilli of the young doctor from abroad, and she had merely come down with the general contagion in an acute but nonfatal form. . . .

One night she dreamt that her friend, the hotel owner's daughter, had persuaded her to enter his room while he was out. She stole the key and tiptoed in, her heart beating loudly: what would he say, what could she answer, if he were to suddenly walk through the door? She wanted him to appear; yet as she stood gazing at all his ties and collars that were hanging by the window, she suddenly panicked and ran away.

This was only a dream; but when her friend innocently told her the following day that her "fiancé," who lived in the Harel too, regularly left notes for her under his pillow which she found when she made his bed, Miriam too decided to rise early the next morning and to look for . . . *what?* And in fact, she lingered like a sleepwalker over the beds and divans in her father's house, as though she absentmindedly half expected to find a message from him . . . *about what?* As a future physician, Hamilin himself would no doubt have exclaimed had he learned of her errant behavior: *Yes, sexual neurosis . . . the neuroticism of our times . . . what pathological proportions it can reach!*

VIII

One evening toward the end of January, Haim asked
Yehezkel to mind the chapel while he went to the Turkish
post office to see if there might be a letter from his son.
"Hanoch, bless him, sends his letters by way of Safed," he
explained, "and the mail from Safed goes through the Turkish
post." *

Yehezkel did as he was asked, filling his temporary position
by sitting on the threshold of the entrance to the chapel's
narrow hallway. Before long Reb Yosef came downstairs,
sat down beside him and struck up a conversation. Yes, Haim's
son Hanoch. He, Reb Yosef, hardly knew him, except, for his
letters to Haim during the last few years. But even if one
agreed with the well-known adage that the style was the
man, in this case it didn't apply, for the letters weren't written
by Hanoch himself (who between the two of them was no
great shakes with a pen) but by a scribe in Safed. In any case,
unlike his namesake in the Bible, this Hanoch did not walk
with God. He seemed to have forgotten his father completely . . . the things that went on these days. . . .

As he spoke, Reb Yosef became the embodiment of moral
indignation. Gradually the topic shifted from Hanoch to his
own family, in particular, to his daughter Miriam. Yes, the

* There were several mail-delivery systems in Ottoman Palestine,
of which the Turkish government's was one.

Rabbis told a story about the young women of Jerusalem, how each was more beautiful than the next, so that whenever enemies besieged the city they would say to one another, "If only Jerusalem is captured, a great lord will be sure to see me and carry me off." The story was in the Midrash. They felt deprived in their fathers' homes—they wanted lords to take them away—nothing less would satisfy them. And today the lord was—America . . . only America . . . nowhere but America. . . .

"America?" queried a Jew passing by in the street, a newcomer in town who had been in the chapel yesterday for the afternoon prayer and now seemed to have lost his way. "Are you bound for America too? I've been looking for the ticket agency. I was at the consul's again today but it wasn't any use. He said he'd help me return to Russia if I wanted . . . royally . . . but he won't help me get to America. I was told that in the agency . . . I've been looking for it for an hour now . . . I can't seem to find a soul to show me the way. . . ."

"Yes, they'll show you the way all right!" snapped Reb Yosef angrily, having hardly listened to a word of what was said. "There's no room for new boarders here. One of these days they'll show me the way from my apartment too . . . yes, indeed. They'll want to start getting it ready for their new school. And they'll move the chapel upstairs too. Haim's Torah in my apartment . . . what paradoxes!"

The stranger stared at Reb Yosef with uncomprehending amazement. Had he said anything about looking for a room? He could see for himself that there was a guesthouse and a chapel here—in fact, he'd come for the afternoon prayer only yesterday—but he wasn't looking for a room at all. He was staying at the Hotel Harel, and paying an arm and a leg for it too. They certainly skinned you there! No, he had simply stopped to inquire about the way to the agency. He didn't live in Jerusalem. He had arrived here just the other day after a tour of the country. He had been in the settlements, in the Galilee, in Tiberias, even in Safed. And this morning he had been in the information bureau for new settlers . . . only what was there to say about it? It was clear to him now that he'd just been wasting his time, which was why he was on his way to the agency to buy a ticket back home.

Reb Yosef realized the nature of his error at last. Loathe to back down too quickly, however, he persisted with school-masterish irritation:

"But what did you come here for in the first place? What did you expect to find?"

A moment later, though, he relented and went on:

"Sit down, my friend. I'd like a word with you. I have a new interpretation for you. It's of the verse, 'And Jacob departed from Beersheba and journeyed to Haran.' The way I see it, the actual meaning is . . ."

But the stranger interrupted him. Not that he wasn't fond of interpretations himself—he too was no ignoramus in the Law, praise God. Only at the moment, he was sorry to say, he hadn't a minute to spare. No, he had no time, he was afraid the agency might close for the day. While as for why he had come this way in the first place—he had come from the hotel. That is, he had been to the bureau . . . in the hotel they had advised him to go there . . . it was a place where they gave information . . . in fact, he had turned to the office in Odessa before setting out and they had advised him there to get in touch with the office here. . . .

"Ach!" Reb Yosef exclaimed short-temperedly. That hadn't been his question at all. Why had the Jew come *to Palestine?* Where was he from?

—Where was he from? From Russia, naturally. Where else

should he be from? He hoped no one would be offended, however, if he pointed out that "where are you from?" was a policeman's expression. *Aktudavo?* *—he hadn't heard the question since leaving Russia and he didn't care to hear it now. The very sound of it gave him goose-pimples! Nevertheless, a question deserved an answer: yes, he was from Russia, that was where he lived. And why had he come to Palestine? He himself wasn't sure any more; in fact, he was beginning to wish that he hadn't, except what alternative had he had? One had to go somewhere, after all. The Jews in Russia were finished, finished and done for. They stole the very bread from your mouth there; the Jew was being shut out of business, it was pointless to go on trying, the situation was hopeless, as he had written at the time in the Holy Tongue to the Odessa office. In fact, he happened to have a copy of the letter right with him, he could show where it was written. . . .

The speaker made a motion to reach into his pocket; glancing up at Reb Yosef, however, he changed his mind for some reason and continued talking instead. No, he was not the only Jew in the hotel who had come to have a look at the country, nor the one with the most money either, yet his was a special case: the others all represented organizations abroad and viewed things from that perspective, whereas he had come on his own and saw in a truer light. That is, he had come on behalf of himself and his family, like those itinerant preachers back home who traveled through the villages to raise doweries for their daughters—how did the analogy strike them, ha ha? No, this was no joking matter for him! He too was an emissary, sent by his own family, he wasn't a free agent at all. True, he had made the trip here himself, but in Russia, praise God, he had a house full of children, grown boys and girls, who were ready for any hardship, any kind of work. In the

* Russian: Where are you from?

beginning, of course, it was hard to adjust to any new place; one had to be ready to suffer; he understood this well enough. In fact, the truth of the matter was that his children had wanted to go to America, but he, their father, had argued against it. Among the Gentiles, he had told them, the horn of plenty would never run out; there would always be time to go to America later, if they still wanted, and turn into pagans then. Whereas here, on the other hand, he was ready to consider anything. Ever since he could remember he had thought of nowhere but Palestine. Since his capital was not large, however, he had written to Odessa to ask whether it mightn't be possible to acquire a small plot of land with it; and the answer had been that no matter how small the sum at his command, he should turn to their office in the Holy Land when he arrived. Several weeks ago he had come to have a look. He had hoped, God willing, that a piece of land would turn up. There were even special organizations, he'd heard, that distributed it.

"Burial plots perhaps!" Reb Yosef sneered with uncharacteristic rudeness. "Well, what happened? What did they tell you in the bureau?"

"What could they tell me? They didn't tell me anything."

"But still . . ."

"They told me that if I were to bring my family here and if we were to work in some settlement, we wouldn't die of hunger."

"Well?"

"Well? A fine prospect, that! I'm to go back to my family with an answer like that? Not on your life! We can work like oxen for someone in America too. What kind of sense does it make? A Jew should come all the way here just to slave for a piece of bread? In America, they say, you have to work too. But in the first place, you save a few hundred or even a few thousand dollars, and in the second, you work for a boss only for the first few years and then you set up on your own. Ask your sexton and he'll tell you. He's been there and I've spoken to him. Of course, what kind of Jew is it who doesn't want to live in Palestine, the land of our fathers, as I wrote to the organization in Odessa. . . ."

This time, however, the stranger went on without offering to produce his letter. Yes, every Jew's soul was bound to the Holy Land, but besides doing something for the Land he wished to do something for himself as well; and it was his opinion that it made all the difference whether one farmed one's own land or worked for some overseer. Was he right or not? In any case, that was how he felt . . . besides which, of course, his children would never think of coming here to work because the wages were so much lower than in America . . . that much went without saying . . . and they weren't used to farming either. Both his sons and daughters, praise God, had received as good an education as money could buy in the town where they lived. They had been taught like the children of a good home that they were. And in Pittsburgh, in America, he had a cousin who worked in a synagogue whose sons were already about to get their English certificates from public school! Of his own sons, who wanted to join their cousins in Pittsburgh, the eldest had come up for army service a year ago and the next eldest was due a year hence, while his three grown daughters embroidered, sewed, and read and wrote Russian to perfection . . . and there were the little ones too, who would still need more schooling . . . what kind of schools could there be in the settlements here? Where could he possibly live? In Odessa they told him that the schools here were excellent, but he didn't believe it. Yes, children had to learn; his elder children had never studied much because they hadn't wanted to and now he was sorry. . . . In addition to which, his capital was small and it was hard to do business here. Even if he were to learn the language in a hurry (he had a special aptitude for this), it would be impossible to peddle goods in the Arab villages— so he had been told and so he had seen for himself. As if he needed to be told! On his first day here he had already observed that one couldn't do business with the natives. It wasn't Russia here. And he had seen how the Jews in the settlements lived too, yes indeed. True, there were those who didn't live badly at all, almost like gentlemen. But not everyone was so lucky, especially now that it was hard to get started and the Baron de Rothschild * was no longer handing out money. Some had filled their pockets while the getting was good, but sorry to say, those times were gone forever. Of course, it was said that with time you could accomplish what with sheer brains you often could not; he, however, was of the opinion that brain-power too was a must. And where was the brainpower, what could be the point, in settling here? To come down with malaria? Yes, he'd seen enough troubles in the last few weeks to last him for many months. In Safed, in fact, he'd actually been an eyewitness. . . .

And the Jew proceeded to relate what had happened in Safed, or more exactly, in the vicinity of Safed. About a half day's walk from the city there was a windmill—he himself had never been there but so he had been told. The mill was owned by an Arab but was run by a Jew who worked there all by himself and was not in the best of health. The past few months had been a slack season and there were times when the mill had lain idle for days on end; then no one, not a soul, had even approached it. To make a long story short, the Jew

* Edmond James de Rothschild (1845–1934), who donated large sums in support of early attempts at Jewish agricultural colonization in Palestine.

fell ill one day. Some said it was sunstroke (it was commonly held that there weren't any winters in Palestine, yet this was plainly not so, it being winter right now . . . in fact, he wished he had taken his other warm coat with him . . . but when the sun shone straight down, he had heard, it could kill you even in winter!), while others thought it was grass poisoning or a fever from drinking bad water. In any case, he lay unconscious on the floor of the mill for four whole days until finally an Arab came to grind meal and found him there. The Arab brought him in his wagon to Safed but it was already too late. They managed to revive him for one day only and now his remains were resting in the Safed cemetery. Indeed he, the Jew from Russia, had nearly seen this charming episode end with his own eyes, for when he arrived at the hospital that day for his treatment (he'd already been there once before for an irritation in his throat), the doctor was attending to the dying man.

A slight, barely visible, almost malicious smile hovered over the stranger's lips when he had finished speaking, the kind of smile that invariably seems to appear when one is relating someone else's misfortunes. Reb Yosef roused himself.

"Wait a minute," he said, turning to Yehezkel. "Isn't the mill where Hanoch works near Safed?"

"But what—!" The Jew from Russia was taken aback. "He's not a relation of yours, is he?" All Jews, after all, were related. In any case, he apologized for having been the one to break the news. Not that he was to blame for it . . . he hadn't meant any harm . . . anyhow, how could they be sure there was only one mill in the Galilee? It hardly seemed possible. . . .

"Shhhh!" Yehezkel broke off the conversation. In the distance he had spied the bereaved father on his way back from the post office.

He hurriedly rose and showed the stranger the way to the ticket agency. He should go straight ahead, on through the Russian Compound.* That is, if they let him pass there. Sometimes Jews weren't allowed to go through.

All the Jew's senses rose in rebellion. "*I* shouldn't be allowed to go where I please in the Land of Israel?"

"Of course, of course, only why make a fuss? . . . "

Haim returned from the post office. Lord! There wasn't any letter. But he would ask Yehezkel to sit down today and write again to his son. The mail went out tomorrow . . . it was all so complicated . . . it had never happened before that Hanoch hadn't written for so long. Yes, he would suggest to him that now that Goldmann's daughter was about to embark on her "grand tour" with Hamilin, perhaps he would like to spend a few days with his son in Jerusalem, as he had always dreamed of doing.

The week that followed was one of preparations and departures. On Friday Henya Goldmann and her uncle, Hamilin, were scheduled to leave for Jaffa, where they would board a ship for Beirut that sailed the next day, while Mister Bassin's party was to set out on Sunday for America, as was reported by the local Hebrew paper in an article headlined "Young Folk to Depart Permanently for America, Eight Men and Women in the Prime of Life" and preceded by an editorial entitled "Jerusalem Depopulated!" To be fully accurate, however, it should have been observed that the party of eight included an octogenarian couple as well, which was not bound for America at all but for England—and not permanently either, but with every intention of returning to die in Jeru-

---

* An area outside of the old walled city of Jerusalem owned by the Russian Orthodox church and containing a cathedral and a hospice for Russian pilgrims.

salem, the old pair having merely been stricken with longing for their children in Manchester, all the more so because life had become unbearable for them in their tiny apartment, which was infected with bedbugs, that eleventh plague not mentioned in the Bible that kept them regularly sitting up every evening past midnight yawning with boredom and thinking of their children and the spacious "flat" in which they lived. During their two years in Jerusalem, in fact, there hadn't been a night, with the exception of Sabbath eves, when they hadn't risen from their beds within an hour of retiring to comb the pillows and pillow cases by candlelight for their bloodthirsty tormentors. Now, once and for all, they had made up their minds to travel to Manchester "for a spell." It was in this manner that they had come to join Mister Bassin's party of "young folk."

A great crowd of relatives turned out to say good-bye to the travelers on the morning of their departure. The farewells, sobs and wails, and last-minute instructions and directions alternately rose above and sank below the din of the station. Mister Bassin's wealthy wife's entire family came out as far as the train, among them a flock of young girls in their colorful best. (Since the day was a Sunday, they had simply folded their Sabbath dresses neatly up the night before and left them out for the morrow instead of putting them back in their wooden chests.) What a delight to the eyes they were, these lovelies of Jerusalem, their sharp noses rosily blooming on flushed faces still webbed with sleep! Between shouts and snatches of advice, the members of the other clans stood whispering about the Bassins:

"It's not as though Jerusalem were a bad place to live when you've got a fat share of the dole. Who needs to have his throat cut in America? She was a fool to have married a man from the Volyhnian charity in the first place!"

Mister Bassin's old mother was present too. She stood trembling to one side like a peasant in city streets for the first time in her life, while a single worry flickered in her burned-out brain, from which the memory of her son's first trip abroad seemed unaccountably to have been erased: He was going away . . . she would be left all alone . . . and soon it would be time for . . . wait a minute . . . Nisan . . . Tammuz . . . the nine fast days of Av when no one ate meat . . . what would she do then? * There would be no work for her . . . she could spend all day in bed . . . the whole week long . . . but she wouldn't earn a penny either. Last year too she had gone without help . . . her son had married into another charity . . . now he was going away . . . what would she do during the nine days when she couldn't earn her keep? There would be no "cuts"—what was she going to do?

Miriam was not at the station; she was not going to America; she was preparing to depart in a few days for Jaffa, as soon as her father left for Tiberias.

Yes, Reb Yosef was off to Tiberias to take the waters— and on Hamilin's prescription. The "examination" had taken place by pure accident, Goldmann having suggested to his brother-in-law that in his capacity as a physician he might be interested in inspecting the rooms that had been set aside for the modern Orthodox school and passing on their hygienic fitness. (The decision to allot the rooms to the school had fully justified itself in recent days, for new arrivals in Jerusalem had all but ceased, so that the guesthouse was able

* Nisan, Tammuz, Av—the Hebrew months corresponding roughly to April, July and August. The Ninth of Av is a fast day commemorating the destruction of the Temple and as a sign of mourning orthodox Jews refrain from eating meat from the first of the month until then.

to make do with the two rooms below, especially since the old sexton and his family were leaving and the new sexton lived by himself.) Hamilin entered the apartment, glanced quickly at Miriam—who for some reason turned as pale as a ghost, though by no means an unattractive one—and then noticed her father, who lay groaning on his back, it being one of his bedridden days. *What was the matter with him?* The question was asked in an impersonal, doctorly tone, as though the two men had never set eyes on each other before, yet Reb Yosef was so intimidated that then and there the entire history of their past relations, imagined as well as real, slipped from his mind, and he answered in a German-sounding sentence: *"Ich kann nicht gewaltigen . . .* control *. . . mit meinem Fuss."* * Needless to say, Hamilin did not even smile. After a moment's debate whether to offer advice without being asked, much less promised a fee, he casually let slip the remark that according to the medical journals the hot springs in Tiberias were recommended for Reb Yosef's complaint, so that Miriam, whose pallor had turned in the meantime to a fiery blush, suddenly concluded that there was no reason to be so afraid. Though the prideful, energetic line of her upper lip had as though been broken and cracked by the news about Henya and Hamilin, her lower lip now dimpled prettily: the young doctor was frightening only from a distance; up close he was not only charming, he was so easy to get along with! Haim, who as sexton had brought up the rear behind Goldmann and the doctor, declared encouragingly to his brother:

"Go, Yosef. Listen to the doctor and go. It's not far from Safed. You may hear something there about Hanoch . . . and of course you'll let me know. . . . "

Esther too was at home at the time, for most of the work for Madame Hamilin, as she had taken to calling Goldmann's

* Broken German: I have no control over my foot.

daughter, had by now been finished, and the remaining odds and ends were in the hands of the assistants. Upon hearing the expedition to Tiberias being urged on her father, however, she suddenly rushed from the house without stopping to put on a hat and went off to look for Yehezkel in his room. He wasn't there. In recent days it had been impossible to find him at home. A person might think he'd been called by the army to judge by the way he was hiding!

And Yehezkel Hefetz was hiding, hiding quite openly, though whenever the two of them met by chance he sought nonetheless, with his last ounce of nervous strength, to conceal the reason for his behavior, that is, the terrible sense of loathing that had lately taken hold of him like an evil demon which he fought in vain to expel.

In itself this loathing had nothing to do with his conflict over the two sisters. That, in fact, though it had tormented him frightfully at one time despite his best efforts to reason with himself, had now abated and all but disappeared of itself. This latest phase in his relations with Esther had an entirely different origin.

Yes, the conflict was over with; it had preceded his involvement with Miriam but the two had vanished together; yet the hour of liberation had not yet come.

Because the conflict did not start with Miriam. As far back as his moments of clarity in the hospital, of which there had been not a few, he had thought each time he saw Esther in her nurse's uniform: *Not so long ago it was you who stretched out your arms to that slender-necked girl and were spurned; now her arms are stretched out to you, lost soul that you are and you spurn her. . . .* It was only later, after his release, while he was on his way to recovery, that he'd begun to take notice of Miriam, which had caused him to feel thoroughly vile and ashamed of himself. *At a time like this,* he had asked himself, *when that tortured, tossed-about woman, who would do so much for you if she could, who thinks only of you, is in agony before you, you dare dream of being happy with her sister, who is merely the same child all over again in a new metamorphosis?*

Of course, he could always excuse himself by replying, *But it's not as though I'm asking anything for myself!* He could always feel less guilty for Esther's unhappiness by thinking of his own. He was no better off than she! They were both in the same boat! Or again, whenever he would be driven to distraction by Miriam's certain indifference, he could think of Esther and console himself: *You're not the only one, you know! What makes her blood any less red than yours? You reach out and are rejected? She reaches out and is rejected too . . . and by you. It's a cruel world. Nature is pitiless . . . it tramples everything like a rogue bull. Why should you be spared if you too trample on her with what nature you have left when she throws herself at your feet? Yes, you: who won't stoop to carry her in her misery on your crooked back; who go on smacking your lips when you see her fainting with hunger. . . .*

He'd struggled with it terribly; sometimes it had seemed to him that even at death's door people like himself were never set free. Yet meanwhile he grew healthier; a brief spell passed, or perhaps a long one—*who was to say?*—in which he'd been gloriously happy like one returned from the dead, from across the border, to kiss the soil of earth once more; and then the wheel had come around again . . . after which, the conflict revived, proceeded to a climax, then vaporized and vanished yet again. The course that it followed reminded him of his teen-age passions, which had also appeared without warning, gathered strength, proceeded to a climax and begun at once to fade away. And here too, of course, Miriam's infatuation with Hamilin had helped hasten things along. At first, it was true, he'd felt he was living in a nightmare, but almost immediately after, he began to forget her. Yes, strange though it may have seemed to the science of psychology, which teaches that jealousy inflames love the more, this was exactly what had happened.

Psychology! Hefetz recalled how then too, during the episode of the widow's daughter, his jealousy had not made him desire her more; on the contrary, he had let himself be convinced by it that he was never really attracted to her in the first place, that he could not possibly love her in the accepted sense of the word; for while love seemed to inspire others with a prideful and conquering ambition, to him it was nothing more than a self-tormenting game. The more he considered it in this light, the surer of it he became. Whenever he'd found himself in the position of being a "lover," his first concern had always been to ask: Was he truly in love? Wasn't he deluding both himself and her by telling her that? At that very moment, didn't his real interests lie elsewhere? And the most tormenting thought of all had been: *How can I say that I really love her, that I can't live without her, when I've lived without her all my life? Not only that, I can remember a time when she didn't even affect me; how do I know, then, that I haven't just talked myself into it, that I don't care for her only because I've willed it?* Yes, what mattered most were his own feelings; whether she loved him, what she thought of him —all this was of the second, if not the third, account; it was as though at bottom it made no difference, it being useless to expect her to love him in any case. What could a mere child know about love? And so when she'd left him for another, he'd felt hurt, of course, but his disillusion had not been great. In the same way that he had been attracted to her in the first place, so he thought neither more nor less of her because of the new situation.

Whereas this time he suffered above all because he was

made to think less of Miriam. Yes, when the inevitable happened this time, what he regretted most was the fact that
she'd tarnished herself, that she, or rather his passing dreams
of her being different, full of a special vitality, not just a
woman but a person in her own right, had been blasted forever. True, his feelings for her during those few days of
health and happiness had been totally, absolutely uncondi-
tional; yet after this, his second encounter with Hamilin, he'd
had the strength to understand for the first time in his life that
this was nature's trodden, its only path. The male of the species
instinctively strove to give, the female to take. A simple
mechanical matter of give and take! And it was only natural
that the bank with the greatest assets should draw the most
customers. More fantasies about the future were worthless in
business; they only counted against you, in the business of
bodies as well. Why should a member of the weaker sex take
up with a man on credit? Why be involved in anything so
problematic?

Yet perhaps he was wrong now too. However one looked
at it . . . perhaps . . . though in any case, it wasn't—no,
it wasn't on account of Miriam that he, Hefetz, had lately
been avoiding Esther. . . .

That conflict *was* over with; the episode with Miriam had
come to an end; yet the hour of liberation had not arrived;
the fear remained as before.

He was afraid that if they should happen to meet, if he
should happen to be alone with her even for a minute, long
enough for her to seize his hand, he would not leave her again
before saying, "Esther, marry me, if that's what you
want. . . . "

He hadn't spent half a year in the house on the outskirts of
town for nothing.

Not for nothing had he come to realize—it was all so clear

to him now!—that there was no such thing as love; what difference did it make, then, if he could not reciprocate the unreal emotions that she felt? Why let it be an obstacle? They could proceed just as well without such figments of the imagination. And she would be better off married to him, really she would; better off anyhow than she was now.

But was this what Hefetz wanted? He was filled with a great, a horrible loathing for it all, the living proof of his damnation. Whenever he thought of her, he wanted to kick out with his last legs. And the thought of this repelled him. He longed to kick out—and was repelled. To kick out! How repulsive! And so he avoided her.

❦ *Part Three*

I

On the moon-bleached rocks across from the Hotel Harel, Goldmann's party continued to be talked about long after it took place. The School of Kahanowitz and the School of Shneirson took opposite points of view. The pessimists of the first group grumbled morosely that festivities of any sort were falsifications of reality, which was why the sages of the Talmud had declared: "In the time of the Messiah all Feast Days will be abolished." All the more so then in the Palestine of today, where conditions were anything but messianic, so that such fetes were the ultimate in sham, hypocrisy, pretentiousness! For example? But what better example could there be than this latest affair that Goldmann had dreamt up?

The optimists on the other side, however, took exception. Life, they insisted, existed only for its celebrations; the latter were the crowning apex of the everyday; they bolstered the morale of the masses, gave them the courage to bear up under hardship and vicissitude, etc., etc. For example? Why, Goldmann's grand public party, which had turned out so splendidly. . . .

Thus held the School of Shneirson.

In point of fact, of course, here too, as in everything else that he did, Goldmann had had nothing more complicated in mind than his own calculations, which, when they weren't being frustrated by "backbiters," "troublemakers," "double-crossers" or competitors who outdid him, never failed to press home invincibly against all odds. He knew one thing only, which was written in the appeals that he personally sent forth to the far ends of Africa, Australia and Canada, namely, that his sacred institutions ("which have been modernized and reorganized to conform to the spirit of the times," as he was careful to insert in the proper place) were "in dire need of support to help meet their extensive commitments." Even when it came to the minor matter of his divorced-daughter-bride-to-be's farewell party, therefore, he mulled it over and over as though it were of vital significance and finally decided to convert the entire affair into a ceremonial banquet presided over by himself. The "program" would be identical in any case: there would still be the same number of guests who had to be invited, the same cakes and sweetmeats, the same wines and fruits of the Holy Land which were listed as far back as the Bible. Nothing would have to be changed but the pretext for the occasion; yet the latter, Goldmann knew, was all-important, for a few lines in the "About Jerusalem" column of the local paper stating that *a ceremonial banquet was held last night in honor of ——— in the home of the well-known public benefactor, his excellency Yakov Goldmann, Chairman of the Board of the General Guesthouse and of the Academy for Torah and Universal Studies* would certainly do no harm, especially if picked up by the foreign press. The only question was—in honor of what? Why a ceremonial banquet? Reb Yakov's first thought had been to announce the formal completion of a study round of all six tractates of the Mishnah; * yet as this artifice, excellent though it was, was

* The Mishnah—The main rabbinic commentary on the Bible, comprising the first half of the Talmud.

bound to lead to an excess of scholarly talk at the table, which would spoil the good fun and the family nature of the event, he was forced to put it aside for another time and occasion. Meanwhile, seeing that her father could be made to back down, Henya, the feature attraction of the evening, began to raise the roof: how dare anyone turn her private affair into a ceremonial banquet to which she couldn't even invite all her female friends, whose eyes she had planned to make "pop right out of their heads"! Goldmann struck the table with his little fist and told her to be still; screaming and swearing, however, the bride-to-be tearily insisted that she would have nothing more to do with it. She would call off the whole *tsunoyprufenish!* * She too had a right to be heard!

Here Goldmann's wife intervened in a tremulous voice to remark that her husband was right; the dinner could no longer be canceled because preparations had already been made; father and daughter, however, could agree to a compromise; Henya could entertain her guests at home, while Goldmann could give his banquet in the hall of the guesthouse. Despite the fact that it came from his wife, the suggestion pleased Goldmann greatly. He reached for his dust-covered volume of the Mishnah, hurriedly glanced at the final page of the sixth and final tractate, lapsed into thought for a moment and suddenly had an idea: he would embellish the occasion, or rather his half of it, by dedicating a new Torah scroll in the little chapel on the guesthouse's top floor where Reb Yosef Hefetz's old apartment had been! Once there was a second scroll it would no longer be just a chapel but—*why not indeed?*—a full-fledged little synagogue. In fact, Reb Yakov already had such a scroll at home, which would help save further and intolerable expenses, so that it only remained to dedicate it properly with a procession and all. There would have to be a

* Yiddish: affair.

bridal canopy for the Torah, he reminded himself, and the press mustn't pass over it in silence. *A new Torah scroll was recently added to the synagogue of The Academy of Torah and Universal Studies amid much pomp and splendor thanks to the beneficence of the esteemed Chairman of the Board, Reb Yakov Goldmann.* No, *it* certainly would do no harm.

The night of the banquet was a moonless night; above and below, all was a single mass of darkness; only directly over the canopy, which rode high on four stilts, did the gloom seem to lift a little. Goldmann strode under it with the Torah in his arms from his home to the guesthouse, his sparse goatee scraping against the jacket of the scroll; in his Sabbath best, by the light of the candles around him, he looked a picture of wrathful zeal for the honor of the Law. A drum and cymbals went before him, but the procession itself was not large: the crowd was led by the boarders of the Harel, while the owner's daughter's fiancé and two disreputable ladies who had recently taken rooms in the hotel brought up the rear. The owner himself was present too; despite the festive nature of the occasion, however, he spoke only of his own depressing *idée fixe*, the frightful costliness of life in Jerusalem, repeating over and over: "I tell you, I know from experience. I tell you, I know from experience." Two Arabs and a Greek who had been spurring their mules down the street were caught in the procession as well and rode slowly along flanking the two ladies, who walked with their arms linked together. (In the "press" the next day it was reported that both Jewish and non-Jewish horsemen rode together in the lavish parade and fired off volleys of rifle shots in tribute.) A small band of Jerusalem's "golden youth," the pale, sleek-faced sons of the sextons and officials of the richer charities, stood to one side in their bright, dandyish caftans; a few of these young worthies held hands like Arab street waifs, fingers intertwined, while their married companions lounged about with the self-satisfied air of the assuredly wealthy and wise. A shiftless Jew passing in the other direction suddenly caught their attention. Beckoning him over, they plucked at him, prodded him and made him the butt of their joke. *Look over there . . . did he see that large empty lot? It belonged to some Frenchman . . . and last night a telegram had arrived—a telegram, did he hear? —appointing him its exclusive agent. Well? What did he say? Did he accept?* The Jew shuffled his feet and sought to escape, to stop his ears, but his tormentors laughingly pursued him until they made his head reel and honestly believed that they had succeeded in taking him in. The fool didn't know his right hand from his left! He could be made to believe anything! How superior they were. . . .

Around the long table in the guesthouse, which was laid with sweets and wine, the boarders of the Harel again took their place at the head. (The more important local residents had already sat down to eat with Goldmann's mother in Reb Yakov's home.) The guests comprised a motley collection of tourists and would-be investors from abroad, moneylenders and speculators, businessmen in unidentifiable professions, unemployed philosophers, women without husbands and aged tycoons on the lookout for nubile young brides. Among the more prominent faces (for even the two lady boarders had managed to get halfway through the door) was the hotel owner's daughter's fiancé, a quick-witted young man from Johannesburg, who in spite of his unknown character had conquered every heart in Jerusalem with his reputation for being "loaded" with money. Present too was his mortal rival, Zeydl the hunchback. Zeydl, who was not a bad-looking chap except for his glassy eyes and the hump on his back, had come to Jerusalem direct from the Transvaal for the purpose of making a match. For success he had counted on his own pounds sterling and the poverty of Jerusalem's young belles, who were desperate to find a rich husband—yet all to no avail; the reason for this being, according to the matchmakers, his insane refusal to reveal to anyone the exact extent of his fortune. Not that Zeydl didn't realize full well that in the end it all boiled down to his money; yet a stubborn something in his glassy eyes kept insisting that his future wife choose him not for his wealth but for himself alone and that she be sensitive enough to overlook his hump and to say: *It's you I want, Zeydl! I want you for your truthfulness, for your honesty!* To be totally truthful and honest, of course, would have required him to have hidden his wealth completely, only this was out of the question, for then no young lady would have consented to consider him at all, as was amply demonstrated by his attempts to arrange a rendezvous with the owner of the Harel's daughter. And so reluctantly he confessed that he did indeed have money . . . he wasn't like the Johannesburgian with his empty boasts . . . yes, he, Zeydl, had money . . . *What? How much? No, no . . . he wasn't the Johannesburgian . . . he wasn't an empty boaster . . . money there was . . . yet not as much as all that . . . he wouldn't say . . . he refused to reveal the whole sum* . . . and precisely this refusal was his downfall. Meanwhile he sat at the banquet table halfheartedly rejoicing in the dedication of the Scroll of the Law.

The sight of so many familiar faces inspired the eldest of the boarders of the Harel, a naturalized citizen of the hotel who was still going strong despite his more than seventy years and had in fact been offered a "good adjustment" only a few weeks before by the one-eyed matchmakeress in the person of a parentless young girl prematurely released from the orphanage. Banging ferociously on the table with his ruddy fist like a beadle silencing a congregation, he began to deliver an unsolicited address on some problems of the day, taking his cue from the words in the *alenu* prayer,* "Who hath not made us like the Gentiles of the Nations nor placed us among the Families of Earth." Why, he asked, did the prayer have to repeat the same idea twice in different words? Clearly, in order to explain why other peoples had vanished into extinction while Israel alone remained mighty and imperishable in its Holy Law! (Here the speaker cast an angry look at the two lady boarders who were loitering by the door.) And why had this happened? Because God hadn't made Israel like so much sand to be sifted as he had the Families of Earth, which were bound to the soil like creeping, crawling things. No, the Gentiles couldn't live without the earth . . . they died for it and perished . . . and why? Because Israel wasn't placed among them! In other words, because they weren't given Israel's portion, the holy Torah, so that they remained the crude, illiterate boors they always had been, while Israel, praise God, became His chosen people whose sole employment it was to rejoice and delight in the delights of His Law. . . .

The preacher concluded in a commanding and by no means elderly voice and resumed his seat, his eyes glistening about him with vitality and fierce pride. His triumph, in fact, would have been complete had it not provoked the envy of the Harel's other learned boarder, the Jew who had been looking for the ticket agency two days before, and who now revealed himself to be an excellent orator and a most ardent Lover of Zion. Recalling in a flash the words of the great Zyslansky at the dinner given for the two *Pionieren* from his native town who were departing for the Land of their Fathers (now, alas, he had looked for them in all the settlements, because he had wished to ask their advice, and hadn't been able to find

* The concluding prayer of the daily service.

them), he jumped on the bench without further ado and began to declaim in a powerful voice, directing the burden of his remarks to the crowd of young idlers surrounding the hotel owner's daughter's fiancé:

"Blessed are ye, O ye pioneers, ye heroes of Israel, whose good fortune it has been to dedicate your lives to our Faith, our Law and the Land of our God! I too have come here. . . . Later I will read you the letter. . . . But not everyone is chosen. . . . Not everyone has the . . . ah . . . good fortune. . . . Yet ye who cling to our sacred ideal—ye have carved an eternal place for yourselves in the blood-red history of our people. . . . "

The speaker looked confusedly about with his blood-red eyes and realized with a shudder that he had forgotten the rest of his speech, that he had nothing more to say in any case . . . and that what he had said so far had failed to accomplish its mission or arouse the slightest enthusiasm or applause. Cold sweat broke out on his forehead. Suddenly a fresh beginning crossed his mind and he snatched at it as though at a lifeline:

"Because of you, er, er . . . because of you, ye pioneers of Israel, the tongues of our enemies and abusers, who slander us by day and by night, shall be silenced forever. . . . 'For the poison of the viper and the asp'—is that the Jew cares only for business, er, er . . . "

"Enough! Enough! We're none of your *Zionisten!*" His rival, speaker number one, sought to shout him down.

Other voices mercilessly joined in. "Enough! Enough!"

Seeing he was hopelessly outnumbered, the Jew lost heart and descended from the bench. His agitation, however, refused to die down, so that some time later, when the guests began to depart, having consumed everything on the table and finished looking in vain for more, he still went about muttering aloud that he had not been permitted to speak and ultimately succeeded in getting Shneirson and Kahanowitz to listen to the full version of his letter to the Odessa office for the third or fourth time "Typical, typical!" Shneirson observed in his fashion with indefatigable pleasure after every sentence, while the Jew read on and on: "Whereas the situation of our brethren in Russia in general, and my own situation in particular, is exceedingly grave, yea, even unto 'chaos, disorder and the shadow of death'; and whereas the wickedness of the Gentiles who oppress us has surpassed all bounds, so that there is no longer the least hope of self-advancement; therefore, in these days of darkness, the desire has awakened amongst us to set out for the Land of Israel; and the fire burning within us has sent forth a fierce new flame to put an end to the long night of our Exile, wherein our lives hang in the balance; wherefore I have resolved to dedicate my life to our People in distress and to labor with all my might for the Country of our Lord, and to set out for the Holy Land, the Land of our Fathers. . . . "

"Set out?" interrupted the hotel owner's fiancé, striking himself on the neck. "Ai, the bastard! He already wanted to set out yesterday and stayed only for the banquet!"

The Jew, however, appeared not to hear. He was completely absorbed with proclaiming that, "Behold, when the great and illustrious Zyslansky was in our midst and counseled us to set out, then did the long-smoldering fire burst forth within us; for he gave us to understand that beyond devoting ourselves to the general good it would not be impossible to improve our position in life through our own labors by the acquisition of a *Kolonie*, to wit, a parcel of land; so that two of our youngsters, the first among their peers, are already setting out and will soon be followed by many men of means who are waiting only for them to depart. . . ."

On the rocks the next day Shneirson recounted all the details of his "liberation" from this insufferable "character"— a liberation, he was glad to say, which came about accidentally and from an unexpected source. Just then Goldmann had stepped into his house to see whether all was in order and whether the time hadn't come to call the party to a close and put out all the lights—and it was at this point that the "incident" with Haim the Sexton took place. It wasn't a very great incident, to be sure, but it turned things in a different direction and freed Shneirson from the clutches of the haranguing Jew.

Haim, who had of course been swamped with work in recent days, was feeling terribly tired and weak, so that having downed a single glass of wine in honor of the occasion, he immediately found himself "drunken and uncovered," as the Bible says of Noah. True, the Holy Writ then adds "within his tent," which Haim was not, but in any case, the moment he spied Goldmann he fell on him importunely:

"In-law! The devil take it! We have a bridal canopy . . . we have musicians . . . lord! Why not a wedding too? You can kill two birds with one stone. A wedding for my son Hanoch's wife . . . in-law! The devil take it. . . . "

"Go to sleep!" ordered the Chairman of the Board, much taken aback.

"A canopy for my daughter—for my *reinigkeit*—and for your daughter too," mumbled the drunken man. "See, he's throwing me out . . . go right ahead . . . and it's still not enough . . . Yosef's been deported down below too . . . therefore, wherefore do I live . . ."

"There's no room here for outsiders," Goldmann declared.

"Outsiders, in-law? Ai, the devil take it! There are no outsiders, in-law. We're all related to each other, we're all in-laws. . . . "

And he fell upon the Lover of Zion and began to embrace him too.

"You come too, my friend. Come to the shelter . . . come see the miracle. It's just like the miracle of the pilgrims in the courtyard of the Temple: *shoulder to shoulder standing there, they bowed to the ground with room to spare* . . . lord! Come to the shelter, my friend . . . here's where we belong . . . there's room here for all of us. . . . "

"And all that from just one glass! He certainly can't hold his liquor . . . what a character!"

With this Shneirson concluded his review on the rocks the next day.

A remarkable change come over Reb Yosef from the moment he moved downstairs to live, or rather "to abide," in the guesthouse below—and not for the better, either. The same man who as recently as the day of Hamilin's visit, when he had been urged to take the cure in Tiberias, had treated both himself and his visitors to an insightful new interpretation of the well-known passage in the Talmud about the mysteries of "that which is above and that which is below" seemed to have withdrawn into an almost total, insightless, interpretationless silence, while his streak of religiosity, which had previously coexisted side by side with his tendency to free thought, now obtained the upper hand. He spent more and more time in his morning, afternoon and evening devotions, while instead of the philosophical *Book of the Kuzari,* which had been his constant companion during his last days upstairs, he had taken to reading the Hasidic wonder tales and commentaries of the followers of the Baal Shem Tov.* His conversation, such as it was (to say nothing, after all, was not always possible), grew

* Israel Baal Shem Tov (1700–1760), founder of the Hasidic movement.

clipped and abrupt; whereas not long ago he had still liked to wander off on long or short digressions about the Holy Land, and to pass from there to his other favorite subject, the Holy Tongue, the mother of all languages, to which so much of his labors had been devoted (not that German too, which he had studied with the help of a "guide," wasn't a lovely language as well—here he would take out the Yiddish letters of his son in Kiev and proceed to read them out loud, Germanizing the words as he went along—yet it couldn't begin to compare with Hebrew, which was all sacredness, all logic, all beauty and grace!), he now preferred to dwell on the cabbalistic arcana concerning the time of the Redemption and the coming of the Messiah, though not with any mystical fervor or even imaginative intensity, but with a rationalistic naïvité, a kind of colorless simplicity that seemed to say: *All's one—yet why not?* After all, didn't it say in the Book of Daniel, "Shut up the words until the time of the end"? * And the numerical value of the letters in the Hebrew words "the time of the end" was six hundred and sixty! † In other words—until the six hundred and sixtieth year of the sixth and current millennium,‡ which was the Christian year nineteen hundred, such matters were not to be discussed. Thereafter, however, the Messiah could be expected yearly, so that whoever knew the secrets of his coming was permitted to divulge them. And there were those who knew! Yes, there were those who knew the time of the end.

"But why the six hundred and sixtieth year of *this* millen-

---

* Daniel 12:4.

† In rabbinic tradition each letter of the Hebrew alphabet bears a numerical equivalent, a fact frequently used for exegetical purposes.

‡ According to rabbinic legend, the life-span of the created universe is seven periods of one-thousand years each, the seventh and last being the age of the Messiah.

nium?" teased Shneirson with undisguised sarcasm. "From the six hundred and sixtieth year on—why, of course . . . the question is, though: of what millennium?"

"Of what millennium!" Reb Yosef addressed his brusque reply not to Shneirson but rather to his friend Kahanowitz. What a foolish question! Didn't everyone know that there were only six millennia? Could anyone seriously believe that the allusion could be to the six hundred and sixtieth year of the seventh millennium, that Sabbath-like aeon of rest and peace? Just to ask such a question, Reb Yosef concluded with a savage polemical thrust, one had to be living in the seventh millennium himself!

For some reason, however, despite Reb Yosef's barbed rejoinders, Shneirson seemed to enjoy calling on him in his new dwelling. Kahanowitz, who had recently joined the ranks of life's sufferers himself, having been turned down by the Teachers Institute as all but an auditor, had his own theory about the "psychological reasons" for his roommate's frequent visits to the guesthouse, which he bitterly expounded to the company on the rocks when Reb Yosef wasn't present and Herr Kauffmann held sway in his stead. The were meant, he explained, to keep anyone from saying that he, Shneirson, had called on Reb Yosef in the past only because of his daughter. Shneirson wanted to show that there had never been anything between him and Miriam in the first place. On his part, of course. In other words, it had never yet happened that a girl whom he cared for had rejected him. It simply wasn't true that he and Miriam had been a pair. The proof of it being that now that she'd left, he continued to see her father even more than before . . . no, not even more . . . just as frequently—for then too he'd come only to see Reb Yosef. . . .

Within the circle of few deeds and much talk to which he belonged, Kahanowitz's tongue had become more and more biting. Most of all, he liked to comment on the irony in human thought and behavior, and when not only Reb Yosef, but Shneirson too, was absent from the discussion, to dwell on the latter's latest romance. At still other times, though, he didn't hesitate to broach the subject subtly to Shneirson's face—yet only to broach it, for in the end he would always steer the allusion to some other, distinctly different anecdote, some story from another time and place, from his days in the Russian army, for example. . . .

(While Kahanowitz was in the army, he had once been assigned to assist his company commander, whose duty it was to open all mail written by the soldiers of his unit and either read it himself or have it read to him. The Yiddish letters were delivered to Kahanowitz, who had to translate them into Russian word for word:

> *With the Help of the Name* *
> *On this* ———————— *day from the Sabbath*
> *To my most honored, revered, illustrious and greatly*
> *learned father, etc., etc. . . .*

This officer had a mistress to whom he was totally in thrall, and once, when he suspected her of having betrayed him with another man, he got hold of a letter that she had received and read it without her permission. To make a long story short, the letter was perfectly blameless and the woman found out all about it. The way she made him get down on his knees and adoringly swallow his medicine for his "unspeakable vileness"! To read someone else's mail! How could he ever have done such a thing? And the way he begged her forgiveness, the way he groveled and pleaded with her to realize that he had done it only because he loved her and was jealous! Ah, the stories one could tell—the irony in human affairs!)

* The Hebrew phrase *be'ezrat ha-shem* (i.e., with God's help), with which letters are regularly commenced.

When Shneirson was not in attendance, however, Kahanowitz proceeded directly to bare all the hidden irony in this latter-day Don Juan. Recently, as everyone knew, after he had been stood up by the hotel owner's daughter (but this was another story), Shneirson had begun to chase after a certain Sephardic girl, an "exotic type," as he put it—though begging everyone's pardon, this too was another story, for the irony did not lie here. No, the irony lay elsewhere: this Sephardic girl, like all the Jews from the Levant who had dealings with the Ashkenazim of Eastern Europe, knew Yiddish perfectly well—as well as Shneirson, in fact. (Abroad every imbecile thought that the Jews in Palestine spoke Hebrew—this too was a story!) Yet despite the fact that she knew, and that Shneirson knew that she knew, and that she knew that Shneirson knew that she knew, and that Shneirson knew that she knew that he knew that she knew—nevertheless, he, Shneirson, and she, the exotic type of his dreams, pretended that . . . *What? They speak that jargon called Yiddish? The idea!* That is, they made believe that as representatives of the two halves of the Jewish people in the Holy Land they could communicate only in Hebrew:

—*Have a piece chocolate, have.*

—*Why 'cause it's good for me? I don't want none!*

—*So when was you going to your aunt already?*

—*I wasn't sleeping there. I was coming to here.*

—*You should only don't forget, I'll pick you up a quarter to nine, wherever you go, me too.*

—*You make me a little hurt and I give you a little kiss.*

In this charming fashion they could be heard conversing with each other in the Holy Tongue every evening. . . .

Of course one could hoist Kahanowitz by his own petard: wasn't it just as ironic of him to vary his story depending on whether Shneirson was present or not? But Herr Kauffmann, who had been terribly busy and "disorientated" as of late ("disorientated" was one of several *Termini** that he had recently come across in the dictionary and taken to using profusely), did not press the point. Where did one not find irony, after all? Besides which, Kahanowitz himself was the first to admit that he was full of contradictions. Take, for instance, the fact that he should never have agreed to be a nonmatriculating student and yet here he was auditing classes. Just try to figure it out!

Be it as it was, the episode of Shneirson and his Sephardic girl friend aroused the God-fearing Jew from East Prussia to touch on the problem of the contemporary lack of faith and its effect on morality. *Weh, weh,* the morals of the younger generation! They corrupted and disorientated the soul! Among all her peers he knew of but one righteous young lady, Herr Hefetz's older daughter, who was a truly modest, moral and not unintelligent woman. (Kahanowitz grimaced; he knew for a fact that no sooner had Herr Kauffmann learned that Esther had two hundred francs to her name than he'd begun to scheme of sending the one-eyed "adjustment-maker" to her, only in the meantime—no doubt because of his disorientation—he had failed to carry this through.) As for the younger daughter, though—*na,* this was something else again. The younger one, *sehen Sie,*† he couldn't make out at all. He, Herr Kauffmann, was rarely in accord with Herr Hefetz, but he agreed entirely with his decision not to say a word to his daughter in the days before her departure. Just as one was commanded to speak when one stood to be heard, so one was commanded not to when one didn't. She had not even come to bid her father good-bye—no doubt it suited her better. *Mit einem Wort, eine hysterische Person!* ‡ And what was to account for all this? Why, the younger genera-

---

* A Latin word used in German: terms.   † German: see here.
‡ German: in a word, a hysterical person!

tion's nonconfessional education, which was lacking the essential—*die Religion!* They learned sciences and what-not but the essential was lacking. They hadn't any understanding of the inner unity of phenomena and events, any knowledge of the identity of all substance, any of their forefathers' faith in Divine Providence. Yes, they were a hellbent lot, these youngsters of Jerusalem, God save and preserve us!

Reb Yosef arrived and sat listening in gloomy silence. Not long ago it would have been out of the question for him to have heard such a conversation and kept quiet. Then he would most certainly have felt obliged to display his knowledge of both rabbinic and philosophical sources; he would have made various invaluable comments on the question of faith and its relation to morality; he would have mentioned Spinoza's *Tractate*, which held that the Mosaic Law was a . . . constitution, and he would have pointed out that not faith but works was the mainstay of the Jewish religion. What greater belief did Judaism have than that in the resurrection of the dead, yet even this was mentioned nowhere in the Bible! Jewish law and Jewish morality were essentially concerned with justice, etc., etc., see such-and-such a page of such-and-such a book . . . whereas now he sat listening without a word. Why speak? It was clear enough that the words that had once been of value to him were no longer any use. The last chapter of his autobiography was simplicity itself. He'd had shining hopes: he would grow old in comfort . . . he would be genuinely, sincerely acknowledged . . . he would influence the younger generation in the spirit of true, unadulterated Judaism . . . he would disseminate unspurious opinions and correct ways of thought . . . yes, he had had great hopes before coming to Palestine! To begin with, of course, he'd had to live in anything but comfort—yet this in itself had not discouraged him; man did not live by comfort alone; he could get along on bread and water too if he had to. For a while the hope for honor and recognition had lingered on—only to vanish in the end too. Not only were there no suitable candidates to instruct in wisdom's ways, but he himself, God help him, had begun to be aware of a great impairment in his own mind, a drying up of inspiration. Yes, a hair's breadth had stood between him and religious collapse. It had happened on the day that he moved downstairs. A temporary weakness . . . all sorts of doubts had risen within him, and worse thoughts too. Thanks be to God, his Rock and Salvation, that he hadn't succumbed . . . but . . . but . . . what metaphor could express his situation? He had been like a little boy with a short-stringed kite which he wished to fly to great heights. The boy can climb a hill but this doesn't mean that his string has grown longer or that his kite has sprouted wings. The hill alone is high; the string is still short, the kite is but paper. Better to sit in solitary silence on the hilltop than to try to descend again. . . .

Reb Yosef kept silent. *For man knoweth not* . . . so began the last will and testament of the great Hatam Sofer, to which the Lev Ivri had written a commentary entitled *The Hebrew Heart.** For man knoweth not* . . . let him sit then in solitary silence.

Silent he sat by himself. His brother Haim was silent too, but he did not sit still: he cleaned the rooms, arranged the mattresses, tended the oil lamp, fetched water from the well— all without a word. Because of his dream he wasn't eating today (he'd dreamt that he dropped a Torah scroll and that Reb Yosef had advised him to fast a day in penance) but he

---

* Hatam Sofer—Moses Samuel Schreiber (1763–1839), German rabbi and scholar.

The Lev Ivri—the 19th-century rabbinical scholar Akiva Yosef ben Yehiel.

went on working and just didn't speak. Yes, he who was always so talkative, was silent now too; he let the argument rage around him without opening his mouth. Not only that, he seemed not even to hear. Yet even if he did hear who could say that he understood? The argument continued: *Judaism . . . justice . . . love of man . . . the law . . . beyond the law. . . .* What were they talking about? Human beings fled from heartache, they wanted to be happy—period! *Love?* Where was Henya's love for her husband? *The Law?* Where was the Law when Goldmann robbed him of his last possession? Last year, when the agent had informed them that it was still not too late to redeem Reb Yosef's books from the customs house—Yosef's books, which were his brother's life, literally his life, so that it would have been like ransoming a living soul!—he, Haim, fool that he was, couldn't get himself to sign over his security to Goldmann as the latter suggested and use the money for the books because—what an ass he had been!—it had seemed to him that he would be exchanging his scroll for something less sacred. In vain he had been reasoned with that Reb Yosef's Slovutian Talmud * was no less holy, that one could dedicate it in a synagogue just like a Torah. Not that he hadn't understood that a Talmud had great holiness, but he had refused to relinquish his scroll all the same. And now Goldmann had gone and donated it in his own name, as though it had always been his! *Justice. . . .*

The weakness brought on by his fast filled Haim with a strange longing; over and over his thoughts kept returning to his son Hanoch. Where was he? Why didn't he send word of himself? His heavy-tongued boy . . . heavy of tongue . . . yes, and heavy of eye too, as though he were looking at you from some deep, dark hole . . . heavy of tongue and heavy of

* A renowned edition of the Talmud printed in the Russian town of Slovuta.

eye . . . yet all this heaviness had been there only when he'd had to speak to his father-in-law, or to his wife, or to strangers, or to anyone important; with himself, with his father, with his own little boy, he had no trouble expressing what he felt. Once—or so Haim recollected—when Hanoch was in Jerusalem at the time of the divorce proceedings, Yosef had been holding forth as usual about how the Law in its wisdom taught that the single individual did not matter at all, but only the collective, Israel as a whole, and Hanoch, bless him, had stubbornly argued back:

"S-s-say w-what you w-w-will . . . what m-matters to m-me is myself."

They had talked about all kinds of ideas that day, just as they were talking today, except that then Yosef had spoken a great deal, and brilliantly at that. He had said—basing himself on the philosophers, of course—that the essential for Jews was not faith in God in itself, as it was for the Christians, who thought it sufficient merely to believe in Him, but rather the study of Him, theo-logy. Of course, the Bible asked in the Book of Job, "Wilt thou ever find knowledge of God?" But to this there could be no sure answer.

"W-well th-th-then, uncle," Hanoch had replied, "if the b-b-believer t-too doesn't know . . . wh-what d-difference does it make? I myself know nothing. I'm a man. I'm alive. It's hard for me to talk. But the Galilee . . . Jezreel . . . camels . . . who made all that? Do you know? God? Fine, God . . . b-b-but who's God? This w-way or that I don't understand it . . . this w-way or that it's b-b-beyond me . . . s-say that it's God . . . He made it . . . b-b-but wh-why did He make it the way He did? You're laughing . . . it's impossible to kn-know . . . fine, it's impossible—but it's n-not necessary, either . . . there's not . . . there isn't . . . there isn't any God. . . . "

"What? What are you saying?"

"I'm s-s-saying," Hanoch stammered, "I'm saying . . . that if God made all this . . . and if He made it so that I shouldn't know about Him—f-fine, then I don't know. B-b-but why did He make it so I sh-shouldn't know? And how d-do I know it was Him? And what difference does it make whether I say that He did or didn't? I'm asking you what difference . . . what difference does it make whether I pray to Him or not . . . will He listen to me if I do? Life is hard for those who b-b-believe and h-hard for those who don't . . . s-so why b-bother? If t-times are hard . . . I'll get by . . . I'll get by without Him. Wh-what? You want me to get on my knees and cry 'm-mercy'? It would be out of p-p-p-place. . . ."

Haim didn't recall that these were his son's exact words. Only the shadow of the conversation that day seemed to hover over him; he couldn't have actually thought of it in whole sentences like these. Unconsciously, he was terrified of the abyss that had opened beneath him. Now that he had seen that the ways of Providence were unfathomable, that good and evil were rewarded unfairly, that the wicked prospered and the just were made to suffer, his faith in God, in a personal heavenly father, no longer sustained him as before; nevertheless, he lived in terrible dread of being left without it; he dreaded the very possibility—dreaded it so that he refused to let himself, to permit himself, even to think of it. One simply didn't think of such things! Without God one couldn't take a single step, dress a single stone, plaster a single wall, carry a single bucket of water, lift a single sack of flour. (In recent days he had begun to think of leaving the sextonship and becoming a porter.) Without faith in God one couldn't breathe even for an instant! Yet something around him, something hovering in the air, something that reached all the way from there, the tedious mill where unknown to him his son Hanoch's life lay buried, to here, the "shelter" in Jerusalem where he and his kinfolk were wasting away, something seemed to grieve: *It isn't so . . . it isn't so at all . . . to breathe is truly impossible . . . but there's nothing to hold on to . . . only empty space . . . and nothing, nothing can ever fill it . . . there isn't any God. . . .*

II

Esther Hefetz tried Yehezkel. She put him to the test—and he failed and was found wanting.

The last time she had spoken to him had been in passing on the day of Mister Bassin's departure. He had said to her then: When a man thinks only of himself, when he sees only himself, and then only from his own point of view, it seems to him that his suffering is immense, that no tragedy can be worse than his, that the sky is about to cave in on top of him. Yet when his field of vision widens to take in the rest of the world, he grows smaller in his own eyes, and his unhappiness and bad luck grow smaller too.

After all that had passed between them, she thought to herself afterwards, to think that a man could be so stone-blind as to say such a thing! If he hadn't simply been talking at random (sometimes when he felt pressed against the wall he had a tendency to do just that), he could only have been telling her that she was too preoccupied with herself, that she should step out of her own petty ego into the world and not be so self-centered. She should have spit in his face for such talk! How could he not have been ashamed of himself? How could he not have turned red? Who was it who had sacrificed everything for him? Who had paid Miriam's way to Jaffa? He?

Yet his face, she recalled, which was the color of old, erased paper, hadn't turned red in the least. And he hadn't blushed the last time that she saw him either, the night of Goldmann's party, when she didn't say a word to him.

No, not a word. She had been one of the hostesses that night. At first she had pretended not to notice him and then —that she was busy. All the while she had waited for him to approach her. But he hadn't, not even to say hello, though he couldn't have not seen her.

She returned to the second-floor room that she had recently rented in a neighborhood far from Sha'arei Yehudah. Shattered and crushed, she debated with herself for hours and finally made up her mind to try one last experiment. She would not go out the next day and would see that word reached him that she was sick. Would he come?

He did not.

For the first two days that followed her only thought had been to shut out the harsh light of reality, to keep the actual history of their involvement from being brought into the open —to keep it not only from others but from herself as well. She still wanted her bit of romanticism, her little "tragedy of love": *Yes, she had loved one man, she had sacrificed all for him, but there had been obstacles in love's way, in the end she had been left all alone, eternally forsaken. . . .* That love should have been out of the question to begin with, however, that there had never been the slightest room for it—the consciousness of this frightened her more than anything, so that she sought to banish all traces of it with the last of her strength. No, it simply wasn't true! She *had* had a romance, a beautiful romance at that, only ah, what could be sadder than a romance that was over!

By the third day, however, she could hold it in no longer and brought it all out into the open herself. Abandoning the silence that had followed her despair, she began to hound her cousin's footsteps wherever she could, to gossip evilly about him in public, to tell all that she had heard about him from the doctor in the asylum—and some things that she hadn't as well. . . .

But this too did not last long. In the end she took to her bed in earnest. Curled like a fetus in its mother's womb, wrapped in worn blankets, she looked a symbol of deterioration and decay.

Yes, she must see him, she must talk with him, no matter what! The first day she could rise from her bed, the minute she could take her first step, she would seek him out, she would find him—and she would have it out with him. Not that she wished to complain, she would tell him. But why had he made believe? Why had he lied to her? Why had he made up to her only to throw her over? Oh, it was nothing that unusual for a man to make a promise of love in order to get what he wanted and then to go back on his word . . . but why had *he* lied?

Why had he lied? The question would undoubtedly have haunted the subject of it too, the teller of the lie himself, had he not meanwhile become involved in yet a new campaign of deception.

Hefetz had come to the decision that Haim must be shielded from the news of Hanoch's death. He mustn't be allowed to hear of it. In order to carry out this subterfuge, it would be necessary to manage things so that Haim would stay in Jerusalem, while he, Yehezkel, would travel to Tiberias with Reb Yosef, from where he would send the bereaved father money and mail as though they came from his son. Once there it would be easy enough to find someone to write letters to Jerusalem and sign them "Hanoch Hefetz."

A lie would stand in the breach. He would make good the loss with it.

He had conceived of this course of action while speaking to Esther about the difference beween those who saw only their own selves and those who saw the whole world. To himself then he'd added the familiar thought: *The whole world? Not really.* It was too much to ask of a man to change the whole world. At any rate, it was a task best left to those universal souls who were on familiar terms with the Whole of Life. He, who knew nothing about the whole, who was only a part himself sitting in his corner, would grope in that corner as best he could, would do what he could in it, wherever and however he could do it.

That same day he decided to try out his latest plan on Esther, to tell her: "Esther, your father has to go to Tiberias, and for your uncle's sake I have to go too. You come too . . . with me . . . we'll live there together . . . I'll find a job teaching children . . . you'll work too . . . we'll manage to get by. . . ."

But he couldn't bring himself to do it.

Suppose it were *her* life? he asked himself all day. That is, suppose someone were to come to him and say, *Which would you rather, that you marry this woman or that she die like Hanoch?*—surely he would marry her and snatch her from death's jaws! Wasn't it the Law of the Corner to treat those who needed you as though death were already upon them?

But he didn't go to her. He heard that she was sick or pretending—and he stayed away. His new plan was either not new enough or not strong enough to override the old objections.

Why do I feel such loathing? he appealed to himself. *Is it just because she's not whom I want—because she, of all people, she, the one woman who loves me, is not whom I want? Yet*

by herself, in herself . . . how can one loathe a person so?
Loathe her for what? Why, she's a living thing too, a human
being, a complete individual world with feelings of its own,
with other living things whom she cares for besides me. And
you, just because she isn't to your taste—you can actually let
yourself loathe her?

Ah well, he had tried to console himself, his "loves" were
never eternal, his "loathings" wouldn't be either.

But it did him no good. When he saw her on the night of
Goldmann's party, all rigged out and corseted together—as
one of the hostesses at the banquet she had felt obliged to dress
up and had even worn a red necktie around the folded white
collar of her blouse—he was stricken again by an unbearable
sense of nausea. The expression of her hands and face made him
think of some one-legged, many-clawed animal that had fallen
into a pit and could no longer fight its way out, though its
nails remained stuck in the dank, rotten walls as though struggling to recover and desperately refusing to admit that all was
over with. . . .

For three straight nights a lean, bedraggled chicken dressed
like a man but with Esther's hands perched on his head and
flapped about between his arms.

On the evening of the fourth night he went to see her and
turned back. He knew what she was saying about him in public. He knew that she was sick.

One morning a few days later he started out again. He
didn't get there this time because something else happened instead.

He strode toward the house where she lived with his mind
firmly made up to tell her: *Esther, this is how it is with me—*
now it's up to you to decide! Not that he was yet sure that he
had the right to do it or that he wouldn't change his mind at the
last minute, yet his determination increased with every step.

No more backing down! As he approached, he caught sight of her standing in her overcoat on the terrace that overlooked the street, a chamber pot in one hand, looking pained and forlorn like a patient venturing out for the first time after a long illness. (The pot must have stood in her room all night long, perhaps the day before too, without anyone to empty it.) Suddenly his confidence grew that he *did* have a right and that he *would* tell her. Yet curiously, when he nodded hello from a distance she didn't reply. Hadn't she seen him? Was she too weak to make him out? But no, she could see him perfectly well, she was even looking straight at him, as if trying to decide whether he had really come for her. (*After all this time* . . .) He greeted her again but still she stood impassively with the pot in her hand. What could be the matter? Feeling strangely, increasingly flustered, he dismissed the question from his mind and hurried to gain access to the doorway beneath the balcony so as not to block the path of her trajectory. But he was too late. The entire contents of the chamber pot had already landed on top of him. Covered with filth, he jumped back without looking up. He could feel that she hadn't yet moved from her place and that the poisonous pallor which had suffused her face a minute ago was still there. He knew that a person choking another to death must look just like that.

He slunk back to his room, wrung out his clothes and lay down in them while they were wet. Even the squeaking of the couch reminded him of the splatter of the slops. *Who needs you*, it seemed to say, *to hell with you!*—and this made him feel better. Yet in it he heard another voice too, like the groan she had groaned the time they had kissed, which now asked: *Why are you torturing me?* Then he grew deathly weary of it all . . . just as he had then . . . three-quarters of a year before . . . in his dream. . . .

It was clear to him now how guilty he'd been all along. As

never before he felt the full horror of the role he had played, realized the full extent of her humiliation at his hands (which was far, far worse than that inflicted on her by all the men who had simply never looked at her twice), was fully conscious of how sinful it had been to think that they could live together when he didn't really want her, knew the full anguish of being an utterly superfluous presence in the world. For the first time he accepted his sentence in full—no longer could there be the slightest extenuating circumstance. Lies! Lies! Words! Words! Suffering made no one any better. Happiness, pleasure, whatever was natural—these alone made one better. It was criminal to suffer, sinful, self-abasing. *Let's hear no more from you then, you wallower in slops! Let's hear no more about the lie that makes better and the right to lie, while you yourself keep running helplessly from the truth that hurts! It's not the whoremasters who are the great sinners . . . there's no such thing . . . it's you who are the sinner, you who are the whore. . . .*

Pity—is that what you want? But when did you ever pity her? A sense of pity is a natural thing in a natural man, but what could you know about that? What makes you think that you even have the ability to have pity? It's all been nothing but a hypocritical lie, nothing but your wanting to be good at her expense, nothing but . . . the devil knows what! She was never even a person to you, just a dry formula— which still didn't keep you from enjoying it when you kissed her. Yes, for a fraction of a second you actually enjoyed it, pitiful though it was—because it made you feel so virtuous. You who paraded your sexual weakness as a pity, a goodness, a sympathy that never existed: damn your soul!

As soon as it grew dark he fled the house to the far ends of the city, yet everything inside him continued to cry out: *Why don't they do away with me? Why do they let me walk around like this alive? Why don't they all realize how despicable I am?*

I? . . . You! You who haven't a sound bone in your aching body, who didn't have the courage to tell her right off and have done with it! She wouldn't have believed you? But why shouldn't she have? Why couldn't you have told her so that she would have? Why did you make up to her? Don't try to get around it, you rotter! You'd like to think that it was none of your doing, wouldn't you? That all the while she felt attracted to you she didn't believe in it herself? That each time you tried to tell the truth about yourself, she thought you were only making excuses? But you who aren't a man, you who never did and never could have loved her if only because you aren't a man, you who insist that the person she loves in you is purely imaginary—why couldn't you have made her get over you once and for all?

Forgiveness—is that what you want? But have you ever forgiven her? Have you forgiven her for not being to your taste? Life can forgive anything and everything—but a worm like you can be forgiven nothing, nothing! Because Life knows only too well . . . because Life sees and asks: "Where is the man who thinks he has seen the other, elysian side of me? Where is the bandier of fine phrases about "the germs of a newer, better existence?" Where is the happy soul that delights in sorrow-filled nights such as these when he walks by himself through the empty streets and his clothes aren't filthy and wet? Where is he who has known the moments when I and my double, Death, kiss and make up? Surely no harm can come to humankind from such a happy worm as thou! But if it could—would!—then the sin and the slops-bucket be on thy head!

"I know thee, worm that thou art!" the voice pursued him further. *"Thou wrigglest most like a worm . . . thou speak-*

est of thy selflessness, thou makest a show of thy purity, thy righteousness, thy benevolence, thy compassion . . . accursed be thy obdurate, weak and contemptible lie . . . on thy knees before Hamilin!"

At midnight Hefetz knocked on the window of the guest-house chapel, woke up Haim the sexton and told him what he knew about his son Hanoch. An end to concealment and deception! An end to lies! Let Haim know everything. Let him come to Tiberias too.

III

Miriam sent a postcard from Jaffa to Jerusalem—to Yehez-kel Hefetz. It was the first letter she had written in her life (she had never sent more than regards to her brother in Russia), and it cost her no little effort, but she hadn't any choice. The money that Esther had given her was about to run out. What would happen when it was gone? She didn't know. She knew only that she must do something, must begin to study—afterwards let come what may. But how did one begin? Her room (she had been recommended to the land-lady by her friend in Jerusalem) was a shambles, yet she never thought of tidying up. In the first place, it wasn't hers, she was only staying in it; and secondly, she hadn't come to Jaffa to spend her time cleaning. She had to study. Only how could a person study if she couldn't even afford her own room?

She put the letter down abruptly and stepped outside. The stretch of sand in front of the house was deserted. Though the sun was already beginning to set, two or three women still sat motionless on the far slope under open parasols. Were they Jewesses or Arabs? It was hard to tell. Either way, they were the same inanimate shapes.

The sky was inanimate too. Looking at it, Miriam thought of the art student in Jerusalem with the suffering eyes who had liked to walk with her and talk about the changing colors in the sky. All the different hues. One after another: gray, blue, *fiolette*. What was *fiolette?*

But the student wasn't here now. Zeydl the hunchback sat on the front steps instead and stared at her like a cat at butter. A shudder of disgust passed over her at the thought that he wished to approach her. She hurried to the seashore, which was not far away. Arabs lolled on the dunes and looked sharply at the young lady who was walking by herself. A ship was setting sail for Europe, but she, Miriam, didn't ask who was on it, met no one to ask. Zeydl was there, someone else was here. The ship was on its way? Bon voyage. To Beirut? Let it be to Beirut. What was it to her? *She* had to study and she was all alone in the world.

Her mouth seemed to hang slightly open, an expression it had noticeably acquired ever since the day of his engagement party.

His engagement . . . now he was in Lebanon again . . . it was as though he had never existed. . . .

Even while he'd still been in Jerusalem, toward the end of his stay there, she had begun to seek out Shneirson again. How she would have liked to speak with him now, to return to the days when she used to ask him all sorts of questions about history and the Bible! Yet when she thought of her friend in the hotel, or of that long-lashed Sephardic ninny—no, she wanted no part of it . . . no part . . . what was it to her? She must do something for herself. Yes, her path was laid out: she must study, study all the time!

She felt suddenly bewildered, as in the time in her dream when she had entered Hamilin's room in the Hotel Harel without permission. Now too, just as then, she ran straight home. Side-stepping Zeydl, she passed quickly inside. The mirror on the wall revealed to her how her eyes had lost their old luster.

Her landlady, the brokeress from Neveh Shalom,* greeted her with news. She had found a job for her with a young couple, both of whom were teachers in the same school. They had no children, took their lunch in the school cafeteria and were away from home all day long, but someone was needed to look after their large apartment, to clean up every morning and to fix them breakfast and dinner.

Miriam would have been only too happy to accept—fifteen francs a month and teachers for employers!—if only she could have been sure that no one would find out. The work would certainly not be too demanding, just a few hours each morning and evening, but technically she would still be a servant and she refused to be thought of as such. What was she to do?

If she were to turn it down . . . Her landlady was candid: if she were to turn it down, her only alternative would be to go to work in an embroidery shop, where for the first few months she would be lucky to earn four bishliks a week. As if anyone could live on four bishliks! And the work was ten hours a day—what would become of her studies?

She must decide. But there was no one to tell her how.

Yes, she needed advice. She picked up her postcard to Yehezkel.

She wrote in a faulty Yiddish, indiscriminately studded with Hebrew words, without proper spelling, punctuation or the like. *Herr Yehezkel Hefetz*, she wrote, *esteemed cousin!* He would no doubt be surprised to receive her letter and would want to know what mysterious person was disturbing his rest; but he need only regard her signature at the bottom to know that it was she, his cousin Miriam. She knew him to be a true friend of the family, a man "with a heart of gold," and

* One of the first Jewish settlements north of Jaffa in the area that later became Tel Aviv.

she hoped he would be good enough to forgive her intrusion.

A sudden tear welled in her eye. Although it fell by itself, it was the drop that presaged the storm to come. Her landlady had gone out. Miriam ran from the window on whose sill she had been writing, threw herself on her unmade bed and buried her face in the crumpled pillow. Bursting into loud sobs, she cried bitterly on and on, for a quarter of an hour, half an hour, an hour. Yes, she would cry, she would cry all alone! A terrible sense of isolation and bereavement, a dreadful fear of her own future, came over her. Not that she was afraid of falling ill in a strange city and a strange woman's house or anything like that. No, she was as strong and healthy as an ox—there was nothing she couldn't endure. But she was lonely, the loneliest person alive. There was nothing left to cling to.

She couldn't think of a single happy memory, couldn't think, in fact, of a single memory at all. What would happen tomorrow, the day after that? How would she live? On what? It was all so hopeless, so hopeless . . . even this postcard . . . it had cost her two piastres . . . but she wouldn't . . . no, she wouldn't send it . . . there was no one to send it to . . . no one would want to help. . . .

Her landlady was sure to be back soon. She must get a grip on herself and stop crying. She sat up on the bed and automatically began to pick at her teeth with a hairpin. As she picked, she thought of what to write. She would write: *How is father? Is he going to Tiberias?* She didn't miss him. She knew he was better off without her. He wouldn't lose his temper so much. And she had a right to live too. A person only lived once. She would write that her life here still left much to be desired. There was a proverb somewhere about choosing the lesser evil but she herself didn't know what to choose. She hadn't arranged her studies yet. But it wasn't just them she'd forgotten—she'd all but forgotten that she was still in this world! Only no, she wouldn't write that. She wouldn't write anything. There was nothing to write!

Cold fingers closed around her heart. Had Zeydl left the stairs yet? There were no more tears left to flow. What, what was she to do?

All of a sudden, without knowing why, she took the hair-pin from between her teeth and pricked the little finger of her left hand with it. A fraction of a second before she'd had a sort of unconscious premonition that something was about to happen that would make everything seem better. At exactly that moment she had thought of Shneirson. Once he had read her a story about a young princess who had done the same thing. In a flash she pricked herself again in the same place. This time it bled and hurt too, hurt more than she'd expected.

The landlady entered the room.

"What's the matter? What have you done?"

"Nothing. I was sewing . . . and I stuck myself."

"Did it bleed?"

"Yes."

"If it bled it will be all right."

The landlady bandaged Miriam's finger with a spider web.

Once again Herr Kauffmann, the Jew from East Prussia, had occasion to see for himself how Providence was against him, how It was bent on his ruin, how It would be the very death of him, heaven forbid! Of course, it was wrong to look upon life through dark glasses; it was all, every bit of it, a war between God and the Devil, a hidden battle whose conduct was invisible and whose outcome could not be foreseen; yet somewhere, after all, there was still a last straw! During all his years in Jerusalem he had never been intimidated by the powers of this world; even when they had sought to humble

him in their fashion, he may have flinched and been afraid
perhaps, but he hadn't resigned from the fray, which he regarded as a mere symbol of the unseen struggle. Foul was fair
and fair was foul, the Devil had his day—yet why worry?
The forces of holiness were ultimately invincible. He, Herr
Kauffmann, need only be patient and fortune would smile
on him by and by. At times Satan might make a man blunder
but this was no reason to be daunted or deterred. The Divine
Presence within was sure to win out in the end.

Such was Herr Kauffmann's theory. Not without justice
did Kahanowitz once remark in the course of an argument
with Shneirson that if he, Herr Kauffmann, had lived two
hundred and fifty years ago in the time of Sabbetai Zevi,* he
would no doubt have been a leader of those factious cabbalists
who crowded around the false Messiah to issue their mystical
fiats and feather their nests with fortune and fame, would
have run after the chariot that carried the "Savior" to Con-
stantinople where he planned to despose the Sultan with a
single breath, would have believed that his master, the Divine
Son, had chosen to apostasize in the end and serve in the
Sultan's court with some deep occult purpose, some hidden
revelation in mind—and all perfectly sincerely, with complete
faith, without a single self-seeking motive! Yes, Herr Kauffmann had the power of his convictions, but this latest blow
dealt him by Providence was unpleasant nonetheless. And the
worst of it was that he himself had given It every chance in
accordance with his theory, had provided It with the perfect
opportunity to work in unmysterious ways Its wonders to
perform. Having heard that Reb Yosef's daughter Esther
was traveling to Jaffa with her father by coach, he'd suddenly

* A Messianic pretender (1626–1676), many of whose followers
remained loyal to him even after his conversion to Islam under duress
upon his imprisonment by the Turkish sultan.

reached the conclusion that he too had to be in Jaffa that very same day, that he had new and urgent business there that could brook no delay, no, not even for an hour. At once he went and reserved a seat on the coach. Far be it from him to make unreasonable demands on Its Excellency, Divine Providence, to expect It to play fast and loose with the laws of nature! No, he had never waited for It to perform miracles. On the contrary, he had always done what he could to help It to bless his endeavors, had allowed things to take their normal, natural course—such had been both his theory and commercial practice. Yet once again Providence played havoc with his plans: nothing took the course it was supposed to. Thank God that he'd been quick enough to realize his mistake before it cost him too much time or money. In general, it was one's duty to welcome the bad with the good, for everything bad contained something good, the Bad being nothing but a step towards the Good—such was his theory. Only *na*—the ways of Providence were beyond him! He, Herr Kauffmann, had meant well, yet no good had come of it. He'd reached for the light—and been burned.

Herr Kauffmann resolved to travel to Jaffa with Reb Yosef Hefetz. The fact of the matter was, of course, that the trip from Jerusalem by train took only four hours, whereas the journey by coach took closer to twenty-four, from the afternoon of one day to the morning of the next, yet Reb Yosef had chosen the coach nonetheless: the railroad might be fine for a single man unencumbered by baggage or a family, but a person quitting Jerusalem for an extended period of time, especially if burdened down with relations, packages, bundles and household possessions, was better off with the coach. Not that the coach was that much cheaper, though when several people traveled together the pennies added up, but Reb Yosef preferred it for a more pressing reason: for the past week not

only his legs but his stomach too—a typical scholar's complaint!—had been feeling indisposed, the two conditions being
in a sense antithetical, for the one called for rest while the other
made you run back and forth. In a word, he was apprehensive
of the train ride where nothing was under a person's control,
the rails having a will of their own which could not be con-
tested, all the more so as getting off at each stop would be a
painful necessity; for since the cars had no provisions for
one's natural needs (Asia and its customs: trains without
w.c.'s!), one had to be laboriously helped down at each station, while before one could manage to board again, whether
because one couldn't find anyone to help one or for some
other reason (in Reb Yosef's case help was not a problem:
Esther, Haim and Yehezkel would all be traveling with him),
the train would like as not be gone. Then what? Whereas
with the coach, one was at least one's own master, and could
get on and off as one pleased with a hand from one's fellow
passengers.

Reb Yosef openly enlarged on all this in the guesthouse
chapel on the eve of his departure, so that Herr Kauffmann,
who sat listening to every word, learned all that he needed to
know; coming after a spell of self-imposed silence, Reb
Yosef's account of his plans appeared to the Jew from East
Prussia to be a sign of some sort—yes, a heaven-sent sign!
The first thing the next morning he ran to buy a ticket on
credit and at the stroke of noon he was off to take his seat
in the carriage with his suitcase in hand, having remembered
to wear his starched, folded collar and to repeatedly scrub his
dirty black tie, after wetting it with his own saliva. Providence helped those who helped themselves! Hot with impatient expectation, bursting with the most fantastic plans, he
excitedly circled the carriage for nearly two hours until
Esther finally arrived with her entourage and belongings. De-

spite the fact that she seemed not a little moody and harassed, he maneuvered at once to engage her in conversation so as "to lay the groundwork," or in the words of the phrase which now ran insinuatingly through his fevered brain (*ach, for shame!*), "to feel her out." Of course, a man was warned in *The Ethics of the Fathers* not to converse too much with women, but he wouldn't overdo it. He would just . . . in moderation . . . one mustn't be rude, after all. True, she was a modest young lady who didn't go fishing for flattery and *Komplimenten* like the rest of them . . . yet nevertheless . . . time would tell. In any case, she would understand . . . although just in case she shouldn't, he'd explain to her that *The Ethics of the Fathers* referred only to married women . . . and they would be traveling together for such a long time—*nicht wahr?* When would he get another such chance?

At first everything went smoothly enough. Herr Kauff-mann plied the coachman with advice about how to arrange the baggage, explained that the cartons of books were not quite as heavy as the latter insisted, and courteously prevailed upon the other passengers to have patience with the delay. The coachman, however, backed away from the books even further, as though fearing to touch them or wishing to view them perhaps from a more distant perspective, and grumbled unyieldingly: "Yes, they'd like this to be my last trip, they would! *Oys balaguleh viln zey mich machn!* * I won't take such heavy things and that's that!" Herr Kauffmann, for his part, tirelessly sought to convince the driver, who was after all the last *Instanz,*† that the truth was the complete opposite of what he was so boorishly claiming. He felt that . . . that . . . yes, that she was looking his way, that he was beginning to make an impression. It was the will of Providence! The voice of the Lord had spoken.

* Yiddish: They'd like to end my career as a coachman!
† German: court of appeal.

A short while later, however, things took a different turn.

The first to clamber up on the carriage was Haim. After roping down what needed to be made fast, he picked out a place for himself up front, exposed to the chilly breezes that heralded the evening; then he jumped down again and together with Yehezkel helped Reb Yosef to a seat in the middle row, which was shielded from the wind on all sides, before reascending. Esther sat down behind him. Reb Yosef spread spaciously out, yet his irritable look was far from auspicious. As though to appeal to his better nature, a fellow passenger inquired:

"Are you off to Jaffa then?"

"Yes, I'm off to Jaffa, that's my first stop," he answered grudgingly, in the tone of a schoolmaster who condescends to reply only for the sake of politeness, which is incumbent upon a man of his stature even if no one deserves it. "It's not as if you have any choice when you're going to Tiberias!"

The inquisitive passenger persisted. "And who, may I ask, do you know in Jaffa?"

"Who in Jaffa? I don't know anyone in Jaffa!" Reb Yosef snapped.

At precisely this awkward juncture Herr Kauffmann slipped forward from his comfortable seat in the back beside the inquisitive passenger and requested that Haim change places with him. Haim, who in the course of his sextonship had suffered more than his share from the guesthouse's permanent "guest," hadn't the faintest idea what the bother was about. How was his own seat, which was out in the open, better than Herr Kauffmann's, which was fully protected? Why switch? Yet Herr Kauffmann, for some reason, stubbornly insisted on it.

It was the impertinent driver who guessed his secret:

"Aha, the pious fellow won't sit behind a woman! I've seen his likes before!"

"There isn't a trouble in the world that doesn't go back to a woman!" joked several of the idlers in the street whose daily entertainment it was to see the coach off.

"As they say in France," Herr Kauffmann guffawed, anxious to retrieve his *Renommee*,* "*cherchez la femme.*"

The coachman grew suddenly respectful. "Don't let him deceive you," he told the others, "I know the man well. He's a real stickler for the Law . . . and speaks languages too. . . ."

"Then the Jew won't sit next to me?" teased Esther coquettishly.

Herr Kauffmann was piqued by the way she referred to him. "Not next to you, behind you!"

Her curiosity was aroused. "Then . . ."

"A nice young lady like you wouldn't want to make me sin now, would you?" Herr Kauffmann pressed on in his best Orthodox-cultured-chivalrous tone of voice.

"Sin?"

Herr Kauffmann stuck to his guns. " 'Sooner behind a lion than a woman,' our Rabbis said. Ask your father, he'll tell you if I'm right."

"But . . ."

The respectful coachman explained it to her.

"And next to me?"

"Next to you? All the more so not!" exclaimed Herr Kauffmann with a peculiar vehemence, while looking straight at her as if to say: *Don't you see, don't you see what kind of man I am, how out of the ordinary? Pay close attention! In these devious, these wayward times, behold a man who puts the fear of God even before knowledge. . . .*

But it was all in vain. Esther's mute answering glance revealed to him *in dem selben Moment*,† as though by means of

* German: reputation.   † German: at the same moment.

a consummate *Offenbarung,** that he hadn't been understood, that these party girls of the young generation were an unregenerate lot, that Providence hadn't really intended . . . how impudently she had addressed him! *And next to me . . . and next to me.* . . . "The Jew," she had called him, as though, heaven help him, he were some dark fanatic and not a modern Orthodox seeker after Truth. . . .

By now he was privately ready to admit that he might have remained sitting where he was, yet he didn't regret in the least having gone to such lengths. In any case, of course, it would have been enough to change places with his neighbor next to him, so that he wouldn't have been directly behind her, only why . . . yes, why make the trip at all if she couldn't even abide his very presence?

Recalling that he still hadn't paid for his ticket and that it wasn't too late to excuse himself entirely, Herr Kauffmann disembarked from the coach.

Then and there he lost the coachman's respect. The hand of Providence was everywhere.

To tell the truth, Herr Kauffmann's miscalculation had been not just psychological but factual: Esther was not accompanying her father to Tiberias, nor was she planning to take a job there in a hospital as he had approvingly heard from some source; she was going no further than Jaffa, and not for her father's sake either, but for her sister Miriam. She had been told in the Hotel Harel that word had arrived from Jaffa that the girl with the letter of recommendation from Jerusalem was critically ill, and that whatever family or true friends she had should hasten to her side.

Esther was doing just that. Say what you will, there was no one else. She was the eldest and the responsibility was hers,

* German: revelation.

especially since it was she who had given Miriam the money to leave home with.

She sat subduedly in the carriage and let her thoughts flit from one thing to another. From time to time a wave of protest swept over her, a wave of protest . . . against men. No, not against men, only against their callousness! Not even against Hefetz, who was sitting in front of her next to her uncle. He couldn't have been coming to see her that time, couldn't even have known that she'd done it on purpose . . . and anyway, she had finished her accounts with him. Perhaps she should have told him . . . but no, there was no need to say anything, it would only have made him think that she was trying to apologize, that she wanted to make up. He wasn't worth it. She no longer even thought of him. He meant nothing to her any more.

Her lips chattered sharply together and she murmured to the inquisitive passenger:

"It's cold."

"Yes, it's cold," he agreed. "In the Talmud it says that a chill wind blows no good."

Esther turned away from him. She didn't want to hear any more, she'd had enough of all these Talmudists. Her father too—always the Talmud, always chapter and verse. And yet he had a heart of stone. It was he she'd had in mind when she'd thought of the callousness of men. Look at him silently sitting there. Just a short while ago he'd said he had no one in Jaffa. In other words, he disowned his own daughter. What did he want from her? What harm had she ever done him? Pure male egotism! Since the day Miriam left home he'd never even asked how she was. Once she had heard him complain, "How can I get along with people if I can't even get along with my own daughter?"—yet even then she hadn't been sure which daughter he was referring to. Perhaps he wouldn't want to see her now either. Perhaps he would refuse, would leave Jaffa tomorrow without even knowing she was in danger. Men were so willful.

But she, Esther, could be willful too. She would pay him back tit for tat. She wouldn't tell him anything, not even why she was making the trip. She wouldn't speak a word to him. Let him get what he deserved.

The coach labored along the mountain grades. Haim and Yehezkel descended from the carriage to ease the horses' load. Esther and the inquisitive passenger conversed about the number of khans between Jerusalem and Jaffa and about how many hours of travel were left before the last of these would be reached. The coachman urged on his horses and accused them in Yiddish of conspiring to drive him out of business with their sloth. *"Oys balaguleh vilt ir mich machn!"* Wrapped in his blanket, Reb Yosef sat without stirring, sunk in "that silence which is the better part of wisdom." His thoughts were, firstly, that in times like the present a man of intellect had no choice but to hold his peace; secondly, that life was a fiery, cleansing furnace—how good it would be then if only one could emerge from it truly purged, yet who knew whether he himself would ever emerge from it at all, whether he wouldn't go on stifling and strangling forever; and thirdly, that the first thing he must do upon arriving in Jaffa was to dash off a letter to his son in Kiev, requesting him "to increase your bounty and goodness to your poor ill father and send me each month care of the holy city of Tiberias double the sum as before to uphold me in my years of eld. God reward you. May you profit from the example of your dear first cousin Yehezkel, who sends you his fond and brotherly regards. . . ."

Once more Reb Yosef resolved to make amends for having

doubled his son's monthly remittance by supplementing his regular letters to him in the future with verse epistles in which he would pour out his innermost feelings and show him what stuff his father was made of. Indeed, he had already tried his hand at this art in days gone by, when there had been much he had wanted to express; if ever he should go through his papers some day, among which were filed away his certificate of marriage to his gentle-souled wife, his entry visa to Palestine and other important documents, he would undoubtedly uncover more than one letter of rhymed couplets in the medieval style which for some reason he had never mailed. Now, however, as long as the creative urge was upon him, he would no longer deny his son the pleasure, for no one could know what the morrow might bring.

The coach rocked back and forth on the gravel road, while fragments of these unsent lines buzzed in and out of Reb Yosef's head:

> *To you, my son,*
> *Is this letter begun,*
> *With a sigh and a tear,*
> *In spirits most drear....*
>
> . . . . .
>
> *I heard a voice say,*
> *"Thy strength's fled away!"*
> *Then quoth I to myself,*
> *"That I still had my health."...*
>
> . . . . .
>
> *Yea, from head to toe*
> *I knew nothing but woe,*
> *And my soul when I sought her,*
> *The King's precious daughter,*
> *Would not dance, would not sing,*
> *But like a bird on the wing,*

Cried out in distress,
O'er the wilderness,
Forsaken, forlorn,
Hither toss'd, thither borne....

He recalled how when he had read these lines over he had been so delighted by them that he had inspiredly toiled to add more:

O Thou, my Creator
Thou also hast made her:
My pure, perfect one,
My soul and bright sun!
The philosopher's stone,
In this world she must roam,
Far, far from her home,
Beyond the blue sky,
Where dwells the All-high
For whom she doth sigh,
While to honor and wealth
She turns a blind eye,
Forever eschewing
All evil-doing....

Later, however, when he had tried to bring his account of himself up to date, he had been dissatisfied with the results, which was perhaps why he had put off mailing them from day to day until finally they remained among his papers. As long as he had confined himself to writing about the soul, or about spiritual life in Jerusalem with its proliferation of different sects and human types, he had been pleased and enthralled with the labors of his imagination; yet when he had sat down the next morning before saying his prayers (he simply couldn't wait another minute) in order to pen a few lines about his own situation, the versification, excellent though it was, seemed somehow not to the point.

Haim's voice sounded in his ears. "Yosef, are you asleep? Do you need to get off? We're coming to a khan soon."

But Reb Yosef didn't answer. His mind was still engrossed in what he had written then.

> *. . . All evil-doing.*
> *Yet why continue reviewing*
> *And further reflecting*
> *And recollecting*
> *The days gone by,*
> *The time that did fly,*
> *Without consolation or gratification?*
> *Yea, I hoped for salvation—*
> *And behold ruination and desolation.*
> *My soul pants for breath before its oppressors,*
> *These Law-transgressors,*
> *And Truth-suppressors,*
> *Doctors, officials and "professors"!*
> *Above all one who struts and brags,*
> *A brazen Mister Moneybags,*
> *A "golden calf" who's quick to gore*
> *Whoever passes by his door.*
> *Yet your father, son, as you're aware,*
> *Knows no reply but to forbear;*
> *Wherefore his soul heaves helplessly*
> *Like Noah's ark upon the sea.*

The coach, in which Reb Yosef's body heaved suddenly back and forth, gave a great lurch and pulled in at the khan. Jaffa was still nowhere near.

IV

In the late hours of summer evenings in Jaffa, the sand in front of the landlady's house served as a squatters' grounds for those who wished to relax from the heat of the day. They lay singly or in groups, spreadeagled on their backs upon the bare sand or on blankets, shawls and the like, staring up into the vastness of space or chatting about the beauty of the sky and the charms of the Palestinian night, which were unrivaled anywhere else in the world, and rising to go home at eleven or twelve with a certain sense of frustration, a feeling of having been somehow let down. At times the younger folk might break into argument about the purposelessness of life, the injustices of the world, the deceitfulness of love, and so on; here and there someone else would complain that people didn't know how to live, to regulate their affairs, to "create the proper atmosphere" and make the best of things; perhaps a group from the Workers Club might choose to debate some question of a moral or otherwise public nature; yet sooner or later, at eleven or twelve or one, the homeward trek would begin, there being no other place to go. . . . From one end of the expanse came the neighborly voices of women: "Oy, if only I had a burner now, I'd make some tea!" "I still have some raisins but they're for the children to have with their bread." "So tell me, did the pill do any good? I can't sleep nights because of the mice." From off in the other direction one sometimes might hear the soft whistling of a girl whose love-life owed its latest diversion to the gathering on the sands, or the horse-play of some reveler reliving the antics of childhood, or the broken, scratchy sounds of a violin coming from the barbershop to the landlady's right (the barber hadn't any work and was teaching himself to fiddle)—all of which helped to relieve the monotony of the evening. And yet home everyone went in the end with the same sense of frustration.

In the winter, however, and earlier in the evening, before the hour of ten, the same sand served not as a haunt to stretch out on but as the thoroughfare of a busy city (Jaffa, after all, was not Jerusalem!), humming not just with young loafers, but here and there with men of affairs out for a serious word. To be sure, the traces of last summer's late-hour lingering still seemed to hover over the practical transactions: now too the promenaders wove their webs of talk; yet these same webs seemed somehow strangely heavy, the spinnings of summer in a wintry garb. The same group *philosophe*, for example, who liked nothing better on a sultry June night than to palaver lightly about the eternal verities, now walked solemnly with his lady friend, who was ready to believe whatever he told her if only he didn't get personal, and unabashedly assured her in an important, and above all, in an involved tone of voice, that "Schopenhauer may have been the first socialist, but even he never thought that the world would amount to a damn." ("I tell you, I heard it with my own ears!" the *philosophe*'s chief rival, the *Intelligenz*, later swore to them all.) The "tragic bard," too, having spent last summer's languorous nights uttering cryptic cries about "the treachery of love" and the like, now strolled side by side with a novice versemaker like himself, to whom he confidentially dropped names with an almost businesslike exactness. Did he, his companion, remember *la coquette* from the sands of last summer and the author of the verses *Where Art Thou Goddess Mine* who was madly in love with her? Did he? Of course he did! How could anyone forget them? Well, then: the harder he'd run after her, the harder she'd fled from him. But your Jewish poet was nobody's fool: eventually he'd simply said to hell with her. And now it was she who ran after him and he who ran from her! Not only that . . . to top it all off, she accused him of having jilted her . . . what a joke! In his latest poem, *Avaunt Ye, No More*, he declared in so many words that his feelings for her to begin with had been nothing but pity for her beauty which was some day bound to fade. The logical question to ask him then was: now that her beauty had actually faded, why did he refuse to have pity?

The hour struck ten. The evening was mild. Disregarding the calendar, which still lagged far from the first day of spring, a few hardy sand squatters began to creep forth. First on the scene was Zeydl, the hunchback from the Transvaal, who had arrived from Jerusalem only a few days before. Stretching himself out on the coat he had brought, he prepared to wait for company while training his glassy eyes in the meantime on every rustling skirt, on every female shadow passing through the dusk, on every little girl-child at play; the worm gnawed and gnawed within him, but he was determined to keep mum. . . . Now the lone figure of the *philosophe* lay down beside him. Early in the debating season though it was, the hunchback threw down the gauntlet. There was no justice or truth in the world! Everybody had his price. It was disgusting how people were out only for themselves, how everyone wanted to get rich. Yes, everyone

wanted to use you. That was the only reason they even
stopped to talk to you. It was a treacherous, lecherous, lying
world. You couldn't even eat in a restaurant without having
to worry about the meat being rotten. Not that he believed in
socialism either . . . cross his palm with pounds sterling, he
still wouldn't believe in it! It was a dream, nothing more.
Yes, socialism was a dream.

"Socialism is socialism!" insisted the *philosophe*.

A group of self-absorbed men passed before them, a gang
of Jewish laborers bound for Marseilles. To pay for their
passage, they were looking to farm out the job they had just
contracted to Arabs who would do it for less. Their loud
voices preceded them: there was trouble ahead! It was said
that a large gang of Jewish builders had arrived by coach
from Jerusalem yesterday and was looking for work. André
from Antwerp had already seen one of them, an old codger
of a Jew with a lunatic son and a sick brother. But what of it?
They were working men, not philanthropists. The idea! Just
let that Jew from Jerusalem stick his nose into their business
and they would give him a proper hiding. The job was theirs.
They had six francs a day coming to them for it. There was
no room for new elements. Scabs keep out!

The group of workers descended the other side of the dune.
If only they could find someone to take the job off their
hands at a profit, everything would be shipshape. Then they
could sail within the week.

"But I'm afraid. They say if we hand over the work to
Arabs there'll be blood."

"What? *They'll* attack *us?* We'll show them!"

The voice of André the anarchist from Antwerp carried
from afar:

"They'll fork up whether they like it or not!"

And furthermore:

"A bourgeois with a belly wrote *Hatikvah* * and I'm supposed to stand here and sing it?"

"The hell . . ."

Following them, a sensitive-looking young couple sat down on the sand and began to speak to each other in Hebrew. The boy seemed about nineteen, the girl sixteen or so; both were students at the National School. Contrary to what might have been expected, however, their Hebrew conversation was not about the importance of Hebrew conversation as such conversations generally were, nor even about the pointlessness and meaninglessness of life, but rather about . . . yes, about art. Their literature teacher had taught them that poetry was the splendor and the beauty in life, that poets and artists found beauty everywhere. Jaffa, for instance, was certainly beautiful at night; but when their class had gone to Jerusalem—how grand that had been! Especially the walled city after dark.

The young man struggled with himself to express his own and his teacher's thoughts. He seemed not so much to speak the strange, unnatural syllables as to stammer them at the top of his voice and stumble all over them. The girl sat there silently, seriously, almost sadly. Her mature breasts hung before her, yet he appeared not even to notice them. As he was saying . . . the walls of Jerusalem at night were . . . were . . . he had seen them when he had gone with his class. It was all that he wanted to talk about.

In his speech and in her silence, in his voice that kept breaking in the middle and in her hot, constricted breathing, there was something troubled and slightly woeful that seemed to spread out before them over the sand.

At twelve o'clock they rose too and frustratedly said goodnight.

* "The Hope," the official Zionist anthem, the words to which were composed by the 19-century Hebrew poet Naphtali Herz Imber.

On Purim eve,* from morning to evening, and again at night after the Scroll of Esther had been read in the synagogue, the conversation on the sand was all about the family from Jersualem. The neighborhood gossips held the center of the stage and played their parts to perfection. "Ah, the pity of it," they chorused all day, "the pity of it. . . ." Zeydl the hunchback was in his element too: after all, he had known the family personally! He mingled among the women with his eyes of glass. "Ah, the Lord have mercy . . . the Lord have mercy . . ." they groaned.

The landlady held court in front of her house. "Oy, what can any of you know about it, what? What can you know about the terrible time that I've had? What have I done to deserve it? Only Zeydl knows what I've been through. The cleverhead came here the same day as she did. He brought me a letter and so did she, from one of my relatives in Jerusalem. . . ."

"Oy!" wailed another commiserator without tears. "Oy! Whenever I think of it . . . the one time I saw her . . . bright as the sunshine she was . . . and hands of gold. . . ."

The landlady refused to be outdone and interrupted. "She was working in the embroidery shop. It was because of me that they took her in there. It wasn't easy to convince them, either. Well, everyone likes to do a good deed! Oy, I thought to myself, she's here all by herself in a strange town. And that's where she had the accident, that's where she stuck herself with the needle."

"It should have been washed right away," Zeydl protested. "All those women and not one knew a thing about hygiene! The needle was rusty . . . a cut should be cleaned. . . ."

"Oy, Zeydl is my witness . . . he lives right here in my

* Purim is the holiday commemorating the events of the Book of Esther, which falls usually in the month of March.

house . . . what haven't I been through, oy! And what was
she to me, after all? I hardly even knew her. She came home
that night from the shop with her finger swollen like a
mountain. And oy, the way she began to cry, to scream:
'What am I going to do? I won't be able to work tomorrow!'
Zeydl heard her and went to get the thermometer."

"Of course I heard!" Zeydl confirmed. "You could hear her
crying three blocks away. A heart of stone could have broken
in half. And what frightened me most was that she had fever.
I put in—she put in the thermometer . . . she had a fever of
forty degrees and was shivering all over."

"Oy, what can any of you know about it?" the landlady
demanded again. "I haven't had a bite to eat. I saved it all for
her. She wasn't any kin of mine but a person is still a person.
Zeydl knows all about it. I wouldn't lie to his face. He took
care of her, he called the doctor and wanted to pay for it
himself. . . . Oy, what can I tell you."

"Oy, the pity of it!" the women groaned bitterly.

But all this was just the prologue. Now the landlady proceeded to describe what happened when the family arrived.
Zeydl had advised her to send word to Jerusalem and she did.
Both the father and the sister came at once but by then
there was nothing they could do. The father never saw her at
all. At first they had tried to keep it from him. But even
when they told him, he refused to believe that she could die.
And when news came that she was sinking fast, he still didn't
come. But what was she saying, "didn't"? Couldn't! Israel's
enemies should only have such luck! That same morning, God
help us, he had still been able to drag his legs about, a step
every quarter of an hour. But when they told him that his
daughter was going, the news paralyzed him completely.

"But you should have seen her elder sister, my good women.
Oy! She was nothing but skin and bones herself, but how

she worked, and what courage! Master of the Universe, she had her transferred on the last day to the hospital, she brought in a specialist, they even gave her injections! Just fifteen minutes before she died they gave her another one. There was nothing she didn't try, oy! And just as the poor thing was passing on . . . Zeydl was there too . . . just as she was passing on—there she was cold as the frost and burning up with a fever of forty-one degrees—for three days she'd been burning and freezing and no one knew what it was . . . her sister starts tearing her hair out—a young girl like that and hair already turned gray!—and she screams: 'Sister, sister! I'm your murderer! It's me who killed you! I stuck the knife in your throat!' As if you could bring a corpse back to life. Oy, what screams . . . one couldn't help hearing. And a smart girl like that too! But of course, she's not well. Zeydl says she takes opium. It's a kind of drink to make you sleep. 'Sister, don't you want to live, don't you want to? Don't die!' "

"And she did want to live," Zeydl assured them. "Just as she lay dying she opened her mouth as though to plead for her life."

"Her mouth! Oy, the pity of it! The pity of it!"

For the first few days after Miriam's death Hefetz was like a tortured man who no longer cares what happens to him, who is even willing to go on being tortured as long as he is allowed to concentrate undisturbedly on his pain.

But the inevitable happened once more. The pain grew less fierce and his memories of her began to dim; he had to worry about the trip to Tiberias, which had been delayed in Jaffa longer than expected, and he soon returned to his senses and his clarity of mind.

He now experienced more strongly the powerful feeling

that he'd already had in Jerusalem, before he could have known that things would end as they did and so quickly: that had he really loved her, he would have been able to save her. Yes, had he really loved Yosef's daughter Miriam as human beings should love one another, he would have kept her from perishing. *How? With what? In what way? By not letting her go away? By going with her to look after her?* He didn't know; yet the feeling persisted and he knew that it was so; just as it was so that had she loved him back even a little, had she looked to him for help at all, she would have been saved by that too.

But it wasn't meant to be.

Don't whimper, Hefetz. Who's there to hear you?

He didn't go to her funeral at the cemetery; but he did make his peace with her once and for all.

He didn't go weep by himself at her graveside, either; instead he opened the grave in his own heart and went early one morning to sit on the empty dune. He directed his thoughts to the window of the house in which she had lived her last days and he said:

"A window. And inside the ceiling is low, so low, and it's all so quiet and dark. But there's nothing to fear. Clear minds have nothing to fear. And we live in times in which our minds are clear. We've got nothing to do with what's not of this world. And this world too, this world of sand, is so naked. The whole universe is so naked and raw. Nothing in it hunts or is hunted. There is no hunt; no cause for alarm; nothing to fear.

"You . . . are no longer among us, you're no longer at all. You aren't. I am—and you aren't. Where are you? In some other world? Of course you're not. My mind is clear. You aren't and there's nothing to fear.

"What then can I say to you? Because you aren't and my

mind is clear. So clear that I know perfectly well that while you were still alive you were never to me what you are now. So clear that I refuse to make a goddess of you even now that you're gone. It doesn't matter, my clear mind tells me. You were a living thing like other living things, a living thing— and you died. Meaninglessly. But is there ever any meaning to death? You died too soon. But how can there be a too soon and too late in life and death?

"No, my dear, nothing is left of you now but a memory, a fragment of a memory. You aren't any more. And I . . . here I sit where once you may have sat, walk where you may have walked, look at your window, your hollow, your hole.

"A hole through which I look and talk. It's possible, it's very possible, that nothing is at all like what I see and say it is. It's possible that I haven't said a single word of truth. But what is truth? I have my hole through which I look . . . can it be that you didn't know that? A black, still hole.

"How sad, my dear, how sad that you're dead! Why couldn't we have lived to spend time together? It's so good to be alive, so pleasant . . . to be alive! Even to be wrapped in spider webs, to live in the spider's web. The possibilities that exist in a single spider's web! Even to lie and miaow like blind, baby kittens. What pleasure could be greater than to lie miaowing together like baby kittens?

"Listen! A rock fell down in a cave-in. A heavy rock. It fell on a dog's head. A lethal blow. He never stood a chance. He took one last great jump, let out one last great howl. But he wasn't a dumb dog. Dogs are smarter than you think. His eyes, his cloudy dog's eyes, stayed calm. He didn't jump or howl any more. He didn't even think of biting anyone. Bite them? He couldn't even see them. Even the cave-in was forgotten. Even the rock. Hurrah for life! Hurrah for breath!

Coolly, collectedly, he hobbled bleeding back to his hole. Spider webs. A quiet place to lie down. For a few more hours, a few more days, even a few more years—he'll lie there and be still."

V

The rainy season was drawing to an end. It was already April, the Hebrew month of Nisan. The words "matzah" * and "baking" began to be heard insistently on the tongues of the women who lived in the rooms above the bathhouse, and when they went down to the lake shore and left their children behind, they would be careful to warn them to watch that the cat, God forbid, didn't get into the house and turn everything set out for the holiday upside down, or that they themselves didn't mix up the Passover and the year-round dishes.

A year had gone by. Once again the Passover was around the corner. In the houses of the holy city of Tiberias, just as in Jerusalem and wherever Jews lived all over the world, there was no end of boiling and washing and scrubbing and rinsing, all with a strict and most scrupulous attention to the provisions of the Law, the better to perform the will of the Maker and put the handful of "Russians" in the neighborhood to shame, those Zionist newcomers who were lax in their customs of observance and hardly any better than Gentiles!

Reb Yosef and his family were not put to shame in Tiberias, for they were staying outside of town in a rented room by the

* Matzah is the unleavened bread eaten on the Passover.

water that belonged to the Arab who ran the hot springs. Only infrequently did they have occasion to venture into the city. Besides which, having no dishes or household goods to speak of, except for the straw mats that covered the floor, there was nothing to be made kosher for the holiday in any case.

The ranks of the bathers were thinning out. The few women who were left regarded Reb Yosef, who had come when the season was already over, with amusement. Two days after his arrival the last male bather departed, a Jew from Hebron who had been living in town for the past two months and coming to bathe every day, rain or shine, despite the doctor's warning to stay home in bad weather, the benefits of the waters being more than canceled out by the dangers of catching cold. All this while he had been waiting for a draft of money so that he too could rent a room next door to the "spa" and not have to run back and forth in the rain and worry about taking sick; but the promised sum had failed to arrive, and with the exception of Sabbaths, of course, he had continued to travel from town day in and day out. Each day in Tiberias, after all, cost him six piastres, which were taken directly from the mouths of his family in Hebron: how could he let even one of them go to waste? Besides which, the bathing lessened his appetite; on days when he failed to take the waters he was forced to eat more; and what could one possibly eat on six piastres a day? Ach, if only he lived next door to the "spa" he would surely have been cured by now!

"But the rooms here are filthy," Esther had said to him. "The windows are all broken and they don't even give you a table."

"A table?" Haim joined the conversation. "What do we need a table for? We didn't come here to sit and write, did we?"

"Of course not!" the Hebronite agreed. One came only to bathe . . . only to bathe . . . if only he lived at the spa he'd bathe three times a day . . . *three?* What was he saying? Ten! He'd take a dip and get dressed and then again—what more did one need? That was the whole cure. True, there were those who said that the waters sapped your strength . . . but he wouldn't let that bother him . . . he would stay in them all day . . . ai, if only . . .

But his dream did not come true. He set out for home without ever having had the good fortune to live four in a room next to the spa. He was forced to remain in town—and even then not forever. His stay in Tiberias had come to an end. Passover was on its way and his family in Hebron could go hungry no longer. He was obliged to think of them too.

"Have the waters at least done you good?"

"The waters are fine, but they're not in good hands," winked the Hebronite in allusion to the Arab manager of the springs, who took advantage of him, as he did of all Jews, by charging four whole piastres for every bath.

"But have they helped any?"

Helped? They had sapped his strength. They had done more harm than good. . . .

"That's good!" declared a woman bather from Safed. "If it hurts a lot, that's a sign that it's helping. The greater the pain to begin with, the greater the cure in the end."

"So they say," shrugged the Hebronite, feeling his side as though to ascertain what the waters had done for him. "In any case, it's time I was off."

"God speed and get better!"

That was the last of him.

On his way to Tiberias exactly one year and a month from the day of his accident while working on the communal farm in

Judea with the hired hand Menahem, Yehezkel Hefetz—and
with a strange kind of wonderment, a wonderment at his own
sense of wonder—ran across the same young man, who was
now employed as a guard in a settlement in the Lower Galilee.
"Is it you?"

"Hel-l-lo there! It's me. What a small world! On your way
to Tiberias? So am I—and on a donkey! The head of our commune's somewhere here too. Only he's got a horse and I don't.
Here, sit behind me. Or in front of me, whichever you prefer.
I'll take you to Tiberias. At this time a year ago, if I remember, I was taking you to another holy city. Everything's a
cycle . . . upon my life! In good times one should always
think of the bad. But you're looking better, damn it all! Time
certainly has flown. Well, how are you feeling? Good? Of
course! And I—I'm the happiest man in all of Palestine. It's no
easy work being a guard, but I swear, I feel twice as strong as
ever!"

And Menahem's appearance confirmed that he was telling
the truth. He was wearing high boots and had wild, curly hair
and the manner of a sworn swashbuckler. As he rode he
played with some pebbles which he held in his whip hand,
while his chatter flew from one thing to the next like a bird
from branch to branch. In the year since he had last seen
Yehezkel in Jerusalem, his feet had trod the length and
breadth of Palestine; there wasn't a hamlet, no matter how
remote, in which he hadn't been. He was one of those people
who knew something about everything, who was both at
home and a stranger everywhere, and yet at bottom he was
a simple, happy-go-lucky fellow. A whole year gone by
—whew! It was just like his tried and trusty revolver—the
incredible hands it had been through. Yes, some day it
would be well worth his, Yehezkel's, while to hear its story:
the biography of a revolver! . . . Only now he was talking

about himself, not his gun. He, Menahem, was staying in the
Galilee, where there was a shortage of accommodations. For
every three people there was only one place, you couldn't
find an empty cot by day or by night. No sooner did one
person get up to go on guard duty then another came in to
lie down. And always the same old squabbles! If one man
was sick in bed, for example, and another well, where was the
sick one to go? The answer was—nowhere; the well man
had to fend for himself. Yes, sickness had a premium over
health, damn it all! . . . Incidentally, on the subject of places
to stay, he had an interesting ancedote to relate from his own
past. Did Yehezkel want to hear something funny? Then
listen, upon his life! It had happened in London. He, Menahem,
was working in the print shop of a Yiddish paper at the time
and had decided to look for room and board in a private home.
It was just one of those things he'd gotten into his head. And
so he put an ad in the paper—typesetters were allowed to
advertise free of cost—which said: *Young man working on
newspaper would like to rent room with meals from private
family. Leave word at paper for M.M.* Sure enough, the letters
began to arrive. Ai, they were well worth reading, some of
those letters! Each of them promised him, M.M., "the very
place" he was looking for. One in particular sounded attractive
and on the third day he went there. It was the home of a "Reverend," that is, of the beadle of a small synagogue. Enter M.M.
"What do you want?" "I was told there's a room here." "Ah,
of course, we've been waiting for you"—and all this while
husband and wife were eating him alive with their eyes. "Have
a seat," the Reverend offered, while the Reverendess for some
reason gave him a wink. "But where's the room?" "What
room?" "What do you mean, what room? You wrote me there
was a room here." "And what do you call what you're sitting
in right now?" "But this is your room. I want a room of my
own." "A separate room? We don't have one. What kind of

work do you do? Are you an editor of the paper?" "An editor? I set type there!" "A *zetzer?!* * I'm sorry, we haven't any room." "But how can that be? Here you've put me to the trouble . . . you wrote . . ." "Put you to the trouble? Tsk, tsk. We thought . . . our daughter said . . . a boarder who'd be one of the family. . . ." "Ah, so that's the kind of boarder you had in mind!" Meanwhile the bride-to-be had begun to peep out of the other room in the middle of her toilette. Good grief, what words could describe her? An absolute horror! *Aha*, he said to himself, *if that's the game you're playing with me I won't let you off so easily*, and out loud:

"Real gentlemen would never have behaved like this. You wrote me that there was a room here."

"But if you're only a *zetzer* what do you need your own room for?"

Add insult to injury, will you? he thought and retorted:

"But I can see that you're pious Jews . . . and I thought that you wouldn't want to have to see me. . . ."

"See you? See you do what?"

"I might want to write on the Sabbath, for example, or smoke a cigarette. . . ."

"How's that? A pox on your head! The rascal! Did you hear him? Oy!"

Menahem let out a mighty roar of laughter over the Sea of Galilee whose echo bounced back from the mountains around them. Wherever the hired hand passed, this laugh of his was the cause of much hearty good humor. He was a frequent visitor to Tiberias and was to help the Hefetz family settle down there. For Esther he was even to find a job in the city.

"Ai, a year, a whole year!" He couldn't get over his pleasure at meeting Yehezkel. "How old are you, friend?"

"I'll be thirty next September."

* Yiddish: a typesetter.

"You mean to say you're not even thirty yet?"

"No, just twenty-nine . . . last September. . . ."

"Ah, I swear to you, Yehezkel, we'll live to see good times yet . . . upon my life!"

That September—in the month of Tishri, under the sign of Libra, the Scales—Yehezkel Hefetz was thirty years old. "In December," he told himself, "it will be a year from my release; in January—the first anniversary of Hanoch's death; and in March—of hers. No, as long as we're still bound by 'the chains of time,' there's meaning enough, 'the common meaning of life,' in every day and turning of the year."

September, December, January, March—winter. The thirty-first winter of his life was about to begin. The sun hadn't set for him yet. With the last of his inner reserves, which he owed to that full and sometimes even unwittingly kind Hand, he had put a few steps between himself and a nasty, hasty oblivion. Yes, he still lay cradled in the sun's, in life's lap. He was still alive.

And on the whole there had been many hours of sun, many hours of light, in those thirty years. Only without bravado now: no brave words! When one was young one tended to think highly of one's own sorrow, to prize it and drain it like a cup of sweet wine, sometimes to the point of self-forget-fulness, even of happiness. But he, Yehezkel Hefetz, at the age of thirty-one, was no longer any youngster. No, no more brave words, no more running away from his accountability to himself! If God had created him twisted, was he any the less accountable? Enough brave words! When things seemed grim, black, hopeless, impossible, why pervert the plain facts with bravado, with the high-flown bluster that stupid, self-in-dulgent little men—and sometimes even not such little men—spouted on every street corner? He, at least, knew his own self.

And he had no illusions about the fact that he was beaten. In every way. A beaten man. Not just by the inevitable death that was yet to come, but by the other, the potentially living side of him too, which had never been able to express itself, though it had gone on existing inside him. He had never had the feeling of being fully alive. Something essential was lacking, something that could never be made good. Alack, a lack! And it was useless, too, to comfort himself with the thought that he still had other qualities with which he could also serve. No, he would never be "a priest of the God most high," never experience the call to rise to such empyrean peaks. Not for him to minister augustly to the destitute father who lived with his children in unendurable want, without food, without heat, without shoes, with nowhere to turn; or to the soldier wounded in battle, breathing his last; or to his comrade in the guardhouse who had just been given fifty stripes; or to the defenseless prisoner whose bullying cell-mate had relieved him of a tooth with a blow to the jaw; or to the toothless, half-blind, dyspeptic, decrepit old man who still clung fiercely to his bond with life; or to the poor, debilitated bachelor whose violent attacks of longing for each female seen and encountered gave him no peace; or to the mother whose son and sole support lay dead at her feet; or to the patient sick with compassion who saw men drowning, drowning all around him yet was powerless to save himself. A man who was not in the best of shape himself, who hovered between light and darkness, letting himself be pulled now forward and now back, and yet who ultimately was all of the above, and ultimately was beaten too—yes, beaten by his own bad times when everything turned against him—such a man had better refrain from brave words, had better not chant any hymns. . . . And yet wasn't it true that there had been many hours of light in his life all the same? Perhaps there had been nothing actual or tangible about them, nothing that could be grasped or put into words. There was no satisfactory way of explaining them. And yet they had existed: they had been flooded with light and warmth and sun! And he was not even thinking of those ecstatic moments from which he had opened his eyes in the end to find himself a hair's breadth away from an infernal paradise; no, the times he had in mind had been quiet and prosaic, like those bright, sunny Friday afternoons in the foster home in Jerusalem where Hanoch's son now was. Even tonight, when they sang "Let us be joyful" * at the Sabbath service, the sorry little orphans would have no fresh clothes to put on; no festive banquet awaited them in the refectory after the prayer; the blisters on the white hands of the warden and on the swarthy hands of the Arab *hajj* † still hadn't healed, not even in honor of the Sabbath. And yet nonetheless—how good it all was! Good? Good wasn't the word for it . . . so good you could laugh like a lunatic . . . ha . . . ha . . . *good!* The children ran chattering about the yard. One little boy had even managed to buy some roasted pumpkin seeds with a piastre he had gotten hold of (a present from grandfather, no doubt) and was giving them out one by one to his friends—to his friends and no one else. *Filth, neglect, abandonment*—all these were empty words used only by the adults in the world outside who sometimes came to visit: they were not what really mattered. What mattered had no meaning, no reason, no purpose, but it was. Here on a Friday afternoon in the orphanage which was the home of Hanoch-the-son-of-Haim's little son *it was.* And whatever it was, it was joyful, it was good, it was life-giving, it was Life itself—blessed be it, selah!

* The opening words of the prayer that begins the Sabbath eve service.

† The title given a Moslem who has made the pilgrimage to Mecca.

A year and a half. First had come the accident . . . then the months shut up in the asylum . . . the two sisters . . . and the many other horrors of Jerusalem . . . then Miriam's death. . . . *Yet have no fear, thou soul of Ezekiel Hefetz! The base of thy cup of sorrows rests firmly on the past. Have no fear of the cloudy future, either . . . of course . . . there'll be more bad times to come . . . you'll lie on a straw mat, though not in a tenement in New York, you'll eat bread that's mostly dust . . . how much better real bread would be . . . but for all that, today you stand on the threshold: bow down with a blessing, bow down with joy. . . .*

On the threshold. Because ultimately nothing was permanent, nothing was assured. There were only thresholds, moments. Seize the day and enjoy it! There was no straight and narrow. There was only a twisting, turning path which was sometimes easy to travel and sometimes not. And all there was to know was the old wisdom: that it was happiness to be lost on this path, happiness to live life and to cherish it, both for its infinite pleasures and for all its rude surprises.

Nothing was permanent. There were always ups and downs. One after another. Like links in a chain. And the future was unpredictable. Which link would turn up next, which link would turn up last, whether it would face up or down—none of this could be known. And yet now, at this juncture, things were looking up again. The going was easier.

It was easier with Esther too. No words had passed between them over the incident that took place; there had been no explanations, no attempts at forgiveness or mutual understanding. Yet he was certain that in making his peace with Miriam he had somehow made his peace with her, Esther, too, certain that the moment seven months ago when he had stood beneath her, soiled and shamed by her hands, had been branded forever in her memory: ever since she had seen him in the disgrace that she had deliberately brought down on him, her unbearable attitude toward him, toward the fact of his being a man, had vanished for good. Now she could choose to be a sister to him or not; he could stay with her in Tiberias or leave for Haifa or Alexandria; the nightmare was finally over.

Of course, here too there were no guarantees, none at all. He was still not made out of steel. He was still as before either all flesh and no spirit or all spirit and no flesh; an unheroic worm; an ordinary mortal struggling with his ephemeral sensations, bound on the whole to his surroundings with all their accidental encounters and involvements; irritable and at war with himself; a stranger to all glimmerings of glory; a soul doomed to descend ever deeper into darkness. He couldn't even enter a plea of idealism or a defense of profundity of thought. Basically he was immoral, yes, immoral. But he did have, he had his higher moments. Not that these made him any more superior in daily life, yet they did exist. Their truth would always stand by him. And most, most important of all —they were no mere products of the intellect: they came to him still smelling freshly of courtyards of sickly, beaten, half-idiot children on Friday afternoons.

Yehezkel Hefetz shut his eyes and said a short prayer: "My Father! Father of Light and of Life, blessed are they, selah! My Father, father of orphans, be good to me: send me a gift of your sunbeams, and I, an orphan among orphans, will gather them gratefully, hopefully, lovingly. I know now to cherish your gifts, your goodness, selah. My heart will rejoice in you, yea, will be jubilant. O Father of Life, blessed art Thou, selah!"

Last Chapter

It was the month of December. In a side street of Tiberias, on the mantle of a window in the home of the two brothers Hefetz, an oil lamp had been burning all night. It was lit by the younger of the brothers in memory of his son Hanoch, whose death, he had learned, had taken place a year ago to the day.

The anniversary happened to fall on a Sabbath when Haim was free and at home. The rest of the week he was busy hauling bathers to the springs outside the city. Yosef, however, was not among them, for the doctor in Tiberias had ruled that his illness was not rheumatism after all: no, it was some condition of the nerves, definitely not rheumatic. Go make your own diagnosis!

The one saving grace, thank the Lord, was that Yosef had become far less irritable. He no longer had any doubts. At last he knew what it was.

Haim gladly shared his earnings with his brother, who sat over his books all day long. From time to time he would think of the sermon he had heard years ago from an itinerant preacher in that town on the Polish border about the two brothers in the Bible, Issachar and Zebulun, who had divided their labors the same way.*

After the evening service, at which he recited the *kaddish* †
for his son, and the Sabbath meal with its hymns, Haim stepped outside with his brother. The two men talked about Yehezkel's suggestion that Hanoch's son be brought from Jerusalem. Reb Yosef agreed that at the end of the bathing season, when Haim would have less to do, he should take some money from Esther and go fetch the child. To tell the truth, he, Reb Yosef, would have preferred to live in Jerusalem himself, for it was a city he loved; but since this was out of the question, it was best to send for the boy. He would be his tutor. Why should he alone not earn his keep? He would teach the boy Torah, the Five Books of Moses. Yes, the Five Books of Moses.

The Tiberian street was alive as usual with the Friday night. Women sat in the doorways, gossiping about this or that in loud or soft voices. *So-and-so had quarreled with so-and-so to-day at the butcher's.* From time to time clusters of children swarmed around them in their play.

The evening was calm and dry. The trickle of moonbeams from above was like a last reflection of the afterglow of the sun as it fell away from the lakeside, that glow which seemed to come from so far off and left a special sense of peacefulness behind it. Still afire with a reddish play of stone, the chain of harp-shaped hills that ringed the city made its unspoken-of presence felt in the streets below.

As the evening wore on, the conversation reached out to become more abstract and universal. Soft- and loud-toned

---

* A reference to rabbinic legends built upon the verse of Jacob's blessing in Genesis 49:13, in which the former of the two brothers is compared to "a servant under taskwork."

† The mourner's prayer.

voices alike ranged far afield to spin somber, sorrowful, heart-splitting tales of distress. Yet though here and there a body unconcealedly sought to melt the hearts of her listeners and move them to pity, for the most part the talk flowed on with the same sublime detachment as before, as if to say: *We mortals have tongues and the power to wag them as long as we live; speech is life's gift to us, so use it we will, good women, to talk —about life . . . which means about everything . . . so whatever we say and whatever we tell you is really all one, the whole point being to say it and not waste the gift that life has given us. . . .*

An old Jewess from Lithuania who had just sat down commenced to tell a group of women in a motherly voice about the woes of raising a son:

"He was studying at the yeshivah in Telz . . . and we too had a yeshivah in Steibitz * . . . and I used to have students over for meals because it made me think of my boy and of how someone there was feeding him too. So when they took him away to the army . . . to the other end of Russia . . . I . . . where we lived . . . I'd never let a Sabbath go by without a soldier at our table. . . ."

Off in another group a young Sephardic girl who had grown up in Safed and married a Tiberian related in broken Yiddish:

"*Ich gezogt* † . . . I didn't know . . . Father he said to me, why do you spend so much time with the Arabs . . . and I spent . . . till three in the morning I used to sit up with them. . . . "

"But how could you? Shame on you!"

"*Ich nit gewusst,*" ‡ the Sephardess innocently apologized. (She's from Safed, thought Haim as he listened. He must go

* Telz, Steibitz—yeshivah towns in Lithuania.
† Broken Yiddish: I said.   ‡ Broken Yiddish: I didn't know.

there . . . he must look for the grave . . . he must put up a tombstone. . . .) "I didn't know from nothing. I didn't even know the sea was so big."

The big sea, the lake of Tiberias, lay tranquil and still. Reb Yosef roused himself and remarked:

"Yedaiah ha-Penini * says that the world is a deep, wide, stormy sea and that time is a rickety bridge thrown over it. Yes, a sea. But perhaps he only meant a sea such as this . . . like the Sea of Galilee. . . ."

His voice bore witness to the fact that he had at last reached the point in his autobiography where he could no longer divide it into periods. The latter had as though run together, everything was all jumbled up. The silence of the sea alone emerged from the confusion.

He continued in halting tones about how good it would be to finally be a free man, completely, totally free. Except for one's religious duties, of course. That is, to have no one at all for whom one was responsible and had to worry about . . . no one in the bare, wide world. . . .

He hadn't always been like this. He had been unbending by nature. No one had ever been good enough for him. And not only that . . . but also . . . at the time, for example . . . when he had needed a napoleon to redeem his books and hadn't had the money, he had thought. . . . *What? Live without his books?* When he had tried to imagine it, it had seemed to him like the end of the world. How was it possible? His precious books which he had acquired and literally sweated over one by one . . . about which he used to jest that half the hairs of his beard were surely buried in them . . . how could he possibly be deprived of them for lack of a single napoleon?

Whereas now it seemed to him . . . everything considered

---

* Yedaiah ben Abraham Bedersi (1270–1340), a medieval Hebrew philosopher.

. . . it was a pity, of course it was . . . but all in all . . . he had painstakingly managed to acquire a few of the more indispensable volumes anew . . . it really hadn't made such a difference. . . .

And with Goldmann too. At first he'd blamed everything on that hypocritical vulture, that wolf in sheep's clothing, who hadn't an ounce of true piety in him from head to toe. Yes, whatever went wrong he had attributed to that wrongdoer, that source of all evil. . . .

And yet now he could see for himself . . . of course, Goldmann was a terror . . . he'd made life unbearable . . . but that was still no excuse to hold him responsible for everything . . . he was certainly not the whole problem. . . .

Why go on? Toward her too, his youngest child, he, Reb Yosef, had been unjust. He'd been too hard on her . . . what had he wanted? For three straight days before she'd left he'd refused to speak a word to her . . . and yet she was blameless . . . what wouldn't he have done for her were she leaving him now! While when it came to himself, he had always had such expensive taste—only ah, why remind himself of his sins? Now he would treat her differently, he would be a better person . . . but alas, there was no undoing what was done. . . .

He had suffered, suffered terribly. He had been practically a corpse when they brought him to Tiberias . . . he had conversed with people without hearing what they said, he had been totally oblivious . . . and even what he'd heard he'd forgotten at once . . . such were the wages of sin. . . .

And now . . . after all these things. . . .

And after all these things, Reb Yosef suddenly found himself humming to the melody of the Book of Esther, *when the wrath of the king had abated. . . .**

The stars sparkled brightly. Over the top of the steep, wide

* Esther 2:1.

drop at the foot of the street, bundles of firewood suddenly appeared to float in thin air, rising and falling with an up-and-down motion. The loaded camels who plodded and swayed beneath them were hidden from sight, so that from a distance the vision of undulating sheaves resembled a scene from some fantastic ballet, like that which Yehezkel Hefetz had seen in the Swiss city the one and only time that he had taken her, the widow's daughter, out to a show. Yes, it all came round in the end. . . .

But he didn't pursue the thought further. For an additional moment the moon and the camels reminded him of still another night, the night of his release from the asylum, but immediately he dismissed this too from his mind and went back to observing the children at play and listening to their cries. Three little girls were chasing a fourth and trying to hit her. They shouted and screamed. Now she was caught by the hem of her Sabbath dress. She scuffled with her captor. The other two caught up and passed her. Now she gave chase to the three of them. The pursuers had become the pursued. Around and around they whirled like birds of the field.

A nine-year-old urchin whose father had died long ago was not playing with the other children. Instead he stood boasting to a friend three years younger than himself that he could see his father whenever he wished and ask him for anything. There was a special trick to it. You had to shut yourself up in a room at night, sit yourself between two mirrors, one in front of you and one in back, light a candle and stare. . . .

One little girl beat on another. "Ooh, I'm scared!"

"G'wan!" The girl who was hit turned at once to her friends. "She's hitting me . . . and it hu-u-rts! I'm dying. . . ."

"Don't talk 'bout dying," cautioned a third. "You mustn't talk 'bout it. You can die for real."

"What's dying?" an even smaller girl wanted to know.

"Don't talk 'bout it!" came the answering shout.

"Soon daddy'll be here," chanted someone else, "soon daddy'll be here."

The stars sparkled. Reb Yosef lifted his head abruptly and said, looking up at the sky:

"The stars . . . the philosopher Kant said two things. . . ."

But for some reason he didn't go on. With strangely expectant longing he continued to stare at the stars. *Who was to say?* Who was to say that deep within him, despite all his knowledge of astronomy and the courses of the heavenly spheres, he did not have the dim intuition that Miriam's soul, the soul of that sinned-against girl, had been turned into one of those stars—yes, that that tiny, brilliant light that twinkled and winked at him up there was not she, she, she, Miriam, his darling daughter?

All of a sudden the urchin's small friend, who had been standing there without moving, came to life, dashed over to Reb Yosef, and raising his lips, stole a kiss from the old man's hand. It was too much for Reb Yosef to fathom but the curious game appealed to him. He softened all over and smiled with contentment.

"Whose boy is this? He must be the same age as your grandson, Haim."

Yehezkel Hefetz's thoughts turned to Haim's grandson. He too was looking forward to the child's arrival. He too, if he didn't decide before then to take to the road once more, would sit and listen to Reb Yosef teaching the Five Books of Moses: "And Enoch—*un Hanoch*—walked—*iz gegangen*—with—*mit*—God—*Gott.** Iz Hanoch gegangen mit Gott.* And he was not . . . *un iz nito* . . . *un iz nit gevorn* . . . *nit gevorn Hanoch.* . . .

Hanoch was not but the Books of Moses still were. Hanoch was gone but Yosef and Haim were not. . . .

* Genesis 5:24.

Yehezkel thought dreamily of the good times that lay ahead for Haim and Yosef. Their own childhood would return to them with the coming of the child, those good schoolboy days of Moses' book when everything was still an impenetrable mystery and each little scholar was a center of creation heedless of the world beyond him, watched over and guarded at every step by an always-near yet omnipotent leader, who could punish and pardon as he pleased, all according to how he, his small pupil, behaved and reacted. *Return to thy mistress and submit thyself under her hands* *—yes return! *And God afflicted Pharaoh with great plagues because of Sarah, Abraham's wife* †—that too was in the text. Hence the rightful insinct of revenge . . . against which the instinct of justice and fair play did not even bother to protest that it was really Abraham's fault for having lied that Sarah was his sister. One simply took it on faith. There was a mysterious world of justice and holiness that was not of this world . . . the mysterious justice and holiness of one's childhood. . . .

"What say we go to bed?" Haim suggested. "I have to be up bright and early tomorrow. It's my turn to lead the first service."

After prayers the next morning Haim went down to the shore. He lay in a hollow scooped out by some Arabs who had camped there with their donkeys and packs and stretched out with his eyes shut for what seemed a long time. Out on the water the mast of the single boat that sailed from Tiberias to the point on the adjacent shore from where one set out for Jerusalem flashed with a gravelly gleam. The craft rode evenly on the surface like the guesthouse chapel on its platform of

---

* From the angel's words to Hagar after her flight from Sarah (Genesis 16:9).

† Genesis 12:17.

rocks. Haim thought of his coming trip to fetch his grandchild and his lips moved silently between his wrinkled cheeks. He fingered the prescribed fringes on the corners of his undershirt * and reflected that clothes wore out quickly in Palestine because of the sweat, so that it was best to lie quietly and not tear them. At the same time he remembered that Hanoch, might he rest in peace, did not bother to wear fringes at all.

Meanwhile the Arabs had returned with their donkeys and packs to dig out and load up. Haim retreated down the beach, a look of pleased amazement coming over his face as he spied a party of Bedouin who had come to take a wintry dip. With a single motion they flung off their cloaks and dove into the chilly water—just as his brother Yosef, in a somewhat different situation, had liked to leap straight into the ritual bath in his younger, devotional days. The spray they sent up rained over him and he whistled under his breath: they didn't seem cold in the least . . . they hadn't the same type of blood. . . .

The Bedouin stroked with cupped hands and drew further and further from shore "What swimmers they are!" marveled the man on land, who had been able to swim once himself. He sat up to watch with a sort of indolent envy.

Almost at once, however, the comical comfort occurred to him: "In a bath . . . ha ha . . . in a bath they couldn't swim either, not even in summer." An odd smile spread over his cheeks as the queer, inexplicable notion flashed through his aging mind. In his eyes there appeared what might have been a vision of mild retribution at the thought that somewhere there were waters as ignoble as those of a bath in which even the Bedouin would have no advantage over his brother or himself.

* The fringed undershawl worn by orthodox Jews in obedience to the Mosaic injunction in Numbers 16:38.

He continued to watch the strong, swarthy, muscular bodies of the swimmers in the distance while strange consolations
whirled through his head. One way or another . . . lord . . .
it was swimmers like these who were always the ones to
get drowned. One didn't drown if one was frightened of the
water. Take Yosef, for example, who bathed only for his
health. Or himself, who waded only in summer and never
strayed far from the shore. People like them never drowned.
People like them kept alive. . . .

A feeling of well-being seeped slowly through the body of
the man on land. One way or another—he picked up a pebble
and putting it under his shirt, began to scratch and scratch
with great gusto. *It won't be hard, it won't be hard,* signaled
the mast of the boat, *soon we'll be on our way, soon, soon
we'll be on our way.*

BREAKDOWN *and*

BEREAVEMENT

Designed by R. E. Rosenbaum.
Composed by Vail-Ballou Press, Inc.
in 11 point linotype Janson, 3 points leaded,
with display lines in Weiss italic and Weiss Series III.
Printed letterpress from type by Vail-Ballou Press
on Warren's 1854 text, 60 pound basis,
with the Cornell University Press watermark.
Bound by Vail-Ballou Press
in Columbia Bayside Vellum
and stamped in All Purpose gold foil.

Date Due

FEB 6 '74			

Demco 38-297